The Vandenberg Diamonds

By John Russo

Twilight Times Books
Kingsport, Tennessee

The Vandenberg Diamonds

Twilight Times Books
P O Box 3340
Kingsport, TN 37664
www.twilighttimesbooks.com/

First paperback printing, December 2006

Library of Congress Cataloging-in-Publication Data

Russo, John
Pending

ISBN: 1-933353-83-X

Cover art by John Russo

Printed in the United States of America

Dedication

To Van
from your buddy
Roscoe

Chapter 1

"Did you radio our position?" Edwin Sharpe shouted to Mark Harris his co-pilot. "I can't keep this bloody thing up much longer."

"I'm trying. I'm try-y-y-i-n-g!" Harris shouted back.

"Captain, number one and number two engines are on fire and the wing looks damaged," Andy Cox, the flight sergeant, and only other member of the crew, yelled into his mouthpiece.

"I know, damn it. I know. The friggin' flack from that Italian gunboat bashed the hell out of us. We're going down."

The Ladybird, a four-engine Halifax bomber, vibrated out of control as her crippled engines billowed ribbons of smoke and flames.

"I knew this bleedin' flight was treacherous from the minute I received orders to make it." Only Sharpe had been briefed on the purpose of their mission. "Did you reach them?" he yelled to Harris, who was still trying frantically to make radio contact.

"I'm not sure. I'm only getting sporadic response. Our antenna must be damaged." He tried again. "Hello Suez, this is flight number thirty-seven. We've been hit. Repeat, we've been hit. Our location is approximately 175 miles south of Crete. We are no longer able to control flight and are preparing to crash land. Repeat. Preparing to crash land."

"Come in flight thirty-seven . . . *static* . . . *static* . . . Your message is not cle . . . *static* . . . *static*. Did you say crashing? Repeat pleas . . . *static* . . . *static* . . ."

"Shit, it's gone dead. I lost them."

"Forget them for now. Grab your controls and hold on as tight as you can. Thank God these Rolls Merlin engines have independent fuel lines. Now that I've cut the fuel supply to those two flaming engines, the fire should die out quickly."

"Yeah, okay." Harris was fighting his jolting controls with all his strength. "But that bloody wing's not going to hold up forever. Some of the topside panels are flapping loose."

"Oh jeez, how can I help?" Cox leaned into the cockpit.

"We're south of the Isle of Crete," the captain shouted. "Quick, figure out the nearest landfall. I'm not going to lay us in the drink if I can help it."

Cox flipped the pages of their route map. "About the closest dry spot would be . . . er . . . let me see now." He studied the map for a moment longer. "T-u-b-r-u-q," he spelled. "Looks like it's on the very edge of Libya about 140 kilometers from here. Just head south, Captain."

"Easier said than done," Harris announced as he fought his pulsating control stick. Sharpe's shoulders were bouncing almost comically as he fought, trying like hell to guide the crippled plane in the direction Cox had indicated.

"It's impossible to keep her on course, damn it," Harris yelled.

"We're dropping steadily," Sharpe said, "but as near as I can figure, at our rate of descent and our current speed, we can make land before she wets her wheels. Cox, pull that red lever to the right of Harris' head. We've got to jettison the extra fuel tank they mounted to increase our range."

Cox reached over and pulled. There was a sudden uplift as the tank released.

All three men were tense as they stared in the direction the battered plane and their weary arms were attempting to take them.

It was turning dusk when Harris shouted, "Look up ahead! See it?"

They could barely make out the flat beach of the North African coastline sprawled a few hundred yards ahead. It looked within reach. Sharpe switched on the landing lights. They were about fifty feet above the water's surface struggling desperately to keep the damaged wing upright. Suddenly, airlift on the good wing flipped them over. The dead wing tip skimmed the water like a shark fin in reverse. In a matter of seconds it hit the packed sand beneath the shallow water two hundred feet from shore.

The impact pitched the fuselage onto its nose. Sharpe and Harris were thrust forward through the windscreen killing them instantly. Cox was slammed against the back of the co-pilot's seat. The plane tumbled and split open coming to a stop just short of the beach. The rear section burst into flames that quickly turned to billowing steam as the Ladybird settled back into the Mediterranean surf. They had no way of knowing that on that September evening in 1941, the Ladybird had drifted eastward from their planned course and had crashed on the northern shore of Italian-occupied Egypt.

The fiery crash drew the attention of the occupants of a Fiat military vehicle patrolling the beach. Recognizing the plane markings as British, they quickly radioed their lieutenant.

Shortly after, Italian soldiers retrieved the three men from the wreckage. They also pulled two large, heavy aluminum cases out of the Ladybird's cargo hold.

Col. Alfonso Marchi was commandant of the Second Italian North Egyptian Brigade stationed along the beach at As-Sallum. His mission was to maintain a safe exit corridor for troops further inland should a retreat be necessary.

After establishing the identity of Sharpe, Harris and Cox as British RAF officers, Marchi ordered an immediate burial for Sharpe and Harris. The brigade's doctor attended to the unconscious and bleeding Cox.

"And these cases?" Lt. Stephano Brazzi, the Colonel's attaché and private pilot, inquired. "Shall I have them broken open, Colonnello?"

Dragging on a cigarette, Marchi, a short, swarthy, ex-teacher from Palermo, kicked one of the chests. "Wait until we are alone, Stephano. They could be of military significance."

⁓☣

It was early morning in London when the news came in from Suez.

"Goddamn bloody bad luck. Those diamonds are worth almost 8,000,000£. Tell me exactly what they said, word for word," demanded Brian Cutler, managing director of Vandenberg Mining, Europe's largest diamond exchange.

Jeremy Waters, his assistant, faced Cutler and two other members of the Exchange as he reread the radio wire. "They say they only got part of the Ladybird's transmission. It was mostly static."

"Go on, man. Go on," Cutler insisted.

"The crew indicated they were somewhere in the Mediterranean near Crete, that they had been hit by anti-aircraft fire and were crashing. That's all they got, sir."

Waters spread a map across Cutler's desk. "With the added fuel tank the Halifax's range had been increased so they could easily reach Suez for refueling." He traced the route with his pen. "After Suez, their next fuel stop was to be Uganda, and from there they were to fly directly to our offices in Pretoria."

"They bloody damn well didn't make it, did they?" Cutler brushed aside the map. "Now tell me how the hell we're going to find two chests of high grade rough diamonds somewhere at the bottom of the bloody Mediterranean." He was so upset that he snapped his Underhill briar in two.

Waters sat down quietly.

"An impossibility," one of his associates offered, "especially with this damn war going on. That whole region is a powder keg of military activity. Any attempt at retrieval will have to wait till this bloody mess is over and the world is back to normal."

"I suppose," Cutler replied, as he filled another pipe.

"Yes," another cut in. "At the club the other day, I heard that Rommel is invading the whole of North Africa. Apparently the Italians are having trouble holding Northern Egypt. There is some military opinion that British control of the Suez could now be in jeopardy."

"I made a real blunder in judgment," Cutler admitted. "I felt it would be better to return the diamonds we had in stock to our South African operation than to have them blown up by those bastardly nightly blitzes or, worse yet, taken by the Nazis if, God forbid, we're invaded."

"We all concurred with you at the time, sir," Waters acknowledged, "particularly since the Government allowed us to ship them on their special flight through Suez."

Cutler couldn't allow them to believe that the Royal Air Force just happened to be flying to Suez now that the flight may have cost three British airmen their lives. "The truth is, gentlemen, the Company coerced a high ranking official to arrange the flight. We reasoned that the diamonds should never be seized to help finance Hitler's world-domination madness. That's why there were only three men on board the Halifax rather than the normal crew of seven."

No one responded to his admission.

Chapter 2

It was nightfall when Lt. Brazzi joined the colonel in Marchi's makeshift office located in a crude building that had originally been a grain storehouse.

"Ah bene, Stephano, you brought tools. Please lock the door and let us see what was so important that it cost those poor Englishmen their lives. The injured one, how is he doing?" In his heart Marchi wasn't really a fascist. He hated the idea of war and the needless dying. As a schoolteacher of mathematics, his world was one of equations and logic, the very opposite of El Duci's control of his beloved country. As a man educated by the state, however, he feared reprisals against himself and his family if he refused the commission bestowed upon him by his local Sicilian Government.

"He is badly hurt, Colonnello, and still unconscious, but the doctor thinks he'll survive."

"Good, when he is able, we'll interrogate him regarding his mission. Now go ahead, Stephano, open them up."

With some difficulty, Stephano slid one of the 18" x 18" x 24" padlocked aluminum cases similar to a miniature steamer trunk directly under the light in the center of the small room. "Dio mio, Colonnello, this must weigh twenty kilos." The lieutenant proceeded to attack the lock with a hammer and heavy screwdriver.

"Be careful, Stephano, there's no telling what could be in there...explosives, a secret weapon. Mama Mia, be careful."

"Si, Colonnello." The lieutenant gently pried the base of the hasp until it gave with a loud click that caused both men to tense up for a moment.

Marchi watched at a distance sensing Stephano's fear of the unknown.

Inside at the very top of this mysterious case was a hinged metal lid that Stephano carefully raised exposing a black felt pad. He slowly peeled that back. Then it exploded into their view . . . a tray full of brilliant white light.

Stephano stepped back at the unexpected sight. "It's glass, Colonnello, hundreds of chunks of glass."

"What kind of military cargo is this? Quick, open the other one." Momentarily confused by the contents of the trays glittering in their awe-struck faces, Col. Marchi looked toward his lieutenant. "Stephano, this is most unusual."

"Si, Colonnello!"

Marchi picked up a large piece and examined it closely under the light. As he rotated it between his fingers it glowed from the light source. "Dio mio, Stephano, I can't believe my eyes. If I'm not mistaken this is a rough, uncut diamond."

"How? How can that be?"

"I remember seeing one that was on display in a jewelry store in Palermo. Ah, and look what is inscribed on the lid."

Stephano read, "Vandenberg Mining, London, UK."

"Then I'm right. They are diamonds, thousands of them. Bello," he whispered returning it to the tray. "You realize what we must do, Stephano?"

"No, Colonnello."

"Close that immediately and let me think."

"Si, Colonnello." Stephano replaced the heavy pad coverings then closed the lids.

Marchi paced the floor of the small room. "Stephano, what I'm about to suggest to you is not between two Italian officers, but rather Alphonso Marchi and Stephano Brazzi, capisce?"

"Si, Colone . . . ahh, capisce."

"Bene, bene. Now, get three men and load these on my plane. And Stephano, because of the weight, casually explain it's captured documents and secret armaments."

"Si, Colonnello, but what of the injured British airman?"

"If he recovers sufficiently, have him transported south to our prisoner of war camp."

"Si, Colonnello,"

Marchi could see his plot sinking into his pilot's brain as the grinning lieutenant slid the heavy cases to the side.

𝄢𝄢

A soft, warm breeze rippled the moonlight's reflection on the surface of the Mediterranean as Lt. Brazzi and three soldiers carried the two silvery chests over the beach toward the Siai S 82, the colonel's private tri-engine plane. As soon as they had loaded and lashed down the cases, Stephano dismissed his three helpers. He could hear them grumbling and cursing about officers as they headed back to their tent encampment.

The following morning as the various patrols made their way to their stations along the beach, they watched the Siai S 82 become airborne after taxiing on the firm sand along the edge of the surf. They envied their Colonnello making one of his occasional forays back to Sicily. The 620 mile flight usually meant he and the lieutenant would spend the night at brigade headquarters in Catania, enjoy good food, vino and a comfortable bed, and return the next day.

ଧୋଓଷ

This trip's destination, however, was different. Stephano had plotted a course for a flight to Venetico, a small farming community located west of Messina. Sitting in the co-pilot's seat, the Colonel leaned back, lit a cigarette and watched the shadow of the Siai follow along on the calm surface of the Mediterranean below them.

"Excuse me for asking, Colonnello, but this farm where you plan on hiding our good fortune, how safe will it be there?"

"Trust me, Stephano. It's my cousin Guido's pig farm. His father and my father were brothers, bless their souls." He made the sign of the cross. "Guido and I saw each other only on special family occasions; you know, like weddings, baptisms and holidays. We played all around the farm. It was a great place for a city boy like me to visit. After my uncle passed away, Guido took over running the farm along with his wife, Stella, and their son, Carlo.

"And your cousin, he is trustworthy?"

"You worry too much, Stephano. Guido is all right. He's not too bright though, only went to school for a short time. I'm not even sure he can read, but I know I can trust him and that's what's important. Capisce?"

"Si, Colonnello, if you say so."

"There it is, Stephano." Marchi pointed as the Siai descended over a large open field. "That's the pig farm up ahead."

Stephano brought the plane down in a level grassy meadow steering it in the direction of the farm buildings. When he was within a few hundred yards, he cut the three engines. A young boy came waving and running toward the plane.

Marchi deplaned first, picked up and hugged the lad. "Ah, Carlo, how you've grown. Now run back to the house and tell your father to come with the horse and wagon."

"Si, Cousin Alfonso." Carlo spun and started running and yelling, "Papa, Papa!"

Stephano secured the plane, then when Guido arrived helped load the two cases onto his wagon.

They drove to one of the farm's smaller barns where the smell and sound of pigs was overwhelming. Inside the barn, Marchi could see how uncomfortable Stephano was standing in pig shit. "But what must I do with military secrets here on the farm, Alfonso?"

"Don't ask questions when it comes to matters of war, Guido. You are one of the fortunate ones allowed to stay home to help raise food for the war effort."

"Colonnello, can we please get on with it?" Stephano complained.

"Ah, what's the matter, young man, you don't like pork chops?" Marchi and his cousin laughed.

They buried the two cases under soft soil and pig manure in a corner of the barn.

After washing up, they enjoyed a lunch of ham, beans and a coarse bread. When they were ready to leave, Guido walked them back to the plane.

"Now remember, Cousin," Marchi cautioned, "forget we were here today, and forget about those military chests. Do nothing until you hear from me. It may be a while, so go about your business and after this stupid war is finished, I'll see to it that you are handsomely rewarded for your patriotic cooperation."

"Grazie, Cousin Alfonso. I do it with pleasure."

After saying their good-byes, Col. Marchi and Lt. Brazzi took off for their official visit to Catania.

"I hope we can trust him," Stephano commented as they circled the farm.

"He's a pig farmer, yes, and not too bright," Marchi replied, "but blood will never betray you. So, my dear ally, until the end of the war when we will be richer than our fondest dreams, it's more of that desert hellhole we're protecting."

"Mama mia, Colonnello, how much do you think those stones are worth?"

"Millions, Stephano, maybe more."

ಬಂದಿ

Six months later, the British pushed the Italians out of Egypt. What was left of Col. Marchi's brigade was ordered to Libya and placed under the command of Field Marshal Rommel. As the last troop truck left As-Sallum, Marchi and Stephano flew out in the Siai S 82.

"I can't take this stupidity forever, Stephano. And the worst of it is to be placed under a German egomaniac who considers himself a fox of the desert."

"Si, Colonnello, all that wealth waiting for us. It makes me think th . . ."

When the first salvo of British fighter fire caught Stephano in the neck, he slumped over the controls. Marchi stared in disbelief as Stephano's blood splattered his shoulder. It seemed like a slow motion sequence of events as the second volley hit the plane and ripped through the cockpit. Stephano's body was literally blown from his seat by the blast of heavy caliber slugs that hit Marchi in the chest. He could feel his own death as the plane spun downward.

"Mama, Mama."

Chapter 3

"But why must we leave the farm?" Carlo asked his grieving mother.

Guido Marchi had died from a heart attack only six months after his cousin, Alfonso, had entrusted him with the two aluminum cases. He never got word that Alfonso and Stephano had been shot to death over the Mediterranean.

"Because without your father, Carlo, we cannot run the farm. You're barely thirteen, I'm not able to do it alone, and the government must have meat for the war. Now please help me pack these things."

"But I don't want to live in the city. I love the farm."

"I know you do, Carlo. And someday when you are a man, it will be yours. Until then, the Balducci brothers will run the farm and give us what they can. Besides, you like my sister, Aunt Marie, Uncle Franco and your cousin Tony. They're glad that we're coming to Palermo. We must hurry now. The wagon will be here soon to take us to the bus station and I must go down and pack food. It's a long trip."

ଔଔ

On the farm the biggest attractions had been the animals and horse cart that Carlo loved to drive, but the city of Palermo was a bazaar of visual curiosities, local activity and throngs of people, all new and captivating to a thirteen-year-old farm boy.

After arriving there, Carlo and his mother shared a room in the DeVito home located in a poorer working class section of the city. For the average citizen, the lack of goods and conveniences caused by the war were nearly unbearable, but to Carlo their meager existence seemed like abundance. In just a few short months, he adjusted to city life mostly due to the companionship of his cousin, Tony, and their life on the streets of Palermo.

Carlo loved his uncle, Franco DeVito, who was tall and slender, clean-shaven, and soft-spoken with a ready smile for everyone he met. He traveled between Palermo and the southern coastal town of Sciacca where he and Bruno Campi, a Palermo baker, owned a small sardine cannery that supplied the war effort.

Carlo was uncomfortable around his uncle's partner, Bruno Campi, who was a stubby man with a burly build and a flat face interrupted by a shaggy mustache. He was coarse, lacked a basic education and everyone said he looked more like a wrestler than a baker of bread. He was selfish and lazy when it came to the cannery. Franco, however, had no choice since it was an inherited partnership for both of them.

It was obvious that for Campi the bakery and the cannery were unwanted inheritances. Carlo had heard his uncle comment that they had been forced onto Campi as a young man to support himself and his mother after his father passed away and that to Campi's way of thinking, baking bread was better than dealing with smelly fish. Besides, Palermo was where many of his newfound interests were developing.

Most of the men of Palermo were away in the Italian army leaving only old men and boys too young for the military to perform many of the local jobs. After school and during the summer Tony had been working for Campi delivering baked goods to his customers. It was after Carlo and his mother moved to Palermo that his uncle persuaded Campi to hire Carlo also.

༄༅

"Happy birthday, Carlo," his mother greeted and kissed him as he came down to breakfast on his fifteenth birthday after they had been living in Palermo for almost two years. "I have no present for you, my son, except my love." She hugged and kissed him again.

"That's all right, Mama. And I love you, too." He dug into the one egg and crusty toast she had prepared.

"Ah, if your papa could only see what a young man you're becoming, bless his soul." She made the sign of the cross.

"I miss him, too, Mama." He finished wolfing down his meal. "I gotta go, Mama, Tony's waiting." He kissed her tear-soaked cheek.

༄༅

"Happy birthday, Cousin." Tony handed Carlo a gift as they headed for the bakery.

"What's this?" Carlo asked as he unwrapped it. "A stiletto! Am I supposed to slice the bread we sell with this?" he joked as he carefully ran his fingers across the sharp sliver of a blade.

"Nah, Sr. Campi just thought that now that we're running all over town with stuff worth a hell of a lot more than a loaf of bread, we might need a little edge." He laughed as he pulled out a duplicate of Carlo's stiletto and made a stabbing gesture.

"I don't know, Tony, grabbing stuff and delivering it for Sr. Campi is one thing, but sticking someone for him is something else."

"You worry too much, Cousin. It's just for show. I'll handle things if they get out of line."

Carlo closed the knife and pocketed it.

಄಄ಚ಼

Carlo and Tony had become inseparable. Each looked out for the other. While Tony was the larger of the two boys, Carlo was the shrewder. Whenever Carlo found himself in a physical situation he couldn't talk himself out of, Tony would intercede, usually with brutal results, a threat, a broken arm, nose or fingers. He was considered by young and old as someone to fear and respect.

The hardships the war had imposed on Italy seemed to have worsened day by day. Everything was in short supply and, seizing the opportunity to make a lot of money quickly, Campi had become connected with the black market. It was a dangerous as well as profitable enterprise, and it had been Campi's idea that Tony and Carlo have some extra protection since they had become much more than mere bread delivery boys. They were now delivering valuable eggs, butter, canned fruit, cigarettes and liquor to special households

From time to time, as a gesture of respect for the boys' family, Campi sent small portions of contraband to the DeVitos. Need overpowered pride because of the difficult times, therefore, Franco overlooked the source of the illegal goods. Having no desire to participate in what his partner was involved in, Franco did, however, worry about the boys working for Campi, but felt he had little choice in the matter for now.

There was an agreement between the two men that each would concentrate on his business and neither would interfere with the other. Consequently, DeVito was completely on his own and totally involved in running the cannery in Sciacca. This suited Campi just fine as long as he got his fifty percent from the sardines.

After the Allies occupied Palermo in 1943, Carlo and Tony began taking on more special tasks for Campi. Considerably more black market materials were floating into Palermo and Campi was edging his way into other distribution channels. It was no surprise that soon his competitors started disappearing as his network grew.

ᏽᏨᏨ

One evening Carlo's mother cornered him as he was leaving the house. "Carlo, you know I never objected to what you were doing for Sr. Campi when you were just delivering bread and a few essentials. You were young and it helped us get through some difficult times."

"Mama, I have to go. Sr.. Campi doesn't like it when I'm late."

"To hell with Sr.. Campi. Sit down and listen." She grabbed his shirtsleeve. He pulled away, but sat.

"I've been hearing very bad things about you and Tony lately, and Uncle Franco is always so busy in Sciacca he doesn't know what's happening here. Aunt Marie and I, we're not so sure we like you and Tony working for that man anymore."

"Mama, please don't say things like that. Sr. Campi's a very powerful man and I've seen him when he's angry. So please, say no more. It's all right. We're not doing anything to hurt anyone, if that's your worry. Now I have to go. Tony's waiting downstairs for me."

"All right, Carlo. For the moment it's your way, but soon the war will be over and I want us to go back to the farm. You loved it there, remember? We can hire help and you can run the place like you papa did."

"Mama, there's no way I'm going back to be a shitty pig farmer." It was the first time he had ever sworn in her presence.

She slapped him hard across the face. "It's a good thing your Aunt Marie can't hear how you speak to me."

He rubbed his red cheek. "I loved papa, but I won't be a pig farmer!"

She made the sign of the cross at the mention of her late husband. "God rest his soul. I'm thankful he can't see what's becoming of you and how you've changed. It would break his heart to see you now. I remember when you loved the pig farm. You didn't want to leave it and come here."

"I'm just delivering stuff and getting paid for it. Besides, Sr. Campi says Tony and me are doing good and he likes us."

"Him? He's becoming Mafioso, for heavens sake, Carlo."

"Mama, I love you, but please not another word about Sr. Campi. Please, Mama."

"I curse the day I made you leave the farm," she told him. "It's all my fault, may the saints forgive me."

"Mama, please. You know the doctor said you're not to get excited."

"You think I don't know what you've done to get us things. Everybody knows. I have no friends. Except for Marie and Franco, I am alone. Carlo, promise me one thing."

"Anything to make you happy, Mama."

"Promise you'll bury me next to your father, God bless his soul, on the farm."

"Why must you speak of death, Mama? You know how it disturbs me. The doctor said, except for a little high blood pressure, you're in good health for your age."

"What do doctors know of dying from a broken heart?"

"Mama, please. You mustn't get upset."

"And the things you do for that devil Campi," she bit her knuckles, "that doesn't upset you?"

"Mama, please. No more."

"Then promise me that when my time comes," she made the sign of the cross, "you'll take me back to the farm to be with your father."

"I promise. Now, I gotta go."

ಬಂಭ

In 1945, Carlo was seventeen and earning as much in a week as his father had in months raising pigs. He and Tony were heavily into Campi's operation from breaking into occupation troop warehouses to intimidating local businesses.

"Have you heard the news?" Tony was driving one of Campi's cars as he and Carlo were delivering several cases of American cigarettes. "The partisans killed Mussolini yesterday. The war is over for us."

"Does that mean we're out of business?" Carlo was disappointed over the prospect of peace and how it would affect their jobs with Campi.

"Nah, Campi says now we're going to expand into supplying anything people are willing to pay for. Hell, now we can do business all over Sicily. Campi says that before the war Palermo was known for its gambling and other vices. He's going to bring them back and play a major role in all of it."

Later that day, Bruno Campi reassured his young protégés of the good life ahead of them. Carlo worried about Campi's criminal ambitions, and deep down he feared the man. On one occasion Carlo and Tony had witnessed Campi break a larger man's arm with little effort and no remorse.

Carlo's own physique was now developing into manhood. Almost 5 feet 10 inches tall, he knew he would become a man much like his father had been, strong and dark skinned with that distinctive large Marchi chin and straight nose.

He hadn't experienced girls yet, but Tony had. Taller than Carlo and two years older, Tony spoke with expertise when it came to young women. In addition to Tony's reputation as a tough, hard head, his typically Sicilian sleek black hair and arrogant swagger aroused many a virgin's passion.

At home Carlo was becoming harder to control. Like Tony, he dressed more elegantly than other boys their age, had money in his pockets and was out until all hours of the night. Tony's father, as busy as he was in Sciacca, was beginning to hear disturbing things about Carlo and Tony. His wife, Marie, as well as Carlo's mother, Stella, were after Franco to do something about it. Carlo was unhappy when one evening Franco told him and Tony that the time had come when they were needed to work with him in the cannery.

"Oh jeez, Pop, I ain't cut out for sardines." Tonyo knew that Carlo hated the idea as well.

"You will be," his father insisted.

Carlo stood next to Tony and remained respectfully silent as his uncle described their future in Sciacca.

"I ain't going down there," Tony snapped at Carlo when they were alone. "And why the hell didn't you back me up, Cousin?"

"Because, I won't disobey your father, Tony. Look what he's done for Mama and me. Besides, I'd rather work in the cannery than go back to pig farming like Mama wants me to do."

"Yeah? Well I'm older than you and I have a choice, Cousin."

Chapter 4

London 1947

Jeremy Waters addressed his staff at Vandenberg Mining's new Diamond Exchange now located on Bond Street. The original exchange building had been totally destroyed by a Nazi fire bombing raid in the winter of 1943. He was standing in the new vault room before a steel table on which sat a large aluminum case and an open bottle of champagne. "Gentlemen, I'm delighted to accept the first shipment of goods from our mines in Pretoria since the war ended. However, I am saddened that our late Managing Director, Mr. Cutler, couldn't be with us to celebrate this important event."

"Here, here," one of the four gentlemen present raised his flute of Dom Perignon.

"And to our new Managing Director, Jeremy Waters," another toasted.

"Thank you, gentlemen. Now let's get these stored properly." He lifted the lid and unfolded a black felt cover. The sheer sparkle of the contents was overwhelming.

ဆာလ

Later that day in his office, Waters spoke privately to his new Assistant Managing Director, Alfred Dunne. "Now that our world is healing its wounds emotionally along with its infrastructure, there is some old business we should pursue." He went on to explain how back in 1941, a British military plane had been secretly assigned to return millions of pounds worth of Vandenberg's diamonds back to the mines in Pretoria for safekeeping. "It was shot down over the Mediterranean and our diamonds are somewhere out there," he continued.

"Sounds like looking for a pin in Grannie's sewing basket, sir. Unless you know the exact location where they went down, those stones may lie there forever. Also, depending on the depth of the water, it could take a crack diving crew or a rather sophisticated submersible to retrieve them."

"When the time comes, Alfred, it'll be worth a try. It'll certainly be worth a try."

Chapter 5

Bruno Campi was fast becoming the head of Sicily's underbelly of crime. Everything and everyone who had stood in the way of his rise to power had somehow disappeared or had been mysteriously murdered. In his power ascent he had attracted an eager following. Sicilian men who had returned from the war could not find decent work other than menial backbreaking construction jobs, and even then there had been five men for every shovel. Therefore, it had been easy pickings for Campi to recruit the type of men he needed to enforce his growing enterprise of crime and corruption. Paramount among them was Carmine Rossi, a brute of a man over six feet tall with a thick shock of grey hair and a long, ugly scar across his lower jaw and running up to his left ear. The wound was the result of an American hand grenade he had encountered in the battle of Salerno Bay. It appeared as a gross grin on his face although Carmine Rossi had no sense of humor. Because of his bulk, fearsome look and brutal demeanor, he had quickly become Campi's number one henchman and bodyguard.

Campi's dominance over gambling, loan-sharking, prostitution, counterfeiting and extortion kept Tony busy running errands and making pickups. Although still not much more than an errand boy, he sported nice clothes, had a car at his disposal and lira in his pockets.

A few months after the disagreement with his father and Carlo regarding his working for Campi, Tony's mother died of a heart ailment. Franco DeVito was devastated and somehow blamed Tony. "Your mother died of a broken heart," he told his son.

"At least I'm not his partner," Tony rebutted.

"You know that's only for the cannery and I'll change that someday."

That's when Tony decided to move out of his father's house and rent a small apartment overlooking the Gulf of Palermo. The day he left he said to Carlo, "Are you coming with me, Cousin?"

"No, I'm not. You're being a damn fool, Tony. Your father loves you and he's been like a father to me. Don't do this, he needs both of us now more than ever."

Ignoring his advice, Tony packed up and, as he left, said to Carlo, "When you get tired of smelling fish, you know where to find me."

"I don't think so, Tony, and here," Carlo handed Tony the stiletto that he never once opened.

ಬಿಂಬ

Heartbroken over the loss of his beloved wife, Franco found the life his son had chosen was now almost too much to bear. He hated Campi and blamed him for his influence over Tony. Wanting to put as much distance between himself and Campi as possible, and seeing no point in remaining in Palermo, he moved to Sciacca along with Carlo and his sister-in-law, Stella.

Before the war, Sciacca, located 100 kilometers south of Palermo, had been considered a growing seaport and vacation area because of its fine beaches and invigorating hot spring spas.

Now as they drove through the tree-lined streets toward Sciacca's waterfront district, Franco thought back to when his father had owned a small sardine fishing boat and how he had convinced Campi's father, who was a good friend and baker in Palermo, to invest with him in buying the old cannery from the owner he had supplied sardines to. Like the elder Campi, his father had considered it a wise investment, not so much for the profit in sardines but for the potential future value of the waterfront property.

ಬಿಂಬ

Carlo studied the entrance of the old stone structure that was to be his future place of employment as his uncle parked below a sign that read, "SICILY PACKING."

Enzio Camerini, a small-framed man with a bushy mustache, wearing a clean white apron, greeted them as they got out of their car.

Franco introduced his sister-in-law and Carlo. "Enzio, this is Signóra Marchi and her son, my nephew, Carlo."

"Benvenuto, Signóra Marchi, Sr. Carlo. Welcome to Sciacca."

"Happy to meet you, Sr. Camerini." Carlo offered his hand to the cheerful man.

"Please, Sr. Carlo, call me Enzio." He wiped his hand against his apron before shaking with Carlo.

Carlo liked this little man immediately. Enzio's bright eyes and sincere smile gave Carlo a sense of trustworthiness and friendship.

"I have arranged everything as you requested, Sr. DeVito. The house you asked me to rent is clean and ready for your family." He handed Franco a set of keys.

"Thanks, Enzio. I'll get them settled in and tomorrow you and I can get young Carlo started in the business of sardines."

Carlo cringed at this depiction of his new career.

But Carlo could see that his mother loved their new home. Franco had arranged for a place not far from the cannery. It was a stucco building common to the area and he had chosen a house with enough land in back for a garden. He knew she had missed gardening during the time they had lived in his house in the city.

On his first day, Carlo was overwhelmed when he entered the building. His ears were assaulted with the sound of hundreds of cans rattling overhead and around him as they made their way to the trimming and packing line. The smell of oil and fish permeated the place.

"You'll get used to it," his uncle shouted. Then he and Enzio gave Carlo a tour of the cannery. They started out on a small pier where fishing boats hoisted nets of flopping small herring they had scooped out of the Mediterranean and dumped them into shoots leading inside. Next they showed him the trimming and cleaning tables where workers were preparing the fish for packing. Further along the line packers hand-placed the sardines in oil filled cans which shuttled into an antiquated looking contraption that sealed the containers.

Carlo couldn't quite see where he would fit into this messy operation. To him it was almost as bad as the pig farm, but at least his shoes were still clean and it wasn't quite as smelly. He could only hope his uncle had considered that he was a relative and would give him a job that suited the boss' nephew.

His hopes were elevated when Franco led the way to a wooden stairwell leading up to a door on the floor above that Carlo figured was some sort of office. Inside it was a little better. At least his uncle and Enzio didn't have to shout to communicate.

"Well now you know how those little flat cans of fish get their start, Carlo," his uncle said. "And the best way for you to get started is to work with Enzio so that you learn the entire operation."

Carlo gulped. He had expected no more than to start at the bottom. His thoughts then turned to Tony riding around Palermo with a young woman by his side and cash to burn. He wondered if Tony was the smart one after all.

ꙮ

Two months passed and, although he did everything expected of him, Carlo knew that his love and respect for his uncle couldn't make up for Tony's absence in Franco's heart. He had learned all the basics of processing fish and had gained a good sense of the costs of running the business. He had learned so well that his uncle put him in charge of daily negotiating with fisherman as well as the payroll for the dozen workers. With Carlo running the office and Enzio supervising the workers, Franco was able to travel and develop business from private food distributors now that army contracts were no longer a market for their sardines.

Carlo sensed his mother's happiness now that he was working hard at a meaningful job. He could also see how much she loved having her garden where she could grow tomatoes and herbs. And, best of all, she hadn't mentioned going back to pig farming since they had moved to Sciacca.

Carlo's new responsibility included delivering Campi's share of the profits to Tony in Palermo. In spite of their different lifestyles, Carlo still enjoyed being with his cousin and he knew the feeling was mutual. He looked forward to these trips for two reasons. He would stay the night with Tony whom he still loved like a brother, and Tony would arrange for the prettiest two working girls from one of Campi's brothels to join them for the evening. Before the girls arrived, the boys would have dinner in a fine Palermo restaurant and laugh and talk about what they'd been up to. Of course Tony always inquired about his father and that gave Carlo the opening to suggest that Tony was always welcome to join him in Sciacca.

"You know, Cousin, I have thought about it, especially lately. Things are much different than when you and I were working for Campi." Tony lit a cigarette. "It's a lot more brutal now."

Carlo leaned back enjoying his second glass of a fine Italian Chianti. "I knew it would be after Campi started recruiting men like Carmine Rossi."

"How the hell do you know about Carmine? And keep your voice down, Cousin."

"Don't you think your father hears things even in Sciacca? He has friends here and they tell him what's going on."

"Friends like that are dangerous and you tell Papa that, Carlo."

"Why the hell don't you tell him yourself, Tony? He's worried about you now more than ever."

Tony crushed out his smoke and waved for the check. "Keep your trap shut till we get out of here," he cautioned.

It was a typical balmy Palermo evening so they walked the several blocks back to Tony's apartment. Making certain there was no one close enough to hear, Tony spoke softly. "I'm in deeper than I want to be, Carlo, but I can't just walk away."

"What are you saying? Oh Christ, Tony, what have you done?"

"Nothing. Just shut the hell up and listen, and swear to me you won't say a word about this, especially to Papa."

"It's not that goddamn stiletto, is it?"

"Just listen."

"About three weeks ago, I'm picking up a package at one of the gaming houses and the guy running the place tells me that Sr. Campi wants to see me at his home as soon as possible. You should see how he's come up in the world, Carlo. He has a small villa on the outskirts of Palermo. When I got there some tough looking paisano frisked me at the door. He took my stiletto and laughed as he told me I'd get my toy back when I left."

"You should have turned and left right then, Tony," Carlo interrupted.

"It ain't that easy. Now do you want to hear what happened or not?"

"Yeah, yeah."

"I get inside and a nice little old lady holding a tray of pastries sees me come into the foyer. She greets me and tells me Sr. Campi is on the terrace having lunch. So I follow her out there and she places the tray on a nearby table. The first guy to greet me when I step outside is Carmine Rossi."

"Just what the hell does he do exactly?"

"You don't want to know, believe me, Cousin."

Tony lit a smoke as they waited to cross the traffic-busy boulevard a few blocks from his apartment.

"Oh great," Carlo grunted.

Ignoring him, Tony continued as soon as they got a break in the traffic and crossed over. "So Carmine told me, 'just sit there until Sr. Campi is through.' He pointed to a fancy iron chair and I sit down. From where I was sitting I couldn't hear what Campi and the guy eating with him were saying, but I could tell by the way Campi kept waving his fork that he wasn't happy. Ten minutes later the guy gets up and bows. He thanks Campi for something and I don't think it was for the lunch. Then as he passed Carmine and me, he says to Carmine, 'Thank you, Sr. Rossi.'

"Next thing I know, Carmine and me, we're standing beside Campi's chair waiting silently as he finishes his espresso. Then he looks at me and says, 'I want you should go with Carmine on a little errand tomorrow, and pay close attention, Tony DeVito, because I'm giving you a chance to do more than delivering. Capisce? That's all, now go. And, Carmine, fix it good,' he says.

"Then Carmine nods, grabs me by the elbow and leads me to the front door where he tells me to meet him the following morning at the corner of Carpello Street and Trago Avenue at nine and warns me not to be late. I asked Carmine just what we were supposed to be doing, and he says, 'You'll know tomorrow.' Then he says to the goon by the door, 'Give him back his knife.' The goon smirks and hands it over."

"So what the hell was it all about, Tony?" Carlo asked as they got to the apartment door.

"I'll finish upstairs. We have a good half hour before the girls arrive."

The apartment was small but well furnished with leather-upholstered seating. There was a bedroom, a kitchenette, a marble and tile bathroom, and a sitting room with a pullout bed that Carlo sat down on. There was also a balcony with a wrought iron railing just large enough for two wooden chairs and a table. There was no direct view of the water although it could be seen from one end of the balcony.

Tony plopped in a chair and kicked off his shoes. Carlo spread his legs across one of the cushioned side chairs and opened a bottle of mineral water. "Still haven't picked up the wine habit, hey, Cousin?" Tony teased, as he opened a bottle of light Claret, filled a glass for himself and continued from where he had left off.

"So it's raining like hell when I get to Carpella Street. I'm fifteen minutes early so I sit in the car, lean back and light a smoke. Suddenly there's a hell of a bang on my roof. I must have jumped right off the car seat. 'You're early, that's good,' Carmine yells at me through the closed window. You should see this guy, Carlo. On a clear day he looks like walking trouble, but there he is standing outside the car in the pouring rain wearing a black slicker and that big scar looks twice as awful with water dripping off it."

"What scar?" Carlo asked as he sipped his water and listened.

"I'll explain that later. So Carmine says to me, 'Leave the car here and come on.' I pull up my raincoat collar, get out and lock the car. 'It's just up the street,' he shouts over the sound of heavy rain splattering on us. So I follow close behind nervous and curious at the same time.

At the end the block we stop at Number 26, a big ornate three-story building that I found out later had been the home of Gilberto Straza, one of Palermo's great opera tenors back in the 1800s. It had tall arched windows and a pillared entrance. It must have been something back then. It still looked in good shape for an old building, but the area had changed after the war. It appeared to be mostly commercial now, but it was still a nice part of the city.

"We go up these worn marble entrance steps and Carmine rings the bell. In about a minute the heavy front door swings partway open and a middle-aged woman sticks her head out as she keeps a firm grip on the brass knob. 'Yes, Signores, may I be of assistance?' she asks.

'Yes, you may, Signora Fasso.' Carmine seemed to know her. 'I'm flattered you know my name, Signore . . . but you have me at a disadvantage.'

"I could see Carmine was getting impatient as we stood out there in the rain. 'It's Rossi, Carmine Rossi. And this is Sr. Anthony DeVito.' He pressed against the door. 'Scusa, scusa, Signores. Sr. Bertoli told us to expect you and to oblige you in any way you wish. Come in please.' She swung the door open wide, bowing slightly. I pieced together then that the guy having lunch with Campi that day was this Sr. Bertoli. 'Grazie, Signora,' Carmine said as we stepped into the entry foyer.

"The interior was classy like in a Neapolitan movie, sculptured side tables, heavy chairs, a shiny crystal chandelier and a curving oak banister following polished marble steps to the upper level. It was the fanciest house I've ever been in. I later learned from Carmine that it was also the most profitable of all Campi's houses."

"It was a Bordello!" Carlo laughed.

"Yeah and a damn fancy one. In fact that's where our girls are coming from tonight, but let me finish, will ya?"

Tony went on to tell how Carmine asked how many girls worked there, and how Signora Fasso seemed surprised by the question and nervously explained that she was only the housekeeper and cook and that they would have to speak to Sr. Tezzo about such matters.

Then Carmine scanned the room and asked where Tezzo was.

She looked up the stairwell then told us that we were not expected so early and that Tezzo was still asleep.

"So what happened then?" Carlo interrupted.

"Carmine snapped back at the old lady that it was nine in the morning. Take it easy on her, I whispered to him. He gives me a dagger look. She shrugged her shoulders and quietly explained that because of the late night hours everyone sleeps till noon. To put her at ease, I asked her to forgive our impatience and explained that our business with Sr. Tezzo was important. She turned, smiled and replied that she understood. She suggested we wait in the salon where she would bring caffe and pastries. She lead us through a huge double doorway with floral stained glass panels into a plush parlor furnished with velour couches, overstuffed chairs and a marble topped bar along one wall. She apologized for the untidiness. There were dirty glasses and overfilled ashtrays strewn about the room, and stale smoke filled the air. Signora Fasso immediately went to a large window, pulled the satin drapes aside and raised the sash. Cool damp air poured in. She picked up several of the dirty glasses and hastened to the kitchen.

"When we were alone, I asked Carmine who this guy Bertoli was. He told me that I gotta learn to ask less questions and that all I needed to know was that Bertoli was in charge of Sr. Campi's Casas Puttana, and Tezzo, who runs this one, is partial to a stiletto. If he thinks the girls aren't working hard enough, he cuts them where it won't affect their appeal. He's sadistic and a problem that we're here to fix and that I should shut up about it. So I quickly changed the subject by saying it was one hell-of-a piece of real estate. But he wasn't interested in our surroundings. He just told me to shut up, and do as I was told.

"Signora Fasso returned with a full tray and set it on the bar. Carmine picked up a cup, and and told her to go tell Sr. Tezzo we were waiting. Then he added that Tezzo should bring a few of the girls down with him. She hesitated for a moment, saying that Tezzo would not be pleased. Carmine insisted saying she shouldn't be concerned and perhaps she should go to the market after she woke him up. She nodded and was gone.

"A few minutes later she returned with her coat on and told us that Sr. Tezzo said to wait and that he would be with us soon. She made the sign of the cross and left for church. Fifteen minutes passed before the double doors the housekeeper had quietly closed behind her swung open abruptly. Tezzo, a big man with long dark hair and a disturbed expression on his mottled face, burst in on us. He was wearing a white silk oriental robe that covered his feet. 'Which one of you is Rossi?' he demanded. 'That's me,' Carmine acknowledged but remained seated.

"He stared at me. 'And you?' I replied, 'Tony Devito, Sr. Tezzo' Then he gave Carmine a dirty look. 'I do not wish to seem impolite to such distinguished guests, but it's too damn early to be calling. We worked till four o'clock this morning. Can't we meet later, Signores?' Tezzo yawned. 'Where are the girls you were asked to bring down?' Carmine snapped. 'Asleep. I just told you they worked until . . .'

Carmine sprung from the couch so quickly it startled me. He reached up and grabbed Tezzo by the collar of his robe. 'What the hell do you think you're doing?' Tezzo was strong enough to break Carmine's grip. He stepped back a few feet and adjusted his robe. 'I don't give a damn who you are, keep your rotten hands off me.' Carmine just smirked and said, 'Those are dangerous words coming from a bordello pimp. We're here to see that you show respect for Sr. Bertoli's and Sr. Campi's interests.' Tezzo shook his hand in Carmine's face. 'I'm the one who should be respected. Do you know how much money I make for them?'

"The muscles on Carmine's neck tightened. 'Yes, and Sr. Bertoli told us the methods you use to get it and that you have been warned about these abuses before. Call some of the girls down here now,' Carmine ordered. 'Do it yourself, you big shit.' Tezzo shouted."

"Jeez, Tony," Carlo interrupted, "Tezzo must be crazy to talk like that to an animal like Carmine. Then what?"

"The next thing I knew Carmine told me to grab Tezzo. So without thinking, I jumped at Tezzo, caught him off balance and he slipped backward tripping over his long robe. Suddenly Carmine jumped onto Tezzo's chest pinning him to the floor. 'You shits,' Tezzo cursed as he struggled to get out from under Carmine. Carmine smacked Tezzo across the face hard and shouted, 'There's only one way you'll learn to have respect.' Then Carmine yelled to me, 'Pull out your blade, kid, and cut the son-of-a-bitch.'

"I pulled out my stiletto but then I froze, Carlo. I didn't know what the hell to do next. Carmine must have sensed my anxiety. He pulled the knife out of my hand and, with Tezzo still squirming, he sliced off his ear. Blood splattered on Tezzo's white robe as well as on Carmine and me. I didn't dare get sick but I came damn close to throwing up."

"Oh, jeez, Tony, you are in deep."

"And it gets deeper, Carlo. So there's Tezzo, blood gushing down his neck, twisting in pain and screaming, 'You no good son's-of-a . . .' Carmine jumped off Tezzo's chest and wiped the bloody blade on Tezzo's white robe. Then he said to me, 'You screwed up, DeVito, you screwed up big time.' I didn't know what to say. Then I turned around and there were two girls in nighties quivering in the doorway traumatized by what they had just witnessed. 'Don't just stand there,' Carmine yelled to them. 'Bring towels, lots of towels. And one of you call an ambulance right away.' Tezzo was rolling on the floor holding what was left of his ear.

"Carmine washed the blood off his hands and wrists at the bar sink. When the girls returned with the towels, he grabbed one and tossed the others to Tezzo who was still crying uncontrollably.

"I just stood there while Carmine poured a glass of red wine from an open bottle at the end of the bar and lit a cigar. Then he looked down and said to Tezzo who was pressing towels against his bloody head, 'Listen good, you disrespectful pig, you're never to come back here or touch any of these girls ever again. And when you get to the hospital, tell them you did this to yourself in a fit of rage. Capisce?' he yelled. Tezzo rolled to one side putting more pressure on the blood soaked towels. Then Carmine walked over and nudged Tezzo hard with his foot. 'Give me a sign that you capisce, you ex-pimp.' Tezzo looked at him and muttered, 'Ca . . pis . . ce.'

"Then Carmine turned to me and I could tell he was really pissed. He yelled, 'DeVito, you chicken shit, pick up that bloody ear and drop it in a whiskey glass for Sr. Tezzo.' I grabbed the ear with the end of a towel and dropped it in a shot glass. 'Call the other girls down here now,' Carmine ordered one of the two standing nearby. Within three minutes, half-clad women were standing around us looking in horror at Tezzo sitting on the floor with bloody towels pressed against his head. One of them stepped forward and spat on Tezzo. 'Good. You got what you deserve, bastardo,' she snarled.

"When we heard the sound of an ambulance coming, Carmine grabbed the whiskey glass with Tezzo's ear in it. 'I want you to see how we deal with those who mistreat our lovely employees.' He held up the glass for all to see. 'As of this moment, Sr. Tezzo is no longer in charge here and will never abuse any of you again. Capisce?' The girls nodded in acknowledgment. 'Good. Now you can go back to bed and forget what happened here or that you ever saw us. Sr. Bertoli will be sending your new manager soon. Now go, except for you,' he pointed to the one nearest him. 'You stay and let the ambulance men in.' She pulled her robe closer around her neck and stood there while her associates made a quick withdrawal. Carmine took the blood stained whiskey glass and placed it next to Tezzo who was now almost in shock. 'Here, maybe they can sew it back on if you're lucky.'

"The doorbell rang then. 'Just let them in to get Tezzo,' he said to the petrified girl, as we headed upstairs to avoid being seen. 'Tell them you don't know what happened, you found him like that and made the call.' She nodded and went to the door, making sure we were out of sight before she opened it. Carmine was satisfied when he heard her follow his instructions to the letter. Ten minutes later Tezzo and the two ambulance attendants where gone.

"When Signora Fasso returned, Carmine explained how Tezzo had injured himself and wouldn't be back. He gave her a handful of lira for the mess she had to mop up and told her that a new manager would arrive soon.

"Then we walked back to my car, and Carmine wiped our prints off the stiletto and slipped it into a sewer drain. 'I can't believe you cut off his goddamn ear, Carmine.' I said. He just stared at me. 'That was supposed to be your job, DeVito, and Sr. Campi isn't going to be pleased when I tell him how you failed to obey.' I figured I had nothing to lose by complaining that it was his fault for not telling me ahead of time. 'I wasn't expecting that, Carmine. You should have told me before we got there.' I must have caught him off guard 'cause all he said was, 'Bullshit, DeVito.'

"Afterward, he leaned close to me and whispered, 'it's what we get paid for, but you don't get shit for today, capisce?' I don't know where I got the balls to talk back to him, but I was more angry than afraid of him then. 'So I was supposed to get extra for today? That's something else you didn't tell me, Carmine.' He grinned and the scar stretched on his face. 'Maybe so, but I'll get your share, too. Just understand one thing about me, DeVito, there's nothing I won't do for money and that includes popping your ass dead if Sr. Campi gives the word.' As he said that he pulled a .45 automatic from his back pocket and shoved it under my nose. Then he laughed, put it back in his pocket, and walked away."

"Jeez, Tony, so what happened then?" Carlo shook his head over the story Tony had just revealed to him. "What did Campi do about it?"

"Nothing really, except a couple of days later Carmine's waiting for me outside one of Campi's gambling houses where I make pick-ups, and he tells me to get into the car."

"Well you're still here, so I guess he didn't cut off anything important . . ."

"Very funny, Carlo. He just told me that Campi was pissed at me and that next time I didn't do what was expected of me . . . well, Carmine just gave me a big knowing grin."

There was a soft knock on the door, Tony crushed out his smoke, smoothed down his hair and declared, "The girls are here."

Chapter 6

London

"Ah yes, Alfred, come in." Jeremy Waters was signing documents when his assistant, Alfred Dunne, entered his office. "By the looks of things, the diamond market is doing extremely well." Waters was obviously pleased with the numbers he was signing off on.

"The tight control on production was a brilliant move on your part, sir."

Waters looked up. "That's all well and good, but we're running into a lesser grade of stones in the new section of the mines, damn it."

"They say timing is everything, sir."

"What do you mean by that bit of philosophical drivel?"

"You will recall that several weeks back, you requested that I find a resourceful person to look into that shipment lost during the war."

"Right. So, get on with it, man."

Dunne was well aware that Waters was not a patient man. "He's here, sir, waiting right outside."

"Who's here?"

"His name is Sean Corklin. He's the head of security for our Pretoria operations."

"Corklin . . . Corklin . . . never heard of him. Doesn't sound British either."

"He's Welsh, sir. And he comes highly recommended by our mining superintendent."

"Dear old Bartholomew, he'll be retiring soon, won't he?"

"Yes, sir. Now about Corklin. He has a jolly good record in the mines, caught any number of lads pilfering stones in unusual ways from ingesting them to inserting them into slits in the soles of their feet."

"Most despicable and disgusting."

"Yes, sir. He even assisted the local Pretorian police in solving the murder of one of our miners. He seems to have a natural instinct for getting to the bottom of things."

"Hm-m-m, we'll see." Waters pressed his intercom button. "Miss Allen, please ask Mr. Corklin to join us."

A tall, robust looking Welshman with a short blonde beard entered. "I'm most happy to meet you, Mr. Waters."

"Yes, well, have a seat then, Mr. Corklin," Waters invited.

"Thank you, sir." Corklin's eyes were steely blue and unblinking, and his voice exuded confidence.

"Alfred here tells me you've quite a record for protecting our interests in Pretoria. Most commendable. And how is old Bartholomew?"

"Mr. Edwards is fine, sir. He has the full respect of all of us who report to him. The workers find him fair and compassionate."

"So I'm told. And he seems to think you're quite the right man for a special assignment we have in mind," Waters stated.

"You've been with the company for over ten years now, is that correct?" Dunne asked, referring to Corklin's profile folder open on his lap.

"Eleven years next month, Mr. Dunne."

Dunne continued reading for Waters' sake. "You're thirty-seven and not married, but living with a South African woman. Your parents settled in Pretoria when your father took a minor Government position there." Dunne looked up. "I'm not embarrassing you am I, Corklin?"

"No, sir. I'm sure it's all there and it's the truth."

Waters studied the Welshman.

"Your parents are deceased and you have no siblings." Dunne picked up where he had left off.

"My one deep regret, sir."

"This woman?" Waters interrupted. "How serious is it?"

"I'm sure your report indicates that Rhonda is black, sir. May I be frank?"

"Of course."

"It's a matter of convenience, nothing more."

"Ahem . . . of course."

Dunne shut the folder, sat back and lit a cigarette.

"I believe you'll do just fine, Corklin. Now I'll briefly explain the misfortune that occurred during the war and the reason why you're here. After which, Mr. Dunne, to whom you are now accountable, will fill you in on all the specific details necessary for you to proceed, if you agree to take on the assignment."

After a ten-minute overview, Corklin expressed interest and excitement in the assignment, particularly the bonus if he were successful. He shook the Managing Director's hand and followed Dunne to his office for further briefing.

Chapter 7

Benniti's specialized in peasant dishes for affluent patrons who wanted to relive their humble mealtime roots at high prices. The ambiance was very old-world as was the cuisine. Carlo had eaten there once before but preferred the more contemporary veal and steak houses in Sciacca.

"Ah, Sr. DeVito, so good to see you again." Benniti himself greeted them and escorted them through the busy main dining room to a small private alcove. When they were seated Benniti suggested the special of the day, polenta with tomatoes and veal shank.

Without consulting Carlo, Franco ordered. "Good, we'll have that and a bottle of Asprino."

"Excellent choice, Sr. DeVito." Benniti bowed and was gone.

"I haven't had polenta since I was a boy," Carlo commented to Franco. "It was a mainstay on the farm. We ate it twice a week, along with pork."

"Ah, then this lunch will be good for your soul and you can tell your mama. Perhaps you should bring her here. I'm sure she would enjoy it."

"Perhaps, I should." Carlo knew his mother would never eat in a place that feigned home cooking. Except for mass, she enjoyed staying home, cooking for Carlo and Franco, and tending her wonderful garden,

After they finished their meal, Franco sat back and sipped more wine. "It's too bad you don't enjoy the fruit of the vine. Asprino is one of the few wines produced in the Basilicata region."

"Papa never developed the taste, and I never did either, Uncle Franco."

"Such a pity." He swirled the dry white in his glass before he drained it. "Now tell me, how is Tony doing? He never calls or visits and I'm becoming very angry over his neglect."

Carlo set his cup of espresso down, not sure how much to tell his uncle.

"Is he well, Carlo?"

"He's okay, Uncle . . . except . . ." Hell, he knew he had to say something, not only out of respect for Franco, but to get Tony out of the mess he had gotten himself into.

"Except what? Is he ill?" Franco sounded more impatient than worried.

For the next several minutes, Carlo told his uncle what Tony had gone through with Carmine and the bordello incident, as well as Campi's inferred warning to Tony. When he finished Carlo could see the fire in his uncle's eyes.

"That son-of a-bitch." Franco fumed quietly. "Campi has caused me enough grief over my association with him. Although we are partners in the cannery only, it appears as though we're partners in all his dirty business."

"Please, Uncle Franco, remain calm. You mustn't do anything that would get Tony in more hot water. Perhaps I shouldn't have said..."

"No, no don't worry, Carlo. You did the right thing. I know your love for Tony and me caused you to speak up."

Just then Benniti approached their table. "And the polenta, it was to your satisfaction, Signores?"

"Very good," Carlo lied.

"Excellent, Sr. Benniti," his uncle said. "If we may have the check, please."

"Of course. I'll have a waiter bring it. The wine, however, is compliments of Benniti's." He walked away with a flourish before Franco could object.

"I'm just worried that if Campi or Carmine think Tony revealed anything...well they're ruthless Uncle."

"I know how to deal with Bruno Campi. I've been wanting to discuss breaking up our partnership for some time now and this is as good a time as any."

"Just be careful, Uncle, please." Carlo grabbed the check when it arrived.

ᏸᎧᏉᏣ

That night Tony DeVito got a call from his father. "Papa, it's good to hear your voice. Is everything all right?"

"Si, Tony, everything is fine. I must be in Palermo on business soon so I thought we should dine together."

Franco's plan was simple. He would see Campi when the next share was due him and propose a buyout. As part of the deal, he would insist that Tony was needed at the cannery.

"Of course, Papa, whenever you say."

"Two weeks from tomorrow, unless, of course, you're ready to come and live in Sciacca."

"That's not possible right now, Papa. Besides I'm making good money and I'm needed here in Palermo."

Franco could sense the frustration in his son's voice. *That won't be true much longer, Tony,* he thought. "I'll call you then. Ciao, Tony."

"Ciao, and Papa, I love you."

Chapter 8

London

"I'm afraid I've run into a bit of a snag, gentlemen." Sean Corklin addressed Jeremy Waters and Alfred Dunne who were seated at one end of an oval table in the privacy of Waters' conference room.

"But you've only just begun," Waters commented.

Dunne sat quietly listening.

"That's the rub, sir. I started by contacting The Office of Military Records. When I inquired as to the details of a missing Halifax bomber during the early stages of the war, I was told that any such information, if it were available, is classified."

"Nonsense. What possible security could be breached now? Hell, we won the bloody war, didn't we?" Waters spouted rhetorically.

"It is a bit unusual," Dunne said, "but the ministry can be dicey about inquiries that concern the armed forces."

"I am aware of that, sir," Corklin explained. "That's why I posed as a relative of the Ladybird's pilot, Captain Edwin Sharpe."

Waters addressed Dunne directly. "There must be a way around this bureaucratic balderdash,"

"Let me look into it, sir. I'm sure I can learn about the proper channels to approach at our club."

Corklin was certain Waters and Dunne would have considerable influence in upper Government circles which was why he had brought this first hurdle to their attention. Although he was quite effective at digging up facts and assembling them coherently, high-ranking contacts were far from his reach.

"Give me a few days," Dunne told Corklin. "Where are you staying?"

"I have a room in Staines." He gave Dunne the number where he could be reached.

"Keep me apprised," Waters said, shaking his head as he exited.

ഇൗരു

"Here it is, September, 1940. The loss of flight number X247, a Halifax bomber, code name Ladybird, piloted by Capt. Edwin Sharpe with a crew of two, Lt. Mark Harris and Flt. Sgt. Andrew Cox," a young female clerk explained. Corklin had been given access to the information he was seeking after presenting the Director of RAF Intelligence with a letter of introduction provided by a member of Dunne's Cricket Club, who was also the Prime Minister's social secretary.

"That's the one I'm looking for."

"According to these transcripts the plane was shot down somewhere over the Mediterranean."

"I believe it was off the coast of North Africa." Corklin knew that much from Waters. He wondered if the record showed the reason for their flight, so he fed out a little line. "A routine mission, as I understand it?"

"It appears that way, sir, except this bit's odd."

"How's that?"

"Well, sir, listed next to the type of aircraft it states that a Halifax normally carries a crew of seven."

"Hmm, you're too young to know about the many shortages that occurred back then, including manpower."

"So I understand. Dad's told us all about the rationing and the blitzkrieg. Thank God we won, sir." The clerk was being politely cooperative because of Corklin's high clearance credentials.

"And you're certain there's nothing indicating where they crashed?"

"Unfortunately the exact location was never determined because of broken transmission between the Halifax and our base in Suez."

"That is unfortunate." Corklin looked up from his notepad. "And, of course, for the crew as well. That's the real tragedy."

"Yes, sir, especially for their families who had no remains for a decent burial and all." Then she pulled out a special appendage to the file. "At least, according to this, Capt. Sharpe and Lt. Harris were cited for bravery posthumously."

As an ex-seaman of Her Majesty's Navy, Corklin bristled. "And why not Cox? Even though he was not an officer, I'm certain he was just as courageous."

"Of course he was, sir. Flt. Sgt. Cox accepted his medal in person."

Corklin stopped writing. "You mean one of them survived?"

"Yes. According to these records Flt. Sgt. Cox was severely injured when they crashed."

"So then you do know where the plane went down?"

"Unfortunately, Flt. Sgt. Cox suffered considerable head trauma. All we have here is that in 1942 he was comatose and convalescing in one of our Veteran's Hospitals in Sheffield."

"And where is he now?"

"That's everything we have, sir. There's nothing further in the file."

"What?"

She politely showed him the last entry she had quoted from.

At least now Corklin felt he had a solid lead to pursue, although he was still far from collecting Waters' promised bonus.

Chapter 9

"Ah, my fish partner, it is good to see you. I am honored that you have decided to visit me," Campi greeted Franco.

"Likewise, Bruno." Franco was there to deliver Campi's share of the month's cannery profits. He also planned to offer to buy Campi out and get Tony the hell out of Palermo.

"Please be seated, Franco, mio casa, suo casa. And what do you think of my villa? Beautiful, no?"

"Very nice, Bruno." *And how many dishonest deeds did it require,* he thought as he chose a leather chair facing Campi. It was then Franco noticed the large man with a horrible scar standing off to one side of the room. "And who is this gentleman?" he asked knowing it had to be the one Carlo described to him.

"Oh, Franco, I should have introduced you. This is my associate, Carmine Rossi."

"Sr. DeVito," Carmine grunted.

Franco acknowledged Carmine with a nod of his head.

"Carmine, please have Signora Quinto bring some refreshments. Wine and fruit perhaps, Franco?"

"Nothing, thank you."

"Never mind, Carmine." Campi held up his hand. "And so, what brings you to Palermo, Franco? Certainly a man of your stature needn't deliver tribute to his partner. I understand your nephew, Carlo, usually makes these deliveries to Tony. How is young Carlo these days?"

"He's fine, working hard in the cannery. But I'm here to visit Tony, and I also have a personal matter to discuss with you, Bruno." Franco gazed toward Carmine as a visual reference to his presence.

"Nothing we speak of leaves this room, Franco. And Carmine is well aware of that."

Franco raised his arms in a beseeching gesture, "It's just between us, Bruno." He detected a smirk across Carmine's scar as he insisted they be alone.

Ignoring Franco's request, Campi asked, "What is it that troubles you, Franco? If it's money, we'll sell more fish." He laughed as he opened the envelope Franco had brought. He waved the lira he removed in Carmine's direction. "That must be it, Carmine, look at the meager share they bring me every three months."

Carmine merely grinned at his boss's comment and Franco's obvious discomfort.

"It's not the damn money, Bruno." Franco was becoming angry. "I want to break up our partnership and I'm willing to buy your half..."

"You what!" Campi screamed. "What the hell are you talking about, DeVito? I don't give a good damn what you want."

"Don't treat me like one of your peons, Bruno. To me you're just a goddamn baker. So let's discuss what I came here for without your Mafioso attitude."

"Be careful how you speak to me, Franco."

"He's got more pallinas than his son," Carmine interjected.

"Be quiet, you fool," Campi snapped at Carmine.

"Si, Sr. Campi."

"Now, let me understand, Franco, you would like to dissolve our partnership, no?"

"That's right, Bruno, and tell your associate to leave my son out of this. Capisce?"

"Carmine does what he's told. I'm the one who's doing the buying out, Franco, so let me see, how much is half a fish business worth?"

"No, Bruno." Franco rose and pointed his finger at Campi. "I want the cannery. It's all I have that my father left me and some day I will leave it to my son. You never gave a damn about it all these years and you know it."

"Sit down, Franco, " Campi ordered. "This display of temper is not healthy...."

A little old woman had quietly entered the room. "Scusa, Sr. Campi, may I bring you and your guest something?"

"Signora Quinto, yes, that would be nice. Some vino and fruit, if you please."

She left as quietly as she had entered.

"Don't threaten me, Bruno. I know too much about what you have been up to lately for you to make an enemy of me now."

"You're a fool, Franco, and beware of what you think you know. Besides, I have future plans for the cannery and it has nothing to do with those stinking fish."

"What plans? You forget, Bruno, I still have a say in whatever those plans might be."

"When the time comes, you will sell me your half. I will be fair about it."

Signora Quito returned with a tray and set it down on a table next to Franco.

"Grazie, Signora," Franco said to her politely. She smiled at him and left.

Campi got up, poured some wine into a glass then handed it to Franco. "Here, this will cool you off, Franco." He poured another for himself. After taking a sip, he stood next to Franco and said, "Now let me explain, something to you p-a-r-t-n-e-r," he emphasized in a derogatory manner. "That cannery sits on a very valuable piece of oceanfront property, and in a couple of years when the world is healed from the war and people travel for pleasure again, I plan to build a hotel and casino there. Do you see the significance of that, you fool?"

"Gambling and puttans. I will never agree to such a venture, nor will I ever sell out to you, Bruno."

"Franco, relax. Who knows what can happen in the next few years? For now run our cannery and be sure I get what's coming to me and I'll see that you get what's coming to you. Now you must forgive me, I'm needed elsewhere."

Franco got up and placed his full glass on the table. "There is one more thing, Bruno."

"Please be quick about it, Franco."

"It's Tony. I need him to help Carlo with the cannery now that I'm doing more traveling to increase business."

"That would cause me some sorrow. Tony has been a great service to me, but I would say it is his choice, no?"

Franco didn't see the cunning grin on Carmine's face as Campi spoke of Tony.

"Then my visit is over, Bruno, and as for the cannery, it will remain such as long as I have anything to say about it."

"Goodbye, Franco. Carmine, see my dear partner out."

ജരു

When Carmine returned, Campi was having more wine. "Join me, Carmine," he pointed to the seat Franco had occupied.

The big man poured himself some wine and sat while Campi lit a cigar. "He has no respect, that one, Sr. Campi."

Campi blew out a billow of blue smoke. "He never did, Carmine, and now he is dangerous and an impediment to our future."

"I could see to it that he disappears, Sr. Campi. It would be a personal pleasure." Carmine wiped his mouth with the back of his hand after draining his
glass.

"No, no. We must be subtle. Everyone knows we are partners. There might
be another way. Let me dwell on it a bit, but it won't take long, I assure you."

"And what of his snot-nosed son?"

"Let's wait to see what he decides. I don't believe he's willing to fool with
fish when he has so much to fool with here in Palermo."

"He does take advantage of our girls," Carmine smirked.

"Let's just leave him alone for the time being, at least until I put my plans
for his papa in motion. I must go now."

"Si, Sr. Campi." Carmine rose when his boss did.

ಐಂಚ

Tony met his father for dinner at a café near his apartment. Franco immediately explained his aggravating meeting with Campi and insisted that he
wanted Tony to leave Palermo and return with him to Sciacca.

"Papa, I'm sorry you had such a bad time with Sr. Campi. But I'm happy here
in Palermo." He hated lying to his father, but after Franco had told him about
their heated discussion and Campi's threatening words, Tony had no choice
but to pretend everything was fine.

"The man is no good, Tony, and the stronger he gets the more evil he be-
comes. I fear he will draw you into bad things, my son."

That damn Carlo, Tony thought, *he must have said something about what
happened with Carmine at the bordello.* "Papa, believe me, I'm not doing anything bad. I just pick up and deliver money at Sr. Campi's different places of
business. I use one of his cars and he pays me well, and that's all I do for him."

"May I refill your wine carafe, Sr. DeVito," the waiter addressed Tony.

"Si, Mario. And this gentleman is also Sr. DeVito, my father," he introduced
Franco to the waiter.

"Saluto, Sr. DeVito." Mario bowed his head slightly as a gesture of respect.

"Grazie," Franco replied.

After Mario refilled the wine bottle, he excused himself and left.

"I take it you eat here often," Franco said as he poured himself some fresh
wine.

"The food is good and it's convenient on nights when I'm not entertaining
a young lady."

Tony was trying to keep the conversation light and avoiding further discussion regarding Campi.

"Anyone special?" Franco inquired.

"No, Papa. Just girls I know."

"So aside from delivering and no special girl in your life, there is not very much to keep you here in Palermo as far as I can see."

"Papa..."

"Tony, Carlo and I need you at the cannery," his father interrupted. "It isn't fair to your cousin, especially since one day the business will be yours."

"You mean mine and Campi's. After what you told me you two argued about today, he isn't ever going to give his share up."

"I'm not worried about him, Tony. Bruno will see things my way when he hears the plans I have for the cannery."

"Papa, I'm not ready to go back. Give me some time, please."

"I'm disappointed that you don't see how much I want you with me, but if you need a little more time, son, I'll be patient, disappointed but patient, because I love you, Tony."

"And I love you, Papa."

Mario returned with the food they had ordered. "Bon appetite, Signores."

Two hours later they embraced, then Franco headed back to Sciacca.

Chapter 10

Sheffield

"The administration office is across the green," a man answered Sean Corklin's inquiry. "Follow me. I'm going in that direction."

Corklin wasn't sure just what the proper etiquette was for a legless man in a wheelchair. "Can I give you a hand?"

"Nah, you don't want to spoil me, now do you? Besides, you're not half as attractive as the help I'm jolly well accustomed to," he joked.

Following along the pathway, Corklin spotted a number of wheelchairs parked under shade trees, while others were grouped together around tables where animated card games were being played.

"Having trouble keeping up, old chap?" the man quipped over his shoulder as he sped toward a three-story building.

Corklin was surprised at the dexterity of the man as he pumped the wheels of his chair.

"Here you are." They stopped at the foot of concrete steps in front of an imposing granite building.

"Thanks."

"Anytime you want to race, let me know." The man laughed as he cruised away toward what appeared to be one of several dormitories.

There was a large veranda at the head of the stairs. More wheelchair occupants and a number of men on crutches were milling around laughing or deep in conversation. Several radios were playing in the background.

Corklin marveled at the bravery of these veterans who, in addition to having defended their country, had the courage to accept the price they had paid for doing so.

Chiseled above the ramp that angled upward to the entrance, he read, "HER MAJESTY'S VETERANS' CARE FACILITY, SHEFFIELD." The double oak and glass doors automatically swung open when he was half way up the ramp. A hint of disinfectant greeted him as he entered.

The interior was filled with overstuffed lounge chairs. Low bookcases lined the walls. Sunlight shafted in from overhead windows creating a cathedral-like ambiance. Convalescents in gray robes occupied several of the seats. It was difficult for Corklin to determine their physical conditions without staring, which he did not do.

Straight ahead he could see what looked like an official area. As he proceeded to it, his shoes tapped on the marble floor. The sound made him feel a bit self-conscious knowing that not many of the residents could do likewise. Stopping at a large metal desk, he spoke to the nurse seated behind it.

"Good morning. My name is Sean Corklin."

"Good day, sir. How may I help you?"

She was a bit matronly, but with a little makeup and street clothes, he imagined she would be rather comely. He shook the thought off. It was obvious to him he was starting to miss his live-in back in Pretoria.

"Yes, I'm making an inquiry regarding a patient."

"Of course, sir. Are you a relative?"

"No. Actually, it's an official matter." He withdrew the letter he had used at the RAF Intelligence Office signed by the Prime Minister's secretary.

After perusing it, she seemed to sit up straighter. "I'm sure the director of our facility will be happy to help you in person. Please excuse me a moment, Mr. Corkley."

"It's Corklin, and I'll be happy to see the gentleman."

She rose from behind the desk. "It's Mrs. Abernath you'll be seeing."

In a matter of minutes she was back. "Please allow me to show you in, Mr. Corklin." She led him into a small, but neatly arranged office. After announcing him, she quietly withdrew.

A woman taller than he, rather slim with a friendly smile, greeted him. "Mr. Corklin, I'm Anne Abernath, director of this facility. Please have a seat." Her voice was soft as she addressed him. With an easy manner, she motioned him into an armchair with an embroidered cushion and returned to the other side of her desk.

"Nice pillow," he commented, adjusting it before sitting.

"It is lovely, isn't it? One of our boys made it for me." There was affection in the way she said it. "You have a rather impressive introduction letter here. I mean, the Prime Minister's secretary." She handed it back to him.

"My employers are well placed in the government," he lied.

As a loyal government official, she did not question the comment. "Just how may I be of assistance, Mr. Corklin?"

"Nothing ominous really. I just need to speak to one of your RAF patients.

His name is Cox, Flt. Sgt. Andrew Cox. He was admitted here in 1942 with head injuries."

"Oh my, I'm afraid I don't recognize the name. But then I've only been here since 1945."

"I'm sure you must keep records..."

"Of course we do, but perhaps we can learn something quicker by checking with Dr. Wilson. He's been here since this facility opened right after the war. I understand it was awful, so many seriously wounded pouring in every day. Were you in the service, Mr. Corklin?"

"Her Majesty's Navy, Atlantic Fleet. I do hope the doctor is about today." He got back to the reason for his visit.

"I'm sure he is. I'll have Gladys, she's the young girl at the desk, locate him." She instructed Gladys through her intercom. "Meanwhile would you care for a tour of our wards?"

Corklin figured she wanted to impress whoever was important enough to obtain a letter from the office of the Prime Minister. "I'd rather not, Mrs. Abernath. I've seen enough of what that damn war did. Please excuse my language."

"With over three hundred painfully mangled souls here, Mr. Corklin, you can imagine we've heard much worse."

After several minutes of small talk, her office door opened and a man in a short green medical coat entered.

"Hello, I'm Martin Wilson, Chief of Staff. What can the Prime Minister's Office possibly want from us?" A well-smoked briar pipe seemed to be growing between his lower lip and a red bushy mustache.

Corklin grasped the firm hand that was offered. Dr. Wilson was shorter than Corklin with a fuller body, but he hardly looked the several years older that he was. Corklin's immediate impression was that if he ever needed a doctor, Dr. Wilson would do nicely.

After their short initial discussion regarding Sgt. Cox, the doctor suggested they return to his office where most of the past and present patient files were kept.

Corklin thanked Mrs. Abernath, then followed the doctor, pipe in hand, into the corridor to an elevator.

As they ascended to the second floor, the doctor explained, "Wasn't this fancy in the beginning. No, sir, no elevators and only three operating rooms.

Did Mrs. Abernath give you the tour?"

"I passed."

"Squeamish?"

"Not at all. Just angry."

"I understand. You must have been in the thick of it."

"Very thick, I'm afraid."

The doors opened. "Ah, here we are then. My office is just a ways down on the left."

Compared to Mrs. Abernath's small neat office, the doctor's was large and overflowing with journals, large x-ray folders, and parts of artificial limbs scattered about. For a moment Corklin regretted thinking this was the doctor of his choice if he ever needed one, until he spotted dozens of prestigious medical diplomas and citations hanging crooked on a good deal of wall space.

"Here, sit down, Mr. Corklin." The doctor shoved a bunch of papers and what looked like a hot water bottle off a chair.

"I do hope we can find Sgt. Cox," Corklin said seriously.

"Oh, don't worry. I take very good care of all my patients. It's just my belongings that clutter my mind and space. All my files are in the next room that a very efficient clerk keeps me out of." He pushed open a side door and spoke to someone Corklin could neither see nor hear. "Rosemary, please find me the file on an RAF flight sergeant name of Cox, Andrew Cox. I believe he was admitted in '42. Severe concussion, if I recall correctly."

Corklin was impressed that the doctor could remember all of his patients and their injuries. He said so as they waited for Rosemary to do her thing.

"It's funny, you know," the doctor explained as he re-lit his pipe. "I remember every injury that I've ever treated but the faces are a blur."

"Must be a medical phenomenon," Corklin commented.

"You think so? Hm-m-m?"

Minutes later Rosemary came in with a file folder. "I believe this is the patient you asked for, Dr. Wilson." She placed it on top of a mess of paper on his desk, shook her head and left.

Ignoring her look of disdain, he picked up the file and opened it. "Hm-m-m." After flipping through several pages, he asked, "What is it you need to know about Sgt. Cox?"

"Quite honestly, doctor, I really only need to speak to him. Is he still a patient here?"

"Oh goodness no. Sgt. Cox was released, let me see . . " He double-checked the file page. "Ah yes, in the spring of 1946. Aside from a rather nasty scar on his temple, his head trauma was completely remedied."

"I'm glad to hear that. Is there anything in his file about where he crashed? We know it was somewhere in the Mediterranean."

He glanced at the file again. "Only this. Apparently Sgt. Cox was transferred to the International Red Cross in Bern, Switzerland, by an Italian medical unit. He was in a coma and, because of his military ID tags, he was sent here from Bern. As I said, that was in 1942."

"Would you know where he . . ."

"Of course, I should have mentioned it earlier," the doctor quickly added. "According to his discharge, he planned to join his only relative, an aunt in Bristol." Before Corklin could ask, the doctor read him her name and address. "It's Mrs. Margaret Smithe, 24 Corry Place, Bristol. There's no telephone number, I'm afraid."

As soon as Corklin finished writing down the information, he stood, thanked the doctor and bid him goodbye. Rosemary escorted him back to Mrs. Abernath. As he took his leave, he assured her that the Prime Minister's Office would be most grateful.

He drove off the facility grounds, his mind focused on getting to Bristol and being one giant step closer to his bonus.

Chapter ii

"So you see, Capt. Tonelli, everyone believes that Franco DeVito is my partner in all my enterprises. By eliminating him, not only will you gain stature as a crime fighter, you will be doing me a very important favor as well. I'm sure you know what that can mean for you personally."

"Si, Sr. Campi, that is true, but what you ask can be very dangerous." James Tonelli sat facing Campi and Carmine Rossi in Propia's Restaurant on the outskirts of Palermo. Captain of Palermo's police, he was also a well-rewarded collaborator of Campi's powerful growing family.

Campi studied the man he had invited to meet with him. Tonelli's mottled face and pug nose gave him the appearance of a boxer. Out of uniform, his clothes fit snugly and his bulky body overfilled the chair. He was a fearsome law enforcement officer who meted out justice cruelly.

"There is no danger involved if the police have a confrontation with DeVito and he is killed as a result of resisting and threatening such authority."

"But how? I have no such authority in Sciacca."

"No, no, here in Palermo, that's where you will do me this favor. Capisce? DeVito was here yesterday and will probably be returning in three months. When the time comes, you will be told. Carmine and I will be with you."

"That sounds easy from a legal standpoint, but killing your partner . . ."

"As I said, it will appear as though you shot him in self-defense when he resisted your interrogation. But then you worry too much, Captain. You will be under my protection and your reward will be generous."

"But still, how can I . . ."

"Who would dare threaten the Police Commissioner of Palermo without my consent."

"You could do that?" Tonelli beamed. "I mean, make me police commissioner?"

"Of course. Am I not controlling these simple city officials already? You have my word on it. In blood."

"How will I accomplish this and where, Sr. Campi?"

"In public," Campi answered. "We will have lunch with DeVito here at

Propia's. When we leave, you and two of your most trusted men will confront him outside in the street. I will make sure that in addition to Carmine and myself, Propia and his nephew will see us to the door and witness everything."

"The more witnesses the better," Tonelli added.

"Exactly, and they will swear that DeVito not only resisted you, but also reached for a weapon."

"That seems dangerous to me . . . I mean, he'll have a gun?".

"Stupido. We will plant the gun on him after you shoot." Campi was becoming impatient with the future Police Commissioner of Palermo, but then again, this was the sort of obedient puppet he wanted in such a high position.

"Just be certain of one thing, Capt. Tonelli," Carmine cautioned, "and this is most important. Be sure that one of your men yells, that he has a gun."

"That is extremely important, Captain," Campi emphasized, "for if there are any other witnesses nearby, they will confirm that you acted in self-defense."

"And I will be ready to shoot as soon as one of them yells out to me," Tonelli boasted like a child who had just memorized his lessons.

"Good, very good." Campi smiled. "Two shots into the heart should do it. Capisce?"

They clinked wine glasses and the plan was set.

Chapter 12

The day after Franco returned from Palermo, he and Carlo were sitting in their small office over the cannery.

"I'm not sure I understand, Uncle Franco. When did you think of this?"

"It was the night you worked late. Sr. Pina Felizi, our distributor from Trapini, had dinner at home with your mama and me."

"And you decided just like that?"

"No, but after my argument with Bruno and I hadn't been able to convince Tony to come home to work in the fish cannery, I decided Felizi was right."

"I still don't understand, Uncle." Carlo got up and closed the office door to muffle the clatter of the canning conveyor.

"When Sr. Felizi tasted your mother's tomato sauce, he raved about it. Then he said to me, 'You know, Franco, you might do better than canning sardines.' I asked him how. Then he said, 'You must have noticed that the canned fish business is now overrun with products. With no more wartime contracts, the prices are so low there's very little profit.' When I told him that I only have the cannery and I didn't know what else I could do, he replied, 'How about Signora Marchi's tomato sauce?' He said it's the best he ever tasted."

"But Uncle," Carlo interrupted, "who would buy Mama's sauce? It's foolish to think any self-respecting Italian will use canned pasta sauce unless they put it up themselves."

Franco could see the confusion and questioning gleam in his nephew's eyes.

"No, no, Carlo, not her pasta sauce, just her canned tomato sauce like she makes now from the tomatoes and herbs she grows in her little garden."

"You know she did the same thing on the pig farm. She canned dozens of jars of tomatoes with basil, garlic, and other herbs for the winter. Then whenever she made pasta, she just added some wine, pork or meatballs to her canned tomato sauce. It was wonderful then and it still is."

"I know. I love her cooking. So did Sr. Felizi."

"Can we really do this, Uncle Franco?"

Franco was anxious that his nephew understand the importance of his decision and be as enthusiastic about it as he was in case he needed Carlo's support in convincing Tony.

"According to the way Felizi explained it to me, there's an expanding export market for Italian foods these days. It seems that in Europe, and especially in Spain, they love cooking with Italian tomatoes. And he says the best Italian tomatoes are grown not too far from here in Arigento. Apparently our Sicilain volcanic soil is not only good for our citrus trees, it's also good for tomato plants."

"Have you told Tony or Sr. Campi of this idea?"

"No. Like I said, it was after I spoke with them that I decided. To hell with Bruno anyway. On my next visit, I will tell him that his bigger share is now coming from canning tomato sauce. He doesn't give a damn about what we do here. And since Tony hates the idea of fish . . . well I thought tomatoes should convince him to come home."

"But how will we accomplish this?" Carlo still sounded skeptical.

"With the lira I have saved and Sr. Felizi's help. He knows about an outfit in Palermo that's been converting factories since the end of the war. They can provide and install the equipment and other materials needed to convert our filling and canning lines. Think of it, Carlo, no more smelly fish, and Sr. Felizi says he can double our business in no time."

Chapter 13

Sheffield

"That's right, Mr. Dunne. Andrew Cox. He was the flight sergeant on the Ladybird mission. I was just as surprised as you are that he survived the crash." Corklin was calling from a pay phone just outside of Sheffield.

"That's great news, Corklin. I'm sure Director Waters will be pleased with your progress. Where did you say he turned up?"

"The Vet's hospital here in Sheffield. According to their records, the International Red Cross turned Cox over to them. He was in a very bad way, I might add."

"And you say he's recovered?" Dunne sounded excited.

"Enough so that they finally released him in '46."

"What's your next move?"

"I'm heading directly to Bristol, sir. With any luck, in very short order we should know exactly where their plane went down."

"Excellent. Call me as soon as you've interviewed Cox. And Corklin, one more thing, if need be you're authorized to compensate the sergeant, let's say up to 15,000£."

"Understood, sir."

"Good man, Corklin."

"Happy to be of service to the company, sir." *And to collect that fat bonus.*

The one thing Corklin hated most about being in England was the bloody weather. He had been born in Wales, but his parents had emigrated to the sun and warmth of South Africa when he was four.

The rain was heavy and had been for most of the 220 kilometer trip from Sheffield to Bristol. After retiring to his room in the small inn where he had dinner, Corklin slipped into a hot bath. He fantasized about the large reward he would soon be getting for locating the downed plane. Most of it would be used to purchase that auto dealership just outside of Johannesburg that he knew was for sale. It would be great to be his own boss and he foresaw a very good life for himself and Rhonda. He lit a cigarette and slid deeper into the tub thinking of home and her smooth dark skin.

ಬಂಚ

The morning sun did little to improve the working class row houses along Corry Place. Both sides of the street looked like a set of bad teeth with several missing, the result of the Nazi blitzes. Although the rubble had long since been cleared, most looked poorly maintained, except for Number 24. Its paint wasn't chipped and flower boxes on either side of the narrow front steps contained a mixture of white and yellow daisies. A green wicker rocker sat to the left of the front door. Corklin grinned as he rotated the door bell key reproducing the jingle of a bicycle ringer. A wrinkled face, with strands of reddish hair hanging over one eye, peered at him through the lacy curtain covering the glass in the door.

"Mrs. Margaret Smithe?" Corklin gave his best "I'm friendly" grin.

"Yes, that's right," came her reply through the door. "Whatever it is you're selling, luv, I'm not interested."

"I'm not a salesman, Mrs. Smithe. I'm here concerning your nephew, Andrew Cox. I need to speak to him. It's a matter of significant importance."

The door pivoted open. Cox's aunt was in her seventies as near as Corklin could guess. Although her hair was slightly untidy, she was neatly dressed in a floral smock with a pressed white apron tied around her full girth.

"Did you say you wished to speak to Andy?"

"That's correct, Mrs. Smithe. Is he at home?"

"This isn't his home," she snapped sarcastically.

The transformation from what he had thought to be a sweet old English lady startled Corklin.

"What would a gentleman like you be wanting with the likes of him?"

Trying to maintain her impression of him as a gentleman, he politely replied, "It has to do with his mates during the war. He may have some information that could be of help to my client." Corklin figured he would play on whatever sympathy she might have for a missing comrade of her nephew.

"You've wasted your time I'm afraid, sir. The no-good scoundrel showed up about a year ago looking for money. As you can see, there's not much of that to be had around here since I'm a widow and all, so he took off pretty quick one night, and I haven't seen him since."

Corklin's early retirement plans suddenly vaporized.

"Any idea where..."

"Like I was telling you, he took off real quick all right with my gold wedding band, a few pieces of anniversary silverware and a cameo broach that once belonged to my mother."

"I'm very sorry to hear that, Mrs. Smi..."

She interrupted again. "If you ever catch up with him I want the bloke arrested."

Corklin had to think fast. "If I knew where to look for him, I'm sure I could oblige you. I'm not without some influence with the police." He could care less about a few trinkets, his goal was far more valuable.

"Last I heard he was headed for London. Least that's what a neighbor heard Andy say when he was trying to sell my silverware at the corner pub."

"Thank you again, Mrs. Smithe. If I locate him, I'll let you know," he lied.

Corklin walked to the corner and entered the Three Feathers Pub. It was a typical English neighborhood gathering place. After the bright sunlight outside, his eyes had to adjust to the dark interior. Several men who looked like chimney sweeps or dust men were gathered along the well-worn wooden bar. An older couple occupied one of the three mismatched tables. He passed a lively dart game as he approached the bar.

"Guinness, a pint," he requested when the young barkeep came over and busily wiped the space in front of him.

"Right, Gov." A moment later the dark lager was placed before him.

Putting down a fiver, Corklin said, "I'm looking for an RAF chum of mine who lived around here." Corklin showed him a photo he had obtained from Cox's medical file.

"Quite a few vets in this neighborhood, sir. Nah, I don't recognize him. What's the chap's name?"

"Cox. Flt. Sgt. Andy Cox."

"Never heard of him, but wait a sec." He addressed his customers aloud, "Any of you blokes know of a lad named Andy Cox? Ex-RAF."

There was a grumbling of negative responses.

"Thanks anyway." Corklin downed his Guinness, left a pound note tip and was soon out the door heading back to London.

Chapter 14

The smell of tomato sauce permeated the air in the newly converted cannery. It had taken the Palermo outfit about two weeks to do a thorough job of cleaning and repainting the factory area. They had purged all the piping and brought in new machinery, cooking vats and liquid fillers. With some adjustments, they were able to utilize the same canning conveyor belts and packing lines. It had cost almost every lira Franco could scrap together with just enough remaining to pay for the first order of plump tomatoes and herbs from Arigenta and other nearby farms.

Once everything had been installed, the conversion people trained Enzio, the foreman, and his crew. After a few trial runs, they had learned to process the tomatoes and operate the new equipment.

Meanwhile Carlo was involved in the precise blending of tomatoes and herbs in several test batches until he and his Mama were satisfied that it was like hers. Finally he beamed with pride as hundreds of cans were filled with her recipe. He was especially proud when he watched the labeling machine applying labels printed with 'Stella's Tomato Sauce' on each can.

Only a month after Pina Felizi had distributed the first sample jars of 'Stella's Tomato Sauce' to food brokers throughout Europe, significant orders were coming in. Carlo and his uncle were definitely in the sauce business, and Franco could hardly wait to get his son involved in their new venture.

Except for a few manufacturing adjustments, the new canning operation worked well. Enzio and his workers were garbed in white uniforms that replaced the street clothes they had worn when they packed sardines.

Carlo also had a good handle on the incoming ingredients and related shipping costs.

"If orders keep increasing, Uncle, Enzio thinks we may need to hire extra help," Carlo told Franco when he returned from an overnight visit with Felizi at his distribution warehouse in Trapani.

"Tell Enzio to hire more, Carlo. From what Felizi showed me, the cases we ship to him go out soon after they arrive. Mama Mia, he was right about doubling our business."

Carlo was pleased to see his uncle in such good spirits. Now if that dumb cousin of his returned home the old man would really be happy. *This might be the right time to broach the subject of Tony,* he thought.

"You know, Uncle, Enzio's not the only one who needs more help, between assisting you with the cash flow and handling all the shipping and receiving, it's becoming too much for me."

"I know what you're leading to, Carlo, and I'm going to get Tony back here soon. In fact, in two weeks I'm planning another trip to Palermo to deliver Campi a larger share than he expects, and I'm not coming back without my son."

"I can't wait to see the surprise on Tony's face when he sees what we've done with this place. I think I'll get him started with the shipping. It'll be the easiest thing for him to start with."

Franco nodded his approval. "But in time, Carlo, I want him to understand it all. After all, someday you boys will be running this place on your own."

A warm feeling entered Carlo's heart when his uncle included him along with Tony in his plans for the future. It was what he had hoped for. "Thank you, Uncle Franco."

"Ah, but you have earned a share in all this, Carlo. Besides, we both have your mama to thank for her wonderful sauce recipe. Now I must perform an unpleasant task and call Bruno. He should know what we've done here, and that once again I will personally bring his increased share and discuss the details with him, if he's interested, which I doubt."

ଽଠେଷ

"Si, Franco, I will expect you then." Campi finished his short conversation with Franco. As soon as he hung up he turned to Carmine who was seated nearby and fumed. "Can you believe it Carmine, that bastard DeVito turned our fish cannery into a tomato cannery without consulting me and he claims our shares are almost double as a result."

"He has no respect, Sr. Campi. I can go down there and end his arrogance."

"No, the plan we have with Tonelli is better. Franco will be in Palermo next Thursday to bring me my share and to explain how he accomplished the change, like I give a good goddamn." Campi stood up and walked to the window of his study. Carmine watched as he looked out over the bay, then lit a cigar and laughed. "Tomatoes, my ass. In a couple of years we'll be hosting well-heeled tourists on that spot."

"It is a beautiful part of Sicily," Carmine declared. "I went there for the hot springs after the war."

Campi turned and faced his henchman. "And that will make it even more of an attraction. Now, first thing tomorrow you get Tonelli here and we'll solidify our plans for Sr. DeVito's end.

"Si, Sr. Campi."

"And, Carmine, get a small pistola that we will plant on DeVito after the shooting."

"Si, Sr. Campi."

Chapter 15

It was nearing August and the Sicilian days were becoming cooler. Franco especially liked this time of year as he drove with the windows rolled down. With the approach of the balmier fall, the heat of summer was diminishing as was the heavy fragrance of olive and citrus trees along the route from Sciacca to Palermo.

Franco had been relieved when Campi suggested they meet at Propia's restaurant. He had been uncomfortable at Campi's villa during his last visit. Besides, it would make it easier to explain the cannery changes he had made since Campi would be less apt to argue and denigrate him in public.

Franco had also called Tony and had arranged to have dinner with him later that evening. Having told his son of the new business, he would wait until they were together to propose that Tony come back to Sciacca to assist in its growth.

Propia himself greeted Franco as soon as he entered the restaurant. "Ah, Sr. DeVito, it's been too long since you've dined with us."

"Thank you, Sr. Propia. I have missed the best Veal Scaloppini in Palermo. Nothing in Sciacca compares to your kitchen." Franco was equally as cordial.

"You are too kind. And here is Sr. Campi's table. I'm sure he will be here shortly. While you wait, my nephew, Mario, will bring you a carafe of my own vino."

"Grazie." Franco sat facing the entrance. He was pleased to see that there were enough other diners to hamper any outbursts by Campi.

༄༅

As Franco was enjoying the rich deep chianti from Propia's cellar, Capt. Tonelli was outside leaning into Carmine's sedan window speaking to Campi. "My two most trusted men are across the plaza waiting for my signal," he assured Campi.

"Bene, molto bene. Now be sure to confront us as soon as you see Carmine come out after we have lunch," Campi told him.

"And you have the gun?" Tonelli asked.

Carmine pulled the small pistol from his pocket. "Si, Captain, don't worry."
He smiled and replaced it.

Campi opened the car door. Tonelli held it as he got out. "And remember to have one of them," he pointed across the plaza, "shout, 'he has a gun,' Captain."

"Si. Then two shots into the heart." Tonelli grimaced.

"Now go and wait," Campi ordered the corrupt cop. "We shall be out in an hour or so."

"Si, Sr. Campi." Tonelli headed across the plaza to where his men waited with a good view of the restaurant entrance.

ဆာ

Franco rose when he spotted his partner approaching. "Bruno, it's good to see you."

Campi grasped Franco's hand, "And I am equally pleased, my friend and partner."

Franco hated the reference, but smiled as he nodded a greeting to Carmine who rudely plopped into a chair and unfolded a napkin.

Seeing his special guests seated, Propia signaled his nephew, Mario, who quickly attended to Campi's table.

After suggesting the specials for the day, Mario took their orders and retreated to the kitchen.

Sampling Propia's homemade wine, Campi wiped his mouth and said, "Bene. Propia's a master with the grape. Don't you agree, Franco?"

"Si, Bruno. This is my second glass."

"It's too delicate for my taste," Carmine complained. He gulped it down and then tore off a piece of crusty bread from the basket on the table.

"You must learn to appreciate the finer things in life, Carmine," Campi teased.

Franco was pleased to see the usually stern Campi in a lighthearted mood. "I don't know, Bruno, Carmine may be right. Sometimes I prefer a good, hearty country vino."

"That's right." Carmine agreed through a mouthful of bread. "My papa used to make a deep red that you could write with."

"So much for your father's course vino," Campi cut him off. "Now, Franco, I hope you have a good explanation for what the hell you did with my papa's half of the fish cannery."

"Here is the first part of my explanation, Bruno." Franco handed Campi an envelope.

Thumbing the thick wad of lira, Campi smiled then handed it to Carmine. "Hmm, I must say this is a hell of a lot better than fish money, hey, Carmine?"

Relieved by Campi's attitude, Franco spent the next several minutes telling them what changes he had made at his own expense to achieve their increased profits. He concluded by saying, "And this is only the beginning, Bruno. As our distribution increases so will the contents of that envelope." He nodded at the one Carmine was now tucking into his pocket.

"Franco, how foolish of you to invest your own money without seeking my advice. But that is your loss, not mine." Campi spoke quietly, "You know I still wish to develop that property someday."

Their food arrived before Franco could once again object to Campi's future plans for the cannery. *To hell with your plans, Bruno,* he thought. *When the time comes, you'll admit I was right.*

Mario and his uncle attentively served the several dishes they had ordered. "Gustare," Propia said as he placed a perfectly prepared veal scaloppini before Franco.

"It smells and looks wonderful, Sr. Propia," Franco complimented the proud owner.

Carmine quickly forked a meatball and grunted, "It's about time."

Campi shook his head at the big man's crude table manners.

"Ah, everything was excellent as usual." Campi wiped his chin as he complimented Propia who was offering them another Espresso. "We are late for another appointment." He signaled Carmine who then started to take some lira from the envelope Franco had delivered.

"No. No, Sr. Campi." Propia shook his hand at Carmine. "There is never a charge for you."

"Grazie, then we go." Campi smiled as Carmine tucked the envelope back into his pocket.

ଚ୦ଙ୍

As planned, Capt. Tonelli and two uniformed policemen quickly crossed the plaza when they spotted Carmine leaving the restaurant followed by Franco and Campi. "Polizia," Tonelli said as he approached them waving his badge and ID wallet.

Carmine and Campi stepped to one side leaving Franco facing Tonelli.

After seeing them to the doorway, Campi was gratified to see that Propia and Mario were watching in awe at what suddenly happened in front of their restaurant. He also noted that several yards up the street two women with shopping bags were looking in a shop window.

"We have had a report of some trouble." Tonelli spoke directly to Franco, one hand in his jacket pocket gripping his Beretta.

"What trouble?" Franco asked looking for Campi to intercede.

The two officers were flanking Franco as Tonelli demanded, "Just show me some identification and be quick about it."

The captain is more clever than I expected, thought Campi as Franco started to reach for his wallet.

The moment Franco's hand touched his wallet, one of the officers shouted loud enough to be heard up the street, "Look out, he has a gun, Captain."

The two shots hit within inches of each other. Franco was dead before he hit the pavement.

The women who were shopping screamed when they heard the gunshots. One of the officers quickly approached them. "It was unavoidable violence, Signoras. However, as you saw, we had no choice but to defend ourselves." They nodded numbly. Then he got their names and assured them it was a police matter that was under control.

Propia and his nephew stepped back inside and explained to their patrons that what they had heard was a police encounter.

As soon as Franco's body fell, Carmine knelt beside him, felt for a pulse, and quickly arranged the pistola in Franco's limp hand.

The second officer went into the restaurant and told Propia to call for an ambulance. Then he addressed the few customers now milling near the door, "Please remain inside until we have cleared the crime scene." Then, turning back to Propia, he suggested, "Perhaps these nervous diners need a drink, Sr. Propia."

"Ah yes, but of course, Officer." Propia signaled his bartender.

Meanwhile, from outside the continuous whining of the ambulance's siren filled their ears.

"There is no need for you to remain, Sr. Campi," Tonelli told him. "We have the names of two women witnesses and the Propias. And I assume you do not wish to be detained any further."

"Very well done, future Police Commissioner Tonelli. Should you need us as additional witnesses . . ."

Beaming at the thought of such a promotion, Tonelli replied, "Only if necessary, Sr. Campi."

Campi nodded as the ambulance left the scene and the restaurant patrons were allowed to leave. He also observed Mario splashing a bucket of water to wash away the last traces of Franco DeVito.

ঠ০০঩

Driving Campi back to his villa, Carmine asked, "How do you plan on telling DeVito's kid about his papa?"

Campi appeared to be in deep thought. Carmine hesitated to break the silence. It was several minutes before Campi replied. "As soon as you drop me off bring him to me before he hears and gets the wrong idea. Do you know where to find him?"

"Si, Sr. Campi. This is the day he picks up at the brothels." Carmine glanced at his watch. "He should be at the Gorgio Street house about now picking up and sampling as usual."

Campi frowned as he fired up a cigar.

Chapter 16

When Carmine entered the Gorgio Street house, Julio, the manager, nervously greeted the big man. "Sr. Rossi, welcome, and how is Sr. Campi?"

"Molto bene, Julio." Carmine enjoyed the fear he put in men. He liked being brusque and intimidating. It gave him a feeling of power.

"Your visit is an honor. How may I serve you, Sr. Rossi?"

"I'm here on business today for Sr. Campi," Carmine said as he walked through the foyer and looked into the empty sitting room.

Julio, right behind him, quickly explained, "Three o-clock is the slow part of the day as you can see, Sr. Rossi."

"Relax, Julio, I understand." He watched the fidgety man wipe his brow. Carmine assumed that Julio had heard about what had happened to Bertoli's ear at the Carpella Street bordello which he figured was the reason for Julio's nervousness.

"Si, and of course the girls are mostly resting now."

"I know that, too, Julio. Just tell me, has Tony DeVito been here for his pick-up?"

"Si. He is still here, Sr. Rossi." Julio looked up the open stairway that rose to the private boudoirs. "The money is still in my office."

Rather than cause Julio any more anxiety, Carmine nodded his head and said, "Would you to go up and tell our young lover that Sr. Campi wishes to see him and that I'm here to take him there." That said, Carmine plopped his bulk into a heavy oak chair by the door, crossed his legs and lit a cigarette.

"Si. Sr. Rossi."

Carmine smirked at the relieved expression on Julio's face as he turned and scurried up the stairs. He knew he wouldn't have long to wait.

Within minutes Julio returned. "Sr. DeVito will be right down, Sr. Rossi. May I offer you a refreshment, some espresso perhaps?"

"No. We had a late lunch." Carmine could hear soft laughter coming from upstairs, then Tony appeared on the landing.

He looked directly at Carmine as he descended. "What's going on?" he asked.

Carmine stood. "You'll know soon enough. Just get the bag from Julio and let's go."

Hearing that, Julio made a beeline for his office and came right back out with a small leather satchel. "Was everything all right, today, Sr. DeVito?" he asked as he handed Tony the bag.

"Thank you, Julio," he replied as he gripped the bag and hurriedly followed Carmine who was already through the doorway.

When they reached the street, Carmine told him, "Leave your car here. You can pick it up later."

𝕰𝕺𝕮𝕾

Upset about being interrupted and by the fact that he was being delivered to Campi with no explanation, Tony blurted as Carmine pulled away, "I hope the hell this isn't another special job like Bertoli."

Suddenly Tony lurched forward as Carmine hit the brakes and grabbed him by the collar. "Look, you'd be smart to learn to do as you're told. You're not paid to question anything. Capisce?"

Tony pulled the big man's hand away, but only because Carmine had released his grip. "Take it easy, Carmine. I just want to know what's going on. Remember you didn't tell me anything before we went to Bertoli's that day. That's all I meant."

Carmine started driving again, "Just shut the hell up and wait. Sr. Campi has something to tell you."

Still pissed, Tony adjusted his shirt collar. He didn't like being man-handled. "You know, Carmine, I don't understand why the hell you're so cruel..."

"I get money for being tough," Carmine snapped back as he looked ahead and kept driving. "You might as well know I'll do anything I'm paid to do. Don't you forget that, Tony."

They made the rest of their trip to Campi's villa in silence.

Campi was in a small office just off his veranda when they arrived. He was seated behind a large hand carved desk made of a light oak. There was a beautiful woven tapestry on the wall behind him. It depicted a Sicilian country scene. Tony had never been in that room before. If he hadn't been literally dragged there, he would have found the room to be warm and pleasant. Standing beside Carmine, he nervously waited until Campi finished his phone call. When he finally hung up Campi motioned Tony to a seat in front of his desk.

Carmine took the leather bag from Tony, "It feels heavy this week, Sr. Campi," he said as he placed it on a side table.

"Bene, Carmine." Campi then focused his attention on Tony who was sitting facing him wondering what the hell he had been summoned for.

"You wish to see me, Sr. Campi?" Tony questioned.

"Si, Tony. There is no easy way to tell you this, so I must be blunt."

Carmine stood quietly next to the table where he had placed the leather bag.

The bastard's going to fire me, was the first thing that entered Tony's mind

"I'm sorry to tell have to you, Tony, your father was killed today."

"No! Don't joke like that, Sr. Campi. I'm having dinner with him tonight."

When Tony saw no change in Campi's serious expression, he started to tremble.

"It's true, Tony, I'm very sorry. Franco was like a brother to me."

Tony didn't see the slight smirk on Carmine's face as a result of Campi's false sentiment.

Saliva started to well up in his throat. "Please, Sr. Campi, you must be mistaken."

When Campi shook his head negatively, Tony's chest started heaving as he fought off hysteria. "Madônne, not my papa. Please, no..."

"I'm sorry, Tony," Campi said softly. He pointed to a pitcher of water and glasses sitting on a tray on his desk. "Carmine, pour him some water."

The big man walked over to the desk, filled a glass, and handed it to Tony who was bent over in a state of shock. "Here, drink this." Carmine shoved the glass into Tony's limp hand.

Lifting his head, Tony brushed the tears from his eyes with the back of his hand and took a sip of water. He didn't want to believe what Campi was telling him.

Campi and Carmine waited impatiently for Tony to compose himself.

Finally Tony gulped, then asked in a sobbing voice, "How was my papa killed?"

"Ah, but this is the worst part of the tragedy," Campi explained. "He was shot by the polizia for resisting..."

"The poliza! How can that be?" Tony shouted.

"Stay calm, Tony," Carmine warned.

"Don't tell me to be calm, goddamn it! My papa's dead."

Carmine started to go for Tony for his insolence but Campi held up his hand stopping his threatening advance.

"How? Why would they want to kill my papa, Sr. Campi?" The news was too painful for him to accept. He needed an explanation.

"We had just finished lunch at Propia's when the polizia approached your papa outside the restaurant."

Tony's eyes welled with tears as he listened intently to Campi.

"One of them was a polizia captain who recognized your papa from our old black market activities. When he asked your papa for identification, your papa pulled out a gun."

"What? That's impossible. My papa never had a gun," Tony insisted as he dried his eyes.

"Of course he owned a gun, we all did back then. You were just too young to know. That's what happened, Tony, believe me. Ask Carmine, he was there as well as several other witnesses who saw it happen, including Propia and his nephew."

"That's right," Carmine grunted. "Your papa shoulda never pulled a gun."

Grief mixed with anger as Tony realized who it was that was telling him all this. After all, he knew his papa and Campi were at odds about the cannery, but he also knew how much Franco hated what Campi had become. He was certain he wasn't getting the whole truth and couldn't wait to get the hell out of there. "Where is my papa now, Sr. Campi?"

"He was taken to a nearby hospital where he was officially pronounced dead."

Tony rose from the chair and stood facing Campi. "I must arrange a proper funeral."

"Of course, Tony, Carmine will take you there. As for the funeral, I have already made all the arrangements with Rizzo's Funeral home here in Palermo."

"Papa wanted to be next to Mama," Tony started sobbing again.

"Those are the arrangements that I have made with Sr. Rizzo. I knew your papa's wishes as well. Now you should go. Carmine will take you."

Riding with Carmine back to his car, Tony asked, "Just who was it that shot papa?"

Tossing his cigarette butt out the car window, Carmine replied, "You know, Tony, your papa had some pallinas to pull a gun on a cop."

You're lying, you bastard, just like Campi. Tony's brain was on fire with anger. "Just tell me who the hell he was, Carmine."

"Capt. Tonelli of the Palermo Polizia. Like Campi said, he only wanted to talk to Franco, but your papa panicked."

Tony didn't respond but remained silent until they reached his car. *Someday they'll pay for this, I swear.*

When Tony got back to his apartment he rushed to the bathroom and vomited. After his nerves settled, he called Carlo at the cannery in Sciacca.

Enzio answered the phone. "Ciao, Tony, it's Enzio. How are you?"

Controlling himself so he wouldn't break down again, Tony replied, "I'm okay, Enzio, but I need to speak to Carlo right away."

"Si, Tony, he's downstairs. I will have to go get him. He'll never hear me yell from up here. Scusi, please."

Tony lit a cigarette while he waited and wondered just how the hell he was going to tell Carlo that his Papa was dead and explain the circumstances the way Campi had explained them to him and which he didn't believe.

When Carlo got to the phone, he teased, "Hey, Palermo big-shot, what's with the phone call. I thought you were meeting your father for dinner?"

At the thought of the pleasant evening he had anticipated spending with his father, all of the grief he was feeling came out in a frenzy of sobbing into the phone. He was bawling so loud that he couldn't hear Carlo questioning what was wrong.

"Tony, what is it?"

"It's papa, Carlo. They killed him." Tony hardly got it out before his voice choked up again.

"What the hell are you talking about? Who killed your father? For God sakes, Tony, get hold of yourself. You're not making any sense."

"I'll try, Carlo. Just listen." For the next few minutes he told Carlo everything that Campi had told him about the shooting, then concluded by saying, "And I don't believe a word of it. I just know that bastard Campi was behind it, and I swear, Carlo, I'm going to get him for what he did . . ."

"Slow down, Tony, don't do or say anything. Oh jeez, how am I going to explain this to mama, she hasn't been in the best of health lately."

"Campi has arranged for papa's funeral and a burial site next to my mama for the day after tomorrow. This will be too much for your mama, Carlo. Maybe you should have Enzio's wife, Esther, stay with her. Aunt Stella likes her a lot."

ೞೊಅ

Carlo's mind was whirling with anxiety over the news of his uncle's death, Tony's emotional instability, and his mother's fragile health. He had been standing when he answered the phone but now he felt his knees buckle so he plopped into the desk chair. "I'm leaving this evening, just stay in your apartment until I get there. I'll call Felizi. I'm certain he'll want to know," he told Tony.

"Just hurry, Carlo, I'm having a tough time with this."

"Stay put, I'll be there tonight. And, Tony, I'm so sorry. I really loved Uncle Franco."

"I know, Carlo."

Carlo heard Tony starting to weep again as he hung up.

Carlo's mother nearly collapsed when he broke the news to her. To ease the shock of it as much as possible, he explained that Franco had died in a car accident.

Chapter 17

It was a cool Palermo morning when Tony, with Carlo by his side, placed a farewell rose on his father's coffin as it was lowered to rest next to his mother. Rizzo's had done a fine job with all the arrangements. A number of old friends of Franco were in attendance as well as Campi, Carmine, Enzio and Felizi.

As soon as the casket was in place, Campi approached Tony and Carlo. "I want you boys to know how sorry I am. Franco and I grew up together and he will be greatly missed."

Fearing an outburst by Tony, Carlo gripped his cousin's elbow tightly and quickly replied, "Thank you, Sr. Campi, for your friendship and the funeral arrangements you made."

"Ah, but it was the least I could do. Now if you will do me the honor, I must speak to both of you. Be at my villa tonight at seven."

It sounded like an order to Carlo, but he was shrewd enough not to annoy this man. "Si, Sr. Campi, we will be there." Thankfully Tony remained silent as Carlo ushered him toward Enzio who were standing by Felizi's car.

"Tony, if there's anything I can do, please call on me." Felizi hugged him.

"Si, Tony, and me as well. I'm heartbroken for you," Enzio added.

"Thank you both, papa loved you, too."

"Enzio, I'm sure Pina will drive you home. Tony and I must stay until tomorrow."

"No problem, Carlo. I'll call you in a few days," Felizi replied as he and Enzio got into the car and drove off.

"Let's get the hell out of here, Carlo," Tony suggested as he took one last look at his parents' resting place.

It was a little after seven when they arrived at Campi's villa. The rough character at the front door greeted them. "You boys are late. Sr. Campi is waiting in his office. Get your asses right in there."

"Who gives a shit if we're late?" Tony snapped as they walked in.

"Watch your mouth, DeVito."

"He's a little upset today," Carlo said as they walked toward the foyer.

"Why are you kissing their asses?" Tony asked when they were alone.

"Because there's no point in causing trouble. Do you understand, Cousin? Whatever he wants from us, we're in no position to bargain. So stay calm and let me handle it. Capisce?"

"Yeah, for now." Tony rapped on Campi's office door.

When he opened it, Carmine was not smiling. "You're late," he snapped.

"Now, Carmine," they heard Campi say, "the boy's have had a rough day." He pointed to a small couch facing the side chair he was seated in. "Come, Tony, Carlo, sit here with me. May I offer you something? Espresso, vino?"

"No, thank you, Sr. Campi. We had supper a short while ago," Carlo said as he sat down.

Tony remained standing.

"Tony, please sit," Campi coaxed. "You must be weary after such an exhausting day."

"Yeah, it was." He plopped down next to Carlo.

"As difficult as this is right now for all of us, there is still the matter of the cannery that we must discuss."

"Si, Sr. Campi," Carlo spoke first. "As you know, my uncle, your partner, invested your interest wisely when he converted to tomato canning."

"That is true, in spite of Franco's decision to do so without my approval. But what is done is done. Of course, Tony, you realize that your father's share is now yours which is why I asked you here."

Tony simply replied, "Carlo was a big part of it, Sr. Campi."

"Of course he was. But now, Tony, you must return to Sciacca with Carlo to continue in your papa's place and look after our business."

Carlo was inwardly relieved. He had hoped Tony would be wise enough to get the hell out from under Campi and it was happening regardless of Campi's true intent.

"Si, Sr. Campi. I need time to adjust to my loss and getting out of Palermo might be best," Tony agreed and Carlo let out a quiet breath of gratitude.

"Then it's settled. Just one more thing, boys, from now on Carmine will visit you in Sciacca from time to time to collect my share of the profits. You may go now." He dismissed them with a wave of his hand.

They rose from the couch as Carlo said, "Thank you for everything, Sr. Campi."

Campi waved his hand in a gesture of generosity.

As they passed Carmine at the door he whispered, "See you soon, boys."

"Looking forward to it," Tony answered when they were out of earshot.

Chapter 18

Corklin was seated in a remarkably comfortable Italian leather chair in Vandenberg Mining's well-appointed reception area.

"Would you care to see the Times, Mr. Corklin?" the equally well-appointed young receptionist inquired.

"Yes, thank you, uh-h-h?"

"It's Muriel, Mr. Corklin."

He watched her step from behind her desk to deliver the paper to him. She was almost as tall as he, had short brown hair and rather full lips. *Whoever selected Muriel for the job knew what they were doing. Her presence makes waiting a pleasure.*

"Mr. Dunne should be with you shortly, Mr. Corklin. He's in an appraisal meeting and they usually don't take very long." She tidied up the magazines on the glass topped table next to him.

Cripes, she smells as good as she looks. He checked her left hand, no ring. *Oh boy, I've been away from home too long.* The idea of fraternizing with a company employee was never a temptation at the mines, but Muriel wasn't like any female who worked in the Pretoria office.

"Can I get you some tea, Mr. Corklin?"

"That would be nice. And please call me Sean. After all, we both work for Vandenberg."

"That's true." She smiled, turned and headed toward a doorway where he assumed the tea was.

"Ah, Corklin," Dunne's sudden appearance broke the spell of Muriel's charming gait. "Sorry to keep you waiting, old chap. Please come in."

"Would you like your tea in Mr. Dunne's office, Sean?" she chirped.

"No thanks, Muriel," he secretly sighed, then lied in an official tone, "I'm fine."

"Efficient young lady," Dunne commented as they entered his office.

Oh, I'll bet she is.

"You say you located Cox and now you've lost him. I must say, Waters wasn't altogether thrilled to hear that bit of news when you called me last night."

Corklin bristled at the implication that he may have blundered. "I never lost what I never had, sir. Apparently our Mr. Cox is a bit of a rogue who robbed his aunt in Bristol and is now somewhere in London."

"Hu-umph. Then what do you propose we do now? I needn't remind you of the financial consequences of failure."

"I haven't failed, sir. We've just come upon a log in our path, and in order to step over it, I need assistance."

"Mine, I presume?"

"Your contacts to be precise."

"I see." Dunne leaned back and fired up a cigarette.

"As a wounded veteran, I'm certain Cox receives a disability pension."

"I would imagine. Go on," Dunne exhaled.

"I understand the military's Financial Services Branch issues all pension benefits."

"Very good, Corklin." Dunne flicked an ash. "I'm sure Mr. Waters or myself can be of assistance in that regard."

I thought you could. "All I need is an address, sir."

"You'll have it by the end of the week. Is there anything else?"

"No, sir. You have my number in Staines. Meantime, I'll enjoy what London has to offer in the way of recreation."

"You do that. And, Corklin, just for the record, Muriel is not included in those plans, I assume. Employee socializing is not good form here at Vandenberg."

I'll be damned, I underestimated old Dunne. "I'm well aware of that rule, sir."

After leaving Dunne's office he stopped at Muriel's desk.

"I'm sorry you missed out on my tea, Sean." She sang his name.

"Me, too, Muriel. I'm sure you brew a wicked cup." His eyes wedged between her cleavage.

"There are several quaint tearooms in Staines."

"You know where I'm staying?"

"Standard procedure."

"I see." He rubbed his beard.

"I occasionally do some shopping in Staines on the weekend, perhaps..."

God would I love to. "Bad idea, Muriel. Company rules, you know."

"Everyone breaks them. It's not a problem, I can assure you."

"You have my number, I assume. If I'm around, I'd love to."

"Ta-ta then."

"See you." He could just imagine those full lips wrapped around a teacup.

જીભ્ય

It was Sunday morning when Corklin received a call from Dunne. "Good news, Corklin. At the cost of a boring evening dining with retired RAF Flight Minister Grimes, I was able to uncover the whereabouts of our man Cox."

"I knew you would, sir."

"Yes, well, it was a rather simple matter for Grimes."

"Just a moment, sir, I'll get a pen." With his hand over the mouthpiece Corklin whispered, "Thank you," as Muriel snickered and handed him her pen. "Go ahead, sir."

"Cox's checks are forwarded to a Miss Irene Hatche, with an 'e,' 133 Charwood Road in Pimlico."

"Got it, sir. That's Hatche with an 'e'."

"I assume you'll be on it first thing?"

"First thing tomorrow, sir. I'm attending to personal needs today."

"Hu-umph, of course. I imagine laundry and such is the price of being a bachelor."

"It's very hard at times, sir. I'll call you as soon as I make contact, tomorrow that is."

Muriel, lying next to him, covered her mouth with both hands to suppress her laughter.

જીભ્ય

The wipers on his rented Fiat fanned monotonously as Corklin tooled his way on A30 toward London. During the 32 kilometer drive, he replayed the highlights of the weekend with Muriel.

He hadn't been surprised when she rang him up mid-morning on Saturday. After meeting her at the zoo that afternoon and having a typical beef dinner in a quiet café not far from the crown jewels, they decided to take tea at his place.

By midnight they were in bed. He had joked at how receptive she was as a receptionist. In addition to a great sense of humor and body, Muriel Swanson proved to be a fiery lover. She had more than made up for his sexual abstinence of the last several weeks to the point where he had been grateful when the weekend ended.

Corklin arrived in Pimlico at noon, found a pub within walking distance of Charwood Street and had a leisurely pint with Shepherd's Pie.

Number 133 was also 135 and 137, an apartment row house. Hatche with an "e" was hand-printed above the buzzer. A window to the right of the porch slid up and a very blond head popped out. "Eer, whatcha looking for?" the blond head screeched.

"Good day, Miss Hatche is it?"

"'Oo wants to know?"

To insure her cooperation, rather than making a direct inquiry regarding Cox, Corklin tempted her by saying, "If this is the residence of Andy Cox, I may have some valuable financial news for him."

"If you mean does he live here, the answer is no."

Damn the luck. Corklin's heart sank a little. "I understood he gets his mail here."

"Oh sure he does. He uses me and me place like it was his. So, if it's money you have for him, you can leave it with me, luv. I'll see that Andy gets it when he shows up again."

I'll bet you will, Irene. "When might that be? I must verify it's Ex RAF Flt. Sgt. Andrew Cox first."

"What's the matter, luv, don't you trust me? He was a flyboy all right. Just a minute, I'll let you in."

The front door cried for oiling as she opened it. "Please, won't you come in, sir."

Irene was short and sensually plump. Though quite pretty, she wore a bit too much mascara. She had on a freshly pressed dark brown skirt and starched tan blouse. He could see the dark roots of her well-coifed blond hair.

"Excuse the crumpled look of the place. I didn't have time to tidy up 'cause I'm running late for work. Exactly what is it Andy has coming?"

"I can only discuss it with Andy. I'm sure after we talk, he'll be happy to share his good fortune with you."

She pulled some linens off a chair, but Corklin remained standing.

"How good is 'good'?"

Corklin was getting tired of playing games. "Now look, Miss Hatche, do you know where I can reach him? It's very important."

"Blast, I'm late. My boss at Boots will be upset with me."

"Cosmetic counter, correct?"

"How'd you know? Ah, you're a kidder, you are. Okay, Andy stops by for his mail, a free meal and well . . . you know, about twice a week. And judging by that government letter he gets regular," she pointed to some mail on a nearby table, "he should be here tonight by supper time for sure. That's all he'll be enjoying tonight, heh, heh, I got me visitor, if you know what I mean."

"Here's a phone number where he can reach me." He scribbled down the number of his rooming house in Staines on a slip of note paper. "Have him ask for Sean Corklin. That's me." He added his name as well.

"And you say there's money involved? I'll be sure he gets this, Mr. Cork."

"It's on the paper, CORKLIN."

He headed out the door with Irene on his heels. She locked up behind them and scurried past him down the stairs.

"I'm really late," she yelled back as she rushed away.

Chapter 19

It had been almost three months since Tony had buried his father. During this time Carlo had been trying to teach him how the cannery worked. The business was growing faster than even Franco had dreamed and Carmine had already made one visit to pick up Campi's share.

In the meantime, however, Carlo's mother's health had failed. She had been hospitalized and it had become necessary for him to spend as much time with her as possible. In her last days with him, she had reminded him often of her desire to be buried next to his father on the pig farm. And each time he had vowed to do as she wished.

During his absence from the cannery, Carlo had to depend on Enzio to continue teaching Tony the basics of running things. Because of his lack of interest, the old man would often lecture him, "You are now the owner, Sr. Tony. You must understand what it is we do here."

The processing, canning, shipping and distribution confused and bored the hell out of Tony. He would throw up his hands in frustration and tell poor Enzio, "Save all that for Sr. Carlo. I'm sure he knows what to do." Then he would leave and go to relax at a local hot bath.

ಬ೦೮೩

The first morning light glittered over the roof tiles as Carlo steered into the cobblestone courtyard of The Saint Ann Hospital in response to the doctor's urgent call. Except for the windows that had been replaced after the war, the centuries-old terra cotta structure had miraculously remained unchanged since its abusive use as barracks by Mussolini's troops.

Within minutes Carlo was at his mother's bedside. A priest was giving her Last Rites. He leaned in and embraced her.

She opened her eyes. "Carlo, my son, I love you. I'll be with your father soon."

He could barely hold back the emotion that threatened to break his heart. "No, Mama, don't say that. You're going to get well."

Tony stood behind his friend, tears welling in his eyes.

"No, my son. Let me go. I miss your father and he is waiting. Remember your promise that you will bury me next to him on the farm. I love you, Carlo . . ."

୫୬

"Stella Marchi was a good woman, beloved mother and a devout catholic." The deep voice of Monsignore Funnaro echoed in Carlo's ears as he cried for his lost mama. The altar of Sciacca's Christ's Heart Church was covered with flowers where her coffin sat during the mass. Tony knelt next to Carlo and several other mourners as the Monsignore intoned the funeral prayers.

Tony had arranged everything including their flight back to Messina. A hearse would be waiting there to take Stella Marchi to their farm in Venetico where she would be buried beside Carlo's father, Guido.

Chapter 20

An undertaker was waiting with a hearse when their flight landed in Messina.

"Thanks for handling everything for me and Mama, Tony." Carlo held back tears and tried to swallow the lump that had formed in his throat. He and Tony stood watching as the dark gray coffin being off-loaded from the plane gently slid into the waiting hearse.

"You did as much for me and Pop. Now all we have is each other."

"Yeah, I know."

୨୦୯୫

Driving a rented Fiat, Tony followed behind the hearse as it sped to the out-skirts of Venetico. He reached over and poked Carlo in the arm. "Hey! Now I finally get to see this famous pig farm of yours."

"Don't expect too much, city boy." Carlo lit a cigarette and puffed out the open window into the landscape that he had loved as a boy. "Jeez, you know I haven't been back since Mama and I left during the war."

"Who's been looking after the place all this time?"

"For a while a man and his wife that Papa knew, but Mama told me they left after the war and the place has been vacant ever since."

"And that's why I also arranged with Sr. Scarpone, the undertaker," Tony pointed to the hearse up ahead, "to get lodging for us in the village for to-night."

"But the farmhouse is still there ..."

"Sure and probably occupied by pigs or whatever. No thanks, Carlo, I prefer indoor plumbing."

Carlo flicked the butt out the window. "I hadn't thought of that."

When they arrived at the farm, Carlo choked up at the sight of his old home. The farmhouse and barns were still standing, but barely. The place was overgrown and what had once been fenced in pigpens was now just rusted wire and a few posts tilted at various angles. The house itself had broken windows with most of the shutters in pieces on the ground. Many of the roof shingles had been blown away and the siding boards were split and paint-peeled. The barns were in no better condition. They had holes in their roofs and the planks were warped with huge gaps where boards were missing. It saddened Carlo to see what his father had once been so proud of falling to pieces.

Sr. Scarpone's assistant had the ground prepared next to Carlo's father's headstone up on a hill several hundred feet from the rear of the house. A village Monsignore said a prayer as Carlo, Tony and Sr. Scarpone stood with heads bowed.

When the last shovels full were returned to the ground over Stella Marchi's coffin, Tony handed envelopes to Sr. Scarpone, his assistant and the Monsignore. They shook Carlo's hand in condolence and departed.

Carlo lingered over the fresh grave. "Mama," he spoke softly, "I kept my promise. Now you can rest peacefully with Papa."

Tony placed his arm over Carlo's shoulder as they walked toward the farmhouse.

The front door hinge popped when they pushed it open. Carlo peered inside. It was in such shambles, it wasn't at all like his memory of the place. "Let's get the hell out of here. I've seen enough. When we get back to the village I'll inquire about selling or giving the place away except for the grave site plot."

Tony scraped the sole of his shoe on a step. "Christ, farms are messy."

As they walked back to the Fiat, Carlo noticed the smaller of the two barns. "You know," he said aloud as he headed toward it. "I remember during the war Papa's cousin, who was in the army, landed here in an airplane."

"Yeah? So what was he doing, picking up some pork?" Tony tried to avoid stepping in areas of soft soil. He imagined it was very old pig shit.

"No really, I remember they loaded some shiny cases from the plane onto Papa's wagon and took them into the barn. They didn't know it but I watched through a knothole and saw them bury those cases in one corner. Jeez, I had completely forgotten about that day until now. Come on, Tony, give me a hand." He grabbed the edge of one of the two old wooden doors that were partially off their hinges.

"Do we have to do this, Carlo? My shoes are getting ruined and I didn't bring another pair."

"Come on, Tony, pull. Let's see what wartime secrets are in here."

Tony grunted as the door gave way. "I'll bet you the cost of dinner it's some old Fascist uniforms or some other worthless wartime crap. Oh jeez!" As he stepped inside, he held his nose. "It's not bad enough my shoes are filthy but it stinks something terrible in here. Phew!"

"It was a pig barn, what the hell did you expect? Let's look over there in the corner, I'm sure that's where I saw them bury those cases."

"I ain't digging in that stuff with my bare hands."

"You won't have to. Look." Carlo pointed to some tools hanging from one of the rafters. He reached up and grabbed a couple of rusty shovels. "Here, start digging."

After two scoops of the moist soil, Tony tossed his shovel down. "Christ, Carlo, it stinks worse than hell. I can't take it. I need air. You dig and satisfy your memories. I'll be outside." He turned and lit a smoke as he hurried out the door leaving Carlo digging intently.

Ten minutes later, Carlo pushed the barn door outward with his rear-end. He was dragging a dirt encrusted aluminum case.

"Give me a hand, Tony, this thing's heavy and there's another one inside just like it." He deposited the case by Tony's feet.

"Great, Carlo. Heavy can mean dangerous . . . like old Italian mines, or grenades or something."

His warning went unheeded. Carlo was already back inside dragging the second case out. When the two cases were side by side, he raised the shovel aiming to break open the padlock.

"Whoa, wait a minute." Tony backed away. "They could be loaded with ammo and old ammo can be very unstable."

"Yeah maybe, except Papa wouldn't have risked having anything like that around our pigs. Here goes."

Tony winced as Carlo drove the shovel blade hard across the top of the lock. Instead of it popping open, the hasp broke off the case. Playing it safe after Tony's repeated warnings, Carlo slowly raised the lid with the shovel exposing a heavy felt pad.

Peering in from a few steps away, Tony exclaimed, "I told you it was probably just old war junk. Looks like army blankets."

"Damn," Carlo uttered in disappointment, as he pulled out the padding. "What the hell? What's with all this glass?"

"Glass?" Tony took a closer look as Carlo unknowingly picked up a five-carat uncut diamond. While he examined it, Tony removed the top tray revealing more stones. "Hey there's lots more of the stuff," he said as he removed all the trays.

"There's more in this one, too," Carlo yelled, after breaking open the second case. "I don't get it, why the hell would they be hidden here?"

"Hey! Look at this." Tony discovered the Vandenberg Mining nameplate under the case lid.

"This stuff's not coal, that's for sure, and if the army buried it here there must be a reason."

"There's only one way to find out," Tony said. "Grab a couple of pieces and when we get back to the village we'll check around."

"They're kinda pretty," Carlo commented as he pocketed two stones.

They dragged the cases to the farmhouse where Carlo's mother had a root cellar and that's where they hid them.

80Q3

The existence of the Hotel Reggenza was quite a surprise to Carlo. It was an exaggerated style of postwar architecture, straight lines of brick broken by rows of prefabricated windows. An artificial balcony hung over the entrance leading into a veneer-paneled lobby with simulated terrazo floors. What was once the peasant Village of Venetico had progressed significantly in the many years since Carlo had left the farm. The agricultural development of the area had had a positive commercial effect on what was now the City of Venetico.

After lunch, Tony and Carlo approached the concierge.

"Si, Signores, there is a fine jewelry shop a block away on the main avenue." He wrote the address and directions out for them.

Twenty minutes later they entered The Gioielleria of Venetico.

A young woman greeted them. "May I be of help, Signores?"

"Perhaps," Carlo replied. "I wonder if you could help us identify this crystal that my late parents left me?" He placed one of the stones on a piece of black felt that was lying on the glass display case.

"Let's have a look." She picked up the stone and peered at it through a jeweler's loup. "Hum-m? I'm not sure, let me have my father examine this. One minute, Signores." She took the stone to a workshop in the rear.

Tony and Carlo could see her and an older man through the open door. They louped the stone several times while having some sort of animated discussion.

She returned following her father. "Signores, I am Signore Bianco, the owner." He placed the stone back onto the felt.

"So?" Tony blurted. "What is it?"

Ignoring his question, the old man asked, "You say your parents left this to you?"

"Not mine," Tony replied. "It's his."

"Yes," Carlo nodded, "but I have no idea what it is exactly."

The old man picked the stone up again and held it toward the overhead light and, as he continued turning and viewing it, said, "I don't know where your parents obtained this, but you are a very fortunate young man." He placed it back on the piece of felt. "This, Signores, is a perfect, m-m-m...I'd estimate three carat uncut diamond."

"You're kidding?" Carlo cried out.

"Are you sure about that?" Tony questioned.

"So sure, Signore, that I'm willing to buy it for...let's say...20,000,000 Lira."

Carlo hadn't gotten beyond the fact that it was a diamond, when the old man's offer registered. "Jeez, you're not kidding, are you?"

"20,000,000 Lira?" Tony repeated.

"It is a fine stone, Signores, and it should cut into a perfect gem, I assure you. I'd be pleased if you sold it to me."

Carlo's head was whirling as he remembered those two cases of them back at the farm.

Tony nudged him, "Gee, Carlo, you don't want to sell the only thing your father left you, do you?"

Carlo got the significance of what his friend was implying.

"He's right, Signore Bianco. I must have time to consider your kind offer." He picked up the diamond and placed it in his pocket along with the other larger one, thankful that he hadn't shown it as well.

"I understand, Signore. Of course my offer stands should you decide to sell. Would you be kind enough to give me your name?"

"It's Sr. ...Cartucci," Carlo lied. "Is there any charge for the inconvenience?"

"None, Sr. Cartucci, and we're open until seven."

They headed to their hotel in a stupor. Tony kept repeating, "It's a dream, it's got to be a damn dream."

"I don't understand," Carlo confessed. "How the hell did my cousin, the Colonnello, get his hands on diamonds? I remember Mama telling me that he was killed a few months after he brought these cases to the farm."

"Who gives a damn? The point is, what the hell do we do now? We're sitting on a fortune, a really big fortune." After they entered the lobby Tony headed straight for the bar, "Madonne, do I need a drink."

৪৩৫৪

The following morning after checking out, Tony and Carlo returned to the farm. Carlo climbed down into the root cellar and removed several more stones from one of the cases.

Driving back to Messina Airport, Carlo rolled over a thought with Tony, "Switzerland."

"What about it?"

"I remember once your father telling a friend who wanted to buy ruby cufflinks, that he had a jewelry connection in Lugano, Switzerland."

"That's terrific. Who's the connection?" Tony steered into the rental lot.

"Either I can't remember or your father never mentioned his name."

"Oh, just great. So now what?"

"I'm thinking, I'm thinking."

Halfway into the flight to Sciacca, Carlo nudged his dozing partner. "I've decided. In a few days, I'm going to Lugano. There must be other jewelers there who would be interested in what we have."

Tony stretched. "How about I go with you? I've never been to Switzerland, and those Swiss misses, I hear they're real friendly."

"Stop thinking with your zipper. We both can't leave together again. I don't want Campi wondering what the hell we're doing away from the cannery so much."

"That bastard, I'd love to get him, Carlo."

"That day may come sooner than you think." Carlo smiled as he hugged his flight bag and its precious contents.

Chapter 21

After waiting an entire day without hearing from either Cox or Irene Hatche, Corklin drove back to Pimlico. When she didn't answer her doorbell, he assumed Irene was at work. Leaving his car parked at the curb, he walked along Charwood Street until he came upon a woman pushing a pram.

"Excuse me, miss, could you tell me where the nearest Boots Chemist might be?"

As soon as the pram stopped moving, the baby inside began crying. "Hush, Billy," she said as she rocked the pram. "Yes. There's one two blocks in the direction you're heading, then take a left. It's right there on Winchester Street."

"Thank you."

"You're welcome." Little Billy hushed the moment he was rolling again.

Boots, the largest chemists in the UK, in addition to drugs, carries sundries ranging from baby items to a huge selection of perfumes and cosmetics, and there she was, behind a tiered glass display of cosmetic items. Irene was applying lip-gloss to the back of a woman's hand when she spotted him.

"I'll be with you in a moment, sir."

"I'm in no hurry, miss."

After a few more smears, the woman made her choice.

"I know why you're here, Mr. Cork... it's not like him. Andy, I mean. He hasn't been back since you visited me. His check is still at my place."

"Call me Sean. Perhaps he's busy somewhere and hasn't gotten to you yet."

"Not likely. He's always been on the dot, so to speak, when it comes to picking up his check." Irene noticed her supervisor heading toward them. "I'm sure we can find a nice fragrance for her, sir. Look, I can't say anymore now. I'll be home by five. Drop by then."

"What's your favorite fragrance?" he asked.

"Cachet. Why?"

"I'll take a bottle. There's no need to gift wrap it, miss."

Irene smiled at him as she rang up the sale.

At six, Corklin and Irene were seated at a small table in the Crown Pub a few doors from her home. The menu boasted "The Best Fish 'n Chips in London."

"It was real nice of you. I just love this scent, don't you?" She leaned close to him.

"Um-m-m. Very tasty." He wasn't only referring to the fragrance. Before he arrived, Irene had changed into a V-neck silk blouse and matching blue skirt. The revealing blouse confirmed her breasts were naturally upright.

As he picked at his dinner, Corklin mentally rephrased the "The Best Fish 'n Chips in London." *Greasiest, would be more appropriate.*

"Like I was saying, Sean. Andy hasn't shown up yet. He's up to no good, I'll wager."

"I don't understand." He stroked his beard.

"I thought you knew Andy!" She wiped her lips after sipping her Guinness.

"All I know is I must find him and that it will be worth his while. Is there something I should know about the elusive Mr. Cox other than he's an ex-flight sergeant collecting a veteran's disability check?" He chose not to say anything about how Andy had treated his aunt in Bristol.

"Well, you're a cute bloke and a generous gentleman, so I'll tell you. Andy has problems with the law from time to time."

Why the hell doesn't that surprise me? "I have nothing to do with the law, Irene. My client just wants to know where Andy got wounded in order to locate his RAF chums."

"You told me that the day we met, and I wish I could be of more help." She slid her unfinished fish and chips away. "Too salty, wouldn't you say?"

"Does Andy do this often, not show up like now?"

"Only once before, and that's because he was in the lock-up for a couple of weeks."

Corklin's vision of his easy bonus started fading again. "What was the charge?"

Irene looked around as though Scotland Yard was at the next table, then leaned in and whispered, "Andy prints and peddles phony racing tickets."

Oh Jeez. "He could be away for some time for counterfeiting"

"I'm not saying they got him, only maybe that's why he hasn't come around."

"I have a thought, Irene."

"I'll bet you do, Sean."

"I'll explain as we go back to your place."

"Tea or Gin?" she offered when they were seated comfortably in her front parlor. She had kicked off her shoes and had her feet tucked under her.

"Tea would be nice. Before you brew any though, I have a proposition for you."

"That cuts it." She jumped up confronting him. "I may be just a plain working girl to you, and Andy's sometimes lover, but I'm not some trollop you can..."

"Forgive me, Irene, you misunderstood. Please let me explain what I have in mind."

She sat, but rigidly.

"It's vital that I talk to Andy, very vital. I'm prepared to pay you for helping me do that."

"I'm not sure I follow what you're suggesting?"

"I'll pay you to let me stay here until Andy shows up. I can't afford to miss him, believe me."

"Oh no, I told you I wasn't like..."

'How does 5£ a day sound? I'll sleep on the floor if need be, and I won't be a bother, I promise."

"You can afford that? Are you some kind of royalty or something?"

"No, but my client is. And I'll pay a week in advance even if Andy shows up tomorrow."

For the first time that evening, she subconsciously pinched her blouse closed. "For 5£ you can have the couch, and I'll make your breakfast."

"Terrific. I'll be back later with a few of my things." *And tomorrow I'll have Dunne check out the gaols for an inmate named Andrew Cox.*

೮೦ℂೞ

By midnight when Corklin was back and curled up asleep on her couch, Irene was lying in her bed wide awake, her cigarette glowing in the dark, staring toward her closed bedroom door. *I just know he'll try something before long. All men are alike. Well 5£ or not, if he tries anything he's out of here. Still he's rather good looking and refined.* "Just as I thought," she said aloud as the door creaked open.

"Irene, are you asleep?"

She remained silent and closed her eyes.

"Irene?"

She heard the door close behind him. A moment later she sensed him leaning over her.

Some gentleman. Couldn't even wait the night. Gripping her covers, she sat bolt upright. "I told you I wasn't that kind of girl, Sean."

"Who the hell is Sean?"

"Andy? For cripes' sake, Andy, what are you doing here?"

"I used me key. I came for me mail and me treats. Shove over, luv." He was already out of most of his clothes.

"Get off of me, you dumb bloke, I've got company."

"What? What are you talking about?"

"'e's in the parlor on me couch."

Before she could explain further, Andy pulled on his pants and was out the door with Irene close behind. She wasn't quick enough, however, to prevent him from yanking Corklin out of a sound sleep and onto the floor.

"What the hell?" Corklin yelled.

"Right, mister, what the hell are you doing on me woman's couch?" Andy's fists were clenched.

Before Corklin could defend himself, Irene, clad only in her undies, grabbed hold of Andy's arm and screamed. "He's been looking for you. Wants to give you some money. Something about your war buddies." When she felt Andy relax, she reached over and turned on a lamp.

Corklin rose from the floor and stood taller than his attacker. "Calm down, Cox, she's right, I'm only here to speak to you. It's extremely important." Corklin adjusted his gray boxer shorts.

"You say you have money for me? Where is it? What's it for?"

"Let me put on my pants, then we'll sit down and discuss it."

"I suppose."

What an idiot. Irene couldn't believe Andy could act so dumb. "Let me put on a robe and I'll make us a pot of tea," she offered.

₧☜

When they were seated around Irene's small dinette table with cups of tea steeping amid swirling cigarette smoke, Corklin observed the object of his future fortune. He hadn't expected Cox to be so scrawny nor his vocabulary so crude. It was possible his long hospital confinement accounted for his unassuming build and perhaps his cockney tongue gave the impression that he was not too literate.

"All right, Mr. Corkney, I'm listening."

"It's CORKLIN."

"Right you are. Go on Gov, I'm all ears." Andy laced his hands around his tea cup and took a loud sucking swig.

"First things first. You are the Andrew Cox who was a flight sergeant assigned to the 409 RAF Light Bomber Brigade?"

" 'oo wants to know?"

"Some very important people here in London." *I could kick your little ass. Keep your head about you, Sean.* "And rich I assume?"

"Yes, that, too. Now can we please get on with it? Are you ex-Flt. Sgt. Andrew Cox?"

"I served me country. So what is it you want from me?"

That head wound must have knocked all the sense out of him. "We just want to know where you crashed and I'm prepared to pay you 5000£ for the exact location." Corklin held back the full amount he was authorized to pay in the event he needed to negotiate further.

"Now that's a right handsome number, Mr. Cork...but I'm afraid I'll need to have a few more facts before I go giving strangers military information."

"You've got to be joking. That was seven years ago. We beat the Gerrys, remember?" *Cripes, I thought Doctor Wilson said he had recovered.* "Look, Andy, I've got no time to waste. All I need to know is where you crashed in the Mediterranean."

"And if I tell you that, you'll give me 5000£, no strings on me?"

"That's right." Corklin signaled Irene for more tea.

"Show me the money."

"I can draw it out at the nearest Barclays Bank. You can trust me."

"All right, 'eres the deal then. We go to Barclay's, you give me the money and I tell you what it is you want to know."

I could strangle this little fool. "It's the middle of the night."

"I know that, so back on the couch with you and we'll do our thing in the morning."

"'ere now," Irene piped in, "I still got 35£ for the week coming, Mr. Corklin."

"That was our deal, Irene, including breakfast."

"Yeah and I'm sure you'll love her cooking. Now it's off to bed for us, luv." Andy yawned, stretched his arms and nudged Irene toward her bedroom.

She jauntily announced aloud her current condition.

"I don't believe me bloomin' luck," he cursed.

Irene laughed and so did Corklin.

ଈଓଔ

After sleeping fitfully for what remained of the night, Corklin was in the loo shaving when Andy entered.

"Good morning, mate. Comfy couch? I've never had the pleasure meself."

As Andy relieved himself, Corklin, carefully trimmed around his beard with a straight razor. "No more pleasure than you enjoyed last night, mate," he replied. *I can't wait to complete my business with this fool.*

Andy ignored the inference. "Irene's making breakfast right now, so as soon as Barclay's opens, we can be on our way."

When he entered the kitchen, Irene was wearing a pale blue nubby robe and had her hair pinned back in a bun. "Morning, Sean. How'd you like your eggs?"

"Cooked," he replied. He couldn't help noticing how fetching she looked in a sensual domestic sort of way. *Too bad Andy showed up so soon. I must be recovering from Muriel.*

As she slid a portion of scrambled eggs onto a dish, he sat and laid 35£ on the table. "That's real gentlemanly of you." Her robe opened a bit as she slipped the money into her pocket, enough for him to really regret Andy showing up so soon.

"'oo's so gentlemanly?" Andy asked when he got to the table.

"Not you, that's for sure." Irene shoveled eggs into his dish, then turned and retreated to the bedroom.

"How did you two meet?" Sean asked as he watched Andy scooping up his eggs.

"Where do you meet lookers like Irene? In the pub, of course. She was working bar before she got all high and snooty selling beauty stuff to women who really need it."

Cynical shit. "Nothing wrong with bettering yourself."

"Stay with your class, I always say." Andy washed down his eggs with a long gulp of tea, then lit a cigarette.

"Tell me, how did you end up in the RAF?"

"Oh no you don't. No money, no information."

"I'm just passing the time."

"Not at my expense, Gov. Let's get going, Barclays is waiting. Then you can ask all you want." He scooped up his allotment check along with the rest of his mail.

Irene was back just as they were going out the door.

"I'll leave my things here until we're through, if that's okay?"

"No problem, Sean. It's me day off so I'll be here."

There was a nip in the air and both Andy and Sean were walking with their hands pocketed and their collars pulled up. When they were about a block from the bank, Andy suddenly raised his collar as high as it would go. "Bloody crap," he sputtered.

It was then that Sean noticed the reason for Andy's concern. A bobby was heading right toward them.

Without saying another word Andy started to cross the street. A second bobby appeared from that direction. Andy spun around picking up the pace back toward Irene's.

Confused, Sean turned and followed shouting, "What the hell is wrong with you?" Then he noticed a third bobby who had apparently been following them.

The bobby coming toward them reached Sean and grabbed him by the arm. "You're under arrest." He had Sean in cuffs before he knew what was happening.

Sean could see the other two bobbies struggling with Andy who was now shouting obscenities. The blast of the bobby's whistle startled him and after what seemed like a slow motion scene from an old movie, he was being shoved into a police wagon behind the kicking and screaming Andy.

When he was seated across from Andy with a bobby on each side blocking the wagon door, Sean tried to explain. "I don't know what this is about, officers. You've made a terrible mistake. We've done nothing wrong. My name is Sean Corklin. If you'll check my wallet you'll see that I'm head of security for Vandenberg Mining."

Andy smiled when he heard that bit of information.

"The only mistake was you getting caught with your mate here. We got a tip he was with his lady friend last night. Looks like, in addition to old Andy here, we got us a bonus—you. Now be quiet or I'll tighten them cuffs."

What the hell did this fool get me into? Corklin gave Andy a nasty look.

"Vandenberg Mining, eh?" Andy beamed at Corklin.

Chapter 22

"How in heaven's name did you get arrested? You can't imagine how upset Mr. Waters was when we received word of it." Corklin was seated next to Alfred Dunne in the company limousine after he had been released through the efforts of Vandenberg Mining's solicitors. "And I do hope you've been discreet regarding our interest in Mr. Cox."

"Of course, sir." Corklin spent the remainder of their trip back to Vandenberg's offices on Bond Street explaining how it all happened. "...so you see, sir, our Mr. Andrew Cox is a rather unscrupulous type."

"And you have no clue as to where their plane went down?"

"That bit of information would have been forthcoming once we withdrew 5000£ from Barclays. Unfortunately we never got there."

"I see. The next step, I suppose, will be to see about getting this Cox chap released, at least long enough to pay him the 5000£ and locate the crash site."

"I'm afraid it may not be quite that simple now, sir. You see when I was cuffed and forced into the police van, I tried to explain that I wasn't a criminal, but in fact a security officer for Vandenberg Mining."

"Egads, Corklin! Well-l-l, no harm really. Identifying yourself under the circumstance seems logical. Besides, I'm sure it was evident when our solicitors contacted the police on your behalf."

"Except...sir..."

"You mean there's more? Egads, man!"

The limo pulled to a stop in front of the office building.

"When I identified myself as an employee of Vandenberg, Cox was seated right across from me and gave me a very expensive, blackmailing grin."

"Damn the luck. Well several more thousand pounds won't matter. You're sure, of course, that he has no idea what was on board that plane?"

"I'm certain he doesn't, sir. He seemed quite content to accept the 5000£ until he became aware that I was representing a wealthy mining company. He's a street hustler who smells more money."

"The scoundrel. But if he has what we're seeking, I'm sure we can meet his demands."

"Yes, sir."

They were now in the lobby waiting for the lift.

"I'm certain we can arrange with Scotland Yard to release Cox in our custody. Nonetheless, be prepared to receive a stand-down from the director."

"Yes, sir." *That damn Andy.*

ഇരു

"It's the truth, Irene. We were walking to the bank when the bobbies picked us up." Andy was explaining to Irene in the visitor's dock where she had brought him some smokes and personal items after he sent word of his incarceration. "Like I always said, you can't trust all that polish and gentlemanly airs. It seems your friend, Mr. Corklin, is some kind of private copper."

"I don't understand what that has to do with your predicament right now, Andy? Are you saying that Sean was the reason for your arrest?"

"Nah, he had nothing to do with it and they let him go real quick. They got me for jumping me bail on an old gambling charge. That's your problem, Irene, you don't get the real picture of the way life works."

"At least my picture ain't got bars in front of me. Serves me right for even coming down here. You'll never change, Andy."

"Easy, luv. You know I mean nothing by it. You're too trusting is all."

"You of all people should be glad I am."

He lit up one of the smokes she had brought, leaned back and puffed toward the ceiling grinning.

She'd seen that conniving look before.

"You're looking at a man who'll soon be rolling in pounds, and I won't forget how good you've been to me, Irene."

"That 5000£ wouldn't last you long, Andy. We both know that."

"That's a mere pittance, luv. I figure old Corklin and his bosses can afford a hell-of-a-lot more than that."

"Times up, miss," the dock guard announced.

As she started to rise, Andy whispered, "Vandenberg Mining."

"Huh?"

"I want you to find out what exactly Vandenberg Mining does."

"I don't understand, Andy."

"That's who Corklin works for. Look 'em up. They gotta be in the directory."

The guard was upon them now. "Go along now, miss. Time is up." He raised Andy by the elbow.

"I'll be back day after tomorrow," she promised as the guard led him out.

"Remember, Irene. It's very important," he shouted after her.

ॐღ

The next two days seemed more like ten to Andy until he was finally returned to the visitor's dock where Irene was waiting.

"You look great, Irene," he said as he sat across from her.

"Humph. You know, Andy, the only time you say sweet things to me is either in my bed or when you want something."

"Can't a chap compliment his girl? Now, did you find out anything about Vandenberg Mining?"

"If I were really your girl, you'd get a job and keep out of trouble."

"I got no time for this, Irene. Come on, out with it. Like I said, it'll be worth your while."

"This is the last time, Andy. If you don't straighten out, we're finished. I've had enough of prison visits."

"If what you tell me works out, you'll never have to make one again, luv. Now, did you look up Vandenberg Mining?"

"They have an office building on Bond Street..."

"I knew it. Jackpot!"

"They own some kind of mines in Africa. That's all me boss could tell me. He dabbles in the stock exchange a little."

"You didn't mention me to him..."

"'Course not. You think I want them at Boots to know I associate with the likes of you."

"Bond Street, huh? I knew it! Well, the likes of me will be getting a lot more respect, and real soon."

"Sounds like another of your bad ideas about to spring out of that small brain of yours. I done what you asked, Andy, but I want no part of what you're scheming."

"Yeah, right, luv." He didn't hear another word she said.

"Time's up, miss," the guard announced.

"Thanks, Irene." Andy got up and anxiously walked away with the guard leaving her still sitting.

ॐღ

Two days later Andy was sitting across from Sean in a pub a few blocks from the prison. Taking a big drag on his cigarette, he smirked at Sean, let the smoke out slowly and said, "I knew you'd be back to git me the hell out of there, Mr. Corklin."

You twit. "It took some doing, Andy. You're not exactly highly thought of by the law."

"The feeling is mutual."

"I'm sure. As soon as you've finished your ale, I'll like to conclude our little financial arrangement. I believe there's a Barclays Bank not too far from here. You give me the location of your crash site and I hand over the 5000£."

Andy showed no sign of being in a hurry. He continued to smirk while sipping his ale. "It took some doing to get me out, eh? I'll wager it did. Those folks you work for must have some pull."

"What's your point, Andy?" Sean's dislike for the man was difficult to conceal. "Let's just get on with it, shall we?"

Andy merely continued in the direction he had planned to take from the moment Irene had informed him about Vandenberg. "I mean to get me out without a fuss must mean you work for some very important people."

"So that's it. You know who my employers are and you figure you can squeeze out a few more pounds. Consider this before you blow your chance at even the 5000£, Andy. We still have no idea that you even have what we're seeking. If you don't, your value could diminish rapidly." Sean knew that Vandenberg was willing to up the ante considerably but he wasn't about to be bullied by this street hustler.

"I want to deal with your superior, not their small fry. That's it. And don't worry, I know exactly where the Ladybird went down. I was on the bloody thing, remember? Now I deal with your boss or I walk. That's it, Gov."

"You dumb...you can't walk, you're in my custody." *I may kick your ass when this is over.*

"Hah, jumping your custody will be a might easier than jumping bail, so it's the big wigs or nothing."

He left Sean little choice. "Okay, I'll arrange it. In the meantime you're to stay at Irene's until I get back to you."

"That won't be a hardship, believe me."

Sean shook his head, tossed some pound notes on the table and got up.

"And Sean, you know how impatient I can be, so don't keep me waiting long or I'll complain to your bosses that you're impolite and tell them how you almost messed up the errand they sent you on." Andy swigged his ale and laughed. "Ta-ta."

Sean retreated before he really did mess up Andy Cox, permanently.

Chapter 23

After a short layover in Rome, Carlo's Alitalia flight continued on to Milano. From there he switched to a Swiss Air shuttle that took him to the small airport outside of Lugano, a medium size city just over the border north of Lake Como. If it hadn't been for the quick passport check, he would have sworn, due to the language and culture, that he was still in Italy.

Alitalia had booked his trip including reservations at a hotel located in the center of the city. "Welcome to the Hotel Fortuna," the desk clerk greeted.

"Thanks." Carlo grinned, and thought, *how ironic*, as he signed in below the hotel name printed in a fine script. He took his key, tipped the bell man, and instructed that his bag be taken directly to his room. Then Carlo walked to the other end of the pink marble reception desk where the concierge was just hanging up the phone.

"May I help you, Signore?"

"It's Marchi. Yes, I hope you can."

"We will try, Sr. Marchi."

"I need the name and location of a reliable jewelry shop. I understand there are several here in Lugano." He had six stones of similar size tucked into spare socks in his leather shoulder bag.

"Si, Signore, Switzerland is known for its fine watch making."

"I'm particularly interested in one that deals in gems as well."

"Ah, of course. You'll find one or two just a short ride from the hotel." He wrote down the names and handed the slip to Carlo. "Shall I arrange a taxi, Signore?"

"Si. Have one out front in an hour. I need to freshen up and have a bite of lunch. Where is your dining room?"

"Just past the elevators, Signore, and, if I may suggest, you might enjoy the terrace. The weather is most agreeable today."

"Thanks." Carlo handed him some lira. "Sorry I haven't exchanged money yet."

"Grazie. There's no problem, Signore, lira or francs, there is very little difference this close to the border."

"One more thing, I'll need a large mailing envelope."

"Si, Signore." The concierge reached under the counter, brought one out and handed it to Carlo.

When he got to his room, Carlo wrote his name on the envelope and slid four of the stones inside, then he licked and sealed it. After washing up and putting on a fresh shirt, he returned to the lobby, had the envelope placed into the hotel safe, and headed for the terrace.

Carlo's first order of business was to open a numbered bank account. The formalities took less than an hour at the Banco Swiss/Italia. He opened the account with a small deposit in both his and Tony's names. From there it was a ten-minute ride to the first jeweler on the list the concierge had given him.

Triangolo Jewelers was located at the beginning of Lugano's main business district. On both sides of the busy thoroughfare were shops of commercial trade from clothiers to professional offices.

A sign in the window read: WE BUY & SELL FINE JEWLERY & TIMEPIECES. He pushed open the heavy glass door and entered. The interior of the shop was long and narrow. The walls were lined with large photo posters of watch mechanisms, springs and dials in abstract compositions. A customer and one of two clerks were having a discussion on either side of a glass showcase. Carlo proceeded toward the rear where the other clerk greeted him with a smile.

"May I be of help, Signore? I am Angelo Silva owner of this shop," he announced proudly.

"Perhaps," Carlo said to the tall thin man. "I'm interested in selling this." Carlo removed one of the stones from his leather bag and placed it on the showcase.

"This appears to be...why yes," Silva exclaimed as he rotated the stone in his hand. "Where did you come by this, Signore?" He was louping it as he spoke. "It's an excellent quality uncut diamond."

"I know," Carlo replied. "I'm afraid I must sell it, along with this one." He removed the second stone and handed it to Silva.

"Madonne. This is also a perfect stone and at least three carats, Signore...I'm afraid I didn't get your name."

Carlo could see the man was waiting for an explanation. "It's Carlo. I never knew my father, who left me these. He was a mining engineer somewhere in India."

"I see, Sr. Carlo." Silva was still examining them.

Carlo didn't bother correcting him. "Are you interested, Sr. Silva? If so, how much will you offer?"

"I could take them off your hands," he studied them again. "Together they're almost six carats, uncut, of course." He pulled over a small adding machine and punched in some numbers. "They will cut much smaller you understand."

Carlo was getting impatient.

"I'm prepared to pay 75,000,000 lira, which will give me a small profit after they are cut."

Carlo knew the offer was low based on the estimates he and Tony had gotten from the jeweler in Venitico, but wanting to avoid undue attention by haggling, he agreed to the unfair price.

"I accept, Sr. Silva." *You deceitful bastard.*

"Very good, Sr. Carlo, I will write you a check."

Normally a check would have been okay with Carlo, but he didn't like or trust this man who was short-changing him. "Cash, Signore."

"I beg your pardon?"

"No check. I want the 75,000,000 lira in cash."

"But, Signore, that's not possible. I mean, we don't keep such a large amount in the shop. I assure you our check will be honored anywhere."

Carlo could see the man's face flushing with anger. "Cash or no deal."

"If you insist, Sr. Carlo, but I'll need until tomorrow. Meanwhile, I'll write you a receipt for these."

Carlo scooped up the stones and put them back into his leather bag. "No receipt. Cash tomorrow, then you get the stones."

"Signore, we are a reputable business."

"What time tomorrow?" Carlo was ready to depart.

"I must make withdrawal arrangements with my bank. I'm not sure how long that will take. Where are you staying, Signore? I'll call you when I have your money."

"The Hotel Fortuna. Just leave a message for room 319 when you are ready."

"Si. Good-day, Sr. Carlo."

৪০৫৪

That evening Carlo decided that he would dine in the hotel since the lunch had been fairly decent. Besides, he didn't particularly care to roam about the city in search of a better restaurant.

The ambiance of the hotel dining room was low-key and comfortable. The room wasn't too crowded at seven when he entered. There was a piano bar in the center of the room and an elderly looking gentleman at the keyboard was rendering a popular love song.

A lone woman was dining several tables away. Carlo couldn't help noticing how attractive she was. *If Tony were here, he'd have made his move by now,* he mused to himself. He was having after-dinner coffee when the woman got up and passed his table heading toward the music. She looked to be twenty-five or twenty-six and her slight figure moved sensually under her dark blue silk dress. She had short, light brown hair and a pretty face. The smoke from her cigarette created a swirling path behind her.

That's the reason Tony wanted to come along on this trip. A real live Swiss miss. So what's wrong with me? It's still early, I've got nothing better to do and it'll really bug Tony if I tell him how I made out for a change.

Carlo carried his coffee cup to the piano bar.

"May I join you?" He sat next to her.

"I was hoping you might." Her voice was soft and friendly. "Italian, aren't you?" she asked in his own tongue.

The piano player, plunking away, looked up and smiled at his audience of two, then concentrated on a light concerto.

"You speak excellent Italian." He studied her closely. She was more like thirty well endowed and not overly made up. It had been a while since the fragrance of a woman's sensuality had entered his nostrils. He was definitely interested.

She laughed, "Of course. I'm Swiss, but Italian is our language in this part of Switzerland."

He surprised himself by laughing back. "I knew that. Hi, my name is Carlo."

"Susanne. Nice to meet you, Carlo."

She was drinking Galliano on the rocks. When she was down to the rocks he offered her another.

"Only if you'll join me, Carlo."

"I don't usually drink, but I do like Galliano. Sure why not?"

After an hour of small talk they had a third round, paying little attention to the man who had taken a seat opposite them.

When the piano player took a break and the man left, she took out a compact to check her lipstick.

"Oh my, I'm a mess. Need to freshen up. Will you excuse me for a moment?"

This was his chance. "You look great to me, but if you must, I'm a guest here and you're welcome to use my room."

She smiled. "You're really nice, you know, and you have been a real gentleman. Why not?"

His heart dropped to his crotch.

Twenty minutes later they were engrossed in sex when there was a knock on the door. He ignored it. There was another knock, this time a bit louder. Again Carlo ignored it. Still another knock, more insistent than the others.

She looked up at him. "I can't concentrate with that going on, Carlo. And you do want my full attention, don't you?" she blinked coyly.

"Shit." He got up. "Just a damn minute." He pulled on a hotel robe and went to the door.

Susanne seized the opportunity and dashed into the bathroom.

As soon as he unhooked the safety latch, the door exploded inward. Carlo was thrown to the floor. A heavyset man Carlo thought he recognized from the piano bar, straddled him and hit him in the temple with a hard object.

He must have been out for a good ten minutes. When he came to, his overnight bag was spilled all over the bed and the leather bag with the two stones was gone. So was Susanne.

"Damn! How stupid of me." He spoke to himself as he soaked a towel with cold water and pressed it against his throbbing head.

He called room service for some aspirin, then nursed his headache and tried to get some sleep. *Tony's never gonna let me forget this.* The thought made his head hurt even more. A bluish black lump over his right eye stared back at him as he shaved in the morning.

For breakfast, Carlo ordered coffee and sweet rolls from room service then called Tony.

"You were set-up, partner. Even I couldn't have gotten the woman you described into bed that quick," Tony confessed.

Carlo quickly changed the subject. "Only one person knew about the diamonds, that goddamn jeweler, Silva."

"Do you want me to come there? I'll fix the bastard."

"What makes you think I couldn't? No, Tony, stay put. There's nothing we can do. I can't call the police. Consider it my screw-up, a 75,000,000 lira screw-up." He then went on to explain the other diamonds were safe and that he'd try another jeweler.

"Good luck, lover boy," Tony teased and hung up.

It was after a light lunch that Carlo felt well enough to try the other jeweler on his list.

Alpine Watches and Fine Jewelry was farther from the hotel at the opposite end of town. Its interior was less extravagant than Carlo would have imagined. Except for the thick pile carpeting, little effort had been put into any semblance of décor. The glass showcases lining each side of the long narrow room were overflowing with merchandise, and had countless Rolex and other Swiss brand display cards sitting on top. Dark paneled walls did little to brighten the place, but the abundance of overhead lighting made up for it. Several customers were negotiating with clerks at the counter as well as at two desks in the rear.

Carlo headed toward the desks hoping that there he would draw less attention to what he had in the hotel envelope. He studied some rather nice looking rings in a showcase nearby as he waited for a clerk to become free. Alpines may have been drab looking but what glittered from its cases wasn't.

"May I be of assistance, Signore?" a clerk who had just finished with his customer inquired.

"Perhaps." Carlo sat before him. "Do you purchase as well as sell?"

"It depends, Signore. We don't normally deal in estate jewelry unless it's of the highest quality. We're primarily retail as you can see." He pointed to the number of salespeople busily engaged with potential buyers. "We do, however, do appraisals. For a fee, of course. What did you have in mind?"

"Of course." Carlo reached into the envelope allowing his fingers to decide which two stones to remove.

The small man peered at him through rimless glasses and stroked his goatee as he waited. "Oh my, one moment." The clerk pulled out a blue velour viewing cloth as Carlo started to place the stones onto the desk. "Now what have we here?" He picked up the larger of the two. After a moment he picked up the other one and holding them both like fragile eggs declared, "Signore, these are beautiful uncut diamonds." As he spoke, he automatically louped them.

"Yes, I know. What I need to know is how much they are worth."

"Where did you get such perfect...." Discretion halted his question.

"Do you purchase raw stones?" Carlo asked as he removed the other two and placed them on the cloth.

"Signore, this is extraordinary. Please wait a moment while I get my partner." He got up before Carlo could reply.

I hope the hell this goes better than yesterday, Carlo thought as he watched the little man interrupt another man who was with a woman customer. After quietly exchanging a few words with his partner, he excused himself and passed her over to a nearby salesman.

When they returned introductions were in order. "Signore, ah, I don't believe you gave me your name?"

"It's Bartucci, Carlo Bartucci." This time he used the same phony name he had given the jeweler in Venetico. "I'm from Potenza." He recalled the town in Italy where he had been told his grandmother was from.

"Sr. Bartucci," the little man extended his hand, "I am Paolo Lanzoni, and this is my partner, Enrico Moro."

Moro was only slightly taller than Lanzoni but was much heavier, rotund actually. He had a cherry-colored face and a smile that seemed permanent.

"Ciao, Sr. Bartucci, may I suggest we step into the office where we can be more comfortable," Moro invited as Lanzoni gathered up the stones.

They passed through a workshop where several tables were occupied by hunched figures busy at work with small, delicate-looking tools. Watch parts and soldering equipment were strewn about the tables. Moro lead the way through a solid steel door into an office containing one teak desk with a couple of chairs angled in front of it. A beautiful tapestry covered the wall where a dark brown leather couch and teak coffee table sat.

"Please, Sr. Bartucci." Lanzoni pointed to the couch.

Carlo obliged and the partners sat as well.

"Café?" Moro offered. "We keep a pot going in the workshop."

"No, thanks. About my stones . . ." He picked one up from the coffee table where Lanzoni had placed them. "I'm most anxious to discuss their value."

"Sr. Bartucci," Moro obviously did the dealing in the partnership, "if we're to make you an offer for these stones, is there any risk on our part? I mean, we are a reputable firm."

"None, Signores, I can assure you. There are no problems attached to them. In fact, if I am treated fairly here today, I can provide several more of similar quality."

"Give us a moment, Signore." They walked to the barred window at the rear of the room where they talked softly but with animated gestures for several minutes.

Carlo wished now he had accepted the coffee.

When they returned to their seats, Moro spoke. "It appears you have here approximately sixteen carats, Sr. Bartucci. At the buying rate of 1,500,000 lira a carat, your stones are worth around 24,000,000 lira."

"That much?"

"Well, not quite, Signore," Lanzoni finally spoke up. "Let me be honest, Signore. You walked in here, a perfect stranger, with four of the best stones either of us has seen in some time and, how shall I put it? You expect us to purchase them without knowing their source."

"That is very dangerous business, Sr. Bartucci," Moro jumped in.

"I see." Carlo proceeded to pick up the diamonds. "Please allow me to pay for your fine appraisal, Signores."

"Aspettare," Moro put his hand on the stones. "I said it was dangerous, but not so much so that we cannot do business. Given the mystery as to the origin of the diamonds, we will buy them for 20,000,000 lira."

"That's a big drop from what you quoted, Signores." Carlo was ready to accept, but had to display some restraint.

"Consider our position, Sr. Bartucci. Without verification of origin and you a stranger, it's a very fair offer. True, we will turn a sizable profit, but only after they are cut and polished."

Carlo stretched back on the couch and crossed his legs. "I understand, and I will accept under two conditions."

"Signore, that is our best offer and we will go no further," Moro stated.

"No, no, you misunderstand. First, I would like the money deposited in my numbered account at Banco Swiss/Italia."

"That will be no problem, a simple transfer of funds. And?" Moro waited.

"That you will consider buying several more pieces of equal or greater value?"

The two partners stared at Carlo then at each other.

"You mean you have more diamonds?" Lanzoni's voice cracked.

"Signore, you have us quite baffled and a bit worried," Moro added.

"Signores, I guarantee that there are no strings attached to our transaction now or later. Do we have a deal?"

They shook their heads in unison. "Very well," Moro said. "Meet us in the morning at the Svizzero Banco Regionale and we will complete our little transaction."

Carlo scooped up the stones and slipped them back into the envelope. "Until tomorrow, Signores."

ဆာဗ

"It's all set, Tony." Carlo called him that evening. "That's what I said, 20,000,000 lira deposited in our numbered account tomorrow morning. I'll catch an afternoon flight back home."

"Christ, Carlo, this is unbelievable. And they're willing to buy more?"

"As much as we're willing to sell. You should have seen them, Tony, they were drooling."

"We can't possibly unload those entire cases on them."

"Of course not, just enough to get the money for the power we need. Then later we'll figure out how to dispose of the bulk of them. Jeez, Tony, do you realize how much that will be?"

"I'm still too damn stunned to think about it. Shall I pick you up at the airport?"

"No. I'll take a taxi. You keep canning tomato sauce."

"I'm too rich to be working now."

"Take it easy, partner. Let's not do anything foolish."

"Yeah, yeah. So do me a favor in the meantime, Carlo, have dinner in your room tonight."

"Very funny. Goodnight."

Chapter 24

"Sir, this is Andrew Cox." Sean introduced Andy to Alfred Dunne.

They were in a small tearoom several blocks from the Vandenberg building. The meeting location was Dunne's idea. "No point in over-emphasizing the extent of our establishment to our pushy friend," he had told Sean when he suggested it.

"I guess I'm not quite good enough to meet in your office," Andy said sarcastically as he took a seat without shaking Dunne's extended hand.

Dunne withdrew his hand. "I just assumed it would be mutually more private this way, Mr. Cox."

"Yeah, well, Mr. What's-your-name," Andy peered around the quiet tearoom with its lacy curtains and fancy bone china, "a pub would have been more to my liking."

"It's Mr. Dunne, Andy. Keep a civil tongue and let's get on with it. You wanted this meeting, remember?" Sean was having a hard time containing himself. He would rather be giving Andy a good thrashing.

"It's quite all right, Sean. If Mr. Cox prefers a pub there's one just a few shops down," Dunne politely offered.

"Nah. We're here now."

"Fine. Now, sir, you understand we are willing to pay for information regarding your unfortunate crash site."

"If you mean do I know where we went down, the answer is yes."

Sean could see the sparkle of excitement in Dunne's eyes, and imagined that his fat bonus was just a few nasty grunts more out of Andy's dumb mouth.

"Very good, Mr. Cox. Now if you can show me . . ." Dunne unfolded a map of the Mediterranean Sea including the northern coast of Africa.

"You must take me for a bloody fool, Gov. What's in all this for me?"

"I beg your pardon, Mr. Cox, I thought you understood. We're prepared to pay you quite handsomely for your assistance in locating the remains of your crewmates."

"Or is it them aluminum cases we was carrying? I figured from the start of that trip, when they shorted our crew, that we was carrying some special government material to Suez. But now this sudden interest from a mining company means value. Big value. Am I right, Mr. Dunne?" Andy winked at the both of them.

"May I, sir?" Sean could see mere politeness was not how to deal with this street hustler.

"Of course." Dunne proceeded to stir his tea.

"Look, Andy, it's simple. You show us right now exactly where you went down and we'll guarantee you 25,000£ whether we find the wreck or not."

"Value. I thought so. Just what was in them damn cases? If I don't get me some straight answers, you'll never find them."

"Ore, Mr. Cox. Unrefined ore, worth nothing to anyone until it's processed by our mill," Dunne lied.

Sean smiled. He was both surprised and pleased at how devious his boss could be.

"Gold, huh? I thought it was something like that. Okay then, 50,000£, Mr. Dunne, and not a shilling less."

"I beg your pardon?"

"You heard me. If the stuff is worth a lot to you then that's cheap considering you'll never find it without me."

"Okay, Andy, you have the advantage," Sean amplified the lie. "But it's not gold. It's a rather valuable mineral used for atomic research."

"What's it all worth when it's refined Mr. Dunne, about 2,000,000£?"

"Or perhaps less, it's hard to know at this point." Dunne continued to down play the real worth. "You're too shrewd a bargainer for us, Andy. I agree, it looks as though you're about to be 50,000£ richer. Now show us where the plane went down and we'll deposit the money in any account you name this afternoon."

Andy started laughing. They assumed it was for his sudden wealth. "I'll do better than that chaps. I'll take you to it."

"Humph. That won't be necessary, Mr. Cox. I'm sure we can find it if you'll just pinpoint where." Dunne stretched the map out further.

"Well, chaps there's a couple of rubs, the first being, how do I know there's not more than what you say? Trust don't go very far when you're talking thousands of pounds."

"My God, man, we're giving you 50,000£ for pointing to a place on this map. I'd venture to say that was one hell-of-a-lot of trust."

"Yeah, well gents you agreed too easily. I want ten percent and that's final."

"That seems quite unreasonable, Mr. Cox."

Sean sensed Dunne's frustration mounting. "Okay, Andy, what's the other rub?" he asked quickly.

"I'm not exactly sure of what part of the coast we hit."

"Coast?" Dunne expressed his sudden excitement. "You mean you actually put down on land and not in the sea?"

"Put down is putting it mildly. We crashed into shallow water. The captain and lieutenant were thrown through the cockpit windscreen. That's the last I remember till I came to in an Italian medical tent in Siwah, Egypt, where I was told I was the only survivor."

Dunne's finger traced along the map to the coast of Egypt and then south. "There it is, by jove, Siwah. Do you have any idea from what point you got there?"

"Me head was cracked. All I can tell you is that it might be somewhere along here." He mistakenly pointed to the coastal area of Al-Alamayn, Egypt.

"That's a might better than we had expected." Dunne was extremely enthused by the possibility of finding the Ladybird and, more importantly, her cargo.

"I believe, sir, that a reconnaissance flight could spot the remains of a plane that size even if it's only partially intact."

"Very good, Corklin. I'll arrange for such a flight and you shall conduct it along with Mr. Cox here."

"But, sir, is Andy still necessary? I'm sure with the proper plane and crew we can..."

"I'm going. That was the deal and you ain't about to short-change me."

"The possibility of Mr. Cox's memory becoming more accurate when he's back in that area is too important to overlook, Mr. Corklin. However, Mr. Cox, I will offer you five percent for your services and not a shilling more."

"You've got a deal, Gov."

"I understand, sir. The value of his presence is a point I hadn't considered." *Maybe I can dump the little bastard overboard after he points the way.*

"Hah. I'll be ready whenever you say, Gov."

"Good enough, Mr. Cox. However, bear in mind that if we don't find what we are seeking..."

"May I, sir?" Sean broke in. He wanted to tell the little creep. "What Mr. Dunne is about to point out, Andy, is if we find nada, you get nada. Just a free plane ride."

"Hey, what about my guarantee?"

Sean smiled, "You waived that when you forced us into agreeing to five percent. You figure it out, Andy, five percent of nothing is nothing."

Dunne set down his teacup and nodded his concurrence.

Chapter 25

A modified Griffon transport with twin Merlin engines was being readied in a private hanger at Gatwick Airport. VANDENBERG MINING was discreetly lettered along the fuselage.

Corklin was helping load provisions when Andy showed up. "You're just in time, Andy. Grab those last few cartons and lash them down in the rear."

"I'm just supposed to navigate this mission, Corklin, understand?"

"Well, Andy, if you're planning on needing rations and water during the next several days, you best navigate those cartons to the rear."

"Oh great, canned goods," he grumbled as he grappled two of the cartons up the stairway.

"Here, I'll take those." The co-pilot relieved Andy of his burden at the doorway.

When he stepped inside, the pilot greeted Andy. "Welcome aboard. I'm Earl Patterson, chief pilot for Vandenberg. And this big fellow is James Craig, co-pilot."

Patterson wasn't exaggerating about Craig's size. He was a good six-two with the bulk of a defensive rugby guard. His cap was worn in reverse and indented by an earphone impression. His large nose overhung a bushy moustache, which overhung a permanent grin.

"Glad to have you with us...Cox, isn't it?" He pushed a huge hand toward Andy.

His grip was gentle.

"Call me Andy." Andy took an immediate liking to the big, cheery Englishmen. Craig reminded him of some of his pub cronies.

The chief pilot was an altogether different matter. Patterson's large dark glasses contrasted with his fair complexion and straight white teeth. His tall erect posture, neatly pressed trousers and flight jacket reminded Andy of so many RAF officers he had disliked.

Corklin boarded and closed the door. "Take your pick." He directed Andy toward two sets of double seats.

Andy buckled in across the aisle from Corklin just as the plane was jerked into motion by a tow vehicle. From his seat he could see Patterson and Craig doing their thing before takeoff. For a moment he had the terrible sensation that he was back in time being taken on another fearful wartime mission. His mind quickly fast-forwarded as the plane thrust down the runway. This mission was one he had waited for all his life, the one that would make him wealthy.

After a smooth lift-off, Andy asked Corklin, "How come only four seats? What's all them built in-bins behind us used for?"

"This ship is used to bring supplies and mining equipment back and forth," Corklin lied.

"Vandenberg must do quite well to have its own airline." He was fishing for information on just how prosperous the company actually was.

"Not really, just this one plane and it's wartime surplus."

ଚ୦ଓଷ

During the next few hours Andy snored loudly while Corklin got part-way through a paperback.

Craig's bulk extruded into the cabin. "We'll be setting down in Marseilles for refueling in about twenty minutes." His booming announcement over the noise of the Merlins woke Andy.

"What's our range in this thing?" Andy stretched as he asked Craig.

"About 1200 km. We'll need full tanks to make it to Malta. We'll spend the night there, refuel and then head on to Damannur, Egypt."

"That's the plan, Andy. Then from there you start earning your keep," Corklin reminded him. "We'll use Damannur as our base of operations and scour east along the coast till we spot what might be left of your old plane, or any familiar landmarks you might recognize."

What Corklin couldn't possibly know was that the next morning when they took off from Malta flying south-west diagonally across the Mediterranean, the treasure they were seeking was only 175 kilometers almost due north hidden in a root cellar on a pig farm just outside of Messina, Sicily.

When they were about halfway there, Andy peered out his window and yelled over to Corklin, "Christ it's eerie, but I think this is just about where we were hit by Italian gunboat fire."

Corklin got up and stretched over Andy to look out. "That's good. What else do you recall?"

"Being bloomin' scared to death. What the hell do you think?"

What an idiot. "I mean about the area. Did you have a fix on your location?"

"At that point, I thought we were in hell. The radio antenna was so badly damaged we couldn't keep contact with Suez, our right engine was on fire and the wing was all torn up."

"Caught it pretty bad, did you?" For a moment Corklin almost felt sympathetic, until Andy continued his babbling.

"Yeah right, but now I realize I had me bloody ass shot at for some dumb ore that your company had us carrying. We wasn't even on a military mission, now was we? Of course those two over-puffed officers of mine never told me a thing. 'Just follow orders Cox' is all they said when I asked about the rest of our crew and those two cases we loaded on board."

"It was for the good of England, nonetheless."

"Bull feathers. Well, it's for the good of old Flt. Sgt. Andy Cox, now."

Corklin went to the rear and opened a carton. He removed four bottles of Perrier water. When he came back, he passed two to Craig in the cockpit, handed one to Andy and took his seat.

"Hey, I remember now," Andy took a swig. "Capt. Sharpe told me to find our position on our flight map. Boy that bump on me head knocked a lot out of me. It just came back to me."

I suppose Dunne was right about bringing him along. "That's good, Andy, do you recall that position?"

"Get me that flight map from the cockpit."

Corklin stuck his head in between Patterson and Craig and explained why he needed the map. He held it open for Andy as they both stared at the Mediterranean from the Isle of Malta to the shoreline of Lebanon. "So what comes to mind?"

"Here. That's what I remember." Andy placed his finger on the paper sea. "I was a gunner, not a navigator, so all I could guess was Tubruq. I told them I thought we were about 150 or 200 kilometers from there." He kept his finger on that spot that was the coast of Libya.

Corklin was confused. "Then why the bloody hell did you tell us Al-Alamayn?" He traced his finger from Tubruq along the coastline to the city of Al-Alamayn. "That's a difference of 500 kilometers."

"Look, Corklin, I'm doing me very best. This trip is important to me. I never said we crashed at Tubruq. It was a guess by a damn frightened gunnery sergeant. I barely remember being turned over to the International Red Cross by some Italian medical unit at Al-Alamayn, so I assumed we crashed somewhere in the area."

"That's one hell of an area, Andy."

Patterson entered the cabin to see what was going on with the map. Corklin gave him a run down on what Andy remembered and guessed regarding their search.

"Looks like we're in for some low flying and coastal hunting," Patterson said as he folded the map. "You better be prepared to be at it for a while, gents. That's a long strip of sand and surf to keep an eye peeled on."

Corklin had the same despondent look on his face as Andy did.

Chapter 26

For two weeks after Carlo's return from Switzerland, he and Tony pondered over what to do with the rest of the diamonds. They needed a plan.

Tony's idea was simple, "Just keep going back to Lugano."

"Not too bright, partner. We can't unload more than a few dozen before the Alpine Jewelers balk at the risk."

"All right, but it's a better damn idea than you've come up with." Tony stretched his feet up on their desk in the cannery office.

"Give me time. There's got to be a way that won't get Campi suspicious." Carlo lit a cigarette. "Meanwhile, we're not exactly poor."

"Yeah, but what the hell good is it doing us? We can't spend it." Tony swung his feet off the desk. "Besides, I want to use part of my share to eliminate that bastard forever."

"Christ, you'll never learn, will you?" Carlo shook his head in amazement. In all the years they'd been together under the tutelage of Franco DeVito, the one thing Carlo had never understood was Tony's reckless approach to problems. The art of subtlety totally escaped him and Carlo feared someday it would be their undoing.

"Yeah, yeah, I know, don't draw any attention to us." As Tony rose to his feet and strode out of the office, he spat out, "Screw it. I'm going to the spa. When you figure it all out, let me know."

৪০০৪

"Si, Pina, but exactly how do we go about such a venture?" Carlo dipped crusty bread into a side dish of olive oil. They were having a quiet dinner meeting with Felizi, their sauce distributor, in the town of Empedocle, just south of Sciacca.

"Yeah, Pina," Tony interjected, "what the hell do we know about America?"

"All you have to know is that they love authentic Italian foods and your sauce would be a guaranteed success."

"That's sounds good, but how?"

"I have a nephew in New York who runs a small distributing company. Of course you'll need to expand the plant to increase production. Can you do that? Financially, I mean?"

"This is crazy." Tony poured more wine.

"Relax, Tony, let me think about it, will ya?"

"Oh boy." Tony raised his palm upward. "Here we go with the thinking again. Go ahead, Mr. Brains, now you have something else to figure out."

Carlo shot Tony a look as a signal not to say more. *Christ he's getting harder to control.* "This nephew, you have confidence in him, Pina?"

"Yes, he's my older sister Donna's boy, Ben. She moved to New York years ago. Her husband was killed fighting in the US Army in France, so after the war I helped finance Ben's start in the business over there."

"Tony and I should discuss this." Carlo ignored Tony nodding his head facetiously. "Give us some time and we will have an answer for you."

"Fair enough. Now let's order, I understand the Calamari is very good here." Felizi tucked his napkin under his chin.

When they parted in the parking lot of the restaurant Felizi embraced them. "Call me when you decide."

"We will, Pina. Goodnight." Carlo slid into the passenger seat of Tony's new Fiat Sportster. "You just had to have a new toy, didn't you?" he teased as he settled himself into the soft leather seat.

Tony peeled out of the driveway. "Why the hell not? What are we supposed to do with the diamond money?"

"Not advertise that we have it."

"Wait a minute, aren't we making good money on the sauce in spite of Campi's fat hands? So who's to know?"

"Shit, Tony, forget it." Carlo didn't want to argue. It was a beautiful night and, as they drove back to Sciacca, a scheme was beginning to evolve in his mind.

A little after midnight they arrived back at their apartment. "That dumb meeting killed the best part of the night," Tony grumbled. "This whole business is boring the hell out of me. Next time you want to discuss cases of tomatoes, do it without me, okay?"

Carlo was so deep in thought, he only half heard Tony's complaint.

"Are you listening, Carlo? We're sitting on a fortune and you're thinking about selling sauce in America. Instead of that bullshit, figure out how we can unload the diamonds, not more tomato sauce."

Tony headed for the phone.

"What are you doing?" Carlo asked.

About to dial, Tony snapped, "It's still not too late to have a little fun."

"Jeez, I don't believe you. Don't you ever think of anything besides dropping you pants?"

"Yeah, I do, like those millions we have, but we don't have . . ."

"Put down the phone. I know how we can do it."

"Oh great." Tony kicked off his shoes, lit a cigarette and plopped into an overstuffed chair. "Okay, Carlo, this I gotta hear and it better be good."

Chapter 27

Corklin leaned into the cockpit to review the best approach to their search for the downed Ladybird with Patterson and Craig.

"Since our friend Cox back there," Patterson tilted his head in the direction of the cabin where Andy was busily opening a can of peaches, "is a bit confused between Tubruq and Al-Alamayn, I suggest we make our base in Tubruq and work our way east."

"Makes sense," Craig agreed.

"That's it then," Corklin agreed. "When we arrive, I'll present Mr. Dunne's letter from the Assistant Prime Minister's office to the Libyan authorities explaining the need to find our downed mining transport plane. I'm sure they will allow us to conduct the search from there."

Craig proceeded to radio Tubruq for landing clearance.

"What the bloody hell was that all about?" Andy asked when Corklin returned to his seat.

"Hopefully we'll be making our base of operation from Tubruq. From there on we'll be straining our eyeballs." *Especially yours, you twit.*

"The sooner the better as far as I'm concerned." Andy watched through the window as Patterson nosed the plane toward the Tubruq airport.

ಬಂಞ

"It will be our pleasure to be your hosts while you search for the unfortunate plane you believe was lost along our coast."

Corklin had presented the introductory letter from the Assistant Prime Minister's office to Sabha Burak, Tubruq's Under Commissioner of Local Visitors. "That is most generous of you, Mr. Burak. Our Government will be pleased with your courteous hospitality."

"Not at all, Mr. Corklin. The Government of Libya is grateful to the British and the Australians for their valiant resistance against the Germans." He returned the letter.

"I believe the Gerrys referred to the Aussies as the Rats of Tubruq," Patterson noted.

"That is true, sir, because those brave men fought them off from deep ground entrenchments."

"So I heard," Corklin said folding the letter. "Thanks again, Commissioner."

"You're quite welcome, and if you require assistance of any nature, I am at your disposal."

"We would appreciate a hotel recommendation," Craig said.

"Ah yes. I suggest you would be most comfortable at Al-Jawf Hotel. The concierge speaks a decent English and the food is more palatable to a visitor's tastes."

"Sounds good, in which case you can reach us there if necessary."

"Very good, sir." Burak nodded and tapped his forehead in a gesture of respect.

୫୦ଔ

After an evening of Andy's complaints about the pissy beer and overcooked lamb, Corklin and Patterson gratefully headed for their room.

Craig, on the other hand, was stuck as Andy's roommate and nursemaid during the remainder of the trip. "This is it, Cox," Craig said firmly. "One more brew for you then it's off to bed. We've an early start in the morning and we'll all need a sharp eye."

"I hear you, mum." Andy took a swig then carried the bottle to their room.

As he was preparing for bed, Craig decided the only way he was going to fulfill his part of the mission was to keep Andy under control. He knew that of the three of them, Andy felt more of a kinship with him than the others probably because, as co-pilot, he held a lower rank with less authority placing him a little nearer Andy's level. Because of his size, Craig never had a problem dealing with so-called street-toughs, so he laid it out clear and simple for his roomy.

"Cox, let's get one thing straight right from the start. I'm here because it's my job. But my job doesn't include taking any bloody crap from you. So, unless you want me to come down hard on your nasty ass, behave and make all our lives easier. Got it, Gov?"

"Yeah, yeah, I got you. Don't get all frazzled, Craig old boy, I'm only here for the blooming reward."

"Good. Now dump the beer and shut the damn light."

Andy switched off the lamp and Craig could hear him take one more gulp before quietly placing the bottle in the dustbin.

୫୦ଔ

It was six when Corklin woke to the clap of thunder. Patterson was already up and showered. "Damn bad luck," he spouted as Corklin stirred.

"Wha...? What's wrong?" Corklin swung out of bed placing his feet onto a small woven floor mat. "What bad luck?"

"The blooming weather, old chap. The whole damn area is socked in. Flying is out of the question, let alone searching. It's like a monsoon out there."

Corklin rubbed his eyes as he gazed toward the rain-swept window. "Shit, is that rain, or are we submerged?"

"Might as well be. I'll meet you in the breakfast room. I'm sure Craig's up. We'll check the local weather station, but you can take your time. You won't be going anywhere today, unless, of course, you're a bloody duck."

"Very funny. How's the hot water?"

"All gone I'm afraid."

"Huh?"

"Just kidding, old boy. See you at breakfast."

ഇ◌ഌ

It had been Friday when the rain started. For the next two days their search was delayed by the weather and, according to the reports, it would be at least another twenty-four hours before conditions improved enough for flying.

Fortunately the hotel had a billiards table. For the first day it kept Andy occupied, but by Sunday night he was driving them crazy.

"Let's get out on the town," he suggested. "Or, how about finding some female companions?"

Both ideas were rebuffed.

"We're not about to start drinking and carousing," Craig told him. "Besides, the Captain and I are happily married."

"And dead as well. Okay, how about you, Corklin? You're not bloody hitched, are you?"

Sean could hardly stand being cooped up with Andy. He grabbed him by the collar, startling Craig and Patterson. "Look, you little twit, it was your idea to come along. No, I'm not married, but any man with half a brain would think twice about messing with women in this part of the world." He released Andy and moved away from him.

Straightening his shirt, Andy snapped, "You bloody well better treat me with respect or your boss'll hear of it. Besides, if you're shy of women, that's your problem."

Craig shoved his face close to Andy's. "For what it's worth, you obnoxious shit, what he's trying to tell you is that these Arabs have funny customs where their women are concerned. If you're stupid enough to be thinking about a whore, just imagine what their sexual health status might be."

"Don't forget," Patterson jumped in, "we're English guests of a government that is not all that stable. Therefore, we're not going to do anything other than what we are here to do. Is that clear, Cox?"

"Yeah, yeah. Piss off, all of you. I'm going up for a nap." He swaggered toward the stairs.

"I'd like to bust his damn head," Corklin threatened as he lit a cigarette.

"You almost did a moment ago, old chap. But we can't have that now, can we?"

"Shall I see after him?" Craig reluctantly offered.

"Nah, let him sulk for awhile."

⁞⁞

After a few hours of billiards with Corklin and Patterson, Craig called it a night. There was no sign of Andy when he entered their room except for his rumpled bed. *That dumb shit must have gone back to the bar. To hell with him. I hope he has a terrible hangover when I get him out of bed at seven.* Craig washed up and hit the sack knowing he needed to be fresh if they were taking off in the morning.

The alarm blasted several times before Craig rolled over facing Andy's bed. "Shake your butt out of there, Cox." When he focused, he realized he was addressing an empty bed. "Don't take all day in there," he shouted as he got up only to find the door open and the john empty. *I'll be damned. He beat me up this morning.*

Thirty minutes later, Craig entered the breakfast room. Patterson was seated alone eating a piece of dark flatbread. "Morning, Craig. Sleep well?"

"Out like a light, Captain. Didn't even hear Cox when he got up. So where is the little creep?" he asked spotting Corklin coming toward the table.

"How the hell should I know? He's your roomy."

⁞⁞

"Morning," Corklin greeted. "Weather seems to have cleared. Where's Cox? Looks like he'll be straining his eyeballs today."

"That's what Craig was just wondering."

"When I woke his bed was empty, so I assumed...."

"What do you mean empty?" Corklin snapped. "Where the hell is he?"

Craig made a beeline for the bar leaving them to assume that Cox was drinking his breakfast.

"That's some character you hooked us up with." Patterson spread a bit of cheese on another piece of flatbread.

"It was Dunne's idea that we bring him along. I was out-voted on the subject." Corklin poured himself some coffee. "Wow!" he blurted as he took the first swig.

"Turkish. I suggest the tea."

Craig returned. "He's not in the bar or the lobby. You don't think he was dumb enough to go out last night, do you?"

"Oh bloody hell," Patterson cursed. "Now what do we do? We've a lot of beachfront to cover and I was hoping for an early start this morning."

When they approached the front desk to inquire about their associate's whereabouts, the clerk informed them that the manager wished to speak with them.

"Now what?" Craig muttered as they headed toward his small office.

The nameplate on his desk read, "R. Brescia, Manager." "Gentlemen," he greeted, "I'm afraid we have a rather delicate problem on our hands."

"Oh?" Corklin bit his lip.

"Is there a problem regarding our flight arrangements?" Patterson naively asked.

"How can I phrase this? I just received a call from our local police."

"Oh jeez," Corklin sighed, certain it had to do with the missing Andy.

"Precisely," the manager continued. "Apparently one of your crew members wandered into a rather unique area of our city last night and, well...approached a young lady rather tastelessly. When he was rebuffed, with a further lack of civility, he tried to make a financial arrangement with her."

Craig shook his head. "Christ, where is he now?"

"As I stated, gentlemen, he is with the police. Had he not insisted on his government status represented by documents he said you are carrying, they would not have bothered to contact me. Needless to say, it is a very ticklish situation."

"You have our deepest apologies for the embarrassment our ignorant associate may have caused you," Corklin said humbly.

"What must we do in order to get him released?" Craig asked.

"I'm afraid it's not that simple. Unfortunately the young lady he accosted is a college student who works as a part-time server in the restaurant. And, to make matters more delicate, she is the daughter of the owner."

"Oh Jeez."

"Our customs regarding young women are quite rigid compared to European standards."

"I understand, sir, and we are sorry. Any advise you can offer to resolve this would be very much appreciated by my company and our government."

Corklin considered offering cash, but thought better of the idea.

Paterson and Craig just stood by appearing too pissed off to offer further comments.

"Since you're guests of my hotel, I feel a certain responsibility, therefore, I will accompany you to the police."

"That's very good of you, sir."

"I will do what I can. Just allow me to deal with this in an appropriate manner which you may not fully understand," Brescia cautioned.

"Of course," Corklin agreed. "Whatever you say."

ⅎ℟

Bardia Road was a clamoring open market street with all kinds of produce venders. Their taxi delivered them to an ominous looking stucco building located at the end of the block.

Brescia spoke in Arabic to an older man wearing a scruffy looking, military-type uniform.

After their brief exchange, Brescia nodded to the old man then translated for the three of them. "This man is merely on entrance duty. We must see the officer in charge about your friend."

"That sounded like quite a heated discussion you two were having," Corklin nervously commented

"Oh no. I'm aware that Arabic always seems a strong language, but in this case, he is somewhat hard of hearing."

In spite of his anger over their dilemma, Corklin couldn't suppress a smile in the direction of Craig and Patterson.

"The officer we must see is at the rear of the building." Brescia led the way.

The sergeant they encountered there was another matter. He was younger and well dressed in a much fancier uniform than the entrance guard. There was only one guest chair, so they stood before his desk while he traded several harsh words in Arabic with Brescia.

"Allow me to introduce Sgt. Davia," Brescia stated. "He is in charge of your friend's detainment and considers it a serous matter."

"Tell him we deeply regret and apologize for our associate's bad behavior and we will do whatever is necessary to correct the situation," Corklin offered.

"Your associate, as you refer to him, has no respect for our people or our customs." The sergeant spoke in almost Oxford English.

"Your English is excellent, Sergeant," Patterson complimented.

"Thank you. I spent five years in your wonderful country. However, the fact remains, your Mr. Fox needs to be taught some manners."

"It's Cox, Andrew Cox," Corklin corrected. Thinking fast he went on, "Under normal circumstances that would be considered appropriate, but unfortunately, Cox is not right in the head, Sergeant. You see, he received a serious head wound in your neighboring country, Egypt, while fighting the Germans. So, as a gesture of generosity for a war veteran, my superiors retained him to assist in our mission here."

For the next ten minutes, Corklin explained about their search for the downed transport plane. As a final touch he presented the Assistant Prime Minister's letter of introduction.

After reading the document, the sergeant handed it back to Corklin. "Your letter is very impressive and, were it up to me, I would release your unfortunate friend, but...."

There's always a but. Corklin smiled. "And what is that?"

"Please understand that the young lady who was offended is the daughter of a respected businessman in our community and a personal friend of our taxation commissioner."

Patterson shrugged his shoulders.

Corklin quietly remarked to him, "Yes, I know."

Then the sergeant spoke at length in their native tongue to Brescia.

Craig plopped into the guest chair while Patterson and Corklin stood waiting patiently.

"As I explained to Mr. Brescia, this matter must be brought to the attention of your embassy. If they will vouch for Mr. Cox's behavior for the remainder of your business here, followed by an appropriate apology to the young lady and her father by the offender, then the matter will be settled."

The last thing Corklin wanted was to involve the British Embassy, but it appeared he had no choice. *Dunne is going to have my ass for this, even though it was his idea to let Andy come along.* "Of course, Sergeant, if that's the only way, then we agree. Now would it be possible to see Mr. Cox while you contact our embassy for a meeting. The sooner the better, I might add, for the sake of the young lady and her father." Corklin's real concern was for the start of their mission that had already been delayed much too long.

"Of course. I will arrange for the visit immediately."

There was a small opening at eye level in the steel-plated door of Andy's cell. Corklin watched as a large gruff guard opened it and allowed him to step into the tiny room that was both primitive and dank. The guard remained outside leaving the door partially open.

Andy was sprawled on a cot below a window so small it didn't require bars. He sprang to his feet the moment Corklin appeared. "It's about bloody well time you got your ass here to get me out," he snapped.

Rather than give Cox the reply he undeniably deserved, Corklin placed his finger across his lips to silence any further outburst. Then he whispered, "Do you know if the guard speaks English?"

"Nah. The dumb bastard only babbles in Arabic. I've been trying to get a smoke out of him every time he eyeballs me through that damn peephole. Now let's get the hell out of here. I'm hungry and I need a shower."

"I'm afraid it's not that simple, you dumb shit." Corklin still spoke in a whisper. *I'd leave you here forever if it were up to me.* "You really screwed up accosting a young girl whose father has a hell-of-a-lot of influence."

"I invited her for a roll in the hay. I even offered to pay her. So what's the big deal? I never laid a bloomin' hand on the bitch."

"This isn't some seedy part of London that you can crawl around in, Cox. These people have an extremely narrow mindset when it comes to their women."

"So I can see by my surroundings. Get me the hell out of here, Corklin."

The big guard stuck his burly head into the doorway. Corklin understood that his time was up.

"Listen, Cox, we've only got a minute. I explained to the sergeant in charge that your wartime head injury made you somewhat loony. The way you've behaved, it could be true."

"Watch your mouth...."

"Shut up and listen. Two things are going to get you out of this mess, the first is to act a little off-center of normal, nothing extreme. And the other is the British Embassy here will arrange for you to formally apologize to the young lady and her father."

"You've got to be pulling me leg."

"That's it, Cox. If you refuse you'll remain here and there's no telling what might happen to your legs."

The guard waved again for Corklin to leave.

He turned without saying another word, almost hoping Andy would refuse.

As the door creaked closed, Cox yelled, "Okay, I'll bloody well do it. Now get me out of here, please."

"As quick as we can arrange it," Corklin said as he handed Andy a pack of cigarettes through the opening in the door.

Later Corklin enjoyed Cox's performance. At first, Andy pretended not to recognize him or Craig or Patterson. Then after vaguely acknowledging them, he acted impassive to his imprisonment. In fact, he complained at having been awakened and removed from his cell. He swore he didn't recall offending any woman, and if he had done so, he was sorry. He was convincing enough so that the sergeant agreed he wasn't in complete control of his mental faculties.

The sergeant addressed Andy directly. "I will arrange to have the young lady and her father meet us at your embassy where we will expect you to apologize to her. Do you understand?"

"If you say so." Andy fumbled with Corklin's almost empty cigarette pack.

Corklin notified the embassy of the situation and obtained permission to meet there. The sergeant contacted the girl's father and made arrangements with him.

Since their presence was no longer needed, Corklin told the manager and Craig to return to the hotel so that Craig could check out the plane in the hope that their search could begin within the next twenty-four hours.

&ᘓ

Two hours later, the sergeant drove Andy, Corklin and Patterson to the British Embassy.

"Sir," Andy meekly questioned the sergeant seated next to him in the police car, "what are these for?" He wriggled the handcuffs on his wrists and began twitching his head as if confused. He hated the whole idea of being arrested for merely trying to entice a woman to sleep with him.

"You are still my prisoner until we complete our business. Then you will be their problem." The sergeant hiked his thumb toward Corklin and Patterson seated in the rear.

"Be a good fellow and remain calm, Cox." Corklin squeezed Andy's shoulder hard. "We'll be at the embassy in just a few more minutes."

"That's right," Patterson added, "and don't worry, Andy, it won't be long before you're back in your room for a good restful nap."

"Thank you." Andy shrugged off Corklin's grip. *I can't wait for this trip to be over and I get my money, so I can tell these two asses what I really think of them.*

Once inside the embassy, they were required to sign-in and show identification before proceeding to meet with the assistant ambassador who was expecting them.

Andy couldn't help but feel a twinge of uneasiness as he eyeballed the large Union Jack on display in the center of the marble entry hall. Except for his tour of duty during the war, he had always felt inadequate as an Englishman. He had been a street hustler throughout his youth with little regard for the law or the government. *Perhaps soon, when he became a man of means, things would be different.*

They were ushered into a room containing a small conference table surrounded by several leather chairs set up for smaller, more intimate meetings. The afternoon sun shone in through tall windows facing a courtyard. Its rays bounced off the highly polished surface of the table onto the walnut paneled wall opposite the windows and illuminated dozens of photos of Merry Old England that hung there.

Seated at the end of the table were two gentlemen. The well-tailored one in brown tweed rose to greet them. His horn-rimmed glasses reflected brightly as he approached.

"Welcome to our embassy." He offered his hand first to the sergeant who had started removing Andy's cuffs out of respect for his surroundings. "Allow me to introduce myself. I'm Walter Twining, assistant to Ambassador Redding. The ambassador apologizes that he is unable to join us. Unfortunately another matter requires his attention at the moment."

"It is most kind of you to see us on such short notice, sir," the sergeant replied, as he pocketed Andy's cuffs.

"Sean Corklin." Corklin offered his hand.

"Ah yes, the South African. Welcome, Mr. Corklin."

"Earl Patterson." Patterson stepped forward.

"The English pilot, correct?"

"Yes sir. It's comforting to see you are well informed regarding us."

"And this young man...Cox, is it?"

That's right you pompous ass save the lowest for last. Nothing ever changes even hundreds of miles from home. The same old crap, there are Englishmen and then there are Brits.

"Yes, sir." The sergeant took a step away from Andy.

"This is Abal Cardul, the restaurant owner." Twining introduced a short man in a black suit and shirt. His features were soft and his smile congenial. The only evidence of his real emotion was a string of beads being tightly drawn through his hands.

With his head slightly bent, Andy nervously scanned the room for the cute little tight-ass who had caused his problem.

After formal greetings, Mr. Cardul explained, "I did not wish to subject my daughter to further embarrassment, therefore she remains at home."

"Understandable," Twining replied. "However, if Mr. Cox is to apologize for his behavior...."

"He may do so to me," Mr. Cardul interrupted sharply, "and I will convey the same to my daughter."

Corklin nudged Andy that it was his cue to speak up.

Andy was silently seething over the entire matter. He considered it all to be nonsense. "Ah, ah, I don't know why I'm here or what is happening," he stammered. *If they want a nut case, I'll give them one.*

Corklin jumped in. "Please understand, Mr. Cardul, our associate has a problem with his memory and often exhibits improper behavior, the result of a serious head wound, which is amplified when he drinks."

"Your ambassador explained all this earlier. In which case, sir, you should be more responsible for him and his crude actions."

Andy couldn't help relishing the fact that Corklin was now suddenly in the hot seat. "Can we go back to the nice hotel now, Mr. Corklin?" He pushed the situation further.

"Obviously, Andy can't apologize because of his condition," Patterson quickly interjected, "so on behalf of our company, Mr. Cardul, please accept our sincerest apology to you and your daughter for the bad behavior of our colleague."

Andy remained standing. He rocked from foot to foot, his head bent and staring trance-like at the floor, enjoying every minute of it.

"Being a man of reason, I accept, gentlemen." He was now gently rotating his beads.

"You're most generous, Mr. Cardul, and you have our assurance that Mr. Cox will be controlled properly during the remainder of their stay in Tubruq," Twining diplomatically added as he turned to Corklin to confirm.

"That's right, you have our word, sir, and again, thank you for your compassion."

After cordial good-byes, Mr. Cardul and the sergeant departed.

"That was the most awkward thing I've ever encountered in all my years in the service." Twining was no longer projecting a calm demeanor. "Cox, you're lucky I didn't allow them to keep your dumb ass in jail, how could you...."

"Get off me case, Gov, it's not my fault. If these two had gone with me for a little fun instead of being such stiff blokes...."

Corklin grabbed him by the collar. "You dumb twit, I can't wait to be rid of you. You've been a thistle in my britches since I first met you." Corklin started to shake Andy.

"You're choking me. Get your bloody hands off." Andy struggled to be released.

"Here, here, none of this," Twining exclaimed. "For God's sake, remember you're in the British embassy. Release him."

Patterson grabbed Corklin's elbow. Corklin let go and shoved Andy away.

"Your boss is going to hear how I'm being treated," Andy threatened as he adjusted his shirt.

"Get him out of here, and keep him out of trouble while you're in Tubruq," Twining ordered shaking his head.

"Don't worry, Gov, I know when I'm not wanted." Andy strode out ahead of them.

Chapter 28

"It's too damn complicated to work."

Tony and Carlo were having espresso at a sidewalk café a few doors from the cannery. They were seated at a corner table some distance from a few other mid-morning patrons.

"Christ, Tony, anything that requires a little effort is always too difficult for you."

"Yeah? Well, according to your plan, you've got the easy part." He sucked up the remainder of his coffee.

"What the hell's wrong with you? I'm the one who has to drag his ass all the way to New York, meet with strangers and start an import company."

"Why the hell can't I do that?"

"Do I really have to tell you why? First of all, you have no business sense and, in case you forgot, I was the one who learned to speak a little English from the GI Joes after the war so we could hustle black market goods. You never made an effort. Remember, Tony? *Besides you would screw it all up in New York. It's bad enough I have to depend on you here in Sciacca.*"

"Yeah, yeah, all right, don't get smart-ass with me. It's just that I figured why should both of us bother learning to speak English?"

"Look, once the diamonds are unloaded, we can go live like princes anywhere in the world. But in order for this to work at all, I need you at this end." Carlo stood for a moment to adjust their table umbrella to shield them from the piercing morning sun. Even with his sunglasses, it was bright.

"Christ, Carlo, I don't know the first damn thing about expanding the factory."

"We're not going to."

"But Felizi said we needed to if we're gonna ship sauce to New York."

"He's just a distributor. He doesn't know about manufacturing. Besides, it's not necessary. I've already worked it out with Enzio. He's going to put on a night shift crew to produce enough sauce to make my plan work. The last thing we want is to have Campi wondering why we're expanding the factory."

"I forgot about that son-of-a-bitch. He'll want a bigger cut for himself. I swear someday I'm going to kill him."

Carlo was sensitive to the fact that he wouldn't be where he was if it hadn't been for his Uncle Franco, but at times like this, he couldn't help being concerned that his only cousin might be more of a liability than an asset.

"Stop thinking dumb ideas like that. Just be satisfied that the best revenge is that we're going to be wealthy beyond belief."

"It's easy for you to think like that. It was my father they murdered."

"Uncle Franco was like a father to me, too, Tony."

"Forget it, Carlo, it's not the same thing. Now what about Felizi?"

Carlo let it drop for the time being. He needed Tony to keep a clear head.

"I'll explain to Pina that we want to start slow with shipping to the States and, if it works out, then we'll expand. That should give us all the time we'll need."

Some of the tables around them were now becoming occupied.

Tony lowered his voice. "I don't know, Carlo, you make it sound so simple. You go to New York, start an import company and I ship cases of sauce to you. I still don't see why we bother." Tony signaled for a piece of pastry. "You want something?"

Carlo shook his head. "It's the only way to unload a large number of the stones. It shouldn't take more than a year at the most."

Tony poured sugar in his coffee and lit a cigarette. "Yeah, a year of me loading them into sauce cans, while you're living it up in the States. How exciting."

"Why are you so damn hard-headed? You've got the easy end. After everything else is set up in New York, I still have to sell the stones and do it carefully. You know, Tony, if you want to be rich, you have to bust your hump a little." Carlo rose and threw several lira on the table. "Now let's get back to the office and call Felizi in Trapani."

Chapter 29

"The gear is up, Captain," Craig declared. The weather was finally clear enough for the low-level flying their search would require.

"We'll skim the coastline at about fifty to sixty meters," Patterson yelled back into the cabin, "so keep a sharp eye starboard."

"Here's where you make up for your damn stupidity. Start looking, Cox." Corklin was still pissed at Andy. "If you spot anything besides a beer bottle or a pair of legs, let us know."

"Bug off, Corklin. Just because you think you saved my pork back there, doesn't give you the right to snap orders at me. I know my job."

Except for spotting an occasional fisherman or beached boat, the first hour of the search was fruitless.

Craig was tracking their progress on the flight map. "We'll be coming up on Bardiyah, soon. It's going to be a bit of a dicey ride along here, the coastline curves sharply south and then again northward."

"Visibility may be in our favor," Corklin announced from his lookout point, "but the tide is dead high and it's pretty choppy down there."

"The nasty weather we've had for the past few days caused rough seas," Patterson explained. "Do the best you can back there. We'll cover about 700 kilometers to Rashid since, according to lover boy back there, somewhere in between is where they went down."

"The tide should be low on our return," Craig added.

"Jeez. You know, I remember now, the water was low when we hit."

"That's the first positive thing you've contributed since this trip began."

"Well I'm about to make another contribution, Corklin. I've got to go to the head."

Andy laughed and left Corklin staring out at the passing coastline.

"Make it quick, Cox, you don't want to miss what could be your fortune." *I'd love to flush you right out, you little twit.*

About 650 kilometers later, they were approaching Alexandria and still hadn't seen anything that looked like plane wreckage. "I'm taking us up to 1000 meters," Patterson declared. "There's no point in checking out this populated area."

Corklin left his post and went aft to get some fruit they had stowed in a small cooler while Cox continued to peer out his window. He sensed Andy was getting discouraged. If this trip hadn't been so important to him, he would have relished the little twit's disappointment.

"Hey the water's calming down," Andy suddenly observed.

"It appears so," Craig agreed.

"I'll drop her back down again when we head for Rashid. From there we'll circle back."

The following two hours were as boring as the first two had been. Now, however, Andy and Corklin were seated on the opposite side of the plane. Just after they passed over Sidi Barrani, there was a yell from the cockpit, "Something up ahead!"

Corklin sprang up poking his head in the cockpit to get a better view.

Andy pressed in against him. "What is it?"

"Get off my back, Cox."

"It could be wreckage." Craig was using binoculars.

"I'm dropping in lower." Ordering Andy and Corklin back to their seats, Patterson reduced speed and nosed closer to shore.

"I'll be damned," Craig exclaimed, the binoculars still pressed firmly against his eyes. "It's a plane, or what's left of one."

Patterson tipped the left wing as they passed over it.

"I see it," Corklin shouted.

"That's it. It must be!" Andy pressed his nose to the glass.

"I'll swing around so we can get another look, but I can't get us much lower."

"It sure as hell looks like the remains of an aircraft," Corklin agreed, his voice revealing the excitement he was finally feeling.

"Remains is right." Craig no longer needed the binoculars. "It looks more like the bony skeleton of a skinny beached whale."

"That's definitely a fuselage," Patterson confirmed.

"We're just about over As-Sallum." Craig checked the map. "The tide was high this morning. I'll bet that's why we missed it."

"What the hell are we waiting for?" Andy yelled. "Let's get to it."

"How about if we drop your butt out right over it, Cox?" Patterson offered.

Then he addressed Corklin. "We could try a beach landing but I'm not sure how firm it is down there."

"It's your call, Captain. Our only other option is to hire a boat back in Tubruq."

"Are you serious, Corklin, a bloomin' boat?"

Andy complained, "That'll take another couple of days."

"Believe me, Cox, the sooner this is over the better, but we're not about to take unnecessary risks."

"Sit tight. I'm going to skim the beach for a better look."

They flew low over the late Ladybird.

"That's our old ship, all right!" Andy whooped.

Patterson was practically at landing gear range when he floated them over the beach. Of course, he had no way of knowing that years earlier Colonel Marchi and his pilot had taken off from and landed many times on that very strip of beach. "It looks pretty solid. I'm going to put us down."

"Damn right!" Andy yelped as he and Corklin cinched up their seat belts.

ʃↃ𝒞ʒ

In order to gain the best angle for landing, Patterson veered upward and out to sea. As he made his approach back over the Ladybird, Andy broke into a cold sweat. It all flashed before him, the final seconds before they had crashed. He clearly recalled the terrifying sight of his pilot and co-pilot being ripped from their seatbelts and smashing through the windscreen. He let out a moan as he relived the moments when he had been thrust forward like a projectile, and the awesome pain as he was smashed into the back of the co-pilot's seat. And then nothing.

"What did you say, Cox?" Corklin shouted over the roar of the engines revving down to landing speed.

"Nothin'." Andy pulled his belt tight as they were about to touch down on the beach.

"Solid," Patterson exclaimed as he maneuvered along the sandy runway. When they slowed and turned to a stop, they were almost facing the purpose of their search lying forty-five meters off shore.

"Let's get out there." Andy was so excited he tried to stand while his belt was still secure.

"Take it easy, Cox. You don't want to return home wealthy but without your family jewels," Corklin laughed.

"You're a real riot, Corklin, a regular Trafalga Square comic."

After dropping the steps, Craig was the first to deplane. Andy elbowed his way out next. As Corklin followed, Patterson indicated he would remain with the plane.

"I don't think we'll need the ship's raft," Craig said. "It looks shallow enough to get out there on foot."

Hearing that, Andy took off toward the Ladybird. He was waist deep and halfway to the wreckage when Corklin and Craig entered the water. "Come on, you two, move you tails!" he screamed excitedly.

The warm Mediterranean was up to his chest when Andy reached what remained of the cockpit. There were still shards of glass stuck to the windscreen frame. Andy pulled himself up onto a piece of wing structure to get a better view.

"See anything?" Corklin was just below him now.

Craig Collins made his way through the ripple of waves to the tail section.

"Not much." Andy squirmed inside the hull and lowered himself back into the water.

"Looks like several years of storms and heavy weather peeled away most of the outer skin," Craig yelled as he reached the tail.

"Well, the storms sure didn't wash away the seats and gun emplacements." Andy threaded his way through the center of the ship. "She's been stripped clean."

"I'm not surprised." Corklin climbed inside with him.

"Nothing out here," Craig declared as he watched them make their way toward him.

Andy was frantically probing with his feet as he moved about the cabin. *Those bloody damn cases have got to be under here somewhere.*

Corklin was doing likewise.

When they got as far back as they could go, Andy turned and disappeared under the surface scattering a school of small fish. Although the water was a bit murky, he could see the bottom well enough to recognize the shape of the flooring and the ship's door. Exploring by hand more than by sight, he was suddenly startled as he came face to face with Corklin who had also submerged.

Craig was outside hanging onto the overhead section of the door frame when they popped up for air. "Anything, Corklin?"

"Not yet. How about outside?"

Hearing their exchange, Andy anxiously dove under again. *Where the hell are those friggin' cases?*

"Busy little seal, isn't he?" Craig quipped.

"Hungry little sucker is more like it. It's possible those crates were thrown free. When we finish searching in here, let's check out the perimeter." Corklin dipped under for another look.

After bobbing in and out of the wreckage for over half an hour, Corklin finally took a breather. He was sitting along the edge of the cabin when Andy surfaced. "Any luck?"

"Yeah, and it's all bad." Andy was gripping what looked like a large rusted belt buckle. "This is all that remains of the rig we used to secure the cases aft." He tossed it to Corklin.

"That's not a good sign." Corklin fingered the piece of harness.

"I take it we're not doing too well," Craig called out as he waded toward them from shore carrying a red bucket.

"What the hell are you gonna do with that?" Andy questioned.

Corklin shoved the buckle Andy had found into his sopping wet pocket.

"It's an old trick we kids who were raised in Brighton used for catching whitefish."

He turned the bucket upside down to reveal a hole in the bottom. "While you two were enjoying your swim, Patterson and I rigged this up."

Craig handed the bucket to Corklin, who tapped the bottom. "Glass," he told Andy.

"A piece of Ladybird's windscreen actually. We cut a hole in the bottom of one of our fire buckets and stuck the glass into place with gasket cement."

Andy still didn't get it. "So now you have a bucket with a piece of glass in its bottom. Bloody dumb, if you ask me."

"Get down here, lover boy, and I'll demonstrate."

Andy slid back into the water and waited.

"Push the bucket into the water a bit and then look inside," Craig instructed.

"You're joking me, right?"

"Just try it, Cox. It won't bite," Corklin insisted.

Reluctantly Andy pressed the base of the bucket into the water and peered in. "I'll be damned," he yelled moving the bucket around as he scanned the sandy bottom, "I can see to the bottom without straining me eyeballs," he declared.

"Okay, Cox." Corklin took back the bucket. "Now that you discovered one of the simple wonders of the world, I suggest we take turns searching around the hull before the tide starts coming back in."

ℬℭ

Waves of incoming tide lapped their calves as they took their last few steps out of the Mediterranean. After nearly an hour of circling around the wreck, they were exhausted. Andy flung the makeshift viewing bucket up onto the beach.

Also disappointed at the loss of Vandenberg's treasure, Corklin somehow accepted the defeat knowing Andy felt worse.

Back on board Patterson suggested that they return to Tubruq and prepare to head for home the following morning.

"Some no-goods copped those chests," Andy grumbled as he removed his wet trousers.

"Looks like you're back to street hustling." Corklin, examining the buckle, the only remnant of Vandenberg's shipment, couldn't help giving Andy a dig.

"And your ass will be shipped back to bloomin' Africa for failing your boss."

Corklin ignored Andy although he knew he was right. Their lack of success had robbed them both of the promised reward.

Patterson took off and circled out to sea.

Making notes of the exact location, Craig snapped a couple of quick photos when they crossed over the Ladybird's bare ribs.

Corklin took one last look, realizing he would again be the bearer of very disappointing news for Jeremy Waters.

Chapter 30

While Felizi was making the necessary sponsorship arrangements with his nephew, Ben, in New York, Carlo realized he still had several things to accomplish before leaving. Aside from obtaining his passport, visa and tickets, he and Tony also had to make a trip to the pig farm.

Carlo was still trying to reassure Tony that his plan was the only way to dispose of the stones. He had this nagging doubt that his temperamental cousin would be able to hold up his end in Sciacca. Tony's cavalier attitude and reckless impulses had really never directly effected Carlo before, but now it was different, and there was no one else he could trust or depend on.

"I hate this damn car of yours. I'd rather be driving my Sportster," Tony complained. He was driving Carlo's Buick to Messina in a heavy downpour.

"For one thing, it's safer in this kind of weather."

"Yeah, yeah. So tell me, what happens if we get caught trying to smuggle gems into the US?"

"Then I go to jail, but they can't touch you since they won't know who's operating at this end. And slow down, I want to live to enjoy our money."

"You mean my money, if they stick your ass in some American prison."

"Don't count on it." Carlo figured it wouldn't bother his partner one damn bit if that did happen, but he wasn't going to let it.

"Okay, so we're going to hide a bag full of them in my car trunk and do what again?"

"Christ, Tony don't you ever listen? All right let's go over it one more time."

"Don't bust my balls, Carlo. You want me to get it right, don't you?"

The rain was letting up when they turned onto the road to the pig farm.

"Once we start a regular routine of shipping to our new importing company, I'll have a chance to learn how US Customs inspects our case goods. Then I'll know exactly what to do."

"You're starting to talk like Felizi does, shipping, importing, case goods ...oh shit! Look at all that mud, I'm gonna ruin another pair of shoes."

"Damn it, Tony, will you pay attention. When I think the time is right, you'll start placing stones in marked cans. Do you remember how we decided to mark them?"

"Yeah, yeah. Christ, what is this a school test?"

"You're damn right. Remember, I'm the one who goes to jail if you screw up."

"I know, I know," Tony griped as they pulled up to the farmhouse.

Once inside, Carlo thought back to his childhood as they removed a number of stones from one of the aluminum chests hidden in his mama's old root cellar. As a boy he had loved sneaking down there and eating apples they had stored for the winter. Now here he was removing a fortune in diamonds from the home where he and his family had lived on the meager income they had made from raising pigs.

"Christ, how'd you keep from going nuts living in this little shack?" Tony commented.

"Country life wasn't all that bad. In fact, it was healthy. We worked hard and ate well, and we were happy. But why am I explaining to you, you were spoiled living in a corrupt city."

"Yeah, well, you've done all right in that city."

"Your father was good to me and I'll never forget it, but it's what's hidden here on this pig farm that will make us both rich."

"Great," Tony exclaimed after they had returned to the car and drove off. "Just as long as I don't have to smell any pig shit."

ଞୠଔ

Three days later they were at Palermo Airport.

Carlo was ticketed to fly from Palermo to Rome, Rome to Lisbon, and from there to New York on Soa Lisbonnia Airlines. Felizi had confirmed that his nephew, Ben, would be meeting him at Immigrations when he arrived at Idlewild.

"Have fun, pig farmer."

Carlo was surprised when Tony embraced him. He suspected his cousin suddenly realized he would be lost without him. "Behave yourself. Remember what we planned, and keep the sauce flowing," he teased.

"Send me sexy postcards from New York," Tony requested as Carlo passed through the boarding gate.

Carlo shot back, "How about one of Lady Liberty?"

"Forget it," Tony replied. "Call me when you get there."

Carlo disappeared into the waiting lounge, and Tony left.

ಜಂಞ

In the Alitalia lounge the magnitude of this new adventure he was embarking on finally registered with Carlo. All sorts of doubts and concerns flooded his mind. Here he was, a twenty-seven year old Sicilian pig farmer's son with no more than a ninth-grade education, flying across the Atlantic to a new world with a very different culture and language to deal with. Now for the first time, after having to make his own choices in life, he would be relying on strangers. He truly believed his plan to dispose of the stones was sound, but starting up and running an importing business was another matter altogether. It was exciting and scary as hell all at the same time. *Screw it. If Tony can handle his part without messing it up, I can handle mine.*

Carlo lit a cigarette, leaned back and opened a guidebook of New York that he had purchased earlier. He was thumbing through photos of Times Square, The Empire State Building, The Brooklyn Bridge, Yankee Stadium, playbills for South Pacific and several movies when he heard his name spoken.

"Carlo Marchi."

"Yes?" When he looked up he was shocked to see the face of Carmine Rossi.

"Carmine!" he stammered. "It's...it's...good to see you."

"I'll bet," Carmine scoffed. "Forget about making your flight, Marchi, Sr. Campi wants to see you."

"He wants to see me? I don't understand."

"We're not stupid. We know what you and that hot head DeVito are up to. Just follow me, and no trouble. Capisce?"

Carlo could just about catch his breath. *How the hell could they have found out where I'm headed?* "But my luggage is checked...."

"It's been taken care of, don't worry. Now move. My car is outside."

As they exited the airport and were heading to Campi's villa, Carlo steadied his nerves enough to ask. "What does Campi want of me?"

"Just sit back, you'll find out why you've been summoned soon enough."

During the next thirty minutes while Carlo's mind labored over who besides Tony, Felizi and Enzio knew of his trip to the States. He had been extra careful getting his passport and making the necessary arrangements for his trip.

His mind in turmoil over this interruption of his plans, Carlo hardly noticed the steep winding private road that led up to Campi's villa. He paid little attention to the beautiful old Roman stone structure with its terraces and white balustrades embracing it. He even ignored the entrance portico that sat above the hillside treetops and overlooked part of the harbor.

Carlo followed Carmine into the huge entry foyer. Then Carmine led him up a flight of marble stairs and into what appeared to be a guest room. He spotted his luggage at the foot of the huge four-poster bed.

"What the hell?" He turned and faced Carmine.

"Relax. I'm sure you'll be comfortable here until Sr. Campi gets back."

"I thought he was already here?"

"Soon. When he gets here, he gets here. Meanwhile you are his guest, so enjoy the villa."

Once alone in the oversized room, Carlo started to panic. He had missed his connection to Lisbon and had no idea what Campi had in mind for him. His eyes scanned the room for a phone but all he discovered was a disconnected line, no receiver. He had no choice but to wait. His fate was in the hands of the unstable people who had executed Franco DeVito.

When Carmine returned Carlo was seated on the edge of the bed. "We'll be dining around six. If you like, you may explore the villa. I see you haven't unpacked. I suggest you do so and if you haven't any swimming trunks there are several pairs in the pool house. Take a cool swim. It will help you to relax."

"Sure, Carmine, and in the meantime, perhaps you can explain why my trip has been interrupted."

"I'm sure Campi has his reasons and, if I were you, I would be respectful. Now go take a swim."

For the next few hours Carlo sweated out his luxurious confinement. Where the hell could he go? The villa was too well guarded for him to slip away. He was lying on the bed when Carmine summoned him and ushered him into a large drawing room.

"Wait in here," he ordered.

Carlo took a seat on one of two silk loveseats flanking a polished glass table. Faded tapestries depicting battle scenes of armored riders on prancing steeds hung on the walls. Carlo had seen similar pieces in the museum in Palermo. There were several matching straight-backed oak chairs strategically placed around the room.

"Carlo, how good to see you," Campi greeted when he entered.

Carlo rose and faced the reason he was there. "Sr. Campi, it is good to see you also."

"I should hope so, Carlo," Campi snapped, "especially since I was kind enough to allow you and DeVito to run my cannery business. And how do you repay me? First by you and Franco, bless his soul," Campi made the sign of the cross, "canning tomato sauce without my approval."

"But it did increase your percentage and we thought . . ."

"The problem is you didn't think," Campi interrupted. "And now you're doing it again," he shouted. "Do you take me for a fool? We know where you are going and why."

Carlo contained himself and allowed Campi to continue.

"I thought it was clear when I let you boys run the cannery that you couldn't take a crap without my blessing, and now you're heading for New York to sell more sauce without permission."

"I told you, Sr. Campi," Carmine who had remained standing chimed in, "these boys are too arrogant for their own damn good."

Carlo was thankful Tony wasn't with him. "Please forgive us, Sr. Campi. We misunderstood the conditions of your generous gift of the cannery. However, since Carmine checks our books regularly and profits have increased as has your deserved share, we assumed that expanding into America would please you."

"The money is good, but there are other things to be considered such as respect." At a signal from Campi, Carmine left the room.

"Please forgive us, Sr. Campi, and may I now have your permission to go to America and increase our business?"

Carmine returned with an elderly woman who placed a tray on the glass table.

"Grazie, Signora," Campi said to the woman.

"Prego! Sr. Campi." She bowed then left.

Campi reached for a cup of coffee. "You see, Marchi, now that's respect. She knows her place."

"I understand, Sr. Campi." Carlo had no idea what to expect. His and Tony's plans and their future were in the hands of this man who had had Tony's father killed. "I apologize for our lack of respect. It won't happen again." Carmine was again standing nearby and from his expression it was obvious to Carlo that he was enjoying his dilemma. He had also figured out that somehow during his last visit to Sciacca, Carmine had gotten wind of his trip to America and that they had been watching and waiting for him to leave.

"If I give you permission to continue with your plans, I will expect a larger percentage." Campi sipped his coffee. "Let's say sixty percent." Without waiting for Carlo to respond, Campi smiled and looked to Carmine. "Is that not fair, Carmine?"

Carmine smiled broadly, "Si. most generous, Sr. Campi."

"Then it's settled. Carmine see that Carlo gets back to the airport safely."

Relieved, Carlo nodded. At this point he didn't give a damn if Campi demanded ninety percent, he just wanted out of there. "Thank you, Sr. Campi. We will do our best to ensure your share. And you have my word, we will seek your counsel and approval on all future matters." Carlo was thankful that Tony was not there to hear him crawl. There was no telling what he would have done.

"So be it. Now get him the hell out of here." Campi waved his hand in dismissal as Carmine escorted Carlo out.

Once in the car, Carmine explained. "I'll drive you back to the airport. You and your luggage are booked on a flight to Lisbon with a new connection to New York. And remember, I will be watching your smart-ass cousin, so don't screw up again. Capisce?"

"We won't and thanks, Carmine."

When Carlo arrived in Lisbon, he called Felizi to inform his nephew of his new flight arrival time without explaining the cause for the delay. Then he called Tony.

"Where the hell have you been? Christ, Felizi and I thought you fell out of the plane or something."

Carlo told him how Carmine pulled him out of the airport and how he had been forced to wait to see Campi.

Tony was livid when Carlo explained. "What the hell do you mean he wants sixty percent? I swear Carlo that bastard is dead."

"Tony, calm down. Think for a moment. We're not in the sauce business, so who gives a shit what they take. Remember what we're really doing."

"How could you kiss their asses like that?"

"For two reasons. I wanted to get out of there in one piece and it was the only way to be allowed to do what needs doing in New York." After what he had just been through, Carlo didn't need Tony out of control. "Promise me you'll calm down. Don't blow this for us. Okay?"

"Yeah, yeah. But someday...."

Carlo changed the subject. "What I can't figure out is how the hell they knew where I was and where I was headed. I know Felizi wouldn't say anything. Hell, he doesn't even know about our involvement with these bastards."

"Oh hell," Tony stammered.

"What? Oh hell what?" Carlo heard his flight being announced. "I gotta go, Tony."

"Ah...maybe I mentioned the reason we needed more sauce when Enzio asked me why we wanted a night shift."

"That's it. He must have accidentally said something and it got back to Carmine. Christ, Tony, from now on not a word to anyone, please."

"Yeah, yeah. Don't worry. Call me from New York."

All Carlo could think about as he entered the boarding gate was how he was going to keep from worrying. Tony was a definitely the insecure strand in the scheme he had woven.

Chapter 31

Corklin stood by silently watching Jeremy Waters gripping the rusted buckle as he studied the photos of the dead Ladybird. His reaction to the news was indiscernible until he startled Corklin by flinging the buckle across his polished walnut desk. Alfred Dunne, seated across from Waters, snatched it before it flew off.

"Gone? You're telling me that the damn plane never sank in the Mediterranean, but crashed into waist deep water and our diamonds are gone? Bloody hell! How can that be?"

Corklin cleared his throat. Although he was not responsible for the loss, he, nonetheless felt a degree of failure. "Obviously they were stolen, sir, and it's impossible to know when or by whom."

"Two billion in uncut stones, gone," Waters repeated.

"There was no trace of them, sir," Dunne, having been briefed earlier, confirmed.

"How about the Tubruq authorities? Did you question them?" Waters persisted.

"We found the wreckage on the coast of Egypt so I had no reason to question the Libyans. Besides, after the furor Cox caused there, I felt there was no point in aggravating the situation."

"Of course, you're right." Waters appeared to have regained his composure.

"Would you believe that gutter trash has had the gall to request a meeting with me," Dunne told them. "He left word with my secretary that he feels he has some compensation coming for his time and effort."

That slimy little twit! "As I reported sir, he caused us considerable trouble and embarrassment. I would just ignore him."

"Indeed we shall," Waters declared. "I just wish there were some way of punishing him for his unseemly behavior."

"The fact that he is no better off than when we started out is, in my opinion, retribution enough, sir."

"Rightly so. I'm sure you're anxious to return home, Corklin."

"Yes, I am. I've checked out of my room and booked a flight back to Pretoria for this evening."

"In spite of the failed mission, we feel you deserve some consideration." Waters nodded to Dunne who handed Corklin an envelope.

"I really didn't expect...."

"Nonsense." Waters made a dismissive gesture with his hand. "You earned it, as did Patterson and Craig."

"Thank you, sir."

Corklin opened the envelope after take-off. It wasn't so much the generous amount that pleased him, but the thought that Cox, *the little twit*, had received nothing and was somewhere below again hustling on the streets of London that really put a grin on his face.

Chapter 32

As soon as Carlo passed through Customs at Idlewild he spotted it, a piece of white cardboard with "Carlo Marchi" hand-lettered on it. He approached the sign holder with a warm grin. If he hadn't known better, except for the younger posture, he would have sworn it was Pina Felizi smiling back.

Ben Tuzzio was tall and slim with a nose that said "proud to be Italian." His brown hair was cropped shorter than Pina's, but the thick curls were unmistakably a Felizi family characteristic. He approached with a smile full of straight white teeth just like those Carlo recalled from his first meeting with Pina. The big difference between them, except for Pina being older, was Ben's attire. He was wearing tan slacks and a brown sweater. Pina always wore a suit and Carlo could never remember seeing him ever remove his jacket or loosen his tie, even during the hottest Sicilian weather.

"Hello. I'm-a the one you wait-a for."

"Welcome, Carlo." Ben folded the sign, then pumped Carlo's hand firmly.

"Grazie." The emotional excitement Carlo felt on arriving in America was further amplified when this familiar looking stranger greeted him so vigorously.

Outside Carlo was even more overwhelmed by the throngs of people and the frenzied airport traffic as Ben led him to a nearby parking lot.

"Madonne," Carlo exclaimed as they dodged a taxi.

"It's like this everyday," Ben shouted as they wove their way through the maze of cars. "America is a land of travelers. Coming and going, working and playing."

After piling Carlo's luggage into the trunk of Ben's new Oldsmobile, they proceeded out of the lot. Carlo couldn't help feeling like a pig farmer come to the big city. He just hoped it didn't show too much to his new friend.

"You speak-a good-a Italian," Carlo complimented.

"And you speak very bad English. Where did you pick it up?"

"GIs after the war," Carlo said in Italian. "It didn't take long to understand their needs, 'hey, kid, how old is your sister?' and 'where's the best wine in town?'"

Ben laughed. "I think we can improve on that. It's a fairly easy language to learn but sometimes difficult to understand."

"I'm a fast learner."

"So Uncle Pina tells me." Ben turned onto the Van Wyck Expressway heading for Forest Hills in Queens.

Carlo stared out the window in complete awe. He had heard and read stories about New York, but to actually encounter the sights and sounds of explosive activity that composed the very nature of the largest city in America made it nearly impossible to imagine what the rest of this marvelous country must be like.

"My home isn't too far," Ben said. "We live on Seventy-First Avenue in the Forest Hills section of Queens."

"Queens? I thought this was New York."

Ben laughed. "It is. Queens is part of New York. You'll soon learn and I'm sure you'll be comfortable with us. Our whole neighborhood is mostly Italian so you won't have too much trouble getting by."

"I couldn't impose on you like that, a hotel will be fine."

"Nonsense. My uncle would never forgive me, and my wife is looking forward to having you as our guest. She loves to fuss over people so you mustn't disappoint her. Besides, with your limited English, you'd starve trying to read a menu."

"I guess you're right, but you must allow me to pay my own way. I had funds transferred to the bank you suggested to your uncle." Carlo was certain that the $50,000 would be enough to set up their front company.

"I'm not worried. Uncle Pina told me that you and your partner, Tony, are very reliable."

"So where is your importing business? Is it nearby?"

"It's across the Hudson River in Jersey City. I lease a small warehouse near Port Newark. I'll take you with me when I go over there in the morning."

"Ah yes, your uncle told me that's where foreign goods come in."

"That's right, from all over the world. There should be enough space at my place for your sauce, at least for a while until you get going good."

"Excuse me," Carlo apologized after a loud yawn.

"It's the time difference. You'll adjust. Take a nap before dinner."

"I'll be okay." Carlo tried suppressing another yawn. He was exhausted, not so much from the time change, but more because of what he had endured while at Campi's. "Yeah, I think you're right, a nap would be good."

The Tuzzio home on Seventy-First Avenue looked like all the others on the block. Although considered one family houses, they were connected like a row of brownstone teeth from porch to porch.

"We're here," Ben yelled as he escorted Carlo down the hall and into the kitchen.

Carlo was surprised at the size and arrangement of the room. The white stove and refrigerator looked new as did the plastic-topped chrome table with chrome legs and matching chairs

Isabella Tuzzio wiped her hands on her apron as she turned to greet them. "Welcome to our home, Carlo."

He hadn't expected her to embrace him and felt a twinge of embarrassment. Not only was she attractive for an older woman, but he was pleasantly surprised by the well-endowed firmness of her body as she pressed against him.

"Thank you, Signora Tuzzio. It's very kind of you to have me."

She smiled as she released him from her motherly hug. "Please, call me Isabella. You're in America now."

"I'll try to remember. Um-m-m, something smells good."

"Isabella is cooking you a real American dinner; roast turkey, sweet potatoes and all the trimmings. She's the best cook on Seventy-First Avenue." Ben reached out and untied his wife's apron strings teasingly.

"That's enough, Ben, you fool. Come, sit, both of you," she invited. "I have coffee and cake ready."

Carlo watched Isabella retie her apron. He couldn't get over her shapely figure. She didn't look like the forty-year old women he was accustomed to. Her straight nose was in perfect proportion to her pretty facial features. Her light brown hair was pinned up in a loose bun and the dark blue dress under her apron contrasted nicely with her ivory complexion. But for her correct Italian, she didn't have any of the typical attributes of a woman named Tuzzio.

When she joined them at the table for coffee, Carlo judged it to be the right time for the gift he had brought her. "Excuse me, I have something in my bag." When he sat back down at the table, he handed Isabella a small loosely wrapped package. "Sorry about the wrappings, I had to open everything in Customs."

"Oh my! It's beautiful, Carlo." She held up the antique cameo brooch for Ben to see, then pinned it on her apron strap. "Thank you, Carlo. How did you know I love old jewelry?"

"Uncle Pina. Right, Carlo?"

Carlo grinned at Ben. "I must confess he helped me. We found it in a small antique shop near his office in Trapani."

"How very thoughtful of you, Carlo." She stood and kissed his forehead. "Now get some rest. We'll call you for dinner."

"That was nice of you, Carlo," Ben echoed. Rising he added, "Come on, I'll show you your room."

At a little after six, Carlo and Ben were seated at the dining room table. Isabella was still busy in the kitchen. Once again Carlo was impressed with the furnishings in America. The highly polished oak table and chairs matched the tall china closet and side table. The venetian blinds projected a striped pattern across the shag carpeting. In contrast to it all, several old faded tintype faces in oval frames stared into the room. He assumed they were family from the old country.

"You're kidding? I don't believe you don't drink wine," Ben exclaimed as he started to pour a dark red for Carlo.

"I know it seems strange but we never had wine when I was a kid on the farm." He purposely omitted pig. "I just never developed a taste for it."

Ben smacked his lips as he sampled the wine and shook his head in amazement. "You don't know what you're missing, Carlo, an old man down the street makes it in his basement."

"I know," Carlo admitted. "It's even harder for my friends back home to understand."

Isabella was placing the golden bird on the table when a voice from the front hall shouted. "I'm home. Hey what's that I smell? Thanksgiving dinner?"

"Anna, we're in the dining room and you're too late to help," Isabella replied.

"Hi, everybody." A young woman entered the room. "Sorry I'm late, Mom. Because dad left the warehouse early, I had to wait for one of the men to give me a ride home."

"Carlo, this is our daughter, Anna. She practically runs the business," Ben said. "Anna, this is Carlo Marchi, the young man Uncle Pina wrote us about."

"Hi, Carlo." She stepped forward and extended her smooth soft hand.

Carlo was aware that his mouth was hanging wide open and he could have sworn they heard it when he snapped it shut. "Hello, it's-a nice-a to meet-a you, Anna." He almost tilted his chair over as he rose to take her hand.

Anna giggled at his awkwardness and his broken English. "It's nice to meet you, too, Carlo," she answered in almost understandable Italian. "I'll wash up and be right back to help, Mom." She dashed away.

"I didn't realize you had a daughter." *And what a daughter.* "She looks very much like you, Isabella." *But more beautiful, if that's possible.*

"So I'm told."

"Yes, Carlo, I'm blessed with two beauties," Ben boasted.

"You sure are," Carlo blurted just as Anna returned.

She had put on an apron and was carrying a bowl of sweet potatoes. As she moved about the table, Carlo studied her every gesture and feature. She was taller than her mother but had the same straight nose, slender neck, and identical hair in texture and color. Also like her mother, Anna had a fine figure though she was sculpted a little tighter with narrower hips and firmer breasts. Her walk was also different from most young girls he had known. There was confidence in the way she moved, like she knew exactly what she was doing.

When they were all seated, Anna leaned over and touched the Cameo brooch pinned to Isabella's apron. "Wow, Mom, this is beautiful, where'd you...."

"Please forgive me," Carlo interrupted, "I had no idea that there were two Tuzzio women or I would have brought two gifts."

"That's all right, Carlo," Ben assured him.

"Of course, and you can be sure I'll be borrowing Mom's from time to time," Anna teased.

"Like everything else," Isabella confirmed straightening the brooch. "Now, Ben, carve the turkey and let's eat."

As Carlo complimented each item on his dish, Isabella explained the custom of Thanksgiving. "So you see, Carlo, this is a traditional American meal usually served in November. Even though it's only June, I wanted to prepare something non-Italian for your first meal in the States."

"Then I look forward to enjoying it again in November, if I'm still welcome."

"I'm sure you will be," Anna said smiling warmly at him.

છ૦ભ

"Christ, Carlo, it's 3:00 a.m. I was sound asleep."

"You wanted me to call when I got here."

"I didn't mean in the middle of the night."

"It's only eight o'clock here and it's the first chance I've had to call. Stop bitching so I can fill you in on the trip and Ben and his family."

Carlo explained, as best he could, his first impressions of America. He described his first turkey dinner and told Tony how warm and hospitable Ben, Isabella and their daughter, Anna, were.

"Ben has a kid?"

Carlo was using the phone in the Tuzzio sunroom. Even though the door was closed he kept his voice low. He could hear Tony lighting a match for a smoke.

"Yeah. Well, she's not exactly a kid."

"Whoa, just how the hell old is this Anna? And why the hell are you whispering?"

"You figure it out, dummy."

"Okay, I get it. So how old is not a kid?"

"About twenty-three or four." Carlo bit his lip the minute he said it.

"And you're their house guest? Son-of-bitch, I knew I should have been the one to go over."

"I don't believe this, you're ready to unzip your fly over a girl you don't know thousands of miles away. You're impossible."

"Yeah, yeah, so what's she look like?"

Carlo just sat there and shook his head. "Hard to describe her, medium size, very pretty, nice personality. Not your type at all."

"You're lying, Marchi. I can always tell when you're lying even this far away. Not my type, I'll bet!"

"Let's change the subject. How are things going? Has Enzio lined up a night crew?"

"He's taken care of it all so we'll be ready when you are."

"Sounds like things are working out. It may take a few weeks before I can give you the okay to start shipping, but as soon as I think the timing is right, you can start packing our stuff."

"A few weeks? Christ, Carlo...."

"You knew the timing when we discussed all this...wait a minute. What's wrong? Something's bugging you. What is it?"

"It's that goddamn Carmine. He came by today to remind me of the arrangement you made with Campi, said he'd be watching me closely. I swear, Carlo, I can hardly stand the bastards. Some day...."

Oh shit, I don't need this right now. I should have had my head examined for leaving an uncontrollable hothead with millions in diamonds. "Tony, come on, think of what we have to look forward to. Don't lose it now. I've got to depend on you. Please don't screw it up."

"Yeah, yeah, don't worry. What I have in mind can wait until I'm wealthy."

"Whatever. Just keep a cool head and we'll have everything we'll ever need."

"Can I get back to sleep now, pig farmer?"

Chapter 33

"Madonne. You mean we are actually going under a river?"

"That's right, we're in the Holland Tunnel and the Hudson River is above us."

"How long will...ah! I see a bit of light up ahead." Carlo hoped he didn't sound too relieved. "What a wondrous thing, a tunnel instead of a bridge!"

"Oh. we've got plenty of those, too," Anna said. She was seated between them. "There's another tunnel called the Lincoln Tunnel farther up the river."

When they left home, Carlo had started to climb into the back seat, but Anna suggested he squeeze in beside her saying it wasn't polite for a passenger to be in the back alone. He gratefully slid in front wondering if that was also an American custom.

Suddenly, like out of the muzzle of a huge cannon, they burst out of the tunnel into bright Jersey sunlight.

"My warehouse is only twenty minutes from here." Ben told Carlo as he steered onto Summit Avenue heading south.

Carlo could feel Anna's hip tight against his. When he tried to move slightly toward the door it seemed as though she shifted, too.

"Pina told me you import olives from Italy and Greece." His voice cracked a little.

"That's how Daddy got started, thanks to Uncle Pina." Anna turned to face him with a smile.

"But now Americans, especially Italian Americans, have a longing for more authentic Italian foods. American processed pasta, rice and cheese don't have that old-world taste they remember," Ben added.

"So now you import pasta, rice and cheese as well?"

"Only pasta and rice in addition to olives. Cheese requires refrigeration and special storage and I'm not equipped for that. But your sauce, that's going to be a perfect item for my wholesalers to carry. You're getting in on the ground floor of what will be a booming import market, Carlo."

A booming diamond market is what I really want. "So your uncle explained. But Tony and I have decided to start cautiously with small shipments to begin with. We can't over-extend ourselves, you understand." Carlo was tempted to light a cigarette but thought better of it.

"Do I ever. Even with Uncle Pina's help, it was slow going. Thank goodness Isabella's father owned a small garage not too far from where I am now. I started by bringing in a couple of hundred pallets of olives my uncle exported to me at cost and stored them in the back area of the garage. Uncle Pina connected me up with a wholesaler he knew. From then on I kept bringing in more and more olives until I took over the whole garage. That was two years ago. Now I own a warehouse and business keeps improving. And you wait and see, Carlo, it'll be the same for you."

"Here we are," Anna announced.

They approached a worn-out looking building. The tin sign beside a double door entrance read "I & A IMPORTING." It reminded Carlo of what the fish cannery looked like when he first saw it, red brick with crudely mortared joints and steel casement windows that were beyond being washed clean. Ben parked in the rear next to a small pick-up with "I & A Distributors" hand-painted on the door panel. Carlo followed as Ben and Anna climbed the steps up onto a heavy timber loading dock. They walked around several empty wooden pallets stacked to one side.

"We sell these for scrap wood," Anna commented as they entered through an open steel overhead door.

The sound of physical activity echoed off the interior brick. Carlo could see three men busily engaged in separating cases from pallets and re-stacking them in different piles lined up near the door.

"They're working on wholesaler orders going out this morning," Ben pointed as they led Carlo toward a small glass enclosure.

Anna moved in ahead of them to answer a ringing phone.

"What time do the men start working?" It was eight-thirty according to Carlo's watch.

"They get in at seven and are through around three if the wholesalers' trucks are running on schedule."

"You don't deliver?" Carlo lit a smoke and took the seat Ben indicated at a desk across from the one Anna was busy at.

"I'm not big enough to afford more than one truck so far. Most wholesalers have a small fleet so I discount my prices for them and they pick up their goods."

"That makes sense."

"Now let's concentrate on you, Carlo. The first thing we'll need are samples of your sauce."

"They should arrive soon. Your uncle is including several cans in with your next shipment of olives."

"Good. That's due in any day now. Once we get the samples, we'll go to see John Collins. He runs Freight Forwarders. They handle everything including getting you an FDA number."

"FDA?"

"Food and Drug Administration. No food or drink comes into America without their approval. Don't worry. John handles all of that including the necessary paperwork required by Customs."

"All for a fee, I'll bet."

"You're learning. I'm guessing it'll be around $5,000 to get your importing permits. Then they will become your freight forwarding agent on every shipment you bring in, and they're well worth it."

"Sounds easy. Tell me what kind of inspection goes on at the pier?"

"Once you're an established importer, they make an occasional spot check as the stuff comes off the boat. It's just routine and, like I said, it's a rare occurrence. Hell, I can't remember the last time they checked one of my pallets. When they did, they only pulled out two cans of olives."

"Is that a serous thing?" *Shit, we'd better not overdo it in the beginning.*

"Hell no, some inspector probably took them home for his salad. Don't give it another thought, that's why you pay your freight forwarder."

"If you say so, Ben. I guess I'm a little nervous. This is all new to me."

"Speaking of new, what's the name of your company?"

"Well you know the sauce is named Stella's Tomato Sauce after my Mama, so I let Tony pick the company name. We're calling it Gemma Importing."

"Hey, I like that. It sounds Italian and is easy to pronounce. Your partner must be a real smart guy."

An unstable time bomb would be closer to the truth. "Yeah, Tony's a bright one all right."

They stepped out of the crammed office leaving Anna on the phone. She waved at Carlo as she was speaking into the receiver.

"She'll be busy like that all day." Ben walked Carlo over to an empty corner of the warehouse. "I had this spot cleared out for you. It should do for a while."

"Thanks, Ben. I'm sure this will be okay. We'll only be bringing in a few pallets at a time, and hopefully that won't interfere with your operation."

"It won't. I'll simply be including your sauce as part of our inventory and offering it to my wholesalers until you decide to go on your own."

"Tony and I would like to keep the arrangement just as you described. We're in no hurry to do otherwise. We should, however, decide what percentage of our profit you will receive for all you're doing for us."

"We'll work out a fair amount. Come on, I'll introduce you to the men and show you exactly how we handle orders."

Chapter 34

Anna answered the kitchen phone where she and Isabella were preparing dinner. "Yes, he's right here, just a moment." Carlo was seated at the table reviewing a book she had given him to study. "It's Tony for you."

"Thanks, I'll take it in the sunroom." He closed the door behind him, then picked up the phone, "Okay, Anna, I've got it." He heard her click off.

"Tony, is everything all...."

"Christ, Carlo, it's been almost three weeks. I haven't heard a damn thing from you. I'm not having an easy time sitting here on my ass waiting for word from you to start shipping."

"I'm glad you called. Guess I should have been in touch with you, but I've been up to my ears getting things lined up. All the paperwork is just now complete. I'll be sending you all the information needed at your end to get the stuff into Port Newark."

"It's about damn time. So that was Anna, she sounded sexy."

"Knock it off. She's been really great helping me with my English. She's even got me enrolled in night classes."

"And what else is she teaching you nights?"

"Keep your mind on business, Tony."

"Yeah, yeah. Everything's set. I even had the stencils made for 'Gemma Importing' and Enzio's ready to start the night crew. Just give us the word."

"I'll check with Ben, but I'm sure I can call you the first of the week to start. And, Tony, we're only talking about the sauce. I'll let you know when to fill the special orders, got it?"

"Yeah, yeah, next week. Gotta go. I've got a late date tonight."

"It figures. Just be careful."

"You, too, and say goodnight to Anna. Know what I mean?"

Now that Carlo was sort of a member of the family, they took their meals in the kitchen. They had already started when he returned from the sunroom. Carlo preferred eating in the kitchen rather than the dining room. The informality of the cooking smells, the pots and pans scattered about reminded him of back home on the farm.

"Sorry that took so long," he apologized to Isabella as she ladled veal stew into his empty dish.

"It's all right," she replied. "Now enjoy your meal."

"Everything okay in Sicily?" Ben passed the breadbasket to him.

"No problems," Carlo smiled. "Tony just gets nervous when things don't move at his speed."

"He sounded nice," Anna commented.

"He said the same about you, Anna." Carlo tore some bread and dug into his stew.

Chapter 35

Carlo was becoming quite close to the Tuzzios. Isabella fussed over him like a son and Ben's hospitality and his advice about importing were invaluable. But Anna Tuzzio, she was another thing entirely.

For weeks she had been tutoring him and helping with his night school homework. He felt a great deal of pride whenever she complimented his learning ability, and was happy to comply when she insisted that they converse in English as much as possible. Slowly it became apparent that her interest in him was more than educational and he was beginning to feel the same way. It was becoming more and more difficult for him to be so close to her while they studied, especially after what happened one morning.

Carlo and Anna shared the bath between their bedrooms on the second floor. Her parents' first floor bedroom had its own bath. In the beginning, Anna had suggested to Carlo that they hang a blue scarf on the bathroom doorknob to indicate one of them was using the facility. Then one morning it happened, he entered the bathroom just as she was wrapping herself in a towel.

"Madonne!" he exclaimed. "Domandare scusa."

To his surprise she didn't appear at all embarrassed. Instead she reprimanded him.

"Speak English, Carlo, remember?"

"Okay, but the scarf was not on the door, Anna. I'm so sorry." He turned to leave.

"Don't be. I was in such a hurry I guess I forgot about it." She started giggling when he tried closing his eyes.

My god, she's even more beautiful than I imagined. "Anna, please forgive me, and be more careful next time."

"Stop it, Carlo. I know you like me and by now you must know how I feel about you."

American girls. I've a lot to learn about this country. What would Tony do? Hell I know what he'd do. "You're right I can't get you off my mind." He stepped forward and embraced her. The towel slipped a little and for the first time in his adult life, Carlo's male instinct was overpowered by an even stronger emotion, respect bordering on love. He released her wet body. "I want you so bad Anna, but not like this."

She adjusted the towel then kissed his lips gently. "I understand. As long as you care as much as I do, that's all that matters for now."

Still twisted between desire and love, he kissed her cheek, turned away quickly and closed the door behind him.

ജ രൂ

Alone and slightly aroused as she toweled herself dry, Anna wondered how far she would have allowed him to go. Thank goodness he had just spared her that difficult decision. It was one of the reasons she was attracted to him. In addition to his Italian good looks, he had an innocent manner about him. He wasn't like the American boys she had dated in high school or later while attending business college. They had been mostly jocks with an attitude. Carlo was different. He was more like a little boy lost in a big world and that appealed to her nurturing feminine side. She was falling in love with this Sicilian and it felt good.

Leaving the bathroom, she spoke through his partially open bedroom door. "Okay, Carlo, it's all yours and don't forget the blue scarf," she called cheerfully.

"Very funny, Anna," he said joining her in the hallway.

She pecked his cheek, then danced into her room.

Now whenever they were alone, their emotional attachment grew stronger and they began to consider the possibilities of a more meaningful relationship.

ജ രൂ

One evening during dinner, Ben commented, "You know, Carlo, Isabella and I can't help noticing how much time you and Anna have been spending together and, even though your English has improved, we wonder if perhaps there's more going on than we realize."

Feeling a bit awkward, Carlo wondered if Anna had said something to her parents about their growing feelings for each other, or was it just that obvious? "You've both been so good to me," he replied. "Please know that I wouldn't do anything disrespectful to upset you, but it's true, I have become very fond of Anna."

"I feel the same way about him, Daddy," Anna jumped in.

"I thought so," Isabella said. "Your father and I love you and believe in your ability to make your own decisions, Anna. We just want both of you to be sure you know exactly what you're doing." Isabella embraced her daughter.

"I know that, Mom." Anna smiled at Carlo over her mother's shoulder.

"Too bad you don't drink wine," Ben said as he toasted them.

Christ what a complicated turn of events, he thought, *I can't tell Anna or the Tuzzios that I came here to sell millions in diamonds instead of sauce, and I can just imagine Tony's reaction when I tell him about Anna and me. You have no choice, Marchi, just stay cool,* he told himself, *there's too much at stake.*

Chapter 36

"Now what the hell do you want?" Tony was seated at his desk reading the local paper when Carmine entered his office.

"Relax, DeVito," Carmine suggested, his bulk overshadowing the desk.

Tony tossed the paper to the side and stood facing the six-foot three-inch mass. He often wondered why Carmine bothered wearing a tie since it always looked short because of his thick neck and large collar size.

"Sit down, DeVito, I'm here for a reason."

"That doesn't give you the right to walk into my private office like this." Tony's courage was bolstered by the Beretta automatic he had recently acquired and kept in the desk drawer.

"Watch that hot temper, DeVito, and don't give me any of your lip. Just shut the hell up and listen." The chair across from Tony creaked as Carmine plopped into it.

"So why the hell are you here?" Tony was seated behind his desk again and inches closer to the weapon.

"Sr. Campi wants to see you."

"What for? You just picked up a few days ago. Campi gets his goddamn money on time and you know it, so what is it now?"

"Just pay attention for a moment."

"Yeah, yeah."

"It's your cousin Carlo... what the hell has he been doing in New York?"

"What about him? You and Campi know what he's doing and what the share will be. We've already agreed to that."

"All I know is Sr. Campi wants me to bring you to his villa and have you explain why the extra money hasn't started yet."

"You tell Sr. Campi it should be easy enough for even him to understand that we haven't started shipping to New York yet. You can go back and tell him that. Can't you?"

Carmine got up and faced Tony. "Look kid, you got pallinas, but I'm still supposed to bring you to see Sr. Campi."

"Okay. But can't it wait awhile? I'm kinda busy here."

"Yeah, sure you are." Carmine walked over and pulled Tony's jacket from the back of a chair, a sure sign Tony was going with him right then.

As they left the cannery, Carmine advised him, "If you don't lose your temper and act and talk respectful, I don't think Sr. Campi will come down on you too hard."

"You're kidding, right? I told you everything I know, for Christ sakes."

"Look, Tony, like I said, I admire courage, even though you didn't show any at the bordello that time. But if you don't do what you're told, I'll have to break something. Capisce?"

"I told you, Carmine, that wasn't my fault at Bertoli's bordello. You should have told me what to do ahead of time. Ah, forget it. Your dragging me to Palermo now is dumb."

"Not to Sr. Campi. He wants you to tell him just where Carlo is and when he'll be getting more money."

"I've already explained it to you. It takes time and that we'll be starting soon."

Carmine just shook his head, remaining silent until they reached Palermo. When they neared the villa, he warned, "Be polite and respectful just like your cousin Carlo was."

"Yeah, yeah, I promise. I'm not Carlo, but I'm also not stupid." *Maybe someday I'll get even with the bastard who killed Pappa and who's now trying to ruin my life.*

ⅎℂℛ

"DeVito, what the hell are we going to do about you?" Campi was in his billiard room when Tony entered.

Tony stood silently waiting to be allowed to answer. *Carmine is right. I have to kiss up to this piece of garbage like Carlo did, but it won't be easy.* When Campi slammed his pool cue down with a bang, Tony pretended to flinch. *I've got to let this son-of-a-bitch think I'm nervous, and that really galls me.*

"I sent him to bring you here to explain about my share of the business." He pointed to Carmine by the veranda door. "What the hell is going on, Tony?"

"May I explain, Sr. Campi?"

"It better be good, Tony. You boys have been nothing but a pain in the ass."

"We're trying not to be, Sr. Campi." *Boy, Carlo would be proud if he could hear me now.*

Campi picked up his pool cue and shook it at Tony. "Go on, tell me."

"Si, Sr. Campi. As Carmine will tell you, I came without hesitation when you sent for me." Tony looked toward Carmine, hoping he wouldn't dispute him. The big man just grinned back at him.

Campi suggested they continue their talk on the veranda. Tony followed him out and took a seat where he indicated at a glass-topped table. He watched in silence as Campi clipped the end off a large cigar, then flamed it until smoke billowed into the clear Palermo evening. Tony took that as I sign that he, too, could light a cigarette.

After a few relaxing puffs skyward, Campi remarked, "What a wonderful view from here. I love looking at it."

Tony nodded in agreement. On a cloudless night like this, it was hard to tell where the Mediterranean Sea and the sky met.

"Now down to business." Campi blew a cloud of smoke in Tony's direction. "We know you've arranged for extra night workers, so why haven't they started yet?"

"We're waiting until Carlo gives us the go-ahead."

"And just what the hell is he doing all this time in New York?"

"I spoke to him two days ago, Sr. Campi, and he told me he's been learning to speak English while all the paperwork was being done. It's almost complete now so we should be starting next week. We'll be keeping a separate set of books for America, and you'll receive the sixty percent we agreed to."

Campi stood and laughed as he tossed his cigar over the balcony. "I'm not a patient man, DeVito. I feel I should have gotten some tribute by now for the generosity we have shown you two."

You son-of-a-bitch. Tony could almost smell what was coming next. "And we are very grateful, Sr. Campi."

"Not grateful enough, I'm afraid. Because of the delay we must endure, you will now pay seventy-five percent. Is that understood?"

"But Sr. Campi, the expenses of the night workers, extra materials, shipping costs, the distributor...that will only leave us with a small...." Suddenly Tony realized, *shit, I'm starting to talk like Carlo and Felizi.*

"You have the balls to complain? This is not negotiable, so you'd better inform your slow-moving partner."

Tony could feel the fury starting to grow within him, then suddenly he thought of the wealth he and Carlo had in diamonds and the power it would give him. He smiled broadly at the man he hated so fiercely. "I'm sure it will be all right, Sr. Campi. I will call Carlo tonight and urge him to proceed quickly for your seventy-five percent."

"Buono." Campi turned to Carmine who had been standing within earshot the entire time, and ordered, "Now get his ass out of here."

෴

On their drive back, Carmine was the first to speak. "You did very good, Tony. Had you not, I don't think you'd be going home now."

Tony lit a cigarette. "How can you stand working for that pig, Carmine?"

"I work for money, Tony. I told you that before and the money is very, very good. You and Carlo are fortunate because of Sr. Campi's respect for your father. But today, things are different. Past loyalties are forgotten. Money and ambition rule now."

"Yeah, I know. Carlo and I are paying more than our share."

"And that's probably what saved your ass this evening, my hot-headed friend."

Chapter 37

"Please, Tony, tell me you're joking." It was the morning following Tony's meeting with Bruno Campi.

"I couldn't help it, Carlo, so don't start lecturing me, goddamn it. That big ape, Carmine, just showed up in the office threatening to bust me up if I didn't go with him."

Carlo could hardly believe what he was hearing and was thankful for the privacy of the sun room phone. "So did you go? Christ, Tony."

"I had no choice, damn it, and I've had just about enough of their crap."

"Okay, now calm down for a minute. Tell me exactly what happened when you met with Campi."

"Nothin', except he wanted to know what the hell was taking us so long."

"And?"

"I kissed his ass just like you would have."

"That was good."

"Not really. Now we have to pay seventy-five percent of our American profits, partly because it's taking you so damn long to get going and partly because he's just a miserable bastard."

"That son-of-bitch. So, did you agree?"

"There was no choice but to agree and to let you know that we better start soon."

"Okay. You did the right thing. Now listen carefully. Start the night crew. Pina will have all the exporting papers for you shortly. Begin with a hundred cases a week for the first few weeks."

"Shit, Carlo, that's not gonna be enough to satisfy Campi, and what about the special sauce?"

"Don't do anything about that yet, and don't worry about Campi. Remember the set of American books I prepared? I'll tell you what amounts to enter to keep them off our backs, and then you draw that much from our Swiss account to cover it. Capisce?"

"You're kidding. Now we have to give the bastard our own money?"

"Tony, think big. For a few thousand our way will be clear for making millions."

"I still want to blow his brains out, and someday I will. I swear it."

Carlo could see Anna waving him to breakfast through the glass of the sun room door. *Christ he's going nuts on me.* "Please, Tony, take it easy. Okay? I've got to go. Start shipping as soon as you can and when I'm sure it's the right time, I'll give you the go-ahead to start packing special sauce."

"Okay, but I'm getting fed up with all the bullshit I'm getting at this end, so hurry up."

"I will. Just behave and promise me you'll keep kissing their asses."

"Okay, but not forever."

As he headed toward the wonderful aroma of breakfast coming from the kitchen, Carlo realized he didn't tell Tony about himself and Anna. But then, given the circumstance of Tony's call, it was probably better that he wait with that bit of news.

The Tuzzios had already started breakfast. Isabella poured his coffee and then cracked a couple of eggs in a skillet for him.

As Anna passed bacon and toast, she asked, "Is Tony all right?"

"Oh yeah. He's just anxious to get started." He loved the way she smiled as he touched her hand. "Someday when you meet him, you'll see how impatient he can be, but he's like a brother to me and I love him in spite of it."

"He won't have long too wait," Ben said. "Uncle Pina should have all the necessary exporting documents by now. Then things will be easier back home."

Carlo dug into his breakfast. As each day passed, he felt more and more like Anna and the Tuzzios were becoming his real family and America was becoming his real home.

Chapter 38

Carlo, Ben and John Collins, Ben's freight forwarder, stood watching outside the Port Newark Customs area as the first shipment of Stella's Tomato Sauce cases where being off-loaded.

"Boy, I can remember how exciting it was for me, Carlo, when my first batch of olives arrived at this very same port of entry," Ben declared.

Collins held a folder with "Gemma Importing" printed on the cover. He had already provided all the documents needed to clear the shipment. "I'll say he was excited, Carlo, and he was also nervous as hell."

Carlo nodded barely acknowledging their comments. His full attention was on the customs agent inspecting the pallet of cases, counting and checking them against a paper attached to a clipboard. When the agent suddenly pulled a case off the pallet, Carlo's heart beat faster.

"What's he doing now?" Carlo nervously asked Collins as the agent tore open the case flaps and pulled out a can of sauce.

"Relax, that's just routine. Sometimes I think they do these random checks just to go through the motions like they're doing their job," Collins assured him.

"Yeah, Carlo, it may not happen again for months."

"He's opening the can!" Carlo caught his anxiety in time. "Is he worried it might be a bad batch?"

"Nah," Collins explained, "the FDA already cleared your product. They're only checking for smuggled goods."

"Like maybe Tony's packing drugs in tomato cans back in Sicily," Ben joked.

Carlo smiled, but inwardly he was far from cheerful.

The agent poured the open can of sauce into a container sifted through it then stamped "APPROVED" on the top case of the pallet.

"That's it, Carlo." Collins shook his hand. "You're now officially an importer. My boys will truck your sauce to Ben's warehouse. Good luck and let's hope we bring in a lot of sauce for you."

On the ride back to the warehouse, Ben told Carlo, "I already have a couple of distributors willing to take on your sauce and, if things go like I think they will, you'll need to bring in more than one pallet next time."

"Thanks, Ben. We'll see. Like I said, Tony and I want to start slow since we only have so much capacity in the cannery."

"I understand, Carlo. But if your sauce takes off, you'll have to make other canning arrangements. American consumers are a strange bunch. If they hate a product, it'll die on the grocer's shelf, but if they like it, they'll drive him crazy for more. We'll know soon enough."

"We're determined to succeed, Ben. Even if it doesn't sell well at first, Tony and I are committed to keep at it." *Long enough to unload a fortune in diamonds, that is.*

೩೦೦೪

The following week Carlo watched his next shipment pass through Customs with no problems and that evening he called Tony.

"Alleluia! It's about goddamn time," Tony shouted. It was noontime in New York and Carlo was alone in the warehouse office. Ben was on a sales call and Anna had run out to get sandwiches for their lunch.

"I know it's been tough waiting, Tony, but now we can start. First, be sure you're not followed, then get enough stones to fill about a dozen cans..."

"All I have to do is get some from the trunk of my car."

"Jeez, Tony, how smart was that?" *Take it easy, Carlo, don't rattle him now.* "You mean you left them there after we returned from the farm? Was that the safest place to keep them?"

"Where else would you suggest? That damn Carmine just barges in on me with no warning, so how safe is the cannery office or the apartment for that matter?"

"You're right. I wasn't thinking."

"Damn right." Tony torched a cigarette. "Okay, Mr. Not-Always-Right, what's next?"

Carlo explained how he had watched the customs agent open a case. "So you see, they grab a top case, pull open the long flaps and remove a can from the middle."

"I don't get it?"

"It's simple, you put the special sauce cans in the four corners of a case where they'll be covered by the shorter inside flaps. And Tony, be sure the special cases aren't on the top of the pallet."

"Do I still mark the cans?"

"No need to. Since they're in the corners, all you'll have to do is mark the case like we planned. You do remember how, don't you?"

"Give me a break, pig farmer, I remember."

"Just be sure to smudge the Gemma Importing stencil on the special case and that's the one I'll watch for."

"Yeah, yeah, don't worry. I practiced on some empties."

"That's it then, partner, just be careful."

"Right. So how's little Anna these days?"

Carlo figured now was as good a time as any. "She's out getting us some lunch. We've become real close, she and I...."

"You did her. Atta boy."

"No. I mean, we're in love." He waited but there was only silence. "Did you hear what I said, Tony?"

"I heard ya, but I can't believe it. Christ, Carlo, you've only been there a couple of months and you think you're in love. Get laid and it'll pass."

"It's not like that. You'll see when you meet her, then you'll understand."

"Understand what?" Anna asked as she entered.

"It's Tony. I was telling him about us."

"Let me say hello." She picked up the extension phone before he could warn Tony to behave.

"Hi, Tony. I can't thank you enough for sending Carlo to me and when we meet I'm going to give you a big hug."

Carlo cringed at the possible response that might come out of Tony.

"Hi, Anna. Hey, you speak pretty good Italian. Yeah, he's a lovable guy all right. I can't wait for that hug."

"That's a promise, here's Carlo." She hung up her receiver.

"She doesn't know why you're really there, does she?"

"No. What can I say? I don't think the time is right for that." Carlo paused. "I guess that's it for now, Tony. I'll call you soon."

"Goodnight, loverboy."

Chapter 39

The clatter of tin cans assaulted Tony's brain as he considered how best to get the diamonds into the sauce cans without being noticed by the few workers scattered along the filling line. He had never spent so much time in the plant. Now he seriously watched the hundreds of pounds of fresh tomatoes going through several washes. From there they were boiled, then strained and blended with various herbs and spices per Stella Marchi's original recipe. After being mixed together, the whole batch was transferred into huge stainless steel vats where the actual cooking into sauce began.

Tony followed the process from the vats to the filling tubes where cans that had been steam-cleaned shuttled along a conveyer toward the fillers. The empty cans reminded Tony of baby birds waiting to be fed. At just the right moment, a funnel-like nozzle spurted the correct capacity into each open can. Following that, the cans passed through a device that crimped on the lids. From there the sealed cans were immersed in an extremely hot water chamber for the final cooking. Then, after passing through drying blowers, they were labeled and delivered for hand-packing into cases.

It was obvious to Tony that the time for inserting the stones had to be just before the lids were crimped on.

"Is everything all right, Tony? You've been down here all morning." Enzio startled him while he was intently watching the labeling operation.

"Yeah, yeah," he yelled back loudly over the din of rattling cans. "I'm just checking things out. I don't want Carlo to think I'm not keeping on top of everything." He started to light a cigarette.

"You can't smoke in here. Sorry, Tony."

"How come?" He held the lit match.

"Sanitary rules. No smoking in a food processing plant."

Tony blew out the match and tucked the unlit cigarette behind his ear.

"You can tell Carlo that everything's running smoothly. For a small operation with only a handful of workers, we're packing almost one hundred cases a shift."

"That's great, Enzio, and what happens between shifts?"

"I'll explain up in the office, Tony. It's too noisy down here."

When they were in the quieter setting of the office, Tony leaned back and lit his cigarette as Enzio proceeded to answer his question. "You know when the day workers quit, right?"

"Yeah. I see them leave around four."

"Well, about a half hour before they leave, we stop production and clean out the fillers. After running for several hours, they can clog up a little. When the night workers come in at five, one of the men I appointed to supervise sees that everything is ready to start up again and then near the end of their shift they clean the fillers so they'll be ready for the day shift."

"So that's how it works. Very good, Enzio."

"After we get the labeling done...." Enzio continued, but Tony had already tuned out the rest of the boring explanation.

"That's terrific, Enzio, keep up the good work," he said. Tony now had his window of opportunity all figured out.

ଥଓଔ

At exactly 4:45, Tony slipped back down to the filling area. The silence was almost as disturbing as the noise when the machinery was running. He was carrying a small sack containing ten stones about the size of olives. Hundred of cans, lined up like tin soldiers were facing the filling nozzle. The whole inanimate scene was like a still photo.

Tony's plan was simple. He dropped two or three diamonds into each of the next four cans to be filled with sauce. To make absolutely certain he wouldn't get them confused with the others, he made a small scratch with a penknife on the side of them. Now all he had to do was stick close by when the night crew turned on the equipment, and visually follow his four cans through filling, lid crimping and labeling. At that point, he pulled the four labeled cans off the line pretending to be spot-checking for quality. Since he was the boss, he wasn't questioned when he interrupted a case packer and personally placed the special cans in each corner of a case that was being filled. While the man packing cases was busy with the next one, Tony discreetly smeared the stencil before placing the case near the bottom of the pallet.

Okay, Carlo, it's up to you now. He lit a cigarette in spite of the rules and headed for home.

Chapter 40

Carlo was checking the new pallets that had arrived that morning when Ben joined him in the corner of the warehouse he had designated for Carlo's sauce.

"Good news, Carlo. The three A&P stores we placed your sauce in are almost sold out. Here's a copy of your first reorder. Congratulations."

"That's wonderful, Ben." There was no way Ben could know that Carlo's exuberance was more for the special case he had just received than for the retail news.

"Looks like most of what you have here will just about fill their order." Ben referred to the two hundred cases stacked in two rows. "You'd better warn Tony to crank things up. One of my distributors thinks he can get you into some Finast Stores, too."

"I'll call him tonight, but like I said in the beginning, we can only handle so much."

"Do the best you can, Carlo," Ben said as he walked away. "But remember, success in this business is as hard to stop as it is to achieve."

When he was certain Ben and his workers were well out of sight, Carlo anxiously pulled open Tony's first special delivery and quickly removed the four corner cans. Then made a beeline for the nearby men's washroom.

Prepared with a can opener and hunched over the toilet, Carlo excitedly poured each can of sauce through his fingers. After almost losing one of them he decided that next time he would need a small strainer. Heart thumping, he rinsed, dried and pocketed the small fortune.

Later in the day, he distributed the remaining eight cans of sauce from the special case to Ben's workers, then discarded the case along with the four empty cans in the trash bin outside.

While riding home that evening with Ben and Anna, Carlo noticed that the uncut stones seemed heavier than when he first hid them in his jacket pocket. As Anna pressed closer to him, Carlo tried to keep his apprehensions under control for reasons he hadn't considered till now. First of all, he could only imagine how hurt the Tuzzios would be if they discovered his real purpose in being there, especially now that he and Anna were so involved. And although the Swiss jewelers had told him about the diamond district on Forty-Seventh Street, he still had to find a reliable outlet there for all the stones. *Christ, and Tony thinks he's got the tough part. Yeah right!*

ঔ৩

The following morning when Carlo had the office to himself he called Tony at his apartment. "Everything arrived okay and with no problems at Customs. The marked case was hardly noticeable. You did a great job, partner."

"Whatcha expect? Look, Carlo, I just got in, and from now on be sure not to call between four and five my time. That's when I do the special loading."

"So you're finally putting in some overtime." Carlo couldn't pass up the opportunity to tease Tony.

"Very funny. I got me a heavy date in about an hour and I was about to take a shower. So tell me, how soon are you selling the first batch of diamonds?"

"I'm working on it. I think I've come up with a plan that will work without the Tuzzios becoming suspicious."

"What about your sweetheart? You're not thinking of letting her know...."

"Hell no. But I hadn't figured on becoming this close to her either. I'll work it out, don't worry. Meanwhile keep doing what you're doing. No more problems with Campi?"

"Nah, I'm behaving and giving Carmine the extra money for Campi like you said. You just take care of your end. Hey! I'll bet you never told her you were a pig farmer either, did you?"

"Goodnight, Tony."

ঔ৩

That evening during dinner, Carlo put his plan into action. "Yes, it was a surprise to me," he explained to Anna and her parents. "When I spoke to Tony this morning, he told me his friend, Roberto from Palermo, was now in New York."

"Isn't that nice," Isabella remarked. "We must have him over for dinner sometime."

"That's right," Ben agreed.

"You must be excited, a friendly face from home." Anna placed her arm around his shoulder.

"Sort of." *Shit!* He hadn't figured on their hospitable nature. "I really don't know him. Tony just asked me to kind of look in on him, see that he's doing okay."

"Where's he staying?" Ben asked.

"Somewhere in Manhattan. I thought maybe I'd go in and see him on Friday."

"I'll drive you," Anna volunteered.

Carlo suppressed a groan. *Now what the hell do I do? I didn't think this idea through far enough. Shit!*

"That would be great, Anna, except, I've got to start getting around on my own sometime, and this could be the beginning."

"But how...." she started to object.

"He's right, Anna, he's got to learn about the city eventually."

Carlo could have kissed Ben for his support. "I'll take a taxi for now. Later, Anna, you can teach me about the subways, and I plan on getting a car of my own soon."

"Your own car? Now you're talking like every red-blooded American man," she quipped.

Chapter 41

As his cab drove along Sixth Avenue, the nearest thing Carlo could equate to Manhattan was the pandemonium of Switzerland where he had sold the first diamonds, but it was much busier and noisier. Taxis and trucks threatened the flow of humanity flooding the streets. Sidewalks knotted with pedestrians and street vendors along with window-shoppers all created the composition of the large vibrant metropolis.

"Here we are, buddy, the Diamond District," the taxi driver announced as he pulled to the curb on Forty-Seventh Street.

Carlo gripped the small sack containing the stones in his jacket pocket as he stared down the famous block toward Fifth Avenue. He immediately sensed that this was the place where he would achieve his goal in America. His eyes jumped from store sign to store sign, all touting their wares with flashing neon depictions of diamonds, rings and watches.

Walking slowly down the block, taking in the spectacle of glittering gems and jewelry in every display window, he began to notice strange looking men milling around outside several of the shops. They were all similarly dressed in long black coats with braided hair growing out from under black felt hats. Carlo observed two of them discussing a small packet of what appeared to be tissue paper. As he drew closer on the crowded street, he saw the object of their interest as one of them examined a diamond with a loupe.

"You look lost," a tall man attired like the others addressed him.

"Not really, sir, more confused I'd say," he replied in his newly acquired language.

"Your accent, Spanish or Italian?"

"Sicilian. I'm from Palermo. Your garment, sir, and those of the other gentlemen, what does it symbolize?" Carlo asked as politely as he could.

"So you won't be confused any longer, I'll tell you. We are Hasidim, or for your benefit, Orthodox Jews."

Carlo had known only two Jews in his life, one worked for the Swiss jeweler in Lugano and the other was a GI he bought cigarettes from after the war. "Just what is it you do here?"

"We deal in diamonds."

A lump formed in Carlo's throat. Could he be lucky enough to have found a buyer so easily. "You mean right here on the street?"

"So why not? It's a free country." Just then another of the Hasidim approached.

"David, excuse me, what's your opinion of this?" The man handed him a half-carat stone he had been holding.

As Carlo stood watching, David pulled out a loupe and eyeballed the diamond. "Poor clarity, Joseph, $1500, no more." He handed the stone back.

When David left, Carlo said, "Perhaps you'd be interested in what I have."

"So show me."

Carlo reached into his pocket and withdrew the first stone he touched in the sack.

"Is this a joke, young man?" Joseph asked when Carlo handed him the rough stone.

Before Carlo could reply, he had his loupe to his eye. "Oy, where did this come from?" he asked as he rotated the stone under the glass.

"Why should it matter?" Carlo answered boldly, thinking that these men were merely street peddlers dealing in gems, perhaps even stolen. "If you're operating in the street, what difference does it make?"

"What is your name, Sicilian?" Joseph asked indignantly.

"Carlo. Just Carlo. So what's the problem?" Carlo thought perhaps his stone was flawed or worse.

"The problem is, Carlo, this rough is a perfect diamond at least a carat and a quarter."

"So what's it worth to you?"

"Nothing to me. We don't deal in unknown goods, especially uncut. I suggest you put it back in your pocket and return to Sicily."

"Now wait a minute, you have no right to...." Just then two other Hasidim joined them.

Carlo took back the stone. "If you're not interested fine, but you insult me by suggesting there's something wrong with me or this stone. I just thought you might want to buy it."

"Try one of these mercenary shops." Joseph pointed to a doorway under a sign that read, "ABRAHAMSON'S, WE BUY, WE SELL, WE APPRAISE."

The word mercenary registered positive in Carlo's brain. He studied the sign for a moment, then went in.

Abrahamson's was a swarm of activity. The store was well lit with fluorescent lights above several extensive glass showcases on either side. People in front of the long narrow room and behind the counters were deep in loud animated discussions. Finding the least crowded counter, Carlo waited eagerly to be acknowledged. As he waited, he watched a small man bent over a work table using a tiny blowtorch on what looked like a heavy gold chain.

"Yes, who are you with?" a heavy-set woman with a bagel in her hand and several large rings on her fingers asked.

"I don't understand. I'm here alone."

"I can see that, sir. Who do you represent? What store or jeweler?"

"I'm not sure I know what you mean...."

"Are you a dealer? Only dealers trade here."

"Not exactly." Lacking a better response, he blurted. "I'd like to see Mr. Abrahamson, please."

"I see. That's his area in the rear, but if you're not a dealer...."

"I want this appraised." Carlo whipped out a stone.

"Oh my!" she said picking up the rough that was a bit larger than the one he had shown the man outside. Before he could speak she was louping it. "Beautiful! Where did you...." She stopped mid-question. "Is Sol expecting you?" She was still fondling the stone.

"Sol?"

"Yes, Sol, Sol Abrahamson. Is he expecting you?"

"Not really, but I was hoping...."

"I see. So you don't know him?"

"That's right. You say he's in the rear?" Carlo reached for his diamond, but she held onto it.

"We can appraise this just as well as Sol," she offered.

"Isn't this his shop?"

"Of course. He's our landlord. We all lease space from him. Each counter is an independent dealer."

It was then Carlo noticed the engraved plastic countertop sign, "A. KISTLER, JEWELERS." Since she was still holding the stone, he asked, "Okay, what's it worth?"

"Let's not stand here, come in." She indicated a metal desk just beyond the small man working with the blowtorch.

Passing through a narrow opening in the counter, Carlo followed her and his diamond.

The moment they were seated she introduced herself. "I'm Barbara Kistler. My husband, Abe, and I own this business. And your name is?"

"Carlo." He spoke it loudly. Even seated further back from the busy show-cases, the sound of passionate voices haggling were several decibels above normal.

"Just Carlo?"

He nodded. He wasn't about to disclose his full name until he was certain he was dealing with a sincere, interested buyer of all his stones.

"Well, Carlo, you have here a perfectly clear, three and a half carat, uncut diamond."

"So what's it worth?" he asked a second time.

"That depends."

"Mrs. Kistler, I'm relatively new at this, so please don't play games with me."

"Call me Barbara. I can tell by your accent, Italian?"

"Sicilian."

"Same difference. Okay, you're right, no games. The price depends on how much information you can give me regarding such a fine stone. The less you can tell me, the bigger the risk and therefore the lower the price. Am I making myself clear, Carlo?"

"Very, Barbara. I can assure you that they are not stolen."

"They? You said they. You have others?"

Regretting the slip, he asked, "How much?"

"Hm-m-m. I'll give you $6,000 cash and no questions asked."

"I said I was new at this, but not stupid. $9,000 cash." He knew it was worth at least $15,000 but he had to establish a source he could trust that could handle a great number of stones.

"Sold." She reached out and shook his hand. "Just so you know, Carlo, a handshake in the district is our bond. Sit tight for a moment." She rose and went over to a heavy-set man with a white scraggly beard. Carlo assumed he was Abe Kistler. After a few moments of discussion they returned together.

"Nice to meet you, Carlo." Abe's grip wasn't nearly as firm as that of his wife. "If you will give me a few moments, I'll return with your money. Would you care for some tea or coffee?"

"No, thank you."

Abe left Carlo, Barbara and the diamond and headed toward the back of the store.

"We all keep our valuables, including large amounts of cash, in private boxes in a common vault," she explained.

A few minutes later Abe rejoined them holding a medium size manila envelope that he handed to Carlo. "Please count it."

"I'm sure it's all there." Carlo felt stupid after saying it, so took out the wads of hundred dollar bills and counted $9,000. Satisfied, he replaced the money and tucked the envelope into his jacket pocket. He remained seated, somewhat assured that the Kistlers were who he was looking for. To their amazement, he spilled the remaining diamonds onto their desk.

"What the hell?" Abe rubbed his beard as his wife, who appeared undaunted, immediately scooped up the largest one.

"How much?" Carlo asked nervously.

"Not here, there's a room in the back we use for private transactions." Abe said guardedly picking up the roughs.

Barbara was still gripping the largest stone as they proceeded to the rear of the building.

Abe hadn't exaggerated about the size of the room they entered. With the door closed it barely held a round plastic-topped table and four metal chairs. The overhead light, however, could have accommodated a much larger room.

Carlo was tempted to smoke but the close, windowless room negated the idea.

"You realize what you have here?" Abe poured the stones onto a piece of black velvet as he reached for the one his wife was still holding.

"Of course, rough cut diamonds of excellent quality which I'm willing to sell for a fair price."

"If there is anything illegal about them, you realize we'd be obliged to notify the police," Barbara Kistler warned.

"I understand. Please believe me, they're not stolen."

Abe shook his head. "Then where the hell did you get them? Exactly who are you anyway? Carlo alone is not enough."

"First, can I assume you're interested in doing business with me?"

"If it's legal, yes," Barbara answered for both of them.

My name is Carlo Marchi. I'm from Sicily and you might say I inherited a treasure in stones like these.

"You mean to say you have more?" Abe asked softly.

"Enough to make us all rich. Now how much are these worth? I understand that under the circumstances your offer will be less than normal."

Abe looked at his wife. "So-o-o?"

"Yes."

"All right then, give us a few minutes to evaluate each one and we'll tell you how much we'll pay you."

"Fair enough. Just remember there are many more where these came from." To conceal his nervousness he pulled out a cigarette. "Do you mind if I smoke?"

"Not in here. Outside in the store." Barbara pointed to the door.

Carlo lit up in the small corridor just outside the small room. He was amazed as he watched the store activity continue at a high pitch.

Half way through his cigarette, Barbara signaled him back in. "We're willing to pay you $50,000 for these."

Abe had the stones lined up before him according to size.

"Barbara and I wish to be honest with you, Carlo. They're worth more, at least half again what we're offering...."

"But since we're dealing with the unknown," Barbara interrupted, "our profit will be much greater, and so will that of the discreet cutters we sell them to."

"It's a deal, on two conditions," Carlo stated, "that we have an ongoing agreement for as many stones as I can provide, and that I be paid by cashier's check."

Abe stood. "Fair enough, with our condition that all your dealings are with us exclusively."

"You have my word."

"If you will return after lunch, we'll have your check ready." Abe offered his hand.

As Carlo shook it, he recalled what Barbara had told him earlier.

By three that afternoon, Carlo was seated at a desk in The Knickerbocker Savings Bank.

"According to your passbook, Mr. Marchi, you have a balance of $33,400."

Carlo couldn't help thinking how all bank people seemed to have the same pallor as though they'd never been out in the daylight. Martin Hilton, Assistant Manager, was no exception. He was peering at the Kistler's cashier's check through reading glasses that were attached to a cord around his neck, which, considering his double chin, was rather tight.

"Yes, and I'd like to deposit this $9,000 in cash plus half of the $50,000 check into my account here and have the other $25,000 transferred to my bank in Lugano, Switzerland." Carlo handed him his Swiss account number card.

"No problem, Mr. Marchi."

Carlo's theory was simple enough. He was transferring Tony's half to their account in Lugano and keeping the other half in his own US account. Although he trusted Tony when they were together, he still had to consider Tony's unstable nature when on his own.

Chapter 42

"I see you had no trouble getting to Roberto and back," Anna commented. They were seated in the living room. Her parents were out with friends for the evening.

"It was easy by taxi. After seeing the way New Yorkers drive, I'm wondering how smart it would be to get a car of my own."

"I'm sure you'll do fine when you decide to get one. So how's Tony's cousin? What's he like and where exactly does he live?" She snuggled as close to Carlo as she could get.

"Quieter than Tony, that's for sure. Why don't I take you out to dinner and fill you in on the rest?"

"Mom left lasagna for us, but eating out sounds better. I'll have to change into something besides these slacks."

"I could use a fresh shirt, but first...." He tilted his head and they kissed. Her lips were warm and moist and partly open. He detected a sweet metallic taste as she pressed hard against his mouth.

When their lips parted she gasped, "Let's go upstairs and you can help me decide what to wear." She led him into her bedroom. "Sit while I choose."

There was no denying he was aroused and how long he could control it depended on her now. His torment ended when Anna removed her clothes as he sat watching. The motion of her firm breasts and inviting thighs as she wiggled out of the last remnant of her undergarments beckoned him.

She stood willingly before him. "I can't wait another day, Carlo. I love you."

He stood and embraced her tenderly. "Anna, I want you now and forever."

Her soft moans as she accepted him created a mixed feeling of tenderness and lust that overcame him as he held her firmly. He had never experienced love sex before. The few women he had had in Sicily had been provided by Tony. Anna's sexual response to him was driven by her love for him and it overwhelmed him. Their passion controlled every move and variation until they lay fulfilled and exhausted. He was convinced they were meant for each other.

ဆာ

"How the hell can anyone eat with these things?" Carlo complained as he fumbled with chopsticks. Anna had suggested he try Chinese. They were in The Teak House Restaurant several blocks from home.

"It's easy, just watch." She showed off as she gripped fried rice between the two wooden slivers and delivered the morsel to her mouth without dropping a grain. She watched as he tried to mimic her finger manipulations. Finally, to her great amusement, he speared a piece of shrimp with a single chopstick.

"Gotcha," he boasted, then gulped it down.

"We'd better get you a fork," she said as they burst into laughter.

"What's the word for thank you in Chinese?"

"I'll settle for prego, ti voglio bene."

"Only English, remember," he teased.

"Yes but 'thank you, I love you,' sounds more sincere in Italian."

At that moment, she realized how grateful she was that fate had sent Carlo to her. Even now, after their intense lovemaking, she could feel his closeness within her. His gentleness with her, and now his warm sensitivity mixed with humor filled her with the hope and desire that this would last forever.

Now that Carlo was able to feed himself properly, she said, "So tell me about Roberto. Where'd you meet him? What's he doing in New York?"

"I met him on Forty-Seventh Street," he replied, as he picked through his sweet and sour shrimp.

She could tell it would be difficult to get him back to Chinese again. "That's the jewelry district."

"Yeah, I found that out when I got there. Roberto does some kind of fine gold filigree for one of the shops."

"That's quite an art. The Florentines are famous for fine gold work. Is he from Florence?" she asked as she started to pour more green tea into his cup.

"I'm not sure, but he must be paid well, 'cause he took me to a fancy restaurant for lunch." Carlo placed his hand over the cup. "I think I'll stick to espresso."

She refilled her cup instead. "Perhaps he'd like to come to Queens for some home cooking."

"We'll see. He seemed kind of distant and shy about meeting people, probably because he speaks very little English. But he did enjoy our visit and hoped we could get together often."

"Just let him know he's welcome at the Tuzzio's anytime."

The waiter delivered a small dish with orange slices and fortune cookies.

"Wisdom and health are more precious than gold." Anna read aloud from the thin slip. "They should have added 'love'," she pouted.

Carlo shook his head as he cracked his cookie open and unfolded the paper. "Well now, this one I agree with."

"What? What's it say?" She tried to take it from him, but he held it out of her reach.

"It says, 'Woman who wishes for love, shall have her way when we return home'."

"Waiter, check please," she requested with excited anticipation.

Chapter 43

For the next several weeks, Carlo found it more and more difficult to explain Tony's fictitious cousin's reluctance to visit them in Queens. He pondered this dilemma while he sat quietly watching Abe and Barbara evaluate his latest batch of stones in their usual meeting place, the back room at Abrahamson's.

Abe finally spoke, "$110,000, for these. The quality that you keep bringing never ceases to amaze me."

"If you're pleased, I'm pleased," Carlo replied.

"No complaints from our end," Abe assured him. "Now let me show you something." He pulled a two and a half-carat marquise cut diamond from a blue velvet pouch and handed it to Carlo between Jeweler's viewing tweezers.

"Wow, Abe, it's beautiful."

"Thought you'd like to see what that large rough you first showed Barbara turned out to be."

"It's worth plenty and I plan on keeping it," Barbara said possessively.

Abe shook his head. "Diamonds and women, Carlo, it's easier separating salt from the sea," he quipped. Then he added, "You never mentioned whether you are married or not."

"Not yet, but someday." He wondered how Anna would have reacted to such a nebulous answer, especially since they were so deeply committed emotionally and physically. Marrying her was the easy part. Explaining the wealth he and Tony were accumulating and the deceptions he had created to conceal that part of his life was going to take the biggest scheme he had ever hatched.

ဆဝင္သ

His weekly visits with the Kistlers had become as routine as his weekly banking business with Martin Hilton.

"You wish half of this cashier's check deposited in your account here and the remaining half transferred to Lugana, is that correct Mr. Marchi?"

"Yes, Martin. And call me Carlo, will you."

"I'll try, sir...I mean Carlo. That gives you a balance of $1,000,047."

"Exactly right, Martin."

In their Swiss account, he and Tony had almost two million dollars on deposit. As it had worked out, the payment to Campi was now coming directly from the sales of 'Stella's Tomato Sauce' which was selling faster than Tony could ship cases.

When Carlo last spoke to Tony, he had instructed him to increase the number of weekly cases to New York to two hundred. After checking with Enzio and Pino, Tony had informed Carlo that was impossible, unless they cut back on the number of cases they were shipping elsewhere. It had been an easy decision. They would reduce their shipments to Spain in favor of the higher price per case being paid in the States.

೮つಅ

Carlo was surprised when Tony called the warehouse the following week.

"Hi, how are you?"

When Carlo heard Anna answer the phone in Italian, he picked up his extension in time to hear Tony's reply.

"I'm okay, Anna, just overworked," he complained. "Maybe I should pay you guys a visit. I need a vacation."

"Oh, that would be wonderful, Tony. I'm dying to meet you and I know Carlo would love it as well."

"Yeah, I miss him, too."

Carlo held on as Anna continued, "I think he gets a little homesick, Tony, but not too often, I'm seeing to that." She smiled across the desk at him.

"I'll bet you are, Anna."

"Well, me and your cousin Roberto, that is."

"Who the hel...."

Carlo jumped in fast, "Roberto DeVito, your friend, dummy, the jeweler who moved here from Palermo." Carlo covered his mouthpiece, shook his head and whispered to Anna who looked confused, "Sometimes he forgets that he has a lot of friends."

"Oh him," Tony obviously caught on. "He's not my best friend, Anna, so he's easy to forget."

"We've invited him for dinner through Carlo, but so far . . ."

"Don't worry about it, Anna, he's kinda shy. But it's nice that Carlo is looking in on him."

"I'll let you boys finish. Bye, Tony, I'm looking forward to your visit."

"Yeah, me, too, Anna."

After she hung up, Tony asked, "Is she still in the room?"

"Yes, that's right." Anna was nearby doing some filing.

"Okay then, just listen. I take it Roberto is your cover to get to the diamond district."

"How clever of you. And where will you get the time to make a trip here?" There was a sting in Carlo's voice that he knew Tony would recognize.

"Look, I'm busting my ass here while you're falling in love, but that's not why I called."

"What is it? No problems, I hope?"

"No, damn it, why do you always think the worst?"

Carlo had a good response but kept it to himself.

"I just need to know if I should start packing two special cases, now that we've doubled the shipments."

"Jeez, Tony, I hadn't thought of that. Do you really think we should?" Carlo was relieved when Anna left the office for a moment.

"Hell, no. I really don't want to come in here between both shifts."

Carlo watched through the glass office wall as Anna talked to one of the warehouse men. "Then don't. We're doing just fine the way things are."

"Good," Tony replied. "I'll tell you what though, how about I just dump a few more stones in what I'm sending now?"

Carlo wondered how the Kistlers would react to the increase. "Sounds okay to me, but don't overdo it. Now what's this crap you were telling Anna? You're coming for a visit?"

"Yeah, goddamn it. I'd like to see New York, maybe blow off a little steam, try one of those American beauties. Yeah, why the hell not?"

"Because, now's not the right time. Christ, Tony, we're just starting to change our luck and build up a fortune."

"I knew damn well you'd object, Carlo. There'll never be a right time, I just know it."

"Give it six months, please. By then we should have millions more socked away. After that we'll get together and you can enjoy a well deserved break." *Like I'm not busting my ass at this end*, he felt like saying.

"Yeah, okay. I gotta go now anyway, it's the Carnevale Festival this week."

"See there, you are having fun. Take some money out of our account and do up the town."

"I already did. You'll be happy to know that you're helping to pay for a grand Carnevale dinner and dance at the Sciacca Garden Hotel for all our employees plus a number of special guests of my own."

"God, the Carnevale, I forgot how much fun that is. What's your costume like?"

"I'm going as Pagliccio."

"You always were a clown, Tony."

"Screw you, pig farmer."

"So when's Tony coming?" Anna asked after they hung up.

"In about six months."

Chapter 44

Ben was pleased when he saw that Carlo's next shipment was double what it had previously been. "Man, you couldn't have timed it better," he said. "Stella's has been selling so well that A & P is placing it in all their New York area stores. At this rate, Tony's going to have to increase production even more."

At that moment, Carlo's thoughts were more concerned about how the Kistlers would react to the extra diamonds Tony had included rather than the success of the sauce business. "That sounds terrific, Ben, but there's no way we can do that right now. We'll just have to limit the distribution till we can."

"Look, Carlo, I don't want to tell you how to run your business, but since I suspect we'll be related one of these days, I feel I can at least advise you..."

"Of course you can, Ben." *Oh boy, Anna must have said something about marriage to her parents.*

"There is a way, Carlo, it's called co-packing."

"I know what that means, Ben, but there's no other cannery in Sciacca we can use."

"Forget Sicily. I mean here in the States. It's done all the time. We simply get a cannery here to duplicate your mother's recipe and who knows how big this could become."

Carlo sensed the excitement in Ben's proposal. Then Ben added, "Hell, I'm even willing to put up half the capital and become a partner."

Carlo could hardly cope with the increasing complications in his life. There was no way he could accept Ben's offer. Damn, he already had an unwanted partner in Sicily, namely Campi. And for sure he would never allow the operating of the business, even a small part of it, out of his realm of control.

"I'll have to discuss it with Tony."

"Fair enough. Meanwhile, we'll make do with what we have."

Anna, busily checking orders, had remained silent during their exchange. However, as soon as her father stepped out into the warehouse, she spoke up, "You realize Daddy knows what he's talking about, don't you? Even from what I've seen processing your invoices, Carlo, you've got the beginning of a very profitable food company in the palm of your hand."

For the first time in his young life, Carlo had to consider something besides trying to abide by his mother's concerns and pacifying Tony's volatile temperament and constant need for reassurance. It suddenly dawned on Carlo what the responsibility of having a woman, no, make that a wife, entailed as far as making decisions that would affect his future.

"Anna, I love you and your folks, and you know how much I want to be your husband someday. But you don't understand how complicated things are back home. Ben's like a father to me already and I appreciate what he's trying to do, but trust me for a while longer and the road ahead will be perfect for us, believe me."

"Whatever you say, Carlo, but you must also understand that I'm walking on that road with you and will have a say in where it takes us."

Christ, he thought, *this is just like the movie we saw last week, "Adam's Rib'" with Spencer Tracy and Katharine Hepburn.* He had been annoyed all through the movie because Hepburn played Tracy's independent, opinionated, self-assured wife. His mother wasn't at all like that, nor was Isabella, but a new generation of women was developing apparently due to the significant role American women had played during the war years. Now Anna was showing that same independent feminine spirit. *Shit.*

Chapter 45

"Up until now, Carlo, we've had no problems selling your stones to a very discreet cutting house, but this increased number may put a burden on our relationship with them." Abe and Barbara were overwhelmed as they scrutinized the larger quantity of roughs Carlo had spread on the viewing felt.

"I'm not sure I understand," Carlo said, as he fingered the empty leather pouch the stones had been in. "Are you saying you can't handle this many?"

"Not at all," Barbara replied, as she handed Abe a two-carat beauty to examine.

"Amazing," Abe exclaimed as he rotated the stone. "As usual, the size and clarity of every piece is exceptional," he added. "No, my friend, we'll continue to take all you have, which simply means that we'll have to expand our base of buyers."

Relieved, Carlo replied, "That's no problem as far as I'm concerned."

"Only if you've not been honest with us regarding the legality of your treasure."

He could sense the seriousness of her warning in her eyes as Barbara said it.

"What we're saying, Carlo, is that bringing in other parties raises more questions. After all, this is a very exotic and competitive business."

"You have my word again, there is no need for concern. They are not stolen but my identity must remain between us. Is that clear?"

"We understand," Barbara assured him.

As Abe started to gather up the stones, Carlo picked one up from the group and requested, "I'd like you to have this one cut and made into an engagement ring as soon as possible."

Surprised, Abe examined the stone. "Very good choice. It should cut round at just under one carat. Of course, I can't say what the final price will be Carlo, but it'll only be a little more than cost for you. Hopefully you'll have it in a couple of weeks."

"Thanks, Abe, whatever the price."

Abe smiled and said, "$224,000 for the remainder of these, Carlo."

Once again Carlo visited his bank where he deposited half of the Kistler check into his New York account. The remaining $112,000 was transferred to the Swiss account.

On his way back to Queens by taxi, he re-examined his Knickerbocker Savings passbook and was amazed at how quickly he had salted away almost $2,000,000, plus the transfers into the Swiss account that boasted an additional balance of roughly $2,000,300, all within five months from the time he had arrived in America. The scary part of the wealth they had accumulated so far was that they had hardly put a dent in the first case of diamonds. At some point they would have to decide how much is enough.

In spite of his financial euphoria, three things were troubling him. First there was Anna. Although their love was strong and the sex unbelievable, Anna was making it abundantly clear she wanted to marry him soon and that children would ultimately be part of that equation. He hoped the ring would take the edge off her desire for wedding bells, at least for a short while.

Then there was the problem of the sauce business. As fast as shipments arrived at the warehouse they were gone. Two hundred cases a week wasn't satisfying the retail demand, and as much as Carlo tried to avoid it, Ben continued to urge him to consider co-packing in the States. He had to do something, either pursue guaranteed growth or let the damn business die. That wouldn't be too healthy though, especially since Tony had informed him that Campi seemed content with their increased monthly payment after they had doubled their shipments to America.

Finally, there were only a few months remaining on his promise that Tony could join him in the US.

That evening when he picked up the phone to call Tony, Carlo was prepared to share with his partner a number of decisions he had reached.

"That's what I think we should do, Tony, cut off the shipments to Europe and arrange with Pina to send everything you produce to the States."

"Are you sure we should do that, Carlo? I mean Pina has done pretty well for us in Europe."

"He'll be the first to agree knowing our markup here is at least twenty-five percent more."

"Do we need to inform Campi? Remember how pissed he was last time we...."

"Tell him when we're ready, then all you'll need to explain is that his share will be more."

"Yeah, the selfish bastard." Carlo could sense the hatred in Tony's voice, then he heard the flare of a match recognizing Tony's habit of lighting up when he was angry.

"Stay calm, especially if you're planning to visit me in a couple of months."

"I'm glad you didn't forget about that because I haven't. Just get those American Beauties lined up for me, partner."

"Speaking of line-ups, you might as well know that I'm giving Anna an engagement ring, which means that eventually you're going to be a best man."

"No shit, pig farmer? Are you really?"

"Yep."

"Does she know about the diamonds?"

"No, and there won't be any need for her to know."

"That's your problem, Carlo."

"I know, and I'll deal with it. I figure that by the time you get here we should have around $5,000,000. Not bad for a couple of Sicilian boys."

"Unbelievable. So what are we going to do with the rest of the stones?"

"We'll leave them stashed in Mama's root cellar until we decide."

Chapter 46

London

"Just where did you say these came from?" Jeremy Waters was examining one of three rough-cut diamonds his assistant, Alfred Dunne, had brought into his office.

"From America, sir. One of our long-time New York buyers brought them to my attention during his packet showing this morning."

After Waters carefully scrutinized all three of the stones, he looked up and exclaimed, "By God, Alfred, these appear to be South African."

"Are you certain, sir?"

"The clarity, texture, even the granular structure suggest that's their origin. Has Corklin reported any thefts recently?"

"Not that we're aware of, and he's always very conscientious about keeping us informed regarding security matters."

Waters reached across his desk and picked up a hand-carved Meerschaum pipe. Dunne watched as he dipped into a Chinese porcelain tobacco humidor.

"Care for a bowl?" Waters offered as he tamped the dark brown strands until they were compacted just enough.

"Thank you, no, sir. I prefer my own Regency Street blend," he replied as the first puffs of pipe smoke curled upward.

"Hm-mph, as you wish, Alfred. Now where the hell did this chap...ah, what's his name... say he got these?"

"It's Rubins, sir. Jason Rubins. He owns a rather lucrative jewelry operation in Manhattan. He's been doing business with us for years."

"Yes, yes, I'm sure he's all of that, but these stones, man?" Waters picked up the largest stone, a flawless one and a half-carat, and pointed it at Dunne. "How did he come by them?"

"I think perhaps Mr. Rubins should explain, sir."

"Is he still here?" Waters re-lit his Meerschaum.

"He's just outside. I thought you would prefer to...."

"Of course. You were right to have him wait. Please show him in," Waters said impatiently.

Waters was still examining the stones when Dunne escorted Jason Rubins into his mahogany-paneled office.

"Come in, please, come in, Mr. Rubins," Waters invited cordially as he rose and shook the man's hand.

Rubins' stout figure contrasted with the slimness of his hosts. His blue gray hair was combed from one side to the other in an attempt to hide his baldness. His smile exaggerated his heavy lips and concealed most of the whiteness of his dentures, while his choice of a conservative navy single-breasted suit seemed most appropriate for the occasion.

"Thank you, sir. It's such a privilege to finally meet you." His nervousness at being in the presence of the head of the largest diamond cartel in the world was obvious by his demeanor as well as his moist hand.

Waters discreetly dabbed his palm with his handkerchief as he indicated they'd be more comfortable at a leather seating arrangement in one corner of the room. A large open credenza revealing several bar accoutrements, as well as a silver tray and tea service, sat against the opposite wall.

"Unfortunately I can't always be available for our more important buyers such as yourself, Mr. Rubins. But let me assure you, we are well aware of your patronage and good standing here at Vandenberg." Waters crossed his legs as he leaned back in a hand-tooled Moroccan leather high-backed chair. Rubins was seated across from him on a matching leather couch. "Tea, Mr. Rubins? Alfred, would you do the honors?" he requested, ignoring Rubins nodding to the contrary.

While Dunne was busy at the credenza, Waters placed Rubins' three stones onto a black ebony coffee table between them. "Mr. Dunne tells me you purchased these roughs in New York."

"Yes, sir, that's correct, and I could have bought more had I chosen to."

Water's face began to flush with agitation as Dunne placed the tea on the table. "More, you say?"

"Oh yes, quite a few more, Mr. Waters, of similar size and clarity."

"According to what Mr. Rubins told me earlier," Dunne interjected, "he purchased these purposely knowing we would be interested."

"We could have cut them into beautiful Marquises and Rounds, possibly for a pendant or clasp which would easily sell at a very generous mark-up. However, knowing the restrictive nature of our industry, I became concerned that the source of these stones might be in conflict with the cartel, even though we were assured they were perfectly legal. Nonetheless, not wanting to jeopardize our good standing with Vandenberg...." Rubins fidgeted as he explained.

"Yes, yes, of course." Waters could hardly contain himself. He sharply banged the remains of his dead pipe into a heavy crystal ashtray. "You were right to do so, Mr. Rubins."

Dunne sat quietly as his superior continued.

"And who, sir, are they, these purveyors of so-called legal diamonds?"

"I'm not certain, Mr. Waters. All I know is that we were offered a small portion of a number of stones that an affiliate of ours was purchasing. Apparently there is an abundance available to the larger cutting houses in New York."

"Did you hear that, Alfred, an abundance? My God, someone in America is dealing in black market diamonds," he shouted.

"You...you, understand we only purchased these assuming you'd wish to be informed. That was our only intention, I assure you," Rubins stammered.

"It's quite all right," Dunne answered approvingly. "Your loyalty is most appreciated."

"Yes, of course." Waters, his mind churning, promptly concurred with Dunne's comment. "This will reflect well in the quality of your packets in the future, Mr. Rubins, I can assure you."

"Thank you, sir."

As Waters stood indicating their meeting was over, he picked up the three stones. "Now, if you'll be kind enough to tell us what you paid for these, Mr. Dunne will reimburse you that amount in addition to the expenses for your trip here."

"That's more than fair. Thank you, Mr. Waters." After another moist handshake, Rubins followed Dunne out.

༄༅

After seeing to it that Rubins received his check, Dunne thanked him again, bid him a safe journey home, and returned to Waters' office.

"Bloody hell, Alfred, do you realize that he paid less than three-quarters of what these are actually worth? Of course you do, man."

Dunne sat across from his boss and loaded a bent briar pipe with his Regency Street blend, obviously waiting to see what Waters had in mind as he buzzed his secretary.

"Mrs. Langford, would you please have Nigel Burns join us at once." When he disconnected he turned to Dunne. "If anyone can tell where these were unearthed, Nigel can."

Less than ten minutes passed before Mrs. Langford announced that Nigel Burns had arrived.

"Nigel, good to see you."

"And you, sir, and you as well, Alfred."

"Are you still running with the beagles?" Dunne inquired.

"Oh yes sir. It's good of you to ask. Every Sunday morning, weather permitting."

Obviously anxious to get on with it, Waters slid the stones across his desk. "Nigel, what do you make of these?" Nigel, Vandenberg's head geologist, automatically louped one of the stones.

"Beautiful," he commented after a moment of studying all three.

"And their origin?" Waters quizzed.

"They're ours, of course. I mean, aren't they?" Nigel replied without hesitation.

"They came from America," Dunne informed him.

"Very humorous, Alfred," Nigel retorted. "You should know full well there really are no diamonds mined in America and the few that are found there are of inferior quality."

Ignoring their dialog, Waters addressed Nigel. "Can you tell us exactly where they were mined?"

"As I said, I assumed they were ours. However, to pinpoint more precisely, I'll need to do a typomorphic test in my lab." He peered through his loupe again then added, "One thing I'm certain of, sir, they're not from Russia, Australia or the Orient."

"How soon can you get back to us?"

"Give me until tomorrow, gentlemen."

Immediately upon Nigel's departure, Waters ordered, "Get Corklin up here as soon as possible, Alfred. Something reeks in America and Sean's going to sniff it out for us."

Chapter 47

Sean Corklin had no idea why he had been summoned back to London. Almost a year had passed since his fruitless assignment to find the lost diamonds. Now here he was again seated with Jeremy Waters and Alfred Dunne in Vandenberg's executive dining room.

"Since your arrival coincided with lunch," Waters explained, "we'll put off our private discussion until after our repast."

Feast is more like it, Corklin thought. The buffet that day boasted cold pheasant and Scottish salmon. Mixed salad and asparagus tips made up the green offering, with a choice of tarts and chocolates for sweets. His usual luncheon fare consisted of potpie and dark ale at a local establishment a short distance from his office at the mine. He knew what Rhonda would think of such gastronomical opulence, especially since she taught reading and writing to the underprivileged children of many of the mineworkers.

As a result of the rich lunch, Corklin's stomach pressed uncomfortably against his belt when they were finally seated in Waters' office. Watching Waters and Dunne both light up their pipes simultaneously, Corklin nonetheless asked as he reached for a cigarette, "May I, sir?"

"Of course. Now, as to the reason we sent for you...." Waters paused as he tamped hot ash deeper into the bowl of his Meerschaum. "Show him," he instructed Dunne.

Dunne placed the three uncut diamonds from America on the table they were seated around.

Having seen thousands of such stones coming out of the bowels of the earth in Pretoria, Corklin took a drag and waited for an explanation.

At that point, Waters rose, went to his desk and returned with a folder. "According to this lab report prepared by Nigel Burns, our geologist...I believe you know him, Sean, do you not?"

"Yes, sir. I personally provided security for Nigel during several of his visits to the mines. A pleasant, agreeable chap, I might add."

"Yes, of course." Waters was impatient to continue. "Nigel is certain," Waters pointed the folder at the three stones on the table, "they're South African. In fact they're from our mine according to his typomorphic analysis."

"I beg your pardon, sir?"

"It's the method employed in determining the origin of rough diamonds," Waters explained.

Corklin acknowledged the information with a shake of his head, then crushed out his smoke, wondering what the hell the old boy was leading up to.

"I'm afraid I don't understand the significance of all this, sir."

Waters raised his voice, "Damn it, man, the bloody things came from America."

"What we're saying, Sean," Dunne interceded calmly, "is they were bought in New York and these are but a few of an abundance of rough cuts being sold to many of our own clients there."

"At ridiculously low prices, damn it," Waters shouted again.

"At first we thought they had somehow been smuggled from our mine..."

Before Dunne could continue, Corklin objected. "There's no way that's possible, sir. I run the tightest security checks you can imagine. We even x-ray the miners and, if anything seems out of the ordinary, we conduct extremely thorough body examinations. It's not possible."

"Relax, Sean, we have every confidence in your ability," Waters assured him. "Alfred and I have come to a startling conclusion regarding these stones. You see, we believe they're part of out lost shipment back in '42."

"Good lord, how is that possible? You mean the cargo from the downed Ladybird we searched for some time ago?"

"Precisely, it's the only possible explanation, and you're going to New York to uncover how, where and who."

"If you don't mind my saying so, sir, that'll be like locating the sour note in a choir."

Dunne smiled at the analogy. "You'll have a better jump on it this time, Sean. The gentleman from New York who brought these to our attention should be able to point you in the right direction. His name is Jason Rubins, a loyal patron of Vandenberg Mining."

"We'll see to it that he assists you in any way you choose, as well as arranging your lodging and transportation while in New York," Waters pledged. "One more thing, Corklin, even if you're not successful, there'll be a tidy sum in it for you. If, however," Waters emphasized, "you locate our diamonds, we'll double your original search bonus."

"I'll do my best, sir." *New York here I come.*

Chapter 48

Carlo brushed the first snow he had ever experienced off his coat before he, Anna and her father hurried into the warm kitchen.

"Wow! It's unbelievable out there," Carlo exclaimed to Isabella. "Everything is covered in white, and boy, the car slipped and slid all over the road."

"I'm glad you're all home safe," Isabella said. "According to the radio they're expecting ten to twelve inches."

"I love it," Anna declared as she hugged him from behind. "Just think, Carlo, your first white Christmas."

"Yeah great," Carlo replied, "cold, dangerous and white is more like it." He rubbed his hands together over the kitchen stove.

"Something smells good." Ben started to open the oven door. "Um-m-m, what is it?"

"Be careful," Isabella cautioned. "Don't you dare make my Panettone fall. I'm making it in honor of Carlo's first Christmas with us."

"Oh jeez, Isabella," Carlo's voice choked up. "Mama baked sweet cake for us as far back I can remember."

"Well, I don't guarantee it'll be as good as your mother's, but I got the recipe from Mrs. Sargento whose husband runs the butcher shop."

"I'm sure it'll be great, and it will remind me of home."

"Oh, I almost forgot. Speaking of home, there's a box for you from Sicily under the Christmas tree."

"Thanks, I'm sure it's from Tony," he said as he headed for the living room with Anna anxiously following close behind.

The six-foot balsam decorated with ornaments, tinsel and lights sat before the large front room window. There, amongst the gift-wrapped packages to be opened in two more days, was a brown shipping carton stamped with foreign postal markings and tied with heavy white cord.

The room was fragrant from the fresh tree and Carlo couldn't help thinking how different the American celebration of the holiday was from the more simple way they celebrated back home. On the farm his father would bring in a huge log for the fireplace and his mother would light candles she had dipped herself. Of course there were gifts, maybe a new sweater, shoes and candy from the village.

And the food, his Mama would bake sweet cake and cookies and his father would trade for a goose from a neighboring farm. The nearest church was miles too far away, so his father would say a special prayer before the meal. It was a wonderful time of year, including the much milder weather. But here, it seemed so overwhelming. Everyone was in a hurry. Stores and shops were crowded with people spending wildly, especially on Forty-Seventh Street where the Kistlers were so busy they hardly had time to deal with him. And the traffic, Carlo was happy he hadn't bought a car yet. His usual trip home from the city had taken almost twice as long as the previous week.

After dinner Carlo and Anna sat together beside the tree facing the package from Tony.

"Open it," Anna said excitedly.

"I thought we had to wait until Christmas morning," he said as he untied the cord.

"That doesn't apply to mailed gifts." She nudged him to hurry.

Carlo was sure she had made that rule up, like so many others. "You're worse than a little child." He stopped opening the box just to tease her.

"Carlo!" She pulled the box away from him and peeled open the flaps. "Darn!" she whimpered, as she pulled out four brightly wrapped presents with crushed bows.

"See there, now we'll have to wait." He read each tag as he placed them under the tree. "I hope Tony will be more patient with his gift."

"From what you told me about him, I doubt it. But I'm sure he'll love the gold cuff links." Before Carlo could stop her she had the giftwrap torn off her present. "Oh Carlo, look, isn't it beautiful?" She held before her a light blue cashmere sweater.

"Very suitable for a spoiled American girl."

"Not as spoiled as you've been lately," she replied as she pulled the sweater on over her blouse. "A perfect fit. You sent him my size, didn't you?" She adjusted herself into it.

"Yeah, and the protrusions are just right, too."

"You would think that." She tossed the empty gift box at him. "Aren't you going to open yours?"

"Sure, why not?" He unwrapped his gift, then began laughing. "Only Tony would send a gift like this," he said as he read the enclosed card then pulled an expensive Swiss gold cigarette lighter out of the box.

"What's so funny about a lighter?" She reached for the card. "Only men would think this is funny," she said after she read, "Carlo use this lighter for that after lovemaking smoke. Enjoy, Tony."

Chapter 49

"Oh my God!" Anna shrieked when she opened the small gift box. It was a Christmas-card morning. A heavy deposit of snow covered Queens and the Tuzzio living room windows were completely frosted over as they all sat near the tree opening their gifts.

"It's so beautiful, Carlo." She jumped up, hugged and kissed her new fiancée. When she released him, she flashed the ring before her parents. The Kistlers had outdone themselves. The perfect stone weighing almost one carat was set in a medium width platinum setting.

Isabella started to weep as she grabbed her daughter. "Congratulations to both of you," she sobbed.

"Welcome to the family," Ben added as he placed an opened gift box containing the usual shirt and tie combination on the coffee table.

"Thanks, Ben, I'm lucky to have such a wonderful new family."

"Oh Carlo." Anna returned to him and nearly crushed him with affection. "June," she said clinging to him, "I want to be a June bride."

"Sounds about right." *Hell, that's months from now. By then Tony will be here and maybe I'll be ready.* He reached into the pocket of his robe for a smoke.

As he was about to light it, Anna gripped his new lighter, "Save that for later, use a match for now." She exaggerated a flirtatious blinking.

Her parents busy opening their presents, missed the meaning of her remark, but Carlo didn't. He happily grabbed a book of matches from a nearby table.

"Oh, Carlo!" Isabella cried as she put on the gold wristwatch. "So expensive. You shouldn't have."

"Wow," Ben exclaimed as he put on a gold watch as well.

"My pleasure. You both have been wonderful to me." He held up a dark blue woolen car coat from Anna and matching scarf and gloves from her parents. "Boy, I'll sure get plenty of use out of these in this weather. Thanks."

Tony had sent a gorgeous Italian leather handbag for Isabella and a pair of soft Italian leather driving gloves for Ben.

"I'll say one thing about Tony, he's got great taste," Carlo declared.

"Not as great as his partner," Anna disagreed, waving her ring hand.

Chapter 50

"My God, is it always this bloody cold in New York?" Corklin had cleared Customs at Idlewild and was in a taxi heading for Manhattan.

"Where've you been, pal?" the taxi driver asked as he negotiated out of the busy terminal area and in between the plowed snow banks that narrowed the roadway. "It's the beginning of January and you ain't seen nothin' yet."

"I'm from South Africa, and I hope I never do." It was bad enough in London with the damp and the rain, but this was unbearable as far as Corklin was concerned. All he could do was hope he could locate whoever was selling Vandenberg's diamonds, resolve it quickly and get the hell out of the US as soon as possible.

Once they were on the Belt Parkway and the traffic lightened up, the driver looked through the rear view mirror and spoke to Corklin. "I hope you have a warmer coat than that, pal, it's supposed to be pretty frigid for the next several days."

Corklin's Burberry raincoat had a thin lining. "I'm afraid it's the only one I brought along." He raised the collar in anticipation of the driver's severe weather forecast.

"Well if you're planning to stay awhile, there's a Macy's down the block from your hotel and they have a good bunch of winter coats there."

"Thanks, what's a Macy's?"

"Man you must be from Africa. It's a big department store."

"I see, like Harrods."

"Huh?"

"Forget it, but thanks for the advice."

They pulled up to the Statler Hotel on Seventh Avenue. "Here we are, pal. Five bucks should do it." He flipped down the meter flag.

Corklin fumbled with the US dollars he had exchanged from pounds before leaving London. He pulled out a five and handed it to the driver. "There you go, and I assume this would be an appropriate gratuity?" He handed him another dollar.

"It's a little light, pal, but that's okay considering you're a foreigner and all."

"South African and I wouldn't want to be considered light." Corklin handed him another dollar.

"You're all right, pal, and don't forget a warmer coat."

As Corklin exited with his bag, he was rudely brushed aside by another fare hustling into the taxi.

The driver shrugged his shoulders at Corklin. "Get used to it pal, you're in New York." He laughed, flipped up the meter flag and sped from the curb.

While waiting at the desk to be checked in, Corklin recorded in his pocket notebook, January 4, 1950, $7 for taxi from airport. Later, after arranging a dinner meeting with Jason Rubins, he followed the cabby's advice, went to Macy's and purchased a hooded, camel-hair coat. Back in his room by five, he made a reservation for seven in the hotel dining room, left a call for six-thirty, then took a short nap.

ಬಂಚ

From the detailed description of Rubins that Dunne had provided, Corklin spotted his contact when he entered the busy dining room. He watched as Rubins was directed to his corner table.

"Mr. Corklin?" Rubins asked so softly Corklin barely heard him.

"Yes, Sean Corklin. I'm happy to meet you, Mr. Rubins. Please sit. I'm having some of your American beer. What would you like?"

Rubins slipped into the chair opposite Corklin. "Ah...red wine, I guess."

Corklin signaled the waiter. While they waited for Rubins' wine Corklin asked, "What sort of American dish would you recommend? I've been reviewing the menu while I waited and there seems to be quite an assortment of main courses."

"That's typical of hotel dining." His wine arrived. "A wide selection but hardly gourmet."

"We could have met somewhere more to your liking."

"No, no, for the purpose of our getting together this will be fine."

"Very well then, perhaps I'll try the Veal Marsala and spaghetti."

"I wouldn't." Rubins shook his head. "Stick to the basics, have the New York strip steak and potatoes."

"Really? I normally eat quite a bit of beef and very little Italian."

"Trust me. Order the steak. Later I'll give you a list of some of the finest Italian restaurants in the city that you might like to try during your stay."

The steak was chewy and the baked potato undercooked. They both left a good portion of their meal on their plates.

When Rubins suggested coffee to help wash away the memory of a poor meal, Corklin replied, "I normally drink tea as you would imagine, but I must say American coffee is rather good."

"Thought you'd like it. Now, I'd like to catch the nine forty-five, so if we can get to the reason for your visit...."

"Of course, I didn't realize you lived out of the city. I'll be as brief as possible."

"No need to rush, I live in New Jersey and my train leaves from Penn Station just across the street. We have a good forty-five minutes before I must leave."

"Very well. I assume if I require further assistance from you we could meet again, perhaps for lunch."

"Of course. Now where would you like me to start?" Rubins asked obviously scanning the more than half-empty room, a testimonial to the lack of popularity of hotel dining among true New Yorkers.

"I'm fully apprised of what you explained to Director Waters and Mr. Dunne, so why not start with who sold you the stones and where I can locate them?"

"It's not quite that simple. Since I run a rather large cutting and polishing house in the heart of the jewelry district, my contacts and discretion are invaluable."

Bloody hell, he's going to take the long way through the bush. "Yes, of course."

"The point is, aside from our semi-annual allotment from Vandenberg, any number of smaller dealers and gem houses approach us to do their cutting. We'll also purchase if the stones are of exceptional quality."

"Then you know which dealer sold you our stones?"

"Yes, of course, but from what I was told they purchased them from someone else."

"And?" *Christ, this is like pulling fat from the fire.* Corklin lit up a cigarette for its calming effect. "Please go on, Mr. Rubins."

"I'm getting to that, but you must understand, I have to be left out of whatever it is you do with such information. I mean, I have a reputation and a rather thriving business and any...."

"Relax. That's no problem." Corklin sucked in a big drag and let it out slowly. "You have the word of Vandenberg Mining that you will not be implicated in any way." Then Corklin slathered on a little more frosting. "In fact, it's my understanding that you will be given special consideration at your next showing in London."

"I got that impression from Director Waters when I was there and I do appreciate it."

Corklin stubbed out his smoke, pulled out his pen and notepad, then leaned a bit forward cocking his head in anticipation of the name of the dealer who had approached Rubins with Vandenberg's stones.

"Simon and Simon. They run a store on Forty-Seventh Street specializing mostly in emeralds and rubies. That's why they approached me, they don't have a big clientele for diamonds."

Corklin was writing as Rubins continued.

"Mel Simon, I've known him for years. In fact, his son and mine were Bar Mitzvahed together...."

"Mr. Rubins, please, remember you've a train to catch."

He glanced at his Patek Philippe and continued. "Well, Mel thought I'd be interested. I mean who wouldn't, such perfect stones? But then when he told me the price I became suspicious and nervous. They've got to be stolen, I told him. He said no they couldn't be, that he got them from a very respectable dealer two doors down from his place, whose wife is related to his cousin. He also knew of more dealers getting in on the bargain. That's when I decided that if so many stones were being sold so cheap, Vandenberg should know about it. After all...."

"The name, Mr. Rubins. What's the name of that dealer?" Corklin's patience was getting as thin as the hair on Rubins' head.

"Kistler. Abe Kistler. He and his wife, I believe her name is, ah...Barbara, yes, that's it, Abe and Barbara Kistler. They lease space at Abrahamson's Jewelers diagonally across the street from my place. I don't know them personally, but from what Mel tells me they handle quality goods."

Unaccustomed as he was to Jewish names, Corklin had Rubins spell them for him as he jotted them down.

"That's everything? That's the connection as far as you know? You have no idea where the...." Corklin referred to his notes, "Kistlers got the stones?"

"As they say in the movies, 'that's the end of the trail'." Rubins checked his watch again. "It's time for my train." He rose and extended his hand to Corklin. "If you need me for anything further come by my shop. I have a private office where we can talk."

Corklin was surprised by the firmness of Rubins' handshake. "Thank you, sir, I will. Sorry about my choice for dining."

"No problem. It's not the first bad meal I've had. Besides, Sarah will have a little something for me when I get home. Here, let me give you some better choices." He proceeded to suggest a couple of New York's finest eating establishments. "They're a bit pricey, but after all, a diamond mining company can afford it."

"Thanks again, Mr. Rubins." Watching as he hurried off to catch his train, Corklin couldn't help chuckling to himself wondering what might be waiting for Rubins at the end of his trail.

Chapter 51

Since the jewelers on Forty-Seventh Street didn't open shop until ten, Corklin had a leisurely breakfast in the hotel coffee shop. After casually thumbing through the Daily News and noting the goings-on of the city, and with absolutely no interest in basketball highlights in the sports section, he left the paper on the table and headed for the street.

After a few steps in the two-inch snowfall from the night before, Corklin again hastened toward Macy's where he purchased a pair of sleek black rubber boots. He added their cost to his expense log right below the camel hair coat.

Dressed for the horrible weather, he took a taxi to Abrahamson's. Strolling along the several counters he discreetly eyeballed the nameplates of the various dealers. It was only 11:00 a.m. but there was a good deal of buying and selling activity. Then, between the traders at one of the counters he spotted the name he was seeking: A & B Kistler.

He studied the man and women in a heated discussion behind the counter. Corklin was certain they were the Kistlers. To avoid drawing attention to himself, he pretended to study the merchandise in a nearby showcase as he observed the Kistlers long enough to recognize them again. Then he left.

Back at his hotel Corklin devoted the remainder of the morning to considering various ways to approach the Kistlers. In the end he decided on a direct confrontation. He had always been most successful at obtaining admissions of guilt by instilling fear of imprisonment in thieving mineworkers back in Pretoria. It was the method he used most in getting to the truth quickly, and he was very good at intimidation.

Recalling that Abrahamson's closed at 5:00 p.m., he taxied back to Forty-Seventh Street. It was around 4:50 p.m. when Corklin positioned himself across the street in the entryway of a deli which appeared to be in the process of closing up as well. Pulling the collar of his new coat up around his neck as a buffer against the cold air whipping around him, he quietly swore as he thought, *Damn this cold, bloomin' climate. The quicker I get this over with, the quicker I can get the bloody hell out of New York.* His hands were getting uncomfortably cold even tucked inside his pockets. *Much more time in this frigid city and it's back to Macy's for a pair of gloves.*

Finally the Kistlers exited the store shortly after 5:30 p.m. At a practical distance, he followed them as they briskly walked up to the end of the block and got into the first taxi in a line of several parked on Seventh Avenue. Quickly occupying the next one in line, he said to the driver, "I just spotted my wife and another man get into that taxi up ahead. There's an extra ten dollar bill for you if you take me where they're headed."

"You got it, pal." He swung out and followed behind the Kistlers' taxi. "Are you gonna bust his ass when we get there. You should, ya' know."

"More likely I'll sue the bloke," Corklin replied with a smile.

"You ain't an American, are you pal? Otherwise you'd bust em' both."

"South African. We don't bust, we decapitate." Corklin made a gesture with his forefinger across his throat.

"Jeez. Aw, you're kiddin', right?"

Before long Corklin recognized the route being taken.

"Looks like they're headed for the Statler, pal. Oops, nope, it's Penn Station they're goin' to."

Quickly paying the fare plus the ten, Corklin followed close behind in the busy terminal as the Kistlers headed for a track entrance with a destination board indicating several towns in New Jersey and a departure time of 6:30 p.m. He thought of Jason Rubins the night before and wondered if everyone who worked in New York lived in New Jersey.

Corklin trailed them along the track platform. When they entered a car, he jumped into the car behind, then walked through and took a seat two rows back from them. The car was almost full, and at several spots along the aisle there were four people seated facing each other in heated cards games. *Strange people these Americans, they seem to work in one area, live in another and play games in between.*

Fifteen minutes later the train jerked forward. Corklin took out a cigarette. As soon as he struck a match to light up, several voices loudly announced that he was in a no smoking car. *So much for being covert, shit.* He tucked the cigarette back into the pack and slid down in his seat.

Since he didn't know their destination, he paid the conductor full fare to Spring Valley, the last stop. After several commuter stops, the Kistlers finally rose to disembark at Westwood. Corklin exited behind several other Westwood passengers. He could see the Kistlers up ahead going toward the station parking lot. Assuming they had a car and seeing no taxis in sight, his only option was to go into the small station house and seek the information he needed. In the short distance from the train to the building, Corklin quickly realized it was even colder away from the city. Inside the station house, the sudden blast of dead, overbearing heat was more of a shock than a relief. Unbuttoning his coat, he approached the only ticket window open and inquired about return times to Penn Station. The agent grunted and handed him a schedule.

"Thanks, chap, but isn't it a bit too hot in here? Bloody uncomfortable, if you ask me."

"Read it outside then," the agent responded.

Obviously New York rudeness extends into New Jersey. "I say, chap, are you from New York by any chance?"

There was no reply. The face in the window disappeared.

Pocketing the schedule, Corklin scanned the small waiting room until he spotted what he was looking for, a New Jersey Bell Telephone directory. With a quick flip through to the letter K and a trace of the finger, he got them. Abraham and B. Kistler, 128 Fanwood Street. Next to the phone tacked on the bulletin board was a taxi company business card.

Ten minutes later, he was parked outside of a large white colonial house with brass numbers 128 attached to a porch pillar. The taxi pulled away as Corklin walked to the front door. The faint sound of melodious chimes when he pressed the doorbell was followed by the illumination of a faux antique carriage light to the right of the door.

A moment later, the heavy-set Barbara Kistler appeared. "Yes? May I help you, sir?"

"I do hope so, dear lady. My name is Sean Corklin. I'm a private investigator here to retrieve the stolen diamonds you've been selling."

"Oh, my God. Abe-e-e, come quick...."

Chapter 52

"Carlo, there's a call for you. It's John Collins," Anna called into the warehouse where he was checking an order for A & P.

"Coming."

She gave him a peck on the cheek as he took the receiver.

"Carlo, there seems to be a problem with your shipment that just arrived," Collins informed him.

"What kind of problem?"

"All I know is that Customs wants us down there as soon as possible."

"That's all you know?"

"They just said some kind of problem. Relax, I'll be by to pick you up within the hour."

Shit. "Yeah, okay. I'll be ready."

Anna started to embrace him when he hung up, but he recoiled. "What's wrong? I thought you liked me touching you."

"I do. I'm sorry, it's just that something's wrong at Customs and you know how nervous I get about official stuff."

She embraced him again. This time he didn't resist. "You worry too much. That's why you pay John Collins. I'm sure whatever small difficulty it is he'll get it straightened out." She kissed his cheek just as her father entered the office.

"Not during business hours you two," he teased.

"I'm just comforting him, Daddy. Seems there's a problem at Customs and my sweet, emotional Sicilian is nervous."

"Hell, I'm sure it's some trivial matter. You've got to remember, Carlo, when you deal with the government everything is blown out of proportion."

"Yeah, I guess, but I'm glad John's going with me. He's picking me up in a few minutes."

"There, you see. He'll get it sorted out in no time. He deals with this kind of stuff all the time."

"I know, it's just that being here on a visa makes me a bit edgy. I'm going to wait for him out on the platform. I need some air and a smoke."

"I'll be here when you get back and we'll go home together," Anna said.

"Yeah, okay." He walked out to the loading platform in a daze. *What the hell could have happened? Maybe they opened the case and checked all the cans. Shit, I could be arrested for smuggling.* The thought of taking off crossed his mind. *So where the hell would I run to? Shit!* Just then he heard John's car horn.

"Carlo, are you deaf? I honked four times," Collins yelled from his car window.

Carlo nervously chain-smoked during the short drive to Port Newark.

"Christ, Carlo, you're acting as jumpy as an expectant father. Try to relax, will you?"

"It's just that everything is going so well with the business and with Anna, that...there's an old Italian saying, 'Even though the sky is clear and the sun is warm, beware, another storm is hiding somewhere,' or something like that. We Sicilians are just too damn superstitious I guess."

Collins pulled into the visitor parking area in front of US Customs.

It seemed to Carlo like they had been waiting an eternity in the pale green, cement-block office when finally an agent that Collins knew vaguely came out and greeted them.

"Collins, right? I believe we met once before. I'm Agent Bill Barton." He extended his hand.

Collins took it. "Good to see you again, Agent Barton. This is Carlo Marchi, the owner of Gemma Importing."

Carlo hoped his palm wasn't as moist as the back of his neck when they shook hands. "Happy to meet you, Mr. Barton."

"You seem rather young to be an importer," Collins commented as he looked Carlo straight in the eyes.

To Carlo it was as though he was peering into his soul. *Calm down, you're only guilty if you appear so.* He remembered his uncle Franco telling that to a paesano once.

"Yes sir, but one ages quickly in business."

Collins chuckled at the quip, but Barton barely grinned.

"I'm sure one does, Mr. Marchi. Now if you'll follow me I'll show you the dilemma we have with your shipment."

Carlo could feel the perspiration flowing down his spine as he and Collins walked behind Agent Barton. They passed through the glass door leading into the general inspection area where Carlo had watched his very first shipment pass through Customs. Beyond that was another door with a sign that read: QUESTIONABLE CARGO.

Carlo imagined the grip of handcuffs as Barton lead the way into the special room. There before them were rows of metal shelves holding all sizes and shapes of crates and cartons. Barton led them past the shelving to an open area and onto a side loading dock.

Carlo's Adam's apple felt like it was about to jump out of his throat when he saw his shipping cases had burst open and cans of Stella's Tomato Sauce strewn about in a heap.

"What the hell . . .?" he started to ask.

"That's the problem, Mr. Marchi," Barton interjected, "the damn unloading net tore open when it came out of the belly of the ship and dumped its contents, including your cases, onto the dock."

"Jeez, what a mess," Collins commented as Carlo walked over to examine his goods.

"You should have seen it before we separated it out from other shippers' merchandise."

As near as Carlo could tell, most of the corrugated cardboard cases were torn apart and a number of cans that had spilled out were dented, but none had burst open. Then he spotted it, the case with the copy GEMMA IMPORTING double smudged by Tony to indicate the special sauce cans. It was hardly damaged just one flap ripped open, but the cans inside were intact. His first instinct was to pick up the special case and leave the rest, but that would have been suspicious, if not down right stupid.

He returned to where Barton and Collins where standing. "Now what, Mr. Barton?" he asked sounding as unconcerned as possible.

"You tell us, Mr. Marchi. As far as Customs is concerned, it's your mess to be dealt with between you and the shipper. Our only interest is that there are no damaged cans that could constitute a health risk."

Oh, shit. They're going to confiscate the load. "It doesn't appear as though any of the cans are badly damaged."

"Let me suggest this, Carlo," Collins jumped in. "If it's okay with Bill, I'll have my people go through the mess and salvage the cases and cans that are marketable. The rest we can destroy under Customs supervision. And we'll get an inventory for the shipper's insurance claim. It's part of our service, Carlo."

"Sounds good to me," Barton agreed. "Only I'd like it done as quickly as possible. This is a very busy dock, and there's another off-loading due tonight."

"No problem, Bill. We'll be back in less than two hours to clean it up."

"If it's okay I'd be glad to lend a hand," Carlo volunteered.

"Sure, why not, Mr. Marchi? It's your money laying there."

&❦

"You'd better go home without me, Anna." Collins had dropped Carlo off back at the warehouse on his way to gather a small crew to help clean up the dock.

"I'll be glad to come along and help," she offered.

Damn it, Anna. He still had a problem with her persistence. "That won't be necessary. John's bringing enough help. Besides, the docks are no place for a good-looking woman wearing a large diamond ring."

"You're right, I guess. I'll wait dinner for you until you get home."

"It might be kinda' late. We've got to return here with whatever we can salvage. I'm sure John will drive me home."

"All right, but try not to be too late. I'll have Mom keep your dinner warm."

"Yeah, okay. That must be John honking, gotta' go." As he pecked her on the cheek, she placed her hand on his butt. *Some persistence ain't all bad.*

&❦

Much to Carlo's relief, they were able to save most of his shipment and by midnight it was stacked safely in the Tuzzio warehouse, including, most importantly, the special sauce case.

With his head tilted back as Collins drove him home, Carlo lit a cigarette, puffed out the partially open window and commented, "Boy, John, I hope that's the last of my problems for a while."

"I remember hearing a saying recently about the weather," Collins replied. "Beware, another storm is hiding somewhere, or something like that."

"I wonder where you heard that."

They both laughed an exhausted laugh.

Chapter 53

"Judging from your wife's reaction a moment ago, you know exactly what I'm referring to, Mr. Kistler." Corklin was facing the Kistlers in their foyer. "I think we'd better sit down and discuss the severity of the trouble you're in."

His demeanor and choice of words had their intended effect. The stunned Kistlers led him into their living room.

It was Corklin's first exposure to the interior of an American home. He studied the room from an ornate wing chair facing a matching velour couch where the Kistlers sat huddled together. The carpeting under his feet was white and thick, the side tables were an oriental style as were the red ginger jar lamps that lit the seating area. The room was too gaudy for his comfort level.

"We haven't done anything illegal," Abe said quietly.

"What makes you think we even have your diamonds? And how do we know you are who you say you are?" Barbara questioned. She was obviously the more outspoken of the two.

"I'm trying to make this easy on you both," Corklin said firmly. "However, if you'd rather I contact the local police, we can continue that way." He pulled out a cigarette.

"We don't allow smoking in our house," Barbara declared.

Corklin tucked it back into the box. "Now look, you're both seriously involved in an international felony by buying and selling stolen diamonds." In actuality, he knew he was on somewhat shaky ground with this threat, especially since the diamonds weren't truly stolen. But except for him, Vandenberg and whoever had retrieved them from the downed Ladybird, who could say it wasn't a crime.

"We're honest merchants," Abe insisted. "We haven't done anything illegal."

"Don't say anything else, Abe," his wife cautioned. "Look here, Mr. Conran, or whatever you said your name is . . ."

"It's Corklin."

"Whatever. You can't come into our home and accuse us of being dishonest. How dare you. You have no proof that we...."

Corklin could see that her defense mechanism had kicked in and that she could be a formidable deterrent in his getting the matter resolved and quickly. "Calm down, Mrs. Kistler, and allow me to get to the real reason I'm here."

"And what's that?" Abe asked softly.

"As for proof, Mrs. Kistler, we have witnesses who will confirm you sold them our uncut diamonds. But that doesn't concern us. All I want from you is the name of the person or persons who sold them to you."

"First, let me make one thing very clear," she replied. "We are bonded and licensed gem dealers and in our business we're constantly on the alert for stolen jewelry. What we purchased were uncut stones and there was no indication or information that such stones were stolen or illegal in any way."

"I understand that, Mrs. Kistler, but weren't you at least curious enough to ask whoever we're speaking of, where they obtained them?"

"Of course," Abe answered. "We were told they were from an inheritance."

"An inheritance? You've got to be kid...."

"Believe what you want, Mr. Corklin, but that's what he told us."

"Okay, if what you're saying is correct, then my interest is with that individual only."

"And supposing we did know his name, just supposing mind you," Barbara replied, "what's in it for us?"

Selfish to the end. "Our business with the Kistlers will be over." Then he played into their greed by adding, "And for good measure you get to keep your ill-gotten profits, no further questions asked."

"His name is Marchi, Carlo Marchi. And all we know about him is that he's Sicilian."

Abe Kistler spilled it out faster than an overflowing bucket on a rocking chair.

Corklin was excited as he wrote the name is his notebook, then looked up. "And where can I find this Marchi chap?"

"We have no idea, and that's the truth, Mr. Corklin."

He noted the sudden change in her disposition. "Then how does he contact you?"

"At the store. He comes to our shop. We evaluate the stones then give him a cashier's check."

Bloody hell, I knew this was going too easily. "Do you know where he cashes your checks?"

"No, because it's a cashier's check, not a personal or business check," Abe explained.

"And what bank did you draw the checks on?" Corklin waited with pen in hand.

"Merchantile Savings, at Sixth Avenue and Fortieth Street. We have our business account there," she replied.

"Very good." He made a note of it. "Now if you'll just describe Marchi to me.

"Good looking, almost handsome, close to six feet, I'd say." She looked at Abe for confirmation.

"That's right. And he was wearing a nice dark blue wool car coat the last time he was in."

Barbara continued. "He has a sturdy body, clean, smooth hands, dark complexion and a firm chin. And his hair is brown, very dark brown."

Corklin was impressed with the details of her description but then he guessed that women always took note of a good-looking man's features. "Well that's it then." He stood up ready to leave, "Except for one other thing."

Abe's face turned grim again. "What else is there?"

"How many stones did you purchase from Marchi?" He waited as they hesitated and stared at each other.

Abe stood silent as his wife answered. "No more than a hundred or so," she said. "Now if there is nothing else...."

Corklin made that his last notation, pocketed his notebook and requested that they call a taxi for him.

Abe made the call and a few minutes later Barbara led the way toward the front door.

As Corklin exited, Barbara stated quite emphatically, "Goodbye, Mr. Corklin. We don't expect to see you or Mr. Marchi ever again. And remember your word, we are not to be involved any further."

As soon as Corklin got out the words, "Of course," she closed the door abruptly.

After he had waited about ten minutes in New Jersey's cold night air, his taxi arrived.

Chapter 54

The streets were slushy when Corklin made his way the few blocks to the Kistlers' bank the next morning. *Damn weather.* He cursed under his breath as he entered the lobby of Mercantile Savings Bank. In spite of his new rubbers, the cuffs of his pants were damp from the walk in the mushy snow.

The interior of the bank was a surprise. Except for the polished marble floors, it was unlike most financial operations he was familiar with. The low ceilings and wooden framed windows absent of any bars seemed more like he was in a large library rather than a monetary establishment. Adding to the incompatible appearance were several wooden desks before him with antique glass desk lamps and a set of chairs at each one. As a security man responsible for extremely valuable material, he was perplexed by their vulnerability until he spotted at the very back of the hundred foot room the reason for the un-fortified front business area. There in the rear, beyond an unobtrusive counter with three teller windows, was a most impressive, huge floor-to-ceiling steel vault with a magnificent, round, carbon-steel door open enough to see its twelve-inch-thick walls.

"May I be of assistance, sir?" the middle-aged woman at the first desk he approached inquired. The blue wool sweater she was wearing seemed quite appropriate given the temperature outside. Her pewter hair was bobbed and a cute nose supported the half glasses she peered over.

"I hope so, Miss..." He referred to the nameplate on her desk, "Miss Reagan." He took the seat opposite her.

"I'll certainly try, Mr....."

"Corklin, ma'am, Sean Corklin."

"And what part of Ireland are your folks...."

"Oh no, ma-am, it's Welsh. That's a common mistake, though."

With a broad Irish smile she asked. "So how can I help you, Mr. Corklin?"

"I just need a bit of information about one of your depositors, Mr. Abraham Kistler."

"What sort of information? We're very discreet regarding our depositors."

"First, let me assure you that I'm not seeking any private financial details concerning Mr. Kistler. I merely need to know the name of the bank where his cashier's checks made out to a Carlo Marchi were cashed. If I'm correct, I believe all checks are eventually returned here stamped with the cashing bank's name."

"And you don't consider that privileged information? I'm sorry, Mr. Corklin, but are you with the police or other official agency?"

"Not exactly. I'm the Security Director for a large international cartel based in London, and I'm here on a very important, unofficial assignment." He tried to make it sound as authoritative as possible. By the doubtful expression on Miss Reagan's face though, she wasn't having any of it.

"Sorry, Mr. Corklin, unless you're with the police or have a court order, that information is still confidential."

"Would it help if I saw the manager?"

"You may, but you'd be wasting your time and his. Believe me, I'm quoting the banking privacy laws of this country and so will he."

"I see."

"Might I suggest you get Mr. Kistler to inquire as to the name of the other bank. It would be quite in order for him to do so."

"Yes, it would, wouldn't it? Thank you, ma'am. Perhaps you've solved my problem after all."

"We're here to help, sir. Goodday."

It was snowing lightly when Corklin hit the street. *Damn banks. Damn weather.*

With no taxis in sight, he trudged back to his hotel where he slipped into a hot bath to soak and think. *No point in trying to have the Kistlers locate Marchi's bank. Other than that, they would be stonewalled regarding any privileged information, like where the hell he is.*

As he picked at a room service lunch, he decided he would have to contact the Kistlers again for just a little more assistance. *And boy, will she be pissed.* He bit into a New York deli pickle.

Chapter 55

"Oui, Monsieur, how my I assist you?"

"Do you speak Italian?" Tony asked.

"Scusi, Signore, but of course."

"I'd like to make a withdrawal." Tony handed him a slip with the amount and account number.

"You realize, Signore, this is over 950,000 Swiss francs."

"Yeah, if that's what a half million American dollars comes to. How much is that in Italian lira?"

The Assistant Manager for Numbered Accounts at the Banco Swiss/Italia where Carlo and Tony had almost $2,300,000 on deposit took a moment to double-check his exchange rate chart. "That would be a little over 1,250,000,000 Italian lira."

"Okay, I'll take it in lira." Tony pushed a soft leather satchel across the man's neatly organized desk.

"It will take some time to arrange, Signore. Perhaps you would care to wait in our lounge. We have espresso and pastries."

"Just how the hell long will it take?"

"At least two hours, Monsieur, scusi, I mean Signore. The hand counting must be checked twice you understand."

"Yeah, okay. I'll just stroll around town. I've never been to Lugano before."

"Then I would suggest, if you prefer an early lunch, you might try the Fondue Trattoria about three blocks from here."

"Thanks, but hot cheese on a stick is not my idea of lunch."

"Ah, then I would recommend the Restaurante Cuomo just a few steps farther."

೭೦೧೩

Back in Sciacca, Tony locked the leather satchel in the cannery office safe. The first part of his scheme was finished. Now all he had to do was enlist Carmine Rossi's help and he was sure the best way to do that was now tucked away in the safe.

At first he thought of offering Carmine a handful of diamonds, but that wasn't too practical, especially if Carmine was discovered unloading them. Then, of course, the fortune in stones they had stashed away could be in jeopardy, not to mention how pissed Carlo would be. No, this way was better. After all, he assumed that half of what was in that Swiss vault was his and Carlo would just have to understand. Besides, after taking care of Campi, he would have to leave for New York much sooner than expected so he could explain it all to Carlo in person.

Screw it, once Campi is eliminated there's no way I'm coming back to this goddamn place, anyway. If I can't remain in the States, then it's off to a good life in South America with or without Carlo. Too bad I can't get that bastard Police Commisioner Tonelli, too, but given the extent of his protection that would be almost impossible. I guess Pop and I will just have to settle for Campi for our revenge.

Chapter 56

After the harrowing incident of the spilled shipment on the Customs dock, Carlo suddenly realized how dangerously fragile his situation was. The thought of being arrested as a foreign smuggler gave him more than a few sleepless nights. Timing was everything, and fortunately the fact that Tony had insisted on visiting New York the following month would now be a blessing. It would ease the sudden threat of his illegal goods being detected. The special shipments would discontinue until Tony returned to Sciacca or until they decided enough was enough.

It was a hell of a quandary for him. There were still diamonds worth many millions in his mama's root cellar and he wasn't sure how pleased the Kistlers would be over the sudden hiatus. He was certain though that they would drool over the quality and size of the stones Tony had selected this time. There were nine exceptional roughs each weighing more than three-and-a-half carats.

What the hell, the Kistlers have made plenty so far and the few months that Tony will be staying won't matter if and when he goes back and we resume. Meanwhile, Enzio will continue our regular shipments to keep Ben, his Uncle Pina and Campi happy.

Carlo decided to visit the Kistlers near the end of the week. As usual, he carefully planned his trip to coincide with a day when he knew Anna would be too busy in the office to suggest she accompany him.

That was another reason it was wise that he and Tony shut down for a while. Her persistent desire to join him and meet Tony's fictitious friend, Roberto, in the city was becoming more and more difficult to evade. Anna had suggested they take Roberto to dinner and then later she and Carlo could make a romantic evening of it. At one point she had even offered to bring a girlfriend along to meet Roberto. *Christ, I can't wait until Tony discovers how different American girls are. Madonne, will I enjoy that little discovery.*

Chapter 57

"You've got one hell-of-a-nerve calling us here," Barbara Kistler quietly cursed into the receiver. "You told us we would no longer be involved with you." Abe was obviously standing nearby. "It's Corklin," he heard her whisper.

"I'm trying to tell you, Mrs. Kistler, if you'll just calm down. Even if I can get the bank name where Marchi cashes your checks, I've been told that giving out his address is against this country's very stringent banking privacy laws."

"And what the hell can we do about that?"

"Just one last thing and you'll never hear from me again." *I hope, you belligerent bitch.*

"What is it?"

"I need you to find out where he lives. That's all."

"That's not possible. He made it very clear in the beginning that we would conduct our transactions confidentially on a name-only basis."

Corklin lit a cigarette, placed his feet up on the bed and watched the first flakes of snow descend outside his hotel window. *Shit, looks like I'm doomed to live in this tundra of a city forever.*

"Okay, then you'll have to point him out to me when you meet next."

"Oh no. Don't you dare think you can come in here to confront him. We're running a business, damn it."

Yeah, a hell-of-a-good business with Vandenberg's stones. "Okay look, is there any particular time he comes in?"

"He wants to know when Marchi comes in," he heard her tell Abe.

After a moment of silence, she said, "Usually on a Thursday or Friday around noon. That gives us enough time to evaluate what he brings and have a cashier's check cut for him."

"Okay, I'll make it as easy as possible for you. Here's what you do. The next time he shows up, one of you call me here at my hotel. I'll rush right over and wait across the street. When you've finished with him, one of you walk him out the front door, shake hands or something, then I'll take it from there."

"Give me your number," she said sounding disgusted. "And remember, this is the last time we want to hear from you."

"Likewise, I'm sure."

Chapter 58

"Mama mia, you are joking, Tony. Where did you get 1,250,000,000 lira? The sauce business can't be that profitable."

"Pop left me with quite a bit," Tony lied to Carmine. It was late in the evening during one of Carmine's unexpected visits and they were alone in the cannery office. The desk was piled high with currency.

"What's so crazy about you making 1,250,000,000 lira and getting out from under Campi?" Tony opened a bottle of wine he kept in the office and filled two glasses. "Ah, pretty good if I do say so." Tony dabbed his mouth with the back of his wrist.

Carmine took a gulp, then nodded his head acknowledging the quality of the wine.

"With that much money, Carmine, you can drink like this every day, and enjoy the other pleasures it can buy, for the rest of your life."

"And be watching over my shoulder for just as long. Forget it, Tony. Keep your money and take the life you have just offered me. What you propose is crazy and deadly."

"I'm not asking you to kill the bastard. I want that pleasure. I have it all worked out. All you need to do for all of this," Tony scooped up a handful of bills, "is to arrange for me to get to Campi when he's alone so I can blow his goddamn brains out. Just like he arranged for my pappa. And you know he did, Carmine."

"I had nothing to do with Tonelli shooting your father."

"Bullshit. You were there."

"I said, I had nothing to do with it, Tony. Capisce?" Carmine took a swig of wine, lit a slender cigar and tossed the match at Tony.

Tony could see that he was pursuing the wrong course by aggravating the big man. "Okay, I understand. But this is your a chance of a lifetime, Carmine." Tony ran his hands over the money.

"And just what do I do if you screw it up? Sr. Campi is bound to suspect me. It's my job to protect him at all times. It would be my death sentence."

Tony lit a cigarette, took a deep drag and poured more wine. He could sense

that Carmine was more than half-interested. "The last thing I want is for anything to happen to you. So here's what you do." *Shit, Carlo would be proud of
me for having planned every detail.* "Starting tomorrow, you begin complaining
to Campi that you're having problems from your war wound, the one from the
shot you took in your stomach. Then for the next few days pretend it's getting
worse. In fact, tell him it's so bad you think you have to see a doctor."

"You're crazy, Tony. I'm in perfect health. No doctor is...."

"Just listen. I will arrange with a lady friend's uncle, a doctor with a small
practice, to confirm your illness as something extremely serious and that you'll
have to be placed in a clinic for the sake of your life."

"Why would any doctor do such a thing?"

"For the 5,000,000 lira I will pay him. Once that's done, you'll ask Campi if
his house bodyguard, that ape Luca, can take you to the clinic because you're
too sick to drive yourself."

"Tony, forget this madness. As much as I would like to get out of all this...."

"You're not thinking, Carmine." Tony poured more wine for him. "You'll
have an excellent alibi. I mean, the doctor will confirm that you are seriously
ill and Luca will verify that he took you to the clinic. In fact, if anyone gets
their ass in a grape press, it will be Luca. All you have to do is call me the day
before and I'll do the rest."

"You really believe it'll work? And what about Carlo? Does he know what
you plan?"

"No, and if he did he would only interfere. Trust me, you and I will be
the only ones to know. Now take your money and stash it somewhere safe,
Sr. Rossi. And get used to being addressed as Sr. Rossi. You're now a wealthy
man."

Carmine finished the last swig of wine, filled the leather satchel and shook
Tony's hand. "I have to leave now," he said with a grin. "Madonne, I'm starting
to get bad stomach pains."

Tony smiled as the big man left gripping his stomach with one hand and
holding the satchel containing the 1,250,000,000 lira in the other.

Chapter 59

It was only a few days after Tony had plotted the demise of Campi, but he was ready when Carmine called. He had a one-way open ticket to New York, sufficient traveling cash and no intention of ever returning. He figured as far as the rest of the diamonds were concerned, they were Carlo's problem.

"Tony, I've arranged everything, but even though I told him I was ill, Sr. Campi wants me to pick up this month's share before Luca has to take me to see the doctor tomorrow. Capisce?"

Carmine is playing it perfectly. "Sorry to hear that, Carmine. But I'll be busy all day. It'll have to be tonight after the night crew leaves."

"I'll be there around ten."

"And Carmine, remember to bring me your key to the Villa."

With his plan now in motion, Tony took the remainder of the day to take care of loose ends. He activated his ticket to New York for the following evening, then went to his apartment and packed. He spent the late afternoon at a spa, and after dinner visited a very cooperative young lady until nine when he returned to the cannery.

After the last of the night crew left, Tony sat alone in his office waiting for Carmine. It always struck him as eerie that, when the filling lines and the can shuttling stopped, the sudden quiet always seemed louder than the noise had been.

In the silence he ran over in his mind just how he would play out his plan. He'd park his car out of sight of the villa, then stay hidden along the driveway until he saw that big ape, Luca, drive Carmine off to the clinic. Then with his Berreta in hand, he would seek out the bastard. He would make Campi admit that he had had his father killed, and then make him beg for his life on bended-knees. Finally, after the pig sweated for a while, Tony would pretend to change his mind and as Campi's face showed signs of relief, he would pop two rounds into his miserable temple. Just the thought of that scenario heated his blood to boiling at the expectation of that long overdue moment.

Carmine arrived on time. He closed the door behind him and sat quietly across from his benefactor.

"Good to see you, my friend," Tony had brought a bottle of good wine for the occasion. He uncorked it and poured.

Carmine smiled as he took the glass Tony offered. "Salute, Tony."

"And to you, too, Sr. Rossi."

They drank.

"Is everything ready as we planned?" Tony asked when he lowered his glass. "If so, I'll need your key to the villa."

"Si, Tony. Sr. Campi thinks I have intestinal damage and the doctor you recommended made arrangements for me at the Veterans Clinic."

"What the hell are you talking about, Carmine? That's not the plan. Now how the hell am I supposed to get to Campi, you dumb shit?"

"That's what I'm about to tell you. I've already been to the doctor. Your plan is perfect."

Tony was so furious he threw his glass against the wall. Then he saw it, Carmine's .45 pointing at him.

"Sorry, Tony, but only half of your plan is working."

"What the hell are you talking about? Put that damn thing away, Carmine."

"I knew you'd loose that stupid temper of yours. Look, Tony, you're forgetting loyalty. I just can't let you kill Sr. Campi, the man I'm sworn to protect. Now shut up, sit down and listen."

Tony was too shocked to comply. He just stood there trembling. He felt no fear just confused rage seething through his pores. "What the hell are you saying, Carmine? I paid you for your loyalty and you screw me like this?"

"I said listen." Carmine pointed the gun at Tony's head. "You were right. I do want out, and you gave me the two things I needed to do it, the money and the reason."

"That's right, you dumb...."

"I said be quiet. Sr. Campi was so concerned about me that he and Luca took me yesterday, and your good doctor told Sr. Campi I may never recover enough to continue working for him as his chauffeur, that I needed considerable medical treatment, after which I'd require a strict diet, rest and quiet. Sr Campi, had no choice but to wish me well and have Luca take me to the clinic. Thanks to your fine plan, Sr. Campi suggested that when I am better I retire someplace far from Sciacca, and when I am settled I should let him know where in case I need any help. But who needs anything? Thanks to you,

Tony, I'm a wealthy man and that's the price you must pay for me to keep your vengeful plan to myself."

"You son-of-a-bitch, Carmine. You're just concerned for yourself."

"That's right, Tony. Remember I told you once I would do anything for money. For years I did everyone else's bidding, first during a war that I didn't understand or give a shit about, and then working for Sr. Campi. Now you must control your damn temper and get on with your life, just like I plan to do." Carmine lowered his .45 hoping his advice would sink in.

Tony could feel his face flush. The last thing he needed right now was this traitor giving him the same old crap about his temper. His Beretta was still in the desk drawer just inches away. He plopped down in his desk chair feigning defeat. "I guess I have no choice, but I'll never forgive you for your betrayal, Carmine." He reached for the wine bottle and took a swig. As he placed the bottle on the edge of the desk, he slowly slid open the drawer and watched as Carmine relaxed his grip on his gun.

"That's your problem, Tony. As for me, I'm going to slip back into the clinic, spend a week or so there, then disappear for good."

Tony could have waited until Carmine turned to leave, but he wanted him to see it coming. He quickly reached into the drawer and gripped the Beretta, but it banged against the front of the drawer as he pulled it out. The delay gave Carmine just enough time to react.

"Goddamn you, Tony."

It was the last thing Tony DeVito heard before his chest exploded.

Chapter 60

"Oh my!" Barbara Kistler exclaimed when Carlo spread the nine large stones on black velvet in the private viewing room to the rear of Abrahamson's.

Abe picked up the heaviest of the group and louped it. "Beautiful, just beautiful."

"They're all beautiful," Barbara agreed as she fingered through them, "the best yet." Then she thought of Corklin and his instructions to call him when Carlo came in again. *Damn the luck. Here we're buying stones for about half their value, and along comes this obnoxious man from England to screw things up. What if I don't call him? No, there's too much at stake not to. Hell, we've already made over $3,000,000 from our dealings with Carlo and, if Corklin represents who he claims he does, why risk it?* She could see the excitement in Abe's eyes as he evaluated the remaining stones.

"Well?" Carlo asked.

"$320,000," Abe finally quoted.

"Terrific. Now I must tell you this will be our last transaction for a while. I'm planning to travel for a few months."

"Oh?" Barbara wondered if he suspected that Corklin was after him. "And where are you off to?"

"We're not sure yet. It's going to be a honeymoon trip."

"Ah, yes," Ben said, "the recipient of the ring we had made for you?"

"That's right. Now if you'll have my check cut...."

"Of course, Carlo. Abe, I'll run to the bank, and while Carlo's waiting, don't forget to call that dealer at his hotel."

"Oh yeah, right, almost forgot about him." As Barbara was leaving, Abe apologized, "Excuse me, Carlo, I'll only be a minute. You can wait here. But if you must smoke...."

"I know, Abe, in the outer hall."

୫୦୯୫

"Just be sure to stall him until I get there. I'm leaving right now," Corklin declared when Abe called him.

"You're not coming in here. I thought Barbara made that perfectly clear."

"Relax, I'll be outside. Give me about fifteen minutes or so, then look out the front window. You'll see me standing across the street in the deli entrance. And don't forget, when he's ready to leave, walk him to the door so I'll know it's him."

"Yes, yes, I understand. It'll take Barbara at least that long at the bank."

"He sold you more stones, did he?" Corklin asked as he slipped into his shoes.

"Yes, but only one large one, around three carats," Abe lied. "I've got to go, he's waiting in our back room. Goodbye forever, Mr. Corklin."

ಬಾಡಿ

To Corklin's surprise the afternoon sun had warmed sufficiently to turn the light dusting of snow from the evening before into liquid. Taking up his vigil in the sunny deli entrance, he appreciated the suddenly mild January day. It was still very cold to a man who loved the heat of the South African sun, but at least that bitter, frigid bite in the air had diminished.

Corklin had only been there a short time when he spotted Barbara Kistler. For a heavy woman, she had a good walking stride as she made her way toward the entrance to Abrahamson's. He mentally prepared himself. It would only be a matter of minutes before he would finally confront the purpose of his visit to America, hopefully be able to recover Vandenberg's stones, and return home with a lucrative bonus.

What the hell do I do? I've got no authority here and the only proof I have that Marchi is the source of the stones is what the Kistlers told me. Shit, I hadn't figured that he might be just one more step in the distribution cycle and not the ultimate possessor of the diamonds. Damn, I hope he's the end of this ball of yarn. Well, there's only one way to deal with it, my usual direct confrontational attack. It worked with the Kistlers, so it's worth a try. If he's the guilty party, he'll show it. And if he is, he's sure to go for the same deal I gave the Kistlers, keep what you've got and I'll go away, provided I get the remainder of the stones, that is.

Corklin watched as the front door of Abrahamson's swung open and a young man in a dark blue car coat appeared followed by Abe Kistler. Abe spoke to him, nervously shook his hand, stared across toward the deli and then made a hasty retreat back inside.

As soon as Carlo headed up the block toward Seventh Avenue, Corklin dashed across the street and followed close behind. When Carlo reached the corner he hailed a taxi.

Shit, not another taxi pursuit. Fortunately Carlo flagged the attention of more than one taxi, and climbed into the first one that reached him at the curb. Corklin jumped into the one behind. "Twenty dollars extra if you take me to where that taxi ahead of us is going."

"That won't be easy in this traffic, mister, but for thirty I'll guarantee it."

Having become somewhat accustomed to the impersonal, profit-driven motivation of New Yorkers, Corklin shouted, "Twenty five and don't loose them, damn it." His neck jerked backward as the driver peeled away skillfully maneuvering through the traffic until they were almost bumper-to-bumper with Carlo's taxi.

Several blocks later, Carlo's taxi drove up to the curb in front of The Knickerbocker Savings Bank. Corklin's taxi pulled in a car length behind.

"Looks like your friend is about to do a little banking," the driver commented as they watched Carlo pay off his driver and head toward the entrance. "Now what, pal?"

"Just sit tight for a moment," Corklin instructed. "I want you to wait while I'm in there. We may be following him again."

"It's your dough, pal." The driver switched off the engine and removed the lid from his coffee thermos.

As soon as Carlo was inside, Corklin jumped out and entered the bank.

The Knickerbocker interior was not at all like the Kistlers' bank. A uniformed guard stood just inside the barred glass double door. On both sides of the center aisle were caged teller windows. *Now this is a bank, damn good security.*

Corklin smiled as he watched a bald-headed man wearing rimless glasses greet Carlo. Standing at a nearby table he fingered a deposit slip and watched as Carlo, now seated at the man's desk, handed him an envelope. It was clear that some sort of transaction was taking place by the exchange of banking documents. Finally Carlo pocketed a bank passbook, rose and shook hands with the man. Then, after passing directly by Corklin, he walked leisurely out of the bank.

Corklin could have stopped him right there, but he was still not certain that Carlo actually had the diamonds. He had to follow him to his final destination to be sure they were in his possession. Making a hasty retreat toward the door, he was prevented from exiting by several people entering. Through the glass doors, he caught a glimpse of Carlo heading toward the taxi Corklin had waiting. By the time he pushed through the few stragglers still blocking his passage, he saw Carlo speak to his driver, then step off the curb and hail another taxi.

By the time Corklin got to his waiting cab, Carlo was already in another one and driving off. "Shit," Corklin yelled as he yanked the door open and piled in. "Get going," he shouted. "Don't loose him now, damn it."

"They've already cleared the stoplight at the corner, pal. Hell, we'll never catch them in this mess anyway. Besides you owe me twenty-five bucks and the meter's still running."

"Try, goddamn it. There's a hundred dollars more for you if you catch up and take me where they're going."

"Hand over the dough first."

"Are you stupid? If you screw around any longer we'll never get...."

"Relax pal, pay up first and you'll get him."

"They're already out of sight, just how the hell are you going to achieve that?"

"I know where they're going. While you were dragging your butt getting out of the bank, your friend tried to hire me."

"And he told you his destination, I'll be damned." Corklin was too pleased to be pissed.

The driver held out his hand for his reward. As he folded Corklin's money, he said, "He's headed for Jersey City, 1011 South Summit Avenue."

Corklin leaned back, lit a cigarette and puffed out a cloud of relief.

"Since the meter's still running, pal, would you like me to drive you to Jersey City now?"

"Hell, yes."

Carlo had arrived at the warehouse a good twenty minutes before Corklin's taxi pulled up across the street from the I & A Importing warehouse.

"That's it pal, number 1011. Now what?"

"Just sit tight for a few minutes." Corklin wrote down the name and address in his notebook along with the two tips of $125 he had given to the driver so far. Then spotting a pay phone at the corner, he got out and walked over to it. He opened the directory that hanging on a chain and thumbed through until he found the number he was searching for.

After two rings a young woman answered, "I & A Importing. How may I help you?"

"Could you tell me how late you're open. I'm interested in some of your merchandise, but I'm on the other side of town."

"We close in about another hour sir, at five," the woman replied. "How far away are you?"

Not knowing anything about New Jersey, Corklin replied, "That's okay, I'll try to stop by in the next day or so."

"That'll be fine, however, we're closed on Saturdays and Sundays."

"Thanks." He hung up

Back in the taxi he asked the driver to take him to the nearest restaurant.

Two blocks away the driver slowed down. "Look, pal, I don't know a damn thing about eating in Jersey, let alone this part of town. Hell, it's an industrial area and I suspect that greasy spoon up ahead is as good as it gets."

"It'll be fine. Park and join me for a cup of coffee."

"Sure, pal, but I'll have to keep the meter running. Are you sure you can cover the fare? You're already up to twelve dollars."

It was getting dark and colder and Corklin was getting fed up with this chiseling driver. For the first time since entering the taxi Corklin read the name on the hack license attached to the back of the driver's seat. He pulled out a twenty. "This should cover it so far, Henry, now turn off the damn thing." Five minutes later they were seated at the counter inside the overheated diner.

Henry ordered a burger. Corklin pointed to an odd looking piece of pastry which the girl behind the counter referred to as a Danish. It tasted better than it looked.

When they had just about finished Corklin checked his watch, it was 4:45 p.m. "We have to leave right now," he said as he paid the check.

Back in the taxi Henry flipped up the meter flag when Corklin instructed him to go back and park across from the warehouse entrance. After several people left, he spotted Carlo getting into a car with a young lady. He watched as they pulled away, then said. "Okay, Henry, let's see where they lead us."

Henry drove far enough back not to be noticed and followed all the way to a home in Queens.

Corklin noted the address then said, "Okay, Henry, that's enough. Take me to my hotel. It's The Statler on Seventh Avenue."

"Yeah right, pal, like I wouldn't know where the Statler is." Henry peeled away.

Corklin sat back making another entry in his notebook: Make a visit to Marchi at the warehouse on Monday.

Chapter 61

It was after midnight in New York when Ben answered his bedside phone and the operator said there was a call for Carlo Marchi from Sicily. Assuming it was merely a thoughtless time for Tony to call, Carlo took it downstairs on the kitchen extension. As soon as he heard Ben hang up, he started to chastise Tony. "You idiot, don't you realize what time it is here?" He was startled when he heard Enzio's distressed voice.

"Sr. Carlo, it's me, Enzio...I...I...it's Sr. Tony. He's in the office. He's...he's dead."

Carlo still wasn't fully awake, and the connection wasn't too clear. "What? What did you say? Calm down, Enzio, speak slower."

"Si, Sr. Carlo. I found him when I went up to the office this morning. Madonne, his chest was covered with blood. I was so frightened, I got sick all over the floor."

"Oh God, Enzio, are you sure it was Tony?" Carlo didn't want to believe that his cousin was dead.

"Si, it was Sr. Tony. He was still in his chair...and there's a pistola on the floor next to him."

As Carlo's eyes started to tear, he recalled Tony's earlier confrontation with Campi's goon, Carmine. He could only conclude that it had happened again, this time with deadly results.

"Enzio, listen carefully. Does anyone else know what happened?"

"Si. At first I called to speak to Sr. Carmine, but Sr. Campi told me he was sick in the hospital. So I told him about finding Sr. Tony. I didn't know what else to do. He told me to wait here, that he was sending someone to take care of things. He also told me to call and tell you to return to Sciacca as soon as possible. Madonne, Sr. Carlo, I'm so frightened."

"Did you tell him about the pistola?"

"No, Sr. Carlo, he made me so nervoso, I forgot."

"That's okay. Now Enzio pay attention to what I tell you. I want you to pick up the pistola, go down to the back dock and throw it out into the water. Capisce?"

"But Sr. Campi...."

"Do what I tell you, Enzio. Sr. Campi will be very upset if he finds the pistola, and you don't want that."

"Si, Sr. Carlo."

"And, Enzio, I want you to call me after Sr. Campi takes care of everything. Now go quickly."

As soon as he hung up, Carlo broke into heavy sobbing. That was when he noticed Anna standing behind him in the kitchen.

"What is it? What's wrong?" she whispered.

He wasn't sure just how much she had heard. *Shit.* He had to think fast. "It's Tony, he had a bad accident. He's dead, Anna, he's dead." He fell into her arms and cried.

"Oh my God, Carlo!" She held onto him tightly. "How did it happen?"

"Speeding. He plunged over a guard rail near Mazaro Del Vallo." Although his explanation wasn't real, Carlo's broken heart was.

With all the commotion coming from their kitchen, the Tuzzios appeared. After Anna explained what had happened, Isabella hugged Carlo as Ben stood close with his hand on Carlo's shoulder. In spite of the way these warm and loving people had accepted him and were now trying to comfort him, Carlo knew there were some things he could never explain. How could he tell them that Tony may have been murdered by the very people they were associated with? It was another lie he would have to live with forever.

After consoling Carlo, Isabella and Ben returned to their bedroom. Anna remained with him holding his hand across the kitchen table as he wiped his reddened eyes. When his mind finally cleared enough to accept that Tony was gone, Carlo gently slipped his hand from Anna's. His emotions alternated from sadness to rage to fear as he recalled the Sicilian life and enemy he had left behind.

"Anna, please get some rest, now. I'll be okay. I need a little time to myself and I'd like to call Enzio back about what arrangements are being made."

"I'm really not that tired if you need me...."

He could see the sadness for him in her eyes, but damn it, right now he needed to know what the hell was going on in Sciacca. "No, please, Anna, I'll be fine."

"I love you, Carlo." She kissed him and headed back upstairs.

As soon as he heard her door close, he checked the kitchen clock. It was now past one o'clock in the morning. He grabbed the phone and had the operator place his call. It rang almost a dozen times. Just as he had about decided to hang up and try later, Enzio answered, "Ciao?"

"What's happening, Enzio? Christ, I thought you had left."

"Oh no, Sr. Carlo. I'm still here, but it is very difficult for me to be cleaning away the bloody mess."

Carlo's throat swelled from the thought. He gulped hard and his hand trembled as he lit a cigarette. "What about Tony, Enzio? Tell me what's going on there."

"Scusi, Sr. Carlo, but I am very nervoso at the moment. Two men took Sr. Tony away. They told me Sr. Campi wanted me to know that he would arrange a quiet cremation and that I should clean up everything here, keep silent and wait for further instructions."

"Did you tell Sr. Campi's men that you called me?"

"Si, Sr. Carlo, just as Sr. Campi had instructed."

"And what did they say?"

"Nothing, they just nodded and said if anyone else asks about Sr. Tony, I'm to say that I have no idea where he is."

"Then do as you were told for now. I'll get a flight as soon as possible. And remember, Enzio, say nothing about the pistola. Capisce?"

"Si, Sr. Carlo. Do not worry."

However, Tony's untimely murder wasn't Carlo's only dilemma. Convincing Anna that he would be returning to Sciacca alone was another problem.

Chapter 62

After entering the cost of his coffee shop breakfast in his notebook on Monday morning, Corklin returned to his room for his Macy's coat, rubbers and gloves. He then waited out front for a taxi. As he entered the yellow vehicle he cringed at the nasal inquiry, "Where to, pal?" He wondered how many more nervy taxi drivers he would have to contend with before he could return home.

Corklin read the driver's name on his hack license displayed on the back of the seat. "Jersey City, Lloyd." He gave him the address of the warehouse.

When the taxi pulled up to the entrance of I & A Importing, Corklin said, "This may take a while, Lloyd, but wait for me anyway."

"Right, pal, but I'll have to keep the meter...."

"I know, you'll have to keep the damn meter running. Just wait."

There was nothing formal about the front entry of the building. It opened directly into the warehouse itself. The only thing that separated visitors from cases of goods and manual activity was the glass-enclosed office space where a young lady was seated across from a man who wasn't Marchi.

When Corklin got her attention by tapping on the door, she came out to greet him.

"May I help you?"

"I hope so. Are you the woman I spoke to on Friday?"

"I'm not sure, sir, we do get a number of calls."

"Of course you do. I asked how late you were open."

"I remember now. How can I help you, Mr.?"

"The name's Corklin, and I'd like to speak to Mr. Carlo Marchi."

"I'm afraid he's not here, but if it's about Stella's Tomato Sauce, I'm sure I can assist you."

"Tomato sauce? I'm not sure I understand?"

"Carlo, I mean Mr. Marchi, is the owner of Gemma Importing. We distribute his sauce from here."

"I see. Well I'm here to see him on a personal matter. When will he return, miss?"

"It's Anna. I'm afraid you've missed him, Mr. Corklin. Carlo left for Sicily last night."

Bloody hell. Corklin could hardly believe the news. It was as though he had suddenly been thrust into the turmoil of a bad traveling dream. After traversing halfway around the globe on this damn diamond hunt, and after getting within arm's length of its conclusion, Marchi was gone. "Sicily! I see. When might he be returning?"

"We're not sure exactly, but it will be at least a few days. His partner had a fatal accident and...."

"I'm sorry to hear that."

"Are you sure I can't be of help?"

Corklin thought for a moment and then decided to stir the pot, so to speak, in the event Marchi contacted her. "I'm afraid it's a rather delicate matter, miss. I represent an international consortium and I'm investigating a possible smuggling operation. I believe Mr. Marchi can be of some assistance." He studied her reaction, but Anna just looked befuddled rather than concerned. Obviously she knew nothing about the diamonds.

"I don't understand how Carlo can be of any help," she stated innocently. "We, I mean he imports tomato sauce from his factory in Sciacca." Then she explained, as she proudly held up her diamond engagement ring, "I guess it'll be we, once we're married."

Corklin congratulated her as he admired the large sparkler on her finger, almost certain the stone had to have come from the Vandenberg mines. "As I said, Miss, he could be of help in our investigation and, since I must get back to Europe, could you provide me with his address in Sicily?"

"Yes, of course. Please step into our office and I'll get it for you."

Thank heaven for minute favors.

Back in his waiting taxi, Corklin studied the address Anna had typed onto a memo sheet. It was Carlo's and Tony's apartment in Sciacca, Sicily. As soon as he returned to his hotel, He planned to find Sciacca on a map and immediately arrange for air passage there. Corklin had little choice but to pursue Carlo, wherever he led. He was the X on the map of the diamonds' location.

Chapter 63

After almost eleven exhausting hours with layovers in London and Rome, Carlo finally arrived at his apartment in Sciacca about six on Monday evening. A lump formed in his throat when he switched on the lights and saw Tony's things strewn all over the place. *Tony, paesano mio, what happened to you? I should never have left you alone.* His memory of his once lively, temperamental cousin and partner was reduced to articles of clothing draped across chairs and hanging from doorknobs. Not only was Carlo exhausted, his heart was breaking. Now he truly had no one left in Sicily.

He picked up the phone and called Anna. She had insisted that he do so when he arrived. Already missing her, he would have called anyway.

She was just having lunch when his call came through. "I'm so relieved you got there okay, but I still feel that I should be with you, Carlo."

Convincing her that he had to leave without her had frustrated him almost to the point of losing his temper until her father, God bless him, had intervened. Ben explained that it wouldn't appear proper for her to accompany Carlo unchaperoned. He told her that attitudes regarding such things were very different in Italy, and that their traveling together would be much frowned upon.

"Anna, it was a long trip, and I'm hungry and tired. After a bite to eat and a shower, I'm going to get a few hours sleep. Once I know more about what's going on here, I'll call you again."

"I still feel terrible that you have to deal with this alone...oh, I almost forgot. A man was here to see you earlier this morning. He said his name was Corklin and that it was important."

"Never heard of him."

"He asked for you by name Carlo. He told me he's investigating a smuggling ring and that he hoped you might be able to help him. I told him I didn't know how you could be of any help that you import tomato...."

The lump that suddenly formed in Carlo's throat almost gagged him. He could hear Anna's voice but his brain blocked out the words. *Who the hell is this guy and just what does he have to do with the diamonds? Oh Christ!*

"Exactly what did he tell you, Anna? Did he say what was being smuggled and what it had to do with me?"

"No, just that you might be able to help him. What's wrong, Carlo? You sound upset. Are you sure you don't know this man or what he wants with you?"

"I'm all right." He had to compose himself. The last thing he needed was for her to start probing. "It's just that I'm tired from the trip, sad about Tony and homesick for you."

"That's sweet."

"So where is Mr. Cort....what's his name, now?"

"It's Corklin. He said he had to get back to Europe and he asked for your address in Sciacca."

"You mean he's coming here?"

"Well yes. I gave him the apartment address. Shouldn't I have?"

Trying to sound at ease, he replied, "Nah, that's okay. He's probably got me confused with someone else. I'll deal with it from here, don't worry about it. I gotta go now, Anna, I'm really wiped out."

"Get some rest Carlo, I love you. Call me as soon as you know what this Corklin is after."

"I will, I love you, too."

Carlo sat staring at the phone he had just hung up. Beads of sweat formed around his mouth and across his forehead. He tried to convince himself it was the stuffy apartment but was certain it was mostly from the news that some-one named Corklin wanted to talk to him about smuggling. Opening the win-dows offered little improvement. The balmy Sicilian air was still and moist. It had to be the damn diamonds, that's all he and Tony had been smuggling. But only he and Tony knew about them. *Maybe it was the Kistlers. But how? All he ever told them was that they weren't stolen.*

He went into the bathroom and splashed cold water on his face, as he tow-eled dry he had an even more nerve-racking thought, *What exactly did Anna say? Had Corklin said anything about smuggling diamonds to her?* He couldn't recall her exact words he had been so intent on hearing that Corklin was look-ing for him and would probably show up in Sciacca. He thought of calling her back but he knew one sign of concern on his part and she would start pressing the issue as she always had with him. *I'll have to deal with her when I return. Hopefully no real damage has been done by Corklin's visit there.*

Visions of Tony being shot, possible imprisonment for smuggling, and explaining it all to Anna kept him from getting the sleep his body craved. After a few hours in his old bed he dragged himself up and showered off his nightmarish perspiration. The bright Sicilian sun did little to raise his spirits as he sat at the small kitchen table where he and Tony had shared so many espressos and croissants. Sicily didn't seem like home anymore. After spending only a few months with the Tuzzios, and especially Anna, he feared his life with them could all dissolve if this Corklin showed up.

⁞⁞

Although his internal timetable was screwed up from lack of sleep, Carlo managed to arrive at the cannery around ten on Tuesday morning. The aroma of his Mama's sauce cooking in big batches compounded his already sad and fearful state as Carlo climbed the stairs to the office.

"Dio mio! Sr. Carlo, you are here!" Enzio acted relieved when Carlo entered the room.

"Enzio, it's good to see you." Carlo embraced his faithful foreman and one of the few people remaining in Sicily for whom he had any true feelings.

"It is good to see you, too, Sr. Carlo." Enzio blew his nose into a huge bandana.

"Is this where you found Tony?" Carlo grasped the back of the new desk chair.

"Si, Sr. Carlo. It was best that I had your old one replaced."

"I understand. Now sit down and tell me exactly what happened."

Enzio reiterated the details just as he had explained to Carlo the night he had called. He explained how two men had come to remove Tony's body. "And then the next day Sr. Campi came to tell me that out of respect for his old friend and partner, Franco DeVito, he had poor Sr. Tony cremated. I was also instructed that when you arrive you are to go to Sr. Campi's villa. I'm sorry there was no service, Sr. Carlo, but I lit some candles at my church."

Carlo knew it would be pointless to press Enzio further and that any answers he needed now would have to come from Campi. "You did well as usual, Enzio."

"I am so saddened by all this, Sr. Carlo. What shall we do now?"

"Just keep things running smoothly until I speak with Sr. Campi."

"Si, Sr. Carlo, whatever you say."

"One other thing, Enzio, where is Tony's car?"

"Still in the back where he always parked it. The extra keys are in one of the desk drawers."

"Grazie." Carlo found the keys.

Tony's car was immaculate. It gleamed from a recent polishing. The interior was also spotless even down to the clean ashtray. Carlo shook his head in sentimental amusement at the inconsistency of the care between Tony's home and car. Making sure he wasn't being observed, He popped open the trunk. Except for the spare tire and related equipment, the space appeared empty. Then Carlo noticed the spare was slightly out of place in the wheel well. And there they were in a suede pouch, four small uncut stones. They were probably the last ones Tony had stashed before Carlo had suggested they temporarily suspend the special sauce shipments. He left them there, closed the trunk, and drove off to Campi's.

Approaching the private road, his uncertainty over the reason he had been summoned reminded Carlo once again of the unpredictable danger that dwelled in the villa up ahead. If Campi had been the cause of Tony's death, he would have to be more tactful than ever in his approach to the treacherous man. But he had to know, and he felt certain his old instincts would detect signs of indifferent arrogance or over-done overtures of grief regarding Tony's death.

Carlo remembered Luca, the hulk who answered Campi's doorbell.

"What can I do for you?" The thin voice didn't match the mass that blocked the entire doorframe.

"My name is Carlo Marchi. I'm a business associate of Sr. Campi."

"He didn't tell me you were coming."

"Just tell him I am here."

"He doesn't see people unless he sends for them. Go away." Luca grasped the edge of the door to close it.

"Look," Carlo pressed his hand against the door to prevent it from closing, "he's expecting me. I came all the way from America, so just tell him I'm here. Capisce?"

Luca's brutish face looked confused, then he leaned into Carlo. "You just wait out here, Mr. Smart Mouth from America. If Sr. Campi says no, I'm going to toss your ass right back to where you came from." He slammed the door in Carlo's face.

Though the threat was ridiculous, Carlo was certain the huge man could, however, give him a good start in that direction. As he waited by the closed door, the faint smell of lemon trees and the warm Sicilian sun on his back momentarily gave him a shudder of nostalgia. Thoughts of the land of his birth, his father and mother, his Uncle Franco, and now Tony, were heartfelt memories of his past. The sudden opening of the big oak door snapped him back to the present as Luca swung it wide and stood aside.

"Sr. Campi will see you. Come in."

"Grazie, I told you that he would." Carlo stepped into the marble foyer that hadn't changed since the last time Campi had summoned him and Tony.

As he led the way, Luca said, "Sr. Campi explained to me who you are. Too bad, I would have enjoyed hurting you."

Carlo approached the ornate writing table where Campi sat reading. His escort stepped to the side leaving Carlo standing there alone where he remained silently waiting until Campi looked up and spoke.

"Damn soccer results." Campi tossed the paper aside. "Ah, Marchi, good you are here."

"Si, Sr. Campi, I came as you requested out of respect for you and Tony's memory." Carlo studied Campi's eyes for any indication of emotion. Nothing.

"As you should have. Sit, Carlo." He waved toward a hand-carved, straight-backed chair.

"Thank you." Carlo gave Luca a quick glare as he accepted the invitation.

"I am sure you were as shocked as we were when Enzio called about Tony. He was shot through the heart at close range. All I could do was arrange that he be cremated quietly."

"But what could he have done to deserve such a thing?"

"The what is easier to answer than the who. Certainly you realize he has given many people cause to dislike him. He was arrogant and had a dangerous temper."

"What are you saying, Sr. Campi?"

"To put your mind at ease, I'm saying that in spite of Tony's problems, I tried looking after him, in fact poor Carmine, who is now gravely ill, looked in on him often."

Yeah, I'll bet you looked after him. Carlo nodded amiably.

"But your partner made enemies with everyone he came into contact with. He was even difficult with Carmine when I sent him with a message that I wished to see him."

Carlo caught a glimpse of Luca nodding in agreement.

"Tony was extremely hotheaded and a womanizer. For all we know, an out-raged husband could have killed him. It's a common vendetta here."

Carlo was momentarily speechless. In spite of his doubts, everything Campi said made sense, and there was little point now in mentioning the pistola he had had Enzio dispose of. "As bad as he was, Sr. Campi, Tony was like a brother to me, and I thank you for your kindness in taking care of him as you did."

"Si, Carlo, but understand, my motives weren't purely compassione. Having a murder investigation by the local authorities even in Sciacca would not ben-efit any of us."

These bastards. Tony and I mean nothing to them but millions of lira. "Si, Sr. Campi, I understand."

"Buono, buono." Campi rose and motioned for Carlo to follow. "Now let us continue our discussion on the terrace. It is a beautiful day, not like the weather back in New York, I'm sure." Once they were seated outdoors, Campi asked, "Caffe?"

"Si. Iced, if it's not too much trouble."

Campi looked toward Luca who had stationed himself nearby. He nodded, and headed for the kitchen.

While they waited, Carlo inquired about Carmine.

"Ah, Carlo, things are not always what they seem. Poor Carmine. For such a strong man on the outside, he is very sick internally. The doctor told me personally that Carmine has an extremely bad intestinal condition that will only get worse. I took him to the clinic myself and assured him that I would provide for his care there."

"Perhaps I will visit him," he lied to seem concerned.

"That would be very respectful and I'm sure he would like that."

Their caffe arrived. Carlo was amused at how awkwardly Luca handled the delicate cups.

Campi took a sip, then began again. "The reason I summoned you, Carlo, has to do with the cannery." He paused to light a cigar.

"Forgive me, Sr. Campi, but without Tony to run it, I have no idea what will happen now."

"You are too presumptuous. The cannery is no longer your concern."

"But Sr. Campi...."

Campi raised his palm to silence Carlo. "Let me tell you what I intend to do. The cannery belongs to me now and I have other plans for it in spite of your financial tribute which was insignificant."

"I'm not sure I understand."

Campi blew on the hot end of his cigar. "It's very simple. Now that the war is far behind us, there is the beginning of a resurgence of tourism in Sicily. Because of this, land values have soared, especially in Sciacca with the thermal spas and the beautiful Mediterranean beaches. Since the cannery is waterfront property and quite near the seaside promenade of the Piazza di Scandaliato, we plan to build an elaborate resort hotel on the site."

"And what of me, Sr. Campi?"

"All that remains for you to do is to shut down the cannery and let everyone go. After that, you can do whatever you wish, remain here or return to America. You are no longer any concern of mine."

Carlo was relieved and pissed all at the same time.

"And now you will excuse me, I have another matter to attend to." Campi rose before Carlo had a chance to respond. "Enjoy your stay in Sicily. Arrivederci, Carlo."

Before Carlo could say more than, "Grazie, Sr. Campi," Luca was beside him ready to escort him out.

It was mid-afternoon when Carlo returned to the cannery. He signaled Enzio to join him in the office as soon as he finished checking a large vat of sauce.

A short time later, the old man joined him. "Your meeting with Sr. Campi went well I hope."

"I suppose so. Sit down, Enzio, I've something to explain to you." Carlo lit a cigarette and leaned back in the new chair. "Sr. Campi is closing the cannery."

"Madonne, I was afraid this would happen someday. And the workers, what do I tell them?"

"Tell them that they will each receive one week's wages." Carlo planned to pay them out of his own pocket. "Also explain that there will be a huge hotel built here soon which may provide new jobs for many of them." Carlo could see the disappointment in Enzio's eyes. "I'm sorry, old friend, but it is out of my hands."

"Si, Sr. Carlo, I understand. My wife's aunt has a bakery in Ficuzza which I can help run."

"Now I must call Sr. Felizi with the same bad news. And Enzio, as far as anyone is concerned, Sr. Tony died in a terrible car crash. Capisce?"

"Si, Sr. Carlo, a car crash. Now, if you will excuse me, I must begin the sad task you have given me."

"One more thing, Enzio, meet me back here tomorrow evening. I've something else to discuss with you."

"Si."

෩෨

"What a terrible tragedy, Carlo. I just spoke to him a few weeks ago about a late shipment. You must be heartbroken."

"Si, Pina. Tony was like a brother to me. I always warned him about his reckless driving." *This should corroborate the story I told the Tuzzios.*

Carlo went on to explain that without Tony he would have to close the cannery. "There is no one to replace him, and besides, my heart is no longer in it."

"I'm sorry to hear this. It was such a good business and growing. I'm sure Ben will be disappointed as well."

"It can't be helped, Pina. My mind is made up. Enzio is telling the workers as we speak."

"Then, Carlo, that's how it must be. Now on to a more pleasant subject, my great-niece, Anna. Ben wrote me that you two are engaged. I've never met her, but if Anna's anything like Isabella, you're a very lucky man."

"When was the last time you saw Ben?"

"Oh, it was before the war. They visited me in Palermo while on their honeymoon."

"Well, mother and daughter are both beautiful, but that's were the similarity ends."

"Meaning?"

"Young American women are very independent and confident, but I'm adjusting to it."

Pina laughed. "If her figure is anything like her mother's at that age, I'm sure it's worth adjusting for. When is the big wedding?"

"We haven't decided yet, but be prepared to attend."

Smiling in anticipation, Pina said, "You know, I've never been to America and I look forward to it. When will you be going back?"

"Much sooner than I had expected. Probably in a couple of days. I've some business to take care of in Lugano first."

"Then I'll wait for the invitation. In the meantime, be well, Carlo, and give my love to the Tuzzios."

"I will, Pina, and thank you for everything."

Sitting alone with his memories of Tony, Carlo wondered what really had transpired in their office several nights earlier. Enzio had told him that Tony's desk drawer was open just wide enough to remove the gun that was on the floor when he found him dead in his chair. If it had been a jealous husband that Tony couldn't reason with, knowing his partner, he probably would have pulled the gun from the desk drawer. Unfortunately he had not been fast enough for his killer, whoever it was.

His thoughts turned to the business of the two aluminum cases of diamonds hidden in his mama's root cellar. Without Tony he had no one to trust with that little enterprise. He already had more than enough money to plan a good future with Anna and he didn't intend to risk that. Besides, until this Corklin guy who was interested in smuggling explained what it had to do with him, those cases could stay burried on the pig farm indefinately. Deep down he feared it had to do with the diamonds, but with Tony gone, it was his word against that of anyone else.

Chapter 64

The following day, Carlo was seated across from the assistant manager of
The Banco Swiss/Italia in Lugano.

"That is your current balance in U.S. dollars, Sr. Marchi, $1,800,000 as of
our last interest posting."

"I don't understand, according to my records there should be a little over
$2,300,000."

"Yes, Signore, that would have been the balance had Sr. DeVito not with-
drawn $500,000 recently."

Damn it, Tony, what the hell was that for?

As surprised as he was at the huge withdrawal, Carlo had to accept the
fact that it was Tony's share of the money. There was, however, no evidence
of what Tony had used it for. Perhaps he had opened his own private account
which was no more than Carlo had done back in New York.

"Yes, of course. I had forgotten my partner had made the withdrawal."

"No problem, Signore. Now, how may we assist you today?"

"I would like to close the account and transfer the funds, except for
30,000,000 lira in cash, to my New York bank." Carlo handed him the account number for The Knickerbocker Savings Bank. He was intrigued by the
assistant manager's cool, typically Swiss, lack of concern at the loss of such a
large account as he handed over the transfer form to be signed.

"Your funds will be available to you in New York by tomorrow. If you will
please wait a moment I will get your cash."

Several minutes later the assistant manager returned to his desk with a large
manila envelope. "Allow me to count it for you, Sr. Marchi." He proceeded to
slide the bills onto his desk.

"That won't be necessary. I'm sure you have already done so."

"Si, twice actually." He tucked the money back into the envelope, sealed
it and handed it to Carlo. "Thank you for trusting in Banco Swiss/Italia, Sr.
Marchi. Is there anything else we can do?"

"No. Thank you."

When Carlo returned from Lugano that evening, he went directly to the cannery. After parking Tony's car in the rear, he removed the suede pouch with the four diamonds from the trunk.

The only sound from the once noisy canning area was Enzio nailing some wooden cases shut. He stopped when Carlo approached. "Just crating some tools I can use," he explained.

"Hell, Enzio, take whatever you want." Carlo sat on a nearby crate and lit a cigarette.

"These tools will be enough. What is it you wished to discuss with me, Sr. Carlo?"

"First of all, Enzio, there's 30,000,000 lira in here." He handed him the manila envelope. "Please see to it that it's shared among the workers."

"That is most generous of you, Sr. Carlo. I will be happy to."

"And this is for you, Enzio." He held up the suede pouch.

"It is not necessary, Sr. Carlo. Sr. Tony was most generous with my salary and I managed to save quite a bit."

"Still, I want you to have these. Hold out your hand."

Carlo could see the confused expression on Enzio's face as he poured the four stones onto his extended palm.

"I do not understand?" Enzio declared as he studied the shiny stones resting in his hand that had been roughened by years of hard work.

"These are uncut diamonds," Carlo told him. "When you get to Ficuzza, take them to a jeweler and he will give you enough lira to retire on. If he asks how you got them, merely say an inheritance. Capisce?"

"Si! Oh, madonne...but why?"

Carlo could see his eyes redden. "For your loyalty to Tony and me."

Enzio clenched his new wealth to his chest. "Grazie, Sr. Carlo."

They embraced, then Carlo left, leaving a grateful old man with a small fortune in stones tucked securely in his pocket while he finished crating his tools.

It was eight in the evening when Carlo returned to his apartment. He placed a call to Anna at the warehouse.

"I've been worried about you, Carlo," Anna started right in. "Is everything going all right? What does Mr. Corklin want with you? I'm very concerned about why he's looking for you, Carlo. Are you sure you're...."

"Haven't seen him yet, but I'm sure he's looking for a different Marchi. So please, Anna, I've just cleared up some business details and...." He was about to tell her he would be home sooner than expected when there was a knock at his door. "Hold on a minute, Anna, there's someone at the door." He set the receiver down, went into the sitting room and opened the door part way. "Si, what is it?" he asked in Italian.

"We need to talk, Carlo Marchi."

Carlo was surprised that the tall man with a trim blonde beard responded in perfect English. He kept his right leg braced firmly against the partially open door, his body instinctively tightened in anticipation of a possible physical confrontation. For only a moment, Carlo regretted having had Enzio dispose of Tony's gun. "Just who the hell are you?"

"The name is Corklin and we've a lot to discuss, you and I."

"About what?"

"The Kistlers in New York to start with."

Carlo's throat knotted, but he still couldn't make a connection. Then it hit him it. This was about the diamonds. "I don't know what you're talking about."

"Okay then, how about Vandenberg? Does that mean anything to you, Marchi?"

"Never heard of him." Suddenly the word VANDENBERG appeared in Carlo's mind. It was the name stamped inside the lid of the aluminum cases containing the diamonds. His body went from a rigid, defensive mode to almost gelatina. A cold sweat flooded under his clothing. "What is it you want?" His hand was trembling as he continued to grip the door.

"I think it would be better if we discuss this in the privacy of your apartment."

Remembering Anna still on the phone, Carlo nervously invited Corklin in. "Just wait one second." He returned to his bedroom and picked up the receiver. "Anna, something important has come up. I'll have to call you back later."

"You sound strange, Carlo. What's going on?"

"Nothing, it's just all the pressure about Tony and all. I'll call you later." He hung up before she could dig further.

Corklin was seated in the sitting room when Carlo returned. He pulled out a cigarette to allay any sign of his nervousness. Corklin did likewise.

"Now what the hell is this all about?" Carlo stood facing him.

Corklin puffed out a cloud of smoke. "I know you've been selling Vandenberg's diamonds to the Kistlers in New York."

"I have no idea what you're referring to." Carlo decided that sitting across from his unwanted guest would gain him more composure.

"Let's cut the bullshit, shall we? I've been chasing these damn diamonds half way around the world. The Kistlers confessed everything to avoid being arrested for dealing in stolen goods."

"I haven't stolen anything, and you can't prove anything you're saying."

"Look we can do this one of two ways. I assume you're planning to return to that nice looking young lady in Jersey City."

"That's none of your concern."

"Assuming you are going back to the States," Corklin quickly continued, "we'll have the British Government arrange for your arrest through the American authorities. With only a green card, you'll end up back here in an Italian prison, which I hear is none too pleasant a place to be incarcerated."

"These people, the Kistlers you're referring to, must be mistaking me for someone else."

"Look Carlo," Corklin continued, ignoring his denials, "we can make the same deal I made with Abe and Barbara."

"A deal? For what? What could we possibly deal over?" Carlo was fighting a losing battle with his own conscience. There was Anna and their future together to consider and he certainly wanted out of Sicily as soon as possible. *Shit, who knows what would happen if Campi got wind of any of this.*

"All we want are the diamonds, and if you return them, I'm willing to allow you to keep the money the Kistlers paid you and forget you ever existed."

"Is that the deal you made with the Kistlers?"

"That's right, Carlo. Now be smart and tell me where they are, and just for my own curiosity, how the hell did you ever get them in the first place?"

"I'll be free and clear? And keep what I have?"

"That's the deal. Now talk."

For the next fifteen minutes Carlo explained how during the war his papa's cousin, Col. Alfonso Marchi, had flown to the pig farm and, along with his papa and the Italian pilot, had carried two small, shiny silver trunks into the pig barn. "My papa died shortly after that. I was only thirteen when Mama and I moved to Palermo. Later we heard that papa's cousin, the Colonnello, and his pilot were both killed somewhere in Egypt." Carlo could see the amazed look on Corklin's face as the tale unfolded. "About a year ago I returned to the farm to bury Mama next to Papa. It was then that I recalled peeking through a crack in the pig barn wall and watching them bury the trunks inside. That's when my partner, Tony, and I dug them up and discovered the fortune."

"Wait a minute," Corklin interrupted, "you mean someone else is involved in this?"

"Not any more. He died in a car crash last week. That's why I came back here."

Corklin shook his head. "Sorry. So how the hell did you get two aluminum cases full of uncut stones to America without being detected?"

"We didn't." Carlo lit another cigarette. He was at a point now where he was beginning to enjoy confusing Corklin with his convoluted, but true, story.

"I don't understand. Where the hell are our diamonds then?"

"Still on the farm," Carlo declared.

"But how did you manage to sell some to the Kistlers?"

"I don't see what that has to do with the deal you offered me." Carlo wasn't about to reveal how he used the cannery to smuggle the stones. "I assure you that most of the stones are still in the cases. They're now hidden in the root cellar under the farmhouse."

"I'll be damned. Well, I guess the next thing is for you to take me to your farm. If it's as you say, you can go your way and I'll return to London with the cases."

"I can drive you there but I don't see how you can get them back easily."

"The same way they got there, by plane. If you don't mind putting me up for the night, I'll call London straight away in the morning."

"My partner's room is a mess, but if you don't mind, you can bed down in there. I'll get you some clean linen."

"Good enough. Of course I'm sure there's no need to remind you that if you take off, I know where to find you. Right, old chap?"

"I'll get the linens. I want this over as quickly as you do."

When Carlo finally retired to his room he called Anna back. The moment she asked about Corklin, he lied that he hadn't shown up and that once he took care of legally disposing of the pig farm he would be home, in a matter of days.

"Okay, Carlo, if you say so, but that man seemed quite intent, so please be careful."

"I will, Anna. Good night."

Chapter 65

After another restless night, Carlo's eyes blinked open to the sound of clattering coming from the kitchenette. He squinted at his alarm clock. It was 10:35 in the morning.

"I hope you don't mind, Marchi, but I needed a cup of tea," Corklin said when Carlo entered the small room.

"We only have espresso." Carlo buckled his trousers as he shuffled to a cabinet.

"No need to bother. Having become a seasoned traveler, I've learned to carry my own." Corklin held up a tea tin.

"Very resourceful of you." Carlo yawned as he proceeded to prepare his caffé. "Did you make your call to London?"

"About an hour ago. Everything is arranged. The company plane should arrive here in Sciacca by midday."

"And then?" Carlo lit a cigarette while he waited for his espresso to brew.

"We fly to the village where your farm is. What's it called again?"

"Venetico. It's a bit west of Messina. Do you think your British pilot can find it?"

"I'm sure Capt. Patterson won't have any trouble. And once we're there you'll only have to direct him to the farm."

ಜಃಛ

On the outskirts of Sciacca at an airstrip once used by the military and now used to fly tourists in for the thermal spas and beautiful white sand beaches, Carlo and Corklin watched the twin engine Griffon taxi to a stop within a few yards of where they stood. In small letters on the fuselage of the plane were the words Vandenberg Mining. When the speed of the props slowed to idle, the door opened and a set of steps were lowered onto the tarmac.

A large man, wearing a worn leather flight jacket waved and yelled from the opening, "Never thought we'd be ferrying you again, Corklin, you old bloke."

Corklin climbed the steps with Carlo right behind him. James Craig took Corklin's canvas travel bag and tossed it into the plane. "It's good to see you again, Craig." Corklin gripped the co-pilot's large hand.

Carlo waited as the two men greeted one another. Then Corklin introduced him. "Craig this is Carlo Marchi. He's going to guide us to the diamonds."

Carlo noticed the inquisitive look on Craig's face.

"Welcome aboard, Mr. Marchi." He reached for Carlo's bag.

"Call me Carlo." He was pleasantly relieved to find that Craig's grip that engulfed his entire hand was quite gentle.

Craig led them into the cabin, then went forward to the cockpit where he took his seat next to the pilot, who Carlo assumed was Capt. Patterson.

Turning partially around from the controls, the pilot yelled above the drone of the engine, "Corklin, I'm bloody glad to see you again, old boy."

The reason for their camaraderie totally escaped Carlo until he was introduced to Capt. Earl Patterson.

"So this is the fellow who is going to put an end to our search for our missing stones. Welcome aboard, Carlo."

"Now chaps, if you'll be seated back there, we have an open clearance for take off," Craig instructed.

Corklin took the first seat back and Carlo occupied the one across the aisle from him. He had no way of knowing it was the same window seat Andy Cox had occupied sometime before.

As Patterson taxied back onto the short runway, Craig leaned into the cabin and told Corklin and Carlo that he had mapped them to Messina, about a forty-minute flight. "From there it'll be a visual to Venetico, then you'll have to guide us to your farm, Carlo."

"I hope I can, I've never seen it from the air before," Carlo replied.

"It shouldn't be too difficult if you recognize the roads and other landmarks in the area."

Once they had leveled off, Corklin left his seat and stood by the cockpit door. Carlo heard him ask, "How much daylight will we have left once we find the place?"

"With any luck at least two hours," Craig replied.

Then he overheard Patterson ask Corklin, "How the bloody hell does our Eye-talian friend back there know where the stones are?"

"It's quite a story which, if we're not on a wild fox chase, I'll explain later."

As Craig had estimated, they were over Messina forty-five minutes after leaving Sciacca airspace. Carlo peered out his window as Patterson took them in a south-westerly direction toward Venetico.

Pangs of emotion overcame Carlo as he studied the countryside below. Although he couldn't accurately identify their exact location, a strong sense of his childhood birthplace rushed through his soul with every tree and roadway they passed over. "There! Up ahead. That's the road we took in and out of Venetico," he shouted.

Upon hearing him, Patterson reduced speed and started a slow descent. Within minutes they passed over the farmhouse.

"That's it. That's our farm. And that big field behind the old barn is where Papa's cousin, the Colonnello, landed."

Corklin studied the place as Patterson made a wide circle. "Can we land here okay, Captain?"

"A piece of Yorkshire Pudding compared to the beach at As-Sallum," Patterson quipped.

Ten minutes later they were on the ground. Patterson stayed by his plane and had a smoke while the others headed toward the farmhouse. The old hinges were barely holding up the door. Time, neglect and weather had continued to erode the building. Most of the windowpanes were shattered and the floor creaked alarmingly under the weight of the three men.

Carlo pulled up the remnants of the worn kitchen floor covering exposing the trapdoor to the root cellar. There, three feet below, under old gunnysacks that he and Tony had used as a cover, lay the two aluminum cases.

"Bloody good!" Corklin shouted as he reached into the hole.

When the two men started to check the contents of the cases, Carlo said, "If you don't need me now, I'll go up the hill behind the house to visit my parents' graves. Just give me a yell when you're ready to leave."

"Sure, Marchi." Corklin excitedly folded back the felt covering inside the second case. "Like you said, they're mostly all here," he declared

"We'll have these on board and lashed down in no time at all, then be on our way with ample daylight," Craig stated as he helped Corklin lift one of the cases.

Carlo knelt on the knoll where his parents had always said they wanted to be laid to rest. He vowed over their small markers that he would never sell the land that embraced the souls of the two people he had loved most in the world.

Teary-eyed he climbed back aboard the plane in time to hear Corklin explaining to the two pilots how a buyer from Manhattan had purchased some uncut stones that were identified as coming from the Vandenberg mines. He described his unpleasant experiences in New York City chasing down the Kistlers and told them how he had ultimately ended up in Sciacca. There he had finally confronted Carlo, who had filled in the details of how the diamonds had come to be hidden on the pig farm, and made a deal to retrieve them.

Carlo sat quietly as Patterson asked, "How do you think Waters and Dunne are going to react to the deal you made?"

Although uncomfortable about being the object of their conversation, Carlo had little choice. All he really wanted now was to return to America as soon as possible and put all this behind him.

"The way I figure it," Corklin continued, "inasmuch as they had pretty much come to believe the diamonds where lost forever, and since technically they were never really stolen, the absence of a few stones won't matter, especially since diamond prices have almost doubled in the past ten years. The increase in value of what we loaded on board today more than compensates for the stones that are missing."

"I suppose you're right," Patterson replied as he prepared for takeoff. "Where exactly are we taking Carlo, back to Sciacca?"

"Palermo would be my choice, if it's not too much trouble," Carlo spoke up. He had no reason to return to Sciacca and a flight to New York would be much easier to obtain from Palermo.

"Makes no difference to us," Craig told him while Patterson was occupied with the flight instruments. "We have to refuel anyway and Palermo will do just fine."

For the next hour little was said between the four men, except for an occasional comment regarding the flight between Patterson and Craig. When they landed at Punta Rasisi Airport in Palermo, Carlo deplaned and watched as the Griffon transport carrying three Vandenberg employees and two aluminum cases of diamonds taxied to a refueling area. He made the sign of the cross and headed for the terminal.

Chapter 66

As Corklin looked down over the English Channel, his thoughts focused on the substantial reward waiting for him in London. Even more rewarding was the knowledge of a job well done and the fact that he would soon be home again in Pretoria.

৪০০৪

The following evening, somewhere over the Atlantic in a Super Constellation winging toward America, Carlo stared out the window into the night sky. He considered himself extremely fortunate except for the loss of Tony. With all things considered, he had now formulated his plan for the future. Ben Tuzzio was right except for one big difference, Stella's Tomato Sauce, his Mama's recipe, could be made in the US but rather than co-packing as Ben had suggested, Carlo now had the financial means to put up his own cannery. Now all he could hope for was that Anna would believe that Corklin never looked him up and that the cash he intended to build a tomato cannery with came from the price of the valuable acrege of the pig farm.

The End

Author Bio

John Russo is a former Creative Director for a Fortune 500 Company. A past member of the American Management Association, he lectured throughout the world and contributed numerous articles to various creative publications. John has had a number of short stories published and has been nominated for a Pushcart Prize Award, a Derringer and an Edgar. His debut novel, "The Bennie Arnoldo File," was published in December, 2002, by Five Star Publishing. His second novel, "Indian Givers," was published in November, 2004. He designed the covers for both books. John is a member of The Mystery Writers of America and The International Association of Crime Writers.

Don't miss any of these other
exciting historical novels

➢ Apache Lance, Franciscan Cross
(1-933353-44-9, $18.50 US)

➢ Harry's Agatha
(1-933353-23-6, $16.95 US)

➢ Mary's Child
(1-933353-11-2, $18.50 US)

➢ The Storks of La Caridad
(1-931201-21-x, $18.50 US)

Twilight Times Books
Kingsport, Tennessee

Order Form

If not available from your local bookstore, send this coupon and a check or money order for the retail price plus $3.50 s&h to Twilight Times Books, Dept. GB906 POB 3340 Kingsport TN 37664. Delivery may take up to four weeks.

Name: _____

Address: _____

_____

Email: _____

I have enclosed a check or money order in the amount

of $_____

for _____ .

If you enjoyed this book, please post a review
at your favorite online bookstore.

Twilight Times Books
P O Box 3340
Kingsport, TN 37664
Phone/Fax: 423-323-0183
www.twilighttimesbooks.com/